## About the Author

The author has been a history teacher, geography teacher and Head Teacher, both in England and abroad. Now retired, he lives in rural England.

His father, Eric Leyland, was a well-known author of several hundred children's books, some appearing as television series in the 1950s and '60s.

Eric's son is now an author himself and has always wanted to write an historical novel, although with the reality slightly twisted to explore what the effect on history might have been.

He has also travelled widely and has had the chance to explore many countries in his life. Rather than American history, he hopes that his next novel will be about a brutal murder in a school in England.

He has five children and two step-children, as well as at least six grandchildren at the last count, and a truly supportive wife, who still works in a school.

*Rally 'Round the Flag* **is dedicated**...

...to the author's wife, Linda, who kept him more or less sane during the research, writing and publication process of this book. She also acted as a valuable secretary while he struggled with editing and is equally a knowledgeable computer expert.

...to his two step-children: Lauren and Jordan, far too old to called "children" and now supporting him in his life and second career. Also his daughter Jo in Australia... and finally...

...to his grandchildren rooted in England: Scarlet, Fin, Jack and Florence.

It is perhaps unusually also dedicated, from the author's own school days in the late 1950s and early 1960s, to an inspiring teacher of history at that time: he was known to his students as 'Sam', although his name was actually Jim (James). This fine teacher engendered a passion for both history and teaching, which have been the cornerstones of this author's teaching career for over forty years. His secondary school years were very happily spent at Sherrardswood School near Welwyn in Hertfordshire. Graham Godsmark was Headmaster at that time; both he and his wife, Mary, are sadly no longer with us and neither is Sam. They will always be kindly remembered as fine educationists.

Jeremy Leyland

# RALLY 'ROUND THE FLAG

AUSTIN MACAULEY PUBLISHERS™

LONDON · CAMBRIDGE · NEW YORK · SHARJAH

A CIP catalogue record for this title is available from the British Library.

ISBN 9781398422186 (Paperback)
ISBN 9781398422193 (ePub e-book)

www.austinmacauley.com

First Published 2022
Austin Macauley Publishers Ltd®
1 Canada Square
Canary Wharf
London
E14 5AA

# Acknowledgements…

…of all those who contributed in so many ways to *Rally 'Round the Flag:* I would like especially to thank Ella Thompson and Rebecca Slack of the production teams at publishers, Austin Macauley, for their belief in the author and their invaluable help and advice from the very outset of the relationship.

…to the man who lived with this book from near the start through to the completion of the published book and who played the most vital of roles: Vinh Tran, whom I thank greatly.

Also my gratitude to Mary, my tireless reader and text advisor.

Of course, and above all, to my wife Linda, who has supported me throughout this book, as well as life itself.

As well, of course, perhaps even more thanks is due to you for buying, borrowing and reading the finished work, since the effort and thrill of writing is in your honour: may you enjoy the read.

My interest in the American Civil War was prompted, as a history teacher, by its being on a syllabus many years ago; this story eventually grew out of that. All the places in England and America are real; their descriptions, however, do change in detail according to the story. The exception to that is fictional Cotton Hall and its plantation, although it is at least imagined from a generic southern type of estate in the 1800s.

Many of the characters depicted were also real people: the majority of the military personnel on both sides of the war, the politicians in England and the USA, but the characters in Oldham and Manchester are imagined, but of generations of the time that are typified by them.

Many people provided invaluable advice during the writing process, but it was followed only as far as it suited the plot; any mistakes are mine alone.

# BACKGROUND TO "RALLY 'ROUND THE FLAG"
*'A timely reminder of how the past colours the future'*
A comment by one of the first readers of the novel

This is the story of an horrendous civil war, carefully reimagined in relation to just one true event that I could have changed in its outcome. It is equally involved, also truthfully, with both slavery in the United States of America in the 1860s as well as the not too different conditions of the working poor in the cotton mills of Lancashire, England, at the same time.

We of the twenty-first century are, of course, aware that slavery had been common and accepted by white Americans since before their country first existed independently in 1775; equally it was accepted by English citizens from the 16th century until slavery's abolition in Britain in 1833.

American slavery ceased in the USA when Abraham Lincoln declared all slaves 'free' by the *Emancipation Act of 1863*; that applied to *all* slaves, since the condition existed in both the Confederate south in great numbers and in the northern Federal Union in rather smaller numbers.

Nevertheless, it is worth remembering that the same Abraham Lincoln was asked at the end of the Civil War if he would still have emancipated the US slaves if he had been able to unite all the states without emancipation? He replied that he was unsure.

Britain had equally accepted the condition and had greatly profited from its *slave trade* with the West Indies, and then the USA, since the early sixteenth century until it was made illegal in Great Britain twenty seven years before the story depicted in *Rally 'Round the Flag* begins.

In other words, although opposition existed, it was present to a lesser extent in earlier times. Slavery was accepted as a 'natural condition' for Africans and West Indians to be traded as possessions by the white Americans and by the many white Europeans who benefitted from it. It also existed in large parts of Asia, South America and Africa from before the colonisation of much of the land of those continents, generally, but not always, by European nations.

By 1860 in the United States of America, slavery was still legal as far as the law was concerned. There was considerable opposition to it, especially in the northern, federal states. Lincoln was the first American president in history to make it clear that by electing him to that exalted position, in November 1860, the nation was giving him the right, even the duty, to make slavery illegal; all existing slaves would thus become free men, women and children. Lincoln famously declared, (1) *"A house divided against itself cannot stand...the government cannot endure half slave and half free."*

The Index on page 412 expands on all sources and quotations in this book

It is undoubtedly true that later many northern American owners of the new industrial *factories* used cheap, manual labourers, who were treated in many ways almost like slaves. Their new and rapidly expanding businesses used this cheap labour of industrial workers while being fully aware that these '*wage earning workers*', although in Pittsburgh or Chicago, rather than Charleston or Savannah, had much in common with a type of 'slavery' in both the USA and Great Britain. Both nations had cotton and wool mills, coal and iron ore mines, whose workers had no rights of employment and wages that kept them in a state of poverty. Both countries had been justifiably called '*slave owning*' by their numerous critics over time.

What we in the century in which we live today believe, and hopefully feel in our hearts and minds, renders us often appalled that the nineteenth and early twentieth centuries still accepted the existence of slavery in all its forms and manifestations, which is now anathema to our way of life and living. One hopes that moral Britons today feel the certain truth that 'slavery' is immoral and must always be illegal, as is prejudice over the colour of a person's skin, but this was not the case for many white Americans in the 1860s.

In the nineteenth century, when *Rally 'Round the Flag* is set, the United States of America was divided by the issue of slavery, as were their British customers with their massive cotton importation from the slave owning States. Both countries seemed generally to agree that slavery was a necessary acceptance to create profitability. We probably believe today that this mantra was likely hidden away in a rarely consulted compartment of many a mind at the time, in favour of material gain for themselves and, it has to be admitted, for their countries and empires as well.

It is against this background that this novel is set. Apart from one event, real characters and truthful situations are included as a large majority of the body of the story. The author will ask you, the reader, once you have read it, to decide what the conclusion might have been as a result. What the story perceives as the potentially first small, but vital fact that is changed and is followed by an inevitable chain of events that could then alter the future history of the USA as depicted in this novel. The shifting of the tectonic plates of truth, just slightly, occurred on Sunday July 21 1861 by a small stream, called the Bull Run. By such small hiccoughs in the outcome of one well-recorded historical event, hundreds of years of history can, indeed, be wiped out and be rewritten.

\*

**The novel is set during the American Civil War of 1861–1865**

The military anthem *Rally 'Round the Flag* was bellowed from thousands of mouths by both the Union and Confederate armies during that Civil War.

(2)Yes, we'll rally 'round the flag boys,
We'll rally 'round again,
Shouting the battle cry of freedom
We'll rally from the hillside,
We'll rally from the plain,
Shouting the battle cry of freedom

# Prologue

The American Civil War began when tempers in both the Confederate southern states and the Union of Federal northern states at last outweighed the previous restraint of those who had had opposing principles for so many years. These same heartfelt principles could finally only be satisfied by physically beating the opposing side of the argument: (whether or not to allow slavery and whether or not to allow states to secede), into defeat and submission by grinding their faces into the dust.

The first, albeit not physically life-taking, outburst replacing more peaceful days when words had been virtually the only weapons, was in January 1861 when seven southern states dramatically seceded from the union.

Far worse came on April 12 1861 when what were generally agreed to have been the first shots of a war were fired by a force of Confederate militia stationed at Charleston, South Carolina. These same men of the Confederate States besieged the Union garrison at Fort Sumpter, a fortified island that guarded the entrance to Charleston bay and harbour. However, during the few days of the siege, the only losses of life were one Union private soldier, very possibly as the result of an accident, and one horse.

The significant month of February 1861 fell in that short period between January and the beginning of April, when no other "organised military force" had yet been used. No one had any realistic idea of what was in truth inevitable. Both North and South held fast to the passionate certainty that each of their own gallant armies would inevitably be overwhelmingly victorious.

In that month, the principals in the forthcoming historic conflict were contemplating how they now found themselves frighteningly close to a killing war in their own back yards. The USA was a new nation in existence for less than eighty years, that now found itself on the brink of a civil war. The principals in this great conflict were Abraham Lincoln, the President, but in reality, soon to be the leader of just the northern United States, and Jefferson

Davis, destined to become leader and then President of the southern Confederate states.

Nearly two thousand miles to the east of the United States of America, Queen Victoria sat firmly on the throne of the world's most powerful nation at that time. It is likely that Her Majesty was unaware of how close civil war was across the Atlantic Ocean.

February 1861 saw both these American factions beginning to realise that they possibly now stood on the brink of a bloody war, a war that was to see more Americans killed than in all previous conflicts on the North American continent.

On a cold winter's day in that month, Abraham Lincoln, elected president of the United States in late 1860, left his large but, as he put it 'not grand' home in Springfield Massachusetts, to take up his Presidency in Washington DC. He spoke to his family and friends that day, perhaps foreseeing the dark events that would surely follow: (3) *"Here [in Springfield] I have passed from a young man to an old man. Here my children have been born and one buried. I now leave, not knowing when or whether I may return, with a task before me greater than that which rested on [George] Washington's shoulders. Without the assistance of that Divine Being who ever attended him, I cannot succeed. With that assistance, I cannot fail... Let us confidently hope that all will yet be well."*

A week later in Washington DC, he reminded a few friends and members of the government of the words first used by him three years earlier: (4) *"A house divided against itself cannot stand. I believe the government could not endure half slave and half free. I do not expect the Union to be dissolved. I do not expect the house to fall. I do expect it will cease to be divided."*

Three weeks later, he spoke to Americans in the southern states: *"We are not enemies, but friends. We must not be enemies."*

On February 18, Jefferson Davis, living on his huge family plantation at Davis Bend, Virginia, received a telegram that informed him he had been elected as Confederate President. However, on that day, he was in Montgomery, before soon moving to Richmond, Virginia, which was to become the Confederate capital. He spoke then to friends and fellow Americans (4) *"...I approach the discharge of the duties you have assigned to me with a humble distrust of my abilities and an abiding faith in the virtue and patriotism of the people and to hope that the beginning of our career as a Confederacy may not be obstructed by hostile opposition... [we are] asserting the rights which the Declaration of Independence of 1776 has defined as 'inalienable'."*

\*

On the same day, the British Prime Minister, Lord Palmerston, had an audience with Queen Victoria at Buckingham Palace. The Queen made no secret of the fact that she much preferred her favoured Prime Minister Lord Melbourne [her 'Lord M'] to Lord Palmerston, who in her view did not keep her truly abreast of what went on in the House of Commons, as he should have done. The lords Palmerston and Melbourne were, in fact, bothers-in-law.

At that somewhat frosty audience, they discussed the recent rail disaster at Salford where eleven people were killed. The Queen wanted to know if Palmerston had yet agreed that his government would financially help the families of those who had died or were injured; he had not.

The Prime Minister moved on to inform Her Majesty that civil war seemed likely in the United States of America, but this was no threat to Great Britain, which commanded the seas between the two nations and that its latest warship, *HMS Prince of Wales*, was now in service, while the next 'ironclad' battleship, *HMS Warrior*, would be in service very shortly. His inference seemed to be that Britain could easily deal with any attempts by the breakaway states to harm Britannia. The Queen let a silence pass, before asking what was perhaps, to her, a more pertinent question.

"Have you read the new novel (7) *Uncle Tom's Cabin* by the American lady, Miss Harriet Beecher Stowe.... my lord?"

Palmerston said he had not read the book, but had heard that it was thought by many members of parliament to be 'a seditious as well as a sentimental lady's novel'.

The Queen showed her displeasure at his reply and added that she felt so 'dreadfully sorry' for poor Tom and had been 'moved to copious tears by the terrible conditions in which slaves in the southern states lived and worked'.

The audience ended coldly after the Queen had expressed her hope that '*my* government' should not interfere on behalf of Mr Lincoln or indeed anyone else'. She received an indistinct reply.

# Part One
# 1860-61

# Chapter One

**Manchester, Known to Many as (8) Cottonopolis: November 1860**

To those living in the metropolis of Manchester in the second half of the nineteenth century, it would have seemed a typical late November afternoon. The rain had been falling since midday. Roads and buildings were streaked with what looked like black tears and the smoke rising from hundreds of tall mill chimneys reduced the afternoon to a dim twilight. Reaching ground level, the murky rainwater was rushing down gutters, blackening windows and reducing even the fine stone of the great public buildings to an ugly grey colour in the matter of a few years after they were born.

(9) *Arthur Tissiman*, a young man of twenty-three, had left Euston Station in London at eleven o'clock that morning on the London and North Western Railway. He pulled his watch from his waistcoat pocket and saw that it showed only ten past four o'clock, meaning the journey had taken about five hours, but in the comfort of a first-class carriage the time had not dragged, thanks to the fascinating book on the campaign to reduce the widespread infection of cholera in cities, which he had finished reading on the journey.

Apparently, according to Dr Partridge, who had studied the 1839 pandemic in Asia, it now took fewer lives in cities like Manchester, Birmingham and London than it had done just twenty years before. Arthur's study of the health of the families in the slums of Manchester and Oldham, near where he lived and in which hoped to teach, had revealed that the doctor's assumptions were, however, far from true there. He had now completed his teacher training and expected to receive notification by the New Year that he was now, indeed, a qualified teacher.

He had lodged in London for the past four years, firstly studying at Kings College for his degree and then at the Westminster Methodist Teacher Training

College. Christmas was almost a month away, but he felt some trepidation as to just how warm this joyful festival might be, realising that the time had come to tell his father what he intended his future career to be.

The light was fading fast and a grim evening was beginning to creep over the city. The gas street lamps merely highlighted the dirty mist that was gathering along the alleyways between the tightly packed back-to-back houses and, with no discrimination, even dared to invade the better paved streets around the city centre and its growing world class architecture. The plans for the fine New Town Hall had already been agreed and work would start soon. Victoria Station, designed by George Stevenson, was already complete and was much admired for both its architecture and its clean bright stone. Both these fine examples of Victorian architecture would inevitably suffer the same process of ageing from bright white to dull grey and black staining. Cynics could be heard to mutter that this was God's punishment on the affluent classes who used stone and iron to boast of their wealth.

As his train pulled into Victoria's modern platforms and concourse, great billows of steam rose to the roof. The driver thrust the braking lever forward so that the locomotive's iron wheels screamed in protest as they gripped the tracks of the railroad and came to a high pitched, iron-on-iron halt. The unholy noise set Arthur's teeth on edge, as it always did however many times he rode the LNWR from Euston. Nevertheless, even arriving on such an unprepossessing afternoon, he still felt pride in this city, more glorious to him than all the sights of London, where he had spent the last four years.

His pride in Manchester was only superseded by his pride in his own ancient family name, the name passed on to him by generations of his ancestors. *Tissiman* was likely a Huguenot name and Arthur's English family stretched back three or four hundred years to the time when they had fled to England during the religious persecutions of non-Roman Catholics in the fourteenth and fifteenth centuries in Europe. Although families like the Tissimans were now labelled broadly as 'Protestants', or perhaps 'Hebrews', they came from many European countries with both Roman Catholic and Protestant religions, such as the Netherlands, Germany, Poland, north and central France and many other scattered enclaves. Arthur was proud of his ancestor's centuries old skills in weaving and tailoring both wool and cotton. The Tissimans had been welcomed to England, as had hundreds, if not thousands, of similar families for their skills. Today they were still at the heart of the booming cloth industries in both Lancashire and Yorkshire.

The carriage windows were now being lowered along the length of the train to allow passengers to reach outside for the handles of the doors, which then swung open with a metallic clang against the bodywork, enabling hundreds, mostly men all in hats, to leave the train to join the mass of humanity that edged and squeezed its way out of the station.

As he stepped down onto the platform, it seemed to Arthur that the voices of the jostling crowd were not actually speaking any known language, but a cacophony of noise that filled the air and drowned even the screaming of escaping high-pressure steam and the crashing of carriage doors. He walked as quickly as he could into the main concourse of the station, where it was a little more peaceful, but still crowded with passengers, many involved in the lucrative business of living and working for *King Cotton* in Manchester and district.

Arthur came to a halt with a sigh of pleasure, raising his eyes to marvel again at the soaring glass and the elaborately designed ironwork of the roof. Back in the neighbourhood of his birth after so many months away, he was in no hurry to leave this modern marvel of the steam age and stood quite still, closing his eyes and breathing in the sweet smell of steam and massed humanity. He felt completely at home here as he had never felt in London.

"Incredible! A young man just arrived at Victoria Station who is actually smiling. A rare sight indeed, possibly even unique, especially on such a miserable afternoon." The remark came loudly and almost angrily from behind him. Arthur opened his eyes and turned to see a well-dressed, well-fed gentleman, somewhat short in stature. He very closely resembled a character Arthur had read about in his early school days, in a story by Mr Charles Dickens. (10) *The Pickwick Papers* had made quite an impression on him at the time and here was the book's namesake, or his verisimilitude, standing directly in front of him, forcing other passengers to avoid him, like a rock in a stream. Caught in a daydream, he felt unnerved, rather as the younger students at his Methodist College must feel when accused by the Head of College, Mr Peterson, of a lack of attention. Inexplicably, Arthur bowed to the obligation of politeness he felt towards this older gentleman.

"My apologies, sir. I must have seemed very selfish just standing and staring like that. I certainly did not intend to impede your progress through this throng."

There was no reply forthcoming, but just an angry stare from slate-grey eyes, which were forced to look up at Arthur. He in turn quickly tipped his hat and forced a smile. Still no words issued from the small mouth, surrounded as it was by the white whiskers of a moustache, side-whiskers and beard. Arthur's nervousness was all too obvious, making him speak far more quickly than he had intended.

He realised too late that he was, uncharacteristically for him, stumbling over his words.

"Yes…yes you are right. I do really apologise… So rude of me standing daydreaming in a crowd like this. I was…just enjoying the sights of our grand station."

Still no reply, just the piercing look.

Arthur struggled on. "You see, sir, I have been absent from home for far too long and I was just enjoying being back here with the sights, sounds and smells of our great city and…" Arthur stammered to a halt, lost for words and looking around anxiously, as if expecting rescue.

This likeness of Mr Pickwick seemed to take yet more time and obvious surprise to digest what must have seemed to be an apology to him, but he finally found the words he thought appropriate.

"That does make you somewhat of a strange young man indeed."

Arthur guessed he must have been at least sixty years old and, like Mr Dickens' original character, was rounded in both head and body. He continued most earnestly, stepping even closer to make his point, which involved his raised finger coming closer and closer to Arthur's chest to emphasise each strongly felt word.

"You, sir, should be ashamed to speak as you do and that makes me doubt you are truly a citizen of Manchester at all." Arthur, raising his right arm rather limply for no reason he could think of, got as far as opening his mouth to disabuse him, but Mr Pickwick lifted his umbrella in response to a perceived attack. Arthur ducked his head, but carried on.

"I can assure you, sir, that Lancashire is my county of birth, although, I must admit to Oldham, rather than to Manchester."

The gentleman, now moving even closer, seemed to puff up his chest in annoyance. "Most who live and work here do not feel the same as you do, I fear. They see our metropolis in its *true* light as the giant leviathan that sucks in the sweat and tears of its people and gives back only pain, infection and hopelessness: coal dust, smoke and the cotton motes that fill our air and drag down the poor."

Arthur feared that he was about to be beaten with the umbrella now being lifted in genuine anger. For once unable, as well as being most out of character and failing to stand up for himself, he turned away and almost ran down the platform. He had felt threatened and ridiculously daunted by the old man, with whom he was in truth in total agreement. He slowed down, as he approached the platform where he hoped his train to Oldham would be waiting.

He tried to shake off all these contrary emotions that had risen within him, feeling an even more urgent need not to delay the rest of his journey home. *Why*, he thought, *should I have not honestly agreed with him?* He began to feel that his homecoming had already been utterly spoiled.

Coming out from under the iron and glass canopy over the main lines, Arthur was soaked within a few yards, as he hurried to the outside platform that carried trains to Oldham Mumps station, a line that had been open for only thirteen years and which had made the journey from Manchester to his home above Oldham so much quicker than in the old days of a horse and carriage or pony and trap all the way from Manchester. The train was already waiting at the platform, belching out what seemed to be angry clouds of frustration at being held stationary in the rain that was now falling even more heavily.

He pulled open the first door he came to and stepped up into a compartment, which seemed barely to have space for him to sit down for the short, eight-mile ride. After his odd encounter and the confusion it had caused him, he was just happy to be out of the rain, even though he now actually found himself in a third-class, no luxury carriage. Yet again, this frustrated his thoughts still further since it was his habit to travel in the comfort of first class.

With a sigh, he reached up to put his small valise on the rack, only to discover there wasn't such a thing above the hard wooden seats. With his case on his knees, he shook the rain off his hat and coat and gratefully sat down. The journey from the London Methodist College had already taken most of the day. He felt exhausted and in need of his own bed, some good Lancashire food and, more significantly, perhaps time to admit what his feelings really were about the poverty that existed almost on his own doorstep in Oldham and what he should be doing about it.

The journey took nearly half an hour, but once the train had left Manchester and its ever-expanding suburbs with their rows of back-to-back houses interspersed with mills and iron foundries, the day grew just a little less dark as the smoke cleared somewhat and Arthur could catch sight of the distant moors rising above Oldham, which he could now occasionally glimpse through the misted windows of the carriage.

Much as he longed to be home, he had to admit that his spirits were dimmed a little as soon as he could see the chimneys sprouting against the skyline in Oldham, each an indication of the site of a cotton mill and each marking its location with plumes of black smoke from the coal-fired boilers. This reinforced his confusion as his Methodist teacher-training came once more into direct opposition to the privileged life he led when at home in the clean moorland air both distant from, as well as high above, the town.

As they pulled into Mumps Station, the sky was growing genuinely dark and the gas lamps were welcome signs that he was almost at his journey's end, with just a half hour ride up the hill towards the moor and his family home at Waterhead Hall. Arthur had written to his father earlier in the week with the time his train was expected and knew that Jenks, the stable lad, would be waiting for him on Station Road. He was cheered even more by the fact that the rain had stopped by the time he stepped out onto the cobbles. It took him a few minutes of searching to realise that Jenks and the carriage were not waiting as he had expected.

As he stood searching the busy road for his ride home, he glimpsed Waterhead Hall's young stable hand hurrying across the station forecourt waving his arms in the air.

"Sir! Mr Arthur, sir!" He reached Arthur's side and touched his cap. Arthur's good humour returned at once.

"Jenks, good to see you. I thought Father had forgotten I was arriving this evening." Young Jenks paused.

"We're just over 'ere sir, be'ind 'awkin's wagon."

Arthur followed Jenks across the forecourt to where the carriage and pair was waiting. His long day's travel, as well as the rain and gloom of Manchester, were all forgotten when he saw Enid leaning out the window smiling and waving. He reached his family's smart maroon coach just as his sister swung the door open and jumped down onto the road, almost stumbling into his arms. As Arthur smiled down at Enid, who still seemed far younger than her twenty-five years and he realised that not even the months away had aged her at all.

"Enid, how lovely of you to come to meet me. I wasn't expecting such a welcome," he laughed, as he took her grey-gloved hand, which she raised so that he could kiss it. Her dark curls escaped from the edges of her bonnet and the smile on that pretty, heart shaped face was just what he needed to realise he was at home. The weight of just how much he had missed her and the family in his last year at college suddenly filled his mind, as he took both her hands and pulled her close so that he could embrace her properly. The homecoming was interrupted by a loud cough from inside the carriage. Arthur grinned, as he let Enid go and muttered, "You still make me feel more than three years your senior."

He glanced into the open carriage door to be met by the unsmiling face of Aunt Josephine, his mother's older sister. She was, as ever, dressed in black from head to foot, which had been her only attire since the death, more than three years ago, of her husband, Arthur's Uncle Charles. The two onerous, to her, roles she now took most seriously in life were as companion to Elizabeth, brother Ernest's wife, and chaperone to Enid, regarded by her as rather more of a challenge than the 'sensible' Elizabeth could ever be.

With the rain now falling again, there followed a great deal of fuss and confusion getting both Arthur and his bag into the confined space left in the coach, once Aunt Josephine had made it clear that it was appropriate for Arthur to sit next to her, all be it that her wide formal black dress and bustle, her umbrella and Chappie, her small and quite vicious terrier, left no more than twelve inches available to Arthur.

"But Aunt Josephine, there's plenty of space..." Enid, trying unsuccessfully to save Arthur from Chappie, ventured to add. Her brother was left struggling to squeeze his body next to the angry small dog now intent upon biting his leg.

"There is no question of that, Enid. There is adequate space next to me. Just sit still, Arthur, and stop annoying, Chappie!"

She then banged on the ceiling of the coach with her umbrella and in spite of the crush inside, they began to move along the street in the direction of the road that would lead through Oldham and up the valley towards Waterhead Hall high above on the edge of the moor.

Enid sulked the whole way, having been deprived of having her brother beside her after such a long absence. Once out of the town's sprawl, they started to climb the moor now travelling on unmade roadways. Arthur, looking out the small rear window, could see the lights coming on in the town below and the occasional bursts of flame as boilers in the mills were opened to receive another helping of coal and the fires in the iron foundries and mills were once more bellowed into life.

Before too much longer, the top of the moor was reached and the road ahead levelled out. The coach turned off the roadway, the wheels hesitating on the stony surface, as Jenks pulled them into the sharp turn, after which the going became a little smoother. Arthur felt his stomach turn over in what he tried to convince himself was excitement, as ten minutes later, he saw the tall stone gate pillars ahead. He tried to dismiss the thought that it was only a small twinge of worry at the prospect that his father might be waiting for him.

The carriage slowed to a crawl, as it navigated the turn through the gateway, then climbed the final slope to come to rest on the sweep of gravel in front of the grand house. After a surprisingly quiet journey up from the station, all was suddenly noise and bustle as servants came down the steps from the front doors carrying lanterns and umbrellas. Enid was first out of the coach and then Aunt Josephine with Chappie straining at his lead to have another grab at Arthur's leg. Arthur let them all go ahead of him, as his mother stood at the top of the steps with open arms. Branson, as ever the perfect butler, stood with the umbrella sheltering Arthur from a sudden squall of rain and nodded with a, *"Nice to see you again, sir."*

Arthur allowed himself a moment to look up at the Hall that had been his home for so many years. The windows on the two main floors glowed with light and all around was the silent evening turning the grounds and woods into deep shadows. He turned away from a vista that reminded him, as it always did, of childhood and hurried up the steps and into the shelter of the portico, where his mother was waiting for him with a warm smile and her arms still held wide. Arthur hugged her and kissed her on both cheeks, while she took his arm and led him into the stately hallway, where a roaring fire threw welcome warmth out to the party of arrivals.

The walls of the huge, double storied hallway rose to enclose the magnificent staircase and the gallery at the top leading towards the main bedrooms and bathrooms. However, on such a cold evening as this, the warmth from the huge fireplace never seemed quite to reach the farthest reaches of the hall and the landings above. This impressive space, like the very best of wealthy homes, was lit by the miracle of gas lighting, while open fires still gave their warmth to all the other family rooms. Arthur was curious to see that revolutionary *radiators* had been installed in his absence that would bring warmth to most of the rooms from a coal-fired boiler in the basement. His mother had written to him several months ago with what she called, 'the thrilling news of this modern invention of comfort for some well-off families, like ourselves'.

Enid managed to disentangle herself from Aunt Josephine, who was trying to persuade the bundle of anger that was Chappie to allow Branson to take him below stairs, where the servants would be expected to tend to his every need. She then handed her hat, umbrella and travelling coat to a maid, squeezed Arthur's arm and turned to his mother, her niece, Dorothy.

"Would you believe that Arthur was late and kept us waiting in the horrible cold rain, but of course we were so pleased to see him…eventually," she said, contorting her pinched features into a somewhat false smile, "now you can get us all into the warmth at long last."

Arthur extricated his arm from Aunt Josephine's grip and put it around his mother's waist.

"It's so very good to be here after what seems such a long time since the summer break. But, where's father? I was expecting him to be pacing the hall because I was just a little late."

Dorothy Tissiman, whose voice tended to rise to a higher octave when she was trying to direct people to the destination she had carefully planned, took her son's arm and, followed by the rest of the party, guided them into the drawing room with some chatter about the draft in the hall and the need to sit down after such a long and tiresome journey. Arthur remained in the dark about his father's absence until his mother had settled them on the sofas on either side of the fire, this time with flames dancing over good Lancashire coal. She was at pains, however, to take him to see and touch the (11) large cast iron radiator attached to the opposite wall.

Then the tea, that had actually been ready for some time, was brought up by two maids in the charge of Branson. The tea itself was poured into Spode cups with similar matching plates for fruitcake. "Made especially by Cook, who knew it was Arthur's favourite," said Dorothy, smiling at her younger son.

Before his mother could demand to hear even more about his journey, Arthur couldn't help repeating his surprise that his father and his brother Ernest were not present. Throughout his childhood and the years of growing into a young man, Arthur feared both his father's silences and his unexpected absences, being certain he had upset or offended him, yet again.

Dorothy was still rather flustered, although Arthur knew full well that his mother, whom he loved dearly, worried if the smooth flow of family life did not go exactly as she had intended. Having touched her crumb-free lips with her linen napkin, she explained, "Well, dear, he has been somewhat busy of late, as poor Ernest has been as well. I never know quite when they will be home and that upsets cook, because dinner could be spoiled… Anyway, as far as I can tell, it is possibly something to do with worries over supplies of cotton? And I think *that* has something to do with the Americas…maybe. Or was it the banks there? Oh dear, I am so silly not to understand. Business seems to muddle my brain even more these days."

A small lace handkerchief now appeared in her hand, replacing the napkin, and the tears that were threatening to run down her cheeks were blotted away before they could show themselves.

Arthur realised, not for the first time that, after many years married to a wealthy mill owner, his mother, a farmer's daughter, was now part of a Victorian society that believed all emotion should be controlled, rather than openly expressed in any way. This was considered appropriate to her role in society that expected all women such as she to follow. Dorothy had long ago become a *lady*. His mother seemed to feel that these ridged rules of society must be applied to the whole family.

She now looked hopefully at the closed drawing room door, but it showed no sign of opening, but Branson was already seeing to the oversight. The room was fashionably cluttered with *objet d'arts*, looked upon with approval by Dorothy's class of friends, a class into which she had not been born, but to which, as time passed and John's wealth grew, she was now accepted, if not fully welcomed. John, however, was happy still occasionally to show a bluff face to all and sundry, regardless of whether they were landed gentry or workers in his mill.

Tea was another excuse to show appropriate manners in the use of the expensive china, silver cutlery, small teatime napkins and the richest cakes to show that there was no shortage of the best food in the Tissiman household, nor a shortage of servants to cater for their every need. The other ladies of the family also showed the appropriate restrained appetite, but the growing awkward silences were, to a general relief, soon abolished with the other men of the family arriving noisily in the hall, as well as the sounds of servants taking coats and hats and the voice of Arthur's father, known to all as his 'bellow', echoing loudly. Dorothy had already hurried through the drawing room door, but her husband remained unaware of this as he stood facing the hall fire, with his back to the sitting room.

John Tissiman's first remark, however, could be heard by all.

"Hurry yourself, Ernest, or we shall be accused of being late by your mother."

He then frowned at Ernest, who was trying with his hands to indicate that his mother now stood silently in the doorway out of his sight, a fixed smile now engraved on her face.

"What! What are you waving at, boy?"

Ernest relieved the awkwardness by hurrying across to his mother, hugged her and said, "So sorry, Mother, we were delayed by some boring chap from the bank when we would have all been much happier with you here."

John glanced over his shoulder, concealing any surprise and muttered, "Ah, there you are."

The tension that had held the whole party in its grip disappeared amid smiles and a welcome home to Arthur. Then more tea was served, cook's cake was praised for its exceptional taste and demands followed that Arthur should tell all about his last year in the city that was at the centre of Britain's vast Empire.

John Tissiman, father of Arthur, Ernest and Enid, looked exactly as a Victorian gentleman of standing and wealth should look, although he was known to claim no interest in either his clothes or appearance. This afternoon, having spent the day conducting business in Manchester, he wore, as usual, a black morning coat, dark trousers that had a faint stripe of grey, a waistcoat and a crisp white shirt with a starched high wing collar and a black cravat; his top hat, overcoat and gloves, had been left with Branson in the hall. On this November Wednesday, he was nine months short of his fifty-first birthday.

Ernest, the eldest child of John and Dorothy, had been born in 1830 and had subsequently married Elizabeth, Betty to her family and friends, just two years ago in 1858; she was within a few days, five years younger than Ernest. She had been born in the Yorkshire dales into an affluent farming family with a huge flock of sheep in their almost one thousand acres of rolling land. Due to the demand for wool in the mills of Yorkshire, the family were considered *comfortable*, although her marriage to Ernest presented her with a step up on the social ladder, so important to those in the ever-expanding middle class of Victorian England.

Aunt Josephine was Betty's mother's elder sister. Eighteen months earlier, she had moved to Waterhead Hall, in reality because the family home had to be sold to pay debts, and she now deeply resented what she perceived as her *charity* status as companion and chaperone. Josephine knew she was now bound for another role, since Elizabeth had announced almost a year ago that she and Ernest were 'expecting'. Sadly, the pregnancy lasted only two months before it was ended by a miscarriage. Josephine, full of appropriate sympathy, was much relieved not to be expected to undertake yet another role that would have included a baby; Josephine had never liked babies.

Although time had now passed since Betty's loss, she was still advised by the family physician, Doctor Foster, to take only light exercise, but had not yet ventured out of doors recently into the cold and wet winter that lay siege to the Hall, where a warm atmosphere was present in all family rooms.

The doctor had spoken privately to Ernest and confidentially advised him that another pregnancy in the near future would be most inadvisable. He discretely suggested that it was up to Ernest to ensure this did not happen. This meant that Aunt Josephine would not then be obliged to take on a mother and new baby, although she had already expressed here opinion that whenever such a time of trial might arise, it would be the Almighty's means to test Betty's faith and stamina. Josephine was grateful that her own faith and stamina were not now to be tested, at least for the time being. Tonight Betty would dine with the family in the dining room for the first time in the several months of her recovery, rather than with Aunt Josephine in the small sitting room off Betty's bedroom.

As in all homes of this class, a single gong was sounded to remind the family that it was time to dress for dinner. They were all obliged to observe the call and to make their way upstairs. They would reassemble in the drawing room in sufficient time to have what tonight, instead of sherry, would be champagne in honour of Arthur's long-awaited presence at the Hall.

The dressing gong having sounded, each member made their way up to bedrooms and dressing rooms to prepare for a dinner to welcome the prodigal son. John and Dorothy had connecting bedrooms with dressing rooms and bathrooms off each, another arrangement that had existed for far longer in aristocratic families, but more recently had been adopted by the wealthy 'upper middle classes', whose wealth came, not from inherited wealth and a stately home, but from earned wealth and large, more modern mansions.

# Chapter Two

Dinner consisted that night of a beef broth followed by roast mallard duck with small, roast potatoes, peas and cabbage and then a dessert of a white wine jelly with poached pears. John Tissiman still preferred the term of his childhood: pudding! And be damned. It was a sign of the special nature of the meal that a savoury of sardines on toast was served after the dessert.

Unfortunately, it was hard for all present not to detect an uneasy feeling just under the surface of the lengthy meal. Not surprisingly, it would have been socially unacceptable to speak of it, even though no one could have been unaware of the reason, which rested on the shoulders of the three gentlemen, who were trying to keep up untroubled conversations throughout what felt a very lengthy occasion. There were silences, not usual at a Tissiman family dinner, followed by several speaking at once, trying to fill the awkward pauses.

It was with some relief to everyone that Dorothy gathered the ladies together as soon as the last mouthful of savoury was eaten, partly full wine glasses were abandoned and the four of the ladies made a speedy departure to the drawing room for coffee, although not before, Dorothy hesitated long enough to look meaningfully at John and then speak quietly to him.

"John, dear, don't you and Ernest keep Arthur for long as I'm sure he must be most weary after such a long journey and…er…the weather, you know."

She left, dabbing her mouth with her napkin, which she had forgotten to leave on the table and which she then handed absently to Aunt Josephine, who looked at it in shock and immediately dropped it on the floor. There followed an overloaded silence in the room as the ladies left and Jervis, the footman, closed the double doors behind them. Branson quickly placed a decanter of port on the table in front of John, followed by the humidor of cigars.

"Will there be anything else, sir?"

"No, nothing until we join the ladies, thank you, Branson." The butler withdrew with the quietness that was expected of all the servants.

Ernest had already moved up the table to sit at his father's right hand, while Arthur remained where he had been sitting next to Dorothy at the other end of the table during dinner.

"Come along, my boy; join us up here for a glass or two and one of my best Havana cigars… Oh, apologies, I forget some times that you don't smoke, unlike the rest of us." John made an obvious effort, but failed to appear the genial host.

Arthur displayed a gesture with both hands that was almost like a truncated wave, looked around the table as if he had failed to notice the departure of the ladies and slowly rose to sit at his father's left hand. The decanter was passed, with a full glass for John and Ernest and a very small dose for Arthur. John raised his eyebrows in surprise, although Arthur knew it was no such thing.

"Easily forgotten, Father," he said, with ill-concealed annoyance.

There followed a painful pause, which John felt it his duty to fill.

"Well, tell us all about your last year at the college, Arthur. We, of course, had your rather occasional letters. You must be most relieved to be home for good at last and keen, I'm sure, to start the long process of learning our ways at Crompton Mill as soon as possible, eh?"

"I'm sure that is true, is it not, Arthur?" Ernest smiled across the rim of his glass, as he raised it to his lips and half the contents disappeared. Both Arthur's father and brother now looked expectantly at him.

Arthur hesitated, glanced into his glass, swilled the shallow draught around and placed it untouched on the table before raising his eyes to both his seniors.

"Actually, Father, I was more interested to hear about what Mother mentioned before you both arrived: something about a shortage of cotton, banking problems and the *Americas?* Is there a problem at Crompton Street?"

John looked briefly at Ernest, but he made no attempt to speak before his father.

"Good Lord, no! Whatever gave her that idea? It's all the same as ever and the same as it will be when you join the family firm."

"Come on, Arthur," Ernest leant forward, laid his smouldering cigar in the cut glass ashtray and leant his elbows on the table so that his unblinking stare was focussed on his brother. "You know perfectly well that Mother, lovely as she is, of course, and whom we all naturally love dearly, does tend to get matters of business, matters that do not really need to concern her, somewhat…how can I put it? Muddled?"

John was nodding; his head now wreathed in blue smoke, but with what Arthur felt was a rather grim smile. Both father and elder son now looked to Arthur, presumably expecting his agreement.

"That may be so and I am well aware that my long absences in London have meant that I am somewhat out of touch with production at the mill. As you know, I have had other things to fill my time. However, we do have newspapers in London, you know, newspapers that report not simply the news in the capital of our country."

"I say, Arthur, that's a bit strong if I may say so. I am sure Father was not criticising your *educational* studies that have kept you, understandably, of course, somewhat at a distance from what you call *our mill in the north*."

Arthur cut Ernest off at that point and with Ernest's voice rising, he, too, found himself almost shouting over his brother.

"What I was about to say was that the London *Times* has reported recently from Washington, which I am sure you are aware is the capital of the United States of America, that there has been a problem with banks failing and worry about a cotton shortage as a result. They actually mention Manchester's suffering as it has always been the supplier of cotton to the whole Empire."

Ernest then got as far as, "What on earth do you think you know about..." before Arthur continued to speak over his brother.

"There are also reports that there is a possibility of Civil War between the southern and northern states and that could cause the northern states, which will be opposed by most of the south, to blockade shipments of cotton from the south to England."

Both brothers now jumped to their feet and John raised the volume of his deep voice. "Boys! Sit down... if you please."

Both did so and each looked across at the other with the smugness that the certainty of righteousness brings with it.

"I sincerely hope that the ladies did not hear this childish outburst," he continued. "You will both apologise to one another this instant." His penetrating blue eyes now settled on Arthur and then Ernest; silence stretched.

Arthur came to his senses first. "Ernest, I apologise for raising my voice. I trust you will forgive my bad manners." He slowly resumed his seat.

Ernest smiled deprecatingly. "Of course I forgive you, brother, and admit I was also partly in the wrong."

Arthur opened his mouth, but closed it abruptly on whatever he might have been tempted to reply. He then stood again, left his crumpled linen napkin and untouched port on the table. He turned to his father.

"Forgive me, Father, but I feel I must retire. I am most tired and it has been a long and weary day. Please convey my apologies to Mother and I will see you all in the morning." He inclined his head, ignored his brother and left the room, closing the door very quietly behind him.

"Oh, my word!" was all Ernest could find to say, attempting to smother the smile on his lips.

John emptied his glass, refilled it again and drank that off as well. He stubbed his cigar out and left the room without a word, leaving the door open. Ernest saw him cross the hall and enter the drawing room, closing the door firmly. The sound of the voices of the ladies could be heard briefly, as he entered and then it stopped as the door closed.

The following morning, which was uncharacteristically bright but still with a cold wind from the north, Miss Maggie Wilkinson was taking a constitutional walk through Alexander Park with her older sister, Agnes. The pair, as daughters of the most senior Methodist Minister in Oldham, were dressed in simple, sombre colours, mostly purples and greys. Their hats were of the same shades, but with somewhat dull cotton flowers sewn around the crown. Agnes, who was nine years older than Margaret and had just celebrated her thirtieth birthday, insisted on treating her sister as if she were her daughter, which annoyed Maggie intensely. As the pair followed the gravel path from the gates towards the lake with its ducks and large lakeside pavilion, Agnes's next remark reinforced Margaret's view.

"Father was surprised that you did not attend the Bible class last evening, Maggie. Has he spoken to you about that yet?"

"I was forced to go back to my room by six o'clock, as you well know, with a most unpleasant headache. I am sure Father was well aware of that and I'm surprised he said anything to the contrary to you." Maggie stopped where the path passed under two giant, but now leafless weeping willow trees and turned to Agnes with a questioning stare. "Well?"

"Perhaps he forgot that. You know only—"

She was interrupted by the appearance of a young man, dressed largely in dull black, but with a most unconventionally deep red waistcoat, rounding the bend in the path and almost colliding with the stationary sisters. He touched his hat to them and Agnes gave him no chance to speak.

"Why, Mr Arthur Tissiman, I do believe. Margaret has spoken of you I seem to recall, in most positive terms, although we have not been introduced have we?"

She looked over her shoulder at Maggie, who was finding it impossible to stop the blush rising slowly up her neck and threatened to spread to her cheeks. "You should introduce us, Margaret."

Maggie, not normally one to be lost for words, nor suffering from shyness, seemed to be finding it difficult to make any words come out of her mouth. Agnes smiled at Arthur and took a step towards him, leaving Maggie in limbo. Arthur took off his hat and inclined his head slightly towards the older sister.

"How remiss of me, Miss Wilkinson. I know of you of course, having heard my father speak of his recent meeting with the minister. I am delighted to meet you myself."

Arthur then offered her his hand. Agnes, surprised to find what she had intended as a rather awkward situation for her young sister, now became a polite meeting and she could do nothing but reluctantly shake Arthur's hand, which had a very firm grip and was accompanied by a broad smile.

"Your sister and I have met from time to time at the Chapel, where I find your father a most stimulating speaker, as I am sure your do." Arthur's firm handshake and direct look prevented Agnes from pursuing the embarrassment she had intended. Meanwhile, Maggie was transfixed by the stones on the path and was pushing them slowly around with her foot.

"And how are you today, Miss Wilkinson?" Arthur was determined to bring Maggie into the conversation. "I find it a little chilly myself, but so pleasant to see even the occasional patch of blue sky in November, don't you agree?"

Maggie managed to pull herself together and look at Arthur for the first time since he arrived.

"Indeed, Mr Tissiman, but I am feeling the cold now myself and my sister and I need to hurry home and get inside where it is a little warmer. Come along, Agnes, we don't want to keep Father fretting if his tea is late."

She linked her arm with Agnes and almost pulled her around to return the way they had come. As they reached the first bend, Arthur was treated to Maggie's hand, enclosed in its lace glove, give a small wave behind her back, while Maggie herself did not turn her head even slightly. Arthur frowned and then a smile spread across his face. What a tease this girl was already proving to be.

Neither sister spoke a word, as they made their way home. The coldness between them seemed reflected in the afternoon's growing colder, as they walked past the grand Anglican church of St Mary & St Peter and then downhill, where streets of back-to-back houses crowded the narrowing road and the pavements disappeared. The day seemed to fade faster now they were 'below town' among the unlit streets, mills, forges, factories, piles of coal dust and tiny courtyards, the only places where water could be pumped and where a washhouse and a lavatory, without water or drainage, existed for anything up to fifty people in a row of two-up-two-down houses. Projecting above the sister's heads in all directions and as far as the eye could see were dozens of tall mill chimneys that belched black coal smoke for all hours of the day and generally at night as well.

They passed three public houses, closed on a Sunday, although the debris of Saturday night still littered the road with filthy sawdust, dog ends and broken pieces of clay pipes, as well as the occasional puddle of drying vomit and ordure attracting scavenging dogs, of which there were many, as well as their own foul droppings.

Although the silence was growing heavy between them, both sisters were determined not to be the first to speak, even though they gripped each other's arms tighter, as they passed the few lighted windows casting a half-hearted glimmer into the darkening street. Turning the last corner into Long Street, with the Manse only a few hundred yards ahead, they both let out a squeal of fear when a dark corner at the end of a terrace moved and then gave a groan...or was it a growl? The sisters stopped and Agnes had one hand over her mouth and the other pulled Maggie tightly against her.

Maggie could make out the shape of a man's body huddled against the wall, his groans sounding as if his life were about to end. She pulled herself from Agnes's grip, even though her sister tried to stop her.

"No, Maggie! Quickly! We must get home at once...He could have a knife! All his kind have them. Come home at once!" The last words were accompanied by her stamping her foot in annoyance.

Maggie had already left her distraught sister with her hands to her mouth, and was kneeling in front of the bedraggled figure. "Come along... John? It is

John Cope, isn't it? It's Margaret Wilkinson, John. You know Minister Wilkinson's daughter? I will help you, so stop making that noise."

The groaning grew a little quieter as Maggie took his hand, ignoring the grime covering both his hands and face and the stench coming from filthy, torn clothes that could not have seen either water or repair for a very long time and were not helped by the vomit stains.

"You remember me, don't you, John? I was here at the Manse just last week and you were in the line for soup?"

She received no reply and his eyes stayed fixed on the ground. Agnes, her hands still held to her mouth, looked at the scene with horror, but could not find the courage to move, nor even to run home, as she so badly wanted to do.

"John? Look at me, John." Maggie noticed that his feet, stained with smudges of what looked like ash or maybe mud, were without clogs or any other covering.

"Where are your shoes, John?"

His response was sudden and totally unexpected. His arm shot out and grabbed Maggie's hand. He seemed much stronger that she would have believed possible. She tried to prise his fingers apart, but he held her tighter still. Agnes now screamed, but stepped further back, away from her sister, then turned and started to run towards the Manse.

Maggie tried not to panic as she realised that Agnes had left her. "John! Stop now and I will help you. You know I will."

The voice, when at last it came, was a tortured and frenzied scream.

"You! You can't help me…you stuck up bitch! Where's your God now? Eh? Not here he ain't."

His lurched forward, grabbed her arm and began to twist it until she yelped with pain. His face was now just a few inches from her own.

"Please, John. You don't need to do this. I promise that God really loves you."

For a moment, she thought he was about to bite her and jerked her head back. It was then that she heard the sound of running feet behind her and the imperious voice of her father.

"Leave her alone, man! Leave her I say!"

The Reverend Nathanial Wilkinson was no giant, but powerfully built and dressed in black, with his frock coat now billowing behind him and his face surrounded by his Old Testament beard, he could have been mistaken for the angel of death. Just before he reached Maggie, John dropped her hand and fell to the ground, his arms protectively covering his head with his body screwed into a ball. From somewhere inside came a whimper of pain.

"Don't hurt me sir! I ain't done nothin'. Please don't…"

Maggie was now in her father's arms, where he held her firmly, while his face showed only pity, as he looked down at the pathetic creature scrabbling on the ground at his feet. There was no sign of Agnes, although when she looked very carefully Maggie could see her standing in the glow of gas light coming from the open door of the Manse, her head cradled in her mother's arms. *Look for the plank in your own eye*, was the angry Biblical quotation that came into her mind.

Maggie's attention quickly moved back to John Cope, the reality of his still howling on the ground at their feet forcing her to quell her own foolish fear and try to become a Good Samaritan. She had, not surprisingly, regularly attended her father's chapel all her life, often more than once on a Sunday and had been happy to help serve a mug of tea and some bread, sometimes soup, to those in the long queue, usually women, who came to the service hoping to take home a meal of sorts for their family.

Maggie had always enjoyed attending Sunday school ever since she was five years old, especially the thrilling stories read by her father or one of the wardens. She clearly remembered sitting on a hard wooden pew, often in the freezing chapel. Now her imagination transferred those stories and parables into the reality today of life in the slums of Oldham. She knew, almost by heart, the tales of David and Goliath or Ruth lonely amid the alien corn or, like this evening, the Good Samaritan stopping to help the poor man who had been attacked by robbers on the road to Jericho, but was ignored by all who passed him by. She could not help the words that swam across the livid picture in her mind: *Just like Agnes!*

So Maggie pulled herself together. "Father, we cannot leave this poor Christian soul, who deserves our pity, here in the gutter."

Her father had dropped John's arm and started to say, "No Maggie, no…" but was ignored by his feisty daughter determined to become the Good Samaritan in her mind's picture from her Bible. She leant down again and touched John's cheek, which was covered in grime smeared by the rivulets of his tears, but he lay unmoving where he had collapsed, like a stone statue, fallen and now broken.

Maggie gagged at the smell coming from his body and clothes, but kept her hand on his face, as she looked up at her father. Her eyes were wide open with a tear in the corners, a look she had cultivated long ago and which she knew full well her father could rarely resist. Her father gave a deep sigh and leant down. He stepped behind John Cope and, using his strong arms, took hold of the shoulders of what he knew he must regard as a poor, lost creature, sadly like many thousands of others, poor and hopeless in this grim town. As gently as he could, he pulled him upright, where he hung like a broken marionette. Between them, Maggie and her father dragged him to the door of the Manse.

Maggie was delighted to push Agnes aside and reassured herself that it was not the pinch she had applied to her sister's arm that caused her to scream again and then run up the stairs. Mrs Wilkinson, clearly seeing the appalling state of the man, helped her husband and daughter move him to the kitchen, where he collapsed on a chair and laid his head on the scrubbed wooden table.

John Cope, aged just thirty-nine years, was one of thousands in Below Town Oldham, who saw no future, just a miserable existence for himself, his wife Jean and his five children, aged from the baby of two months to George now eight years old. John had had several short-lived jobs since losing his place at Crompton Mill, from collecting night soil to dying cloth in the huge vats on Cart Row, but none had lasted more than a few days. The more employment he lost, the more he drank in the dozen or so public houses, taverns and gin palaces within walking distance of their rented tenement behind Frederick Street. He had tried daily to borrow a few coins to buy a beer, which for a time made the world seem brighter. Having run out of other drinkers to beg for money, he ran up a 'slate' at every drinking place and was now barred from all of them. He was starving and filthy and had lost any pride he might once have had.

He was angry with his family for their expectations of him as the provider, although it was Jean who worked at Crompton Mill six days a week and brought home five shillings every Saturday. George, their eight-year-old, had been lucky enough to get a job as a scavenger last week at the Mill, working between the never stopping looms, cleaning and looking for *cloggings*. The job was highly dangerous, as his friend Donny had found out a month ago when he had to have his hand amputated, without expensive anaesthetic, above the wrist after it was jammed in one of the steam-powered looms; he would never work again. God knew what his future held.

Even George's one shilling a week was welcome. The rent for their two-up, one down, with use of the water pump and the overflowing privy in the yard, already came to shillings a week. Starvation loomed continually for this and for so many other families.

Rachel Wilkinson, the Reverend's wife of thirty-five years, looked pleadingly at her husband.

"What do we do now, Nathanial? He cannot stay here and I know Jean Cope from Chapel. She will be distraught by now. Those five children have little to eat and no…"

A knock at the front door stopped her in mid-sentence. Nathanial simply said, "Wait here."

He opened the heavy front door of the Manse, causing those outside to jump back. The dim light in the street revealed a woman with a black shawl covering her head and shoulders with a baby in her arms while several other ragged children clung to her skirts. Nathanial realised she must be young, but her sunken cheeks and stooped body looked more like a fifty or sixty-year-old. The children stared open mouthed at the clergyman. Nathanial was used to such sights on the streets of Oldham, but had still never grown used to such desperate poverty on his doorstep.

"Would you be looking for John Cope?"

The children huddled closer to their mother at the sight of the man who looked like one of the angry prophets they had heard about at Sunday school. They simply stared up at him and the warmth and light that glowed behind him.

Reverend Wilkinson was never short of words and now continued, "Come inside where it is warmer. I recognise you from chapel, Mrs Cope."

Still no response and so he put his arm out to Jean, whom he well knew was John's wife. Gradually, he persuaded the frozen group of human detritus, washed up on his doorstep, to move inside. Both mother and children looked truly terrified, as they moved hesitantly into the kitchen to be greeted by a sight they knew only too well.

Their father looked up and glared at them. He tried to stand, but staggered back and clung to the mantle shelf above the range which glowed with bright heat. "You! Git yourself and yer bloody brats out of 'ere or you'll feel me belt when I get 'ome."

He swayed towards them. The children screamed, the baby yelled as they tried to move themselves out of John Cope's intended lunge. Nathanial caught

41

him by the arm and stopped him falling. Agnes's scream added to the cacophony, as she peered into the room from the bottom of the stairs. Nathanial still held John's arm and with Maggie's help lowered him back onto the chair. Maggie then turned her attention to Jean and the children, gently guiding them towards the parlour.

It was several hours later, after Jean and her children had drunk a mug of tea and greedily gulped down some bread and cheese, that Nathanial and Maggie accompanied them back to their house just a few streets away. Maggie handed Jean a basket with the rest of the bread and some milk. Nathanial sent a message to one of his churchwardens to fetch John Cope and make sure he also got home.

Once back inside the Manse, Maggie and Nathanial, with Agnes joining them and, having assured herself that all the Cope family had left, Rachel made tea for the family. No one made any attempt to speak about what had happened until Nathanial put down his cup with a sigh and looked at his family, warm and without hunger, sitting around the open range in the kitchen. He acutely felt the chasm of difference that lay between even their meagre life in the chapel and the Manse and the desperate poverty of families like the Copes, who lived all around them. His gaze settled on his two daughters.

"I think we could all learn something from what happened here this evening. It is less of a shock to me than you, I suspect, although I am pleased that, of course, your mother always accompanies me, and sometimes Maggie, in arranging soup and bread as often as we can in the chapel." Maggie glared at her sister who smiled and looked her in the eye as her father said this and then went on with his eyes still on his family.

"Margaret, you have seen some of the little help we can give our many starving brothers and sisters. There are so many and not just here in Oldham."

"But, Father," interrupted Agnes, "surely this is because men like John Cope won't work to feed their families. They are idle and drunk and—"

"Agnes! How dare you make light of poverty and starvation."

The Reverend Nathanial glared at both of his daughters. "Agnes, I blame myself I suppose for not making sure you see this world as it truly is. And Margaret, you are too hasty to blame others for the evil that surrounds us. You need to take the plank out of your own eye and look to yourself first."

Both girls looked at the floor and their mother glanced from one to the other. Maggie felt a surge of guilt rising inside, as she recalled what she had silently accused Agnes of a very short time before.

"You should know better, girls," he continued. "We are *all* sinners in our way, you as much as anyone else. When we all learn to help each other, perhaps then we shall be allowed to see the Promised Land. Until then, I would like you both to go to bed and to remember John Cope and all like him in your prayers."

# Chapter Three

The Cope family, seven in all, lived in a terrace house on Frederick Street, just around the corner from Crompton Mill in Werneth, an area all too typical of Below Town. Nevertheless, Werneth, with its many adjoining streets, was one of the poorest and roughest parts of Oldham in 1860, the twenty-third year of the reign of Victoria, Queen and Empress of India, monarch of cities from Calcutta to Mandalay, from Cape Town to Birmingham, and even Oldham. Those like the Cope family could never comprehend the riches that were accumulated in Victoria's Britain by the wealthy and land-owning classes, who were, in their eyes, people of a different species of humanity to ordinary, poor folk like themselves.

Thomas Robinson, one of the wardens of the Methodist Chapel, half carried, half walked John Cope from the Manse that cold November evening, when darkness combined with coal smoke from the mills to turn the night black, with only dim patches of light from oil lamps and candles in some of the few windows of the back-to-back terraces.

The street was airless, as well as dark with motes of coal dust in the air. Thomas and his human burden passed pieces of dismal waste ground covered with mud and blackened bricks and rubbish. The bricks, which in their virgin state were red Accrington stock, were left over from building the terraces of houses. The two men also came across, even at that time of night, others out of work, gaunt and dirty, unshaven and with greasy hair and often no shoes or clogs, hanging around street corners, with nowhere else to go.

As they reached the far end of Frederick Street, Thomas dragged John Cope to a stop in front of a dark, long terrace of houses where he half-remembered John's family lived. John showed no recognition of where he was. The houses were blackened and looked as exhausted as the people who rented them. (12) *'Mean looking and straggling, shabby and looking underdone'* as one young minister, new to the region, had recently described the area in a letter to his mother in far off Lyme Regis.

"Where's the passage into your yard, John? I can't see anything. There are no lights."

John, who had sobered a little on his enforced walk, tried to shake off Thomas's arm that was supporting him and stumbled as a result. Thomas caught him before he fell into what looked like mud along the side of the street, but which Thomas knew only too well contained far worse material than mud.

"Take your fucking hands off me!" John yelled into his face and Thomas grabbed his arm away and wiped his own face of the spittle. John veered to the side of the road and then disappeared. Thomas quickly realised that he must have wandered down one of the narrow passages, the *jitties* that led to the courts that served anything up to twenty of the dozens of back-to-back houses along both sides of the street. Thomas Robinson tried hard to regard all men as basically good, which is what the Reverend Wilkinson commanded him to do every Sunday, and so he followed John Cope into the passage, albeit with some trepidation.

As he came to the other end, light glowed dimly from windows on the far side of the yard. He was able to distinguish the pump in the middle of the filthy space and the doors along both sides that he knew led into what he knew would be numerous houses. Thomas gagged at the stench that was now reaching his nostrils. He pulled out his handkerchief which, although none too clean, did help him to breathe more easily. He knew the smell of human excrement came from the single outhouse lavatory that would serve the fifty or sixty people living here.

He heard a door slam and then John Cope shouting, although he could not make out what he said. He crossed the yard to one of the darkened lodgings, from where the shouting still seemed to come. He knocked at the door and then stood well back, as he felt might be advisable.

The door was opened wide enough for him to distinguish a woman's face, her head covered in a shawl. She was gripping the door with one hand and hiding something at her side with the other. He could see that she was being pulled back from behind.

"Get back from me, you drunkard! Get back John or, God help me, I'll smash yer 'ead in with this pan!"

Whoever had been trying to pull her away from the door must have seen sense, because she relaxed her grip and glared through the murk at Thomas.

"And what do you want, Thomas Robinson, disturbin' law abidin' folk?"

She got no further, as a child now started to scream. "Mam! Mam! E's got Georgie down on't floor…"

The door then slammed and the woman he had spoken to a moment before now yelled through the closed door. "An' you get out of 'ere!"

Thomas felt he had done as much, or even more, than was his Christian duty and turned, felt his way out of the court, through the passage and, at a brisk trot, headed for home.


The steam whistles of dozens of mills sounded, more or less together, ten minutes before six o'clock the next morning and no mill manager would ever consider even a little leniency in meeting that iron-clad hour to start work on any morning, bar Sunday. When the whistles screamed Below Town, it was the signal that it was time to hurry to work. The workers themselves, aged from as young as eight years old, or even younger, up to the dreaded age when a worker was no longer able, through illness, disability or simply old age to continue rushing through the streets to meet the six o'clock deadline. Once the whistle had ceased its call, the gates would be closed within a few minutes and locked until the fourteen-hour shift ended.

At the two up and one down terrace house that the Cope family rented, it was still pitch dark at half past five that Wednesday morning when Jean came down the narrow wooden stairway to try to catch the embers of the range before they died. Firstly, she had to find a candle stub that still had enough wax to light so that she could see what she was doing. Having rummaged through the box of small candle ends and found one that had about half its original life remaining, she lit it and then pulled open the range door to be met with just a little suggestion of warmth. She raked the old coals over to find a spark of light, hoping that the screwed-up piece of old newspaper in her hand could persuade it to come to life again. She tried blowing onto the tiny glow she had uncovered and prayed that today of all days, it would catch. She then put two or three small lumps of coal carefully against the flickering flame, closed the door and stood back up, gasping, as her knees reminded her she was now nearer forty rather than thirty years old.

That was all she could do to get some warmth into the dark, freezing kitchen. She stood the candle on a saucer on the table and then, by its dim light, opened the cupboard where any food in the house was kept. She always knew what she would find, but that never stopped the thought that some miracle may have sought out her family overnight and more would be there than there was yesterday, which had been virtually nothing. Today there was at least a heel of bread that, although now hard, she would moisten with hot water once the kettle boiled. There was also a potato in reasonable shape that she was saving for John's breakfast once it had sat in the oven for long enough to make it at least edible.

As her precious clock, which had been left to her by her mother nearly twenty years ago and was now back on the mantle after a long spell in the pawn shop, ticked around to twenty minutes to six. Jean took the candle and went back up the stairs to wake George, the only other person who would work today. She could still hear John snoring in the tiny bedroom on one side of the tiny landing and trod as quietly as she could to avoid waking him. The children's door was partly open, but thank God there was no sound from them. Three-month-old Gertrude had been awake off and on in their room throughout the night and the only blessing was that John had still been too drunk to wake.

She stood the candle on the floor just outside the open door and by its faint glow, stepped carefully around the narrow bed where Jess and Letty slept. George shared the other single bed with Nat, who was two years younger than George's eight years. Because George always had to sleep next to the wall, she had to reach over Nat to wake him. After eight years, she was used to the fact that he was terrified of not being enclosed safely between his brother and a solid wall at night. She put her hand over his mouth as she gently shook him and whispered his name. The ginger haired boy came awake with a jerk and flung his arm across Nat, who woke with a cry of 'Mam'!

Ignoring him Jean dragged George out of bed into the cold room. As usual at this time of year, the children slept in all their clothes and so she pushed him towards the stairs.

"Bloody 'ell, Mam! It ain't mornin'. Stop pushin' me!"

Nat was by now also complaining loudly, Gert was awake and screaming, while Jess and Letty pulled the thin old blanket over their heads and stayed where they were.

"George! 'Ow many times must I tell you 'bout swearin'? Now get down them stairs."

As she closed the door, picked up the candle and put her foot on the top step, John bellowed from their bedroom.

"Fuck the hell up! All of yer! If you don't fucking be quiet, you'll feel me belt, yer little buggers!"

George was downstairs by now. Jean turned back, opened the door again, scooped up the still screaming Gertrude and also pushed Nat ahead of her down the stairs. She slammed the door at the bottom.

"'ere George, you take Gert...no, no jus' do it."

George for all his bravado was used to looking after his baby sister and, although he wouldn't admit it, rather liked her warmth and the smell of her soft skin.

Nat was standing in a sort of daze, but at least he was quiet.

"Now yer both sit there by the range. There's a bit o' bread 'ere I've softened and the kettle's boilin' for some tea. Nat you pour that out, there's a good lad. I'm goin' to put me apron and shawl on and then I'm outside to the lavvy for a minute. Anyone else wants it, come with me or 'old it in."

When she got outside to the court, there was enough pale light in the eastern sky to make out the terrace at the back of the court, the pump and the door to the outhouse lavatory where a rough wooden seat with a hole in the middle was wedged over the pit. The boys had obviously decided to wait until it was lighter; George had another terrible fear, this time of the rats and 'roaches that he thought were waiting for him in the dark. Jean rattled the door as hard as she could and waited as she heard the scurrying of tiny feet beat a retreat. She used the lavatory as quickly as possible and knew that the next break at the mill would still be many hours away.

Pulling her shawl back over her head and around her shoulders, checking her apron was the right way around in the growing light, then pushing her feet into her clogs, she opened the kitchen door and to her relief found a quiet baby in George's arms and no sound from above. The clock now showed a quarter to six. Crompton Mill was ten minute's fast walk away.

"George, give Nat the baby." George hated parting from his sister like this every morning, but handed her over.

"Nat, when the clock says six," here she pointed carefully to where the hand s must be, "you take Gert over to Jane 'cross the court. She's expectin' her as usual…and don't no one wake yer dad."

"But, Mam, it'll be dark yet and I'm frightened of…" He was forced into silence, as the whistles from the mills all over the town filled the streets with the insistent scream that drove thousands to rush outside and head together down the streets to work, like rats running from a flood.

Jean and George were already out the door and half walking, half running down towards the mill. The huge clock over Crompton Mill gateway was showing three minutes to six, as they arrived outside the huge cotton mill that stretched for over two hundred yards along the street from the gateway. It was built of red Accrington brick, six floors high with windows that that were not designed to open. A giant chimney, tapering upwards for over sixty feet, belched black smoke to join that of all the other Oldham mills, blowing away in the direction of the rest of Below Town. Crompton Mill was a twenty-four-hour mill and had shifts at night as well as during the day.

It was a vast, imposing place, even more so to someone of George's age. To Jean, it simply meant a way to keep her family from starvation, provided she and George worked hard enough for fourteen hours, six days every week.

# Chapter Four

Jean Cope, nee Peake, had been born in Oldham almost thirty-five years ago, only a matter of four streets away from Crompton Mill in Werneth, Oldham. She had married John Cope at an age considered quite late for Below Town: just nineteen years old. On days like today, Jean could not remember what had persuaded her to marry John, although ten years ago, aged twenty-four, he seemed to have good prospects with a job as an overseer at the Mill. At that time, John was a very different man. He was good looking, tall with ginger hair, a moustache and a muscular body. Even though he was an overseer, all the workers on his floor of the mill liked and respected him. Although he did have a reputation of never putting up with slackers, he was considered a fair man. He was secretly proud to have grown up in a strictly Christian home, mainly thanks to his mother, who ran a teetotal family and had the reputation as a harridan.

George had already gone off with a crowd of other boys into the mill. Jean stopped inside the archway watching Mr Groom slam the iron gates behind them, turn the large key in the lock and hurry back into the mill. Jean suddenly felt the weight of the years on her shoulders thinking back to the first few years of her marriage, of how thrilled they both were when George arrived after almost two years, but by the time Jess was born a year later, everything had changed. Almost two years ago, John had got into a fight on the machine floor he supervised. He had never told Jean what the fight was about, but he had shattered Bob Scudder's jaw and, more seriously, smashed into one of the looms, causing eight of them to be stopped. Mr Ernest sacked him on the spot and threw him out of the mill. The immediate loss of his ten shillings a week changed everything for the Cope family and they had never recovered.

It took John only a few days to turn to drink, which he funded by regularly taking George's one and sixpence off him on a Saturday night, leaving Jean with her five-shilling wage that hardly paid the rent. Even this, however, was far from sacred to John, who now needed drink as his only friend. Jean had started to take in clothes from neighbours that needed mending or patching. As soon as Jess was old enough, she helped with this and also looked after Gert when Jane Ernshaw, across the court, wasn't working herself at the mill; Jane was twelve years old and worked night shifts.

There were so many weeks when Jean had to try to avoid the rent man, but that led in the end to pawning something she was unlikely ever to redeem: her clock. They often lived without candles and more often without food. Inevitably, she always gave the children what she could scrape together or maybe even *beg*, her own hated word, outside the Methodist chapel on a Sunday. That Methodist girl gave her a shilling, under the Rectory table, and now Mam's clock was back, at least for a week or two.

Luckily for Jean, it was Jacob Ernshaw who spotted her that morning as she was lost in thought just outside the mill doors. "Hey! Jean! What you dreamin' of, girl? Git yerself inside double quick afore old Bluebeard spots you."

John Tissiman was known to most workers as 'Bluebeard' and had the nasty habit of being at the mill himself on some days before the six o'clock whistle so that he could catch any late arrivals.

"I 'eard that your John was in a sorry state ag'in yesterday evenin', 'cause my 'ettie saw that creep Robinson draggin' him 'ome," Jacob sounded pleased to point out.

Jean had no time for anything other than a nod as she now rushed through the doors and up the stairs to the second floor. Once inside the mill, the noise hit her like one of those steam trains. Many workers on the floors became partly, or even wholly, deaf after a few years. There were one thousand three hundred steam powered looms on each floor and they were in operation twenty-four hours a day. Running up the stairs for fear of being noticed as late, Jean was gasping for breath within minutes.

Jean had worked at Crompton Mill for twenty years, starting as a ten-year-old child whose job it was to get under the looms, which never stopped, to pull out waste cotton, slap on grease where needed and watch for bobbins that had stuck, threatening to close down a loom. This had to be done at lightning speed and injury was common, even if often reasonably minor, maybe twisting a wrist or an arm, or more seriously drawing blood on exposed limbs; even having a hand or arm partly torn off was not unknown. Jean was more worried about George than herself, as he scurried on his hands and knees under the machines all day. They all worked on the day shift for fourteen hours with only two short breaks of about fifteen minutes to eat whatever snacks they might have brought from home. However, in this break, the women were expected to maintain their looms, which often involved re-greasing at least some of them.

The noise was so great that the one hundred and sixty women operating the looms on each floor quickly learned sign language of a sort and on this Monday morning Jean, as she took over charge of eight looms from Elsie Long, signed 'hello', understood a question of 'how's your old man this morning' and answered with a shrug of her shoulders.

She had long since ceased to notice the air filled with what could have been a snow storm, but were actually fine spots of cotton lint that inevitably they breathed in all day, every day for six days a week. This was made worse by the warm, damp atmosphere created by steam being sent to every floor to keep the thread from breaking and windows that were not made to open. Jean's congested lungs were so common that no one remarked on it any longer and they all knew better than to seek out a doctor, whose fees were way beyond the reach of the workers at Crompton Mill.

Jacob Ernshaw was one of several overseers on her floor and now, as he made his rounds of the machines, he gave Jean a pat on the shoulder and a look of understanding. She had known both Jacob and Hettie ever since she joined the mill. Both of them were several years older than she was.

She and Jacob were alerted, not so much by a scream, which could hardly be heard, but by another overseer several rows of looms away: there were two hundred and fifty looms to a row with just enough room between each row to squeeze through. The man, now the focus of attention, was dragging a lad of about eight years old out from under a loom and, as he did so, ripping the sleeve off his shirt, which now hung down from a loom that had ground to a halt. He then delivered a blow to the lad's head and threw him on to the floor. It would not have occurred to Jean or anyone else to move from their machines and all quickly lowered their eyes back to their racing bobbins. Even Jacob shrugged as the boy was dragged off towards the manager's office. It would be no surprise to anyone that he would inevitably be thrown out into the street and his wage stopped immediately. Jacob was well aware that the boy's accident was bound to mean that the family would no longer be able to take the one shilling train ride on the next August Bank Holiday to Blackpool, which most families working at Crompton Mill had been trying to save for. However, although that was hardly of importance compared to the instant drop in wages, meaning that now that the struggle to have enough food to stay alive would most likely no longer be possible and the workhouse would threaten.

All the machinery was powered by a huge steam engine that was housed in the engine room in the basement, below the far end of the ground floor. A giant chimney then rose for sixty feet carrying the exhaust smoke of the engine, which touched against the outside wall of each of the six floors.

Each row of looms had strong cotton belts, about six inches wide, looped around the horizontal iron poles above the end of each loom that, via cogs on the looms, moved the two alternate cotton threads, weft and warp, up and down at lighting speed as the shuttles shot backwards and forwards between them. The belt then ran upwards towards the ceiling and there it looped around another spinning iron pole that was connected down to the giant power of the engine in the basement. This arrangement caused the threads in all thirteen hundred looms to clatter their growing sheet of cotton cloth up and down more than ninety times a minute.

The cotton or, more likely, leather belts themselves were inevitably slightly flexible and the noise of slapping from them, as they rotated rapidly, would have been bad enough, but this sound was made even more deafening by the additional crashing of the wood and metal loom frames, as they moved backwards and forwards at such speed for fourteen hours a day without ceasing and then continued for another ten hours with the night shift.

The engine itself never stopped, unless there were a breakdown. Its constant demand to be fed with coal took the work of a team of four stokers labouring in the unbelievable heat of the engine room. These were mostly younger men, stripped to the waist and covered in coal dust, like any coal miner in the labyrinth of pits that spread out underground from the edge of the town.

In addition to the weaving looms in the main wing of the mill that produced the cloth, there was another wing that made the thousands of yards of cotton thread that either fed the looms or was sold separately. The machines in this wing were no quieter and were driven by the same steam engine. Thousands of large bobbins collecting the thread were in rows that spread above the spinning machines along the whole length of the floor and each row of such spinning machines was operated by one woman, adding another hundred mill employees to the labour force.

The huge mill employed almost six hundred workers, the majority of whom were women who operated all the thousands of looms and spinning machines, each floor holding more than a thousand of the clanking, deafening machines. These 'girls', always had their hair covered to prevent its being caught in a machine, although no girl or woman of any age would ever dream of having her hair uncovered wherever she was, except in her own home. This was simply a natural part of life as it had been for centuries, for men and boys out of doors in hats, just as it was for girls and women.

The women learned how to operate the leviathan machines either by watching when they were children working in the mill or often by a friend or family member giving a quick demonstration and then hopefully trying to keep a weather eye open for a few days afterwards. The unbreakable rule, however, was that they had to keep up with the looms or the spinning machines, which set the pace at which everyone on the floor had to work. Failure to do so meant that a machine could 'crash' and work for the whole line would come to a halt. In some mills, the first time this happened, it would be treated as a mistake, but, apart from possibly this one chance, it would mean instant dismissal.

Jean Cope worked almost by instinct on the lines of looms, as did all the other women. Jean had worked at Crompton Mill for more than twelve years. Her floor also employed several men as overseers and dozens of children, who risked injury or even death. They all had to keep pace with the speed the machinery set unless, heaven help them, they suffered injury or fell behind the pace and caused a loom to stop. In any such instance, they were likely to be laid off immediately. As well as all these rules to remember, no visit to the rudimentary lavatory was allowed, except in the two short breaks in each day.

It was only just after ten o'clock on the Wednesday morning and four hours into the shift. The air Jean was breathing was damp and so was she. All the girls here wore full length white aprons, tightly fixed around their waists, covering a dress or shirt and skirt that was either cut off above the wrist or buttoned tightly in an attempt to stop the cotton lint from settling on any part of the body that was not covered or, worse still, carelessly allowing loose clothing to snag the loom. Wooden clogs helped to protect their feet from the thundering iron skeletons of the looms themselves.

Jean couldn't risk being spotted by an overseer as slowing down or missing the shuttles as they flew along the looms, from the first minute of the shift to the last. Her face and hands were sweating and the lint in the air had a nasty habit of sticking to these exposed body parts. After ten years, the work required no real thought; it became as automatic an act as breathing.

Jean worked at the first group of looms on her row and was able to glance across to where Ethel Carter was still struggling to keep up the pace. Ethel was just fifteen and had been taken on last week because Jean and Elsie vouched for her and could watch her. This morning, like other girls recently started, Ethel found it a nightmare to get into the rhythm of the looms and the time was fast approaching when a bobbin needed to be replaced. Jean could see the growing panic in her eyes. As she had done several times yesterday, Jean waited for a few minutes when she dared to leave her own looms, ran across the aisle and removed the empty bobbin on Ethel's loom and replaced it with a full one; it took her less than a minute and without any loom stopping.

She would have sworn that Jacob hadn't had time to see her helping Ethel, but her heart sank into her clogs, as she saw him hurrying in her direction. Without words, but by his angry look and the mill sign language, she realised she had been seriously warned. To her enormous relief, he then turned away, but immediately swung around to face her again. The signs were clear enough: "*I saw you doing that yesterday.*" His meaty fore finger was thrust under her nose and she knew she had received the only warning she was likely to get.

Sweating over her looms Jean was, of course, unaware of anything more than a few yards away, but in the offices that adjoined the mill John Tissiman and both his sons had just arrived. In John's case, this was much later than usual.

There were several offices in Crompton mill: one was dedicated to John Tissiman, the Chairman of the company. Another was the Board Room, while a much smaller room was in a separate part of the building from the other two on the far side. In that same building, there were also smaller offices for the book keeping clerks and others who dealt with correspondence. These offices could hardly be called 'grand' and were definitely utilitarian in construction and contents since John Tissiman could never see any sense in paying out hard earned money for a simple working space.

The Board Room contained a fine eighteenth century oak table, ten feet long and four feet wide, with walnut chairs that could seat, at the table's head, the senior Mr Tissiman as Chairman and ninety percent shareholder. Then Ernest, the Mill Manager and a ten percent shareholder, would be to his right and the two other places were for the remaining directors, one of whom was

John's cousin, Richard, who had not attended a meeting for twenty years, as he was a farmer over the Pennine Hills in Yorkshire and hated to leave his farm. Finally, there was one empty place; Ernest had never dared to ask whom that might be for. The four chairs looked rather lonely against such a large table.

These rooms all had oak doors with engraved boards stating: 'The Chairman of the Board' for the first and 'Company Board Room' for the second, while the third, not located too close to the other two, simply had 'Mill Manager' on the door.

John Tissiman's office naturally held the largest desk, with a comfortable leather chair, designed for a gentleman of importance and girth. In front of his desk were two other, smaller chairs. The Board Room was next door. Both these rooms had windows looking out onto the mill yard. However, the Manager's Office, where Ernest had his kingdom, adjoined the mill's first floor and its only window looked down on that huge floor below with its rows of weaving looms stretching as far as his eyes could see. This window had two sheets of glass in its frame to help reduce the noise from the mill and was also fitted with robust wooden doors which, when closed, ensured that the room remained comparatively quiet.

There was a raised platform below the window, which was located more than four feet off the ground and thus enabled Ernest to look down on the whole floor and watch work in progress, while being assured that the workers could not see him looking down on them. However, unknown to him, the workers below knew full well that Mr Ernest 'spied' on them, which added to the dislike they already had for him, due to his position in a class so far above their own.

This Wednesday morning, Ernest was already standing on the platform beneath the window. Its height above the mill workers seemed for most to confirm his importance and hence the lowly condition of those working below for fourteen hours on the day shift and ten hours on the night shift, six days a week. His eagle eyes ensured that there was no slacking and that workers earned every penny of their wage.

The earnings of a typical mill worker's family, consisting of father, mother and anything from one to five or more children, would just about allow them to rent the mean accommodation of just one room or, for the slightly more fortunate, a meagre one room down and two rooms up in a terrace and, if they were careful, put a little food on the table. A good wife, or more likely one with side lines not known to the employer, could also barter, steal or exchange enough food to keep the family alive when mill wages were not enough.

As Ernest's sharply focussed eyes looked for anyone who was starting to lose pace or engage in carelessness, he was unconcerned that their desperately hard and precarious work enabled his own family to live in comfort and security. In fact, he considered the workers to be most fortunate to have paid employment made available by Crompton Mill.

Ernest stood on the shoulders of several generations of Tissimans, from William Thomas Tissiman in the late eighteenth century to Ernest's family today, all of whom believed that their lives were entitled to grow more and more comfortable with each generation and could charitably give employment to the poor working in the town's mills, factories and coal mines, the opportunity of working to survive in England in the second half of the greatest century in history. Ernest accepted without query that their Queen and Empress, ruler of a quarter of the world's population, had a similarly inalienable right to look down on him.

Arthur, now resting himself against the front of his brother's desk, watched Ernest scrutinising those labouring below. Over the years he had spent at the Methodist College in London, he had tried to learn how to persuade the children in communities in such poverty as this that the ability to read and write could provide them with a way out of penury. He realised even more clearly that his own privileged life, when set against those who never knew where the next half loaf of bread was coming from was, in fact, hypocrisy. He and many of his fellow students in London were determined to change this state of affairs which, when argued over coffee in his rooms in Westminster, sounded entirely reasonable and possible for those who believed, as he did, in the need for a real change in the way society pretended to be unaware of the disgrace of so few being able to feed off the many. And yet on every visit to his own home and family above Oldham, this determination became diluted. How could he ever speak such heresy to his father, let alone his elder brother?

He pushed himself off his perch against the desk and mounted the steps to stand beside his brother. Looking down on such labour, he could understand how so many of his friends in London could describe it as '*the evil of the powerful and rich over the poor and weak*'. Ernest glanced at him and then back to watch the floor with its almost super-human activity. Even behind a sheet of thick glass, he could hear the voice of poverty.

"How do you feel standing here, Ernest, watching your fellow humans working to exhaustion to put those good quality clothes on your back?"

He couldn't resist picking up the collar of his brother's immaculate coat between his thumb and forefinger, but let it go as Ernest turned and angrily shook him off.

"For God's sake, little brother, what makes *you* so pious all of a sudden? The rags on your back perhaps? The meagre breakfast you enjoyed this morning in the warmed air of the morning room? The shoes you put on that were polished to a shine by the boy whose name you don't even know, while you slept beneath fine sheets and blankets. The dinner you ate last night?" Ernest pushed past his brother, in danger for a moment of knocking him over the railing.

"Get out of my way, Arthur. I feel I am talking to a mere child."

Arthur became increasingly annoyed that his concern over the state of his country was being taken so lightly. He wished his friend Henry, who had, like Ernest, also been at school at Harrow, were here now. He was so intelligent, so impossible to disagree with when these same honestly felt concerns were being thrashed out in the White Hart after a long day at college. Why did Ernest always make him feel so inferior, just as he had done when his brother as a child, called him '*stupid*' and a '*baby*' before using his powerful body to knock him easily to the playroom floor?

While Arthur tried to think of something clever and cutting to reply, the bell in the corner of the room, connected by a wire to his father's office below, sprang into life. There was no doubt in Ernest's mind that this was the summons he had expected and meant that his father required his wealth of experience over some matter of business, while Arthur, not expecting to be summoned himself, watched his brother hurry out and slam the door behind him.

However, a few minutes later, the bell sounded again, a longer, almost angry and louder noise than before. A glance at the clock above Ernest's desk assured him it was not yet time for luncheon and so, much to his surprise, his father must require *his* presence. He automatically straightened his stock, tugged down his waistcoat and tried to brush back his wiry head of hair that refused to assume a civilised style. He tried to stop himself from running towards his father's summons, stopped to catch his breath and finally walked down the stairs and along the corridor to knock on The Chairman's office door.

He waited for the bellow of '*Come!*' and entered the domain of the man he loved and feared in equal measure.

With its pervading smell of cigar smoke, as well as that of the coal fire that gave the room a pleasant warmth, Arthur could not help the brief cramp in his stomach that he had always experienced as a youngster when summoned to his father's study at Waterhead Hall John was standing in front of the fire, while Ernest was sitting in one of the chairs by his desk. John's face looked somewhat wary, but had a smile for Arthur; Ernest did not.

"My apologies for keeping you waiting, sir. I didn't realise the bell was for me."

"Of course we wanted you, my boy, to welcome you on this auspicious day to the board of Crompton Mill Limited Company as our new under-manager."

Although there was no response from Arthur, John quickly stepped forward and grasped his son's hand and placed his other hand on his shoulder; Ernest remained seated. Arthur was not surprised and had, indeed, expected something similar now he was back in Oldham, but he was very genuinely surprised and somewhat disturbed by the timing and tone of his father's welcome. Nor could he overlook Ernest's failure to take any part in the one-sided conversation. He was also aware that he was still holding his father's handshake and had not yet found any words to match the occasion.

John, buoyed by his certainty that his younger son could not fail to be delighted by his welcome remarks, drew him towards his desk and indicated the second chair. He then clapped the silent Arthur on the shoulder again and walked around the desk to take his place opposite his two sons.

John Tissiman found silence an awkward partner at any time and it weighted on him now. He looked from one young man to the other. "Well then, we need to toast the occasion."

In his hurry to place a stamp on the moment, he jumped up again and opened the doors of a cabinet behind his desk. Arthur could see a cut glass decanter, half-full of what he took to be brandy, and several equally expensive glasses. Those in John Tissiman's employ certainly did not regard him as a nervous man, but today he spilled some of the brandy, as he handed glasses to Arthur and Ernest, then took a third glass himself and raised it in a toast. His smile was starting to look uncertain.

"Well, let us firstly toast Arthur joining the family firm and then raise a glass to Crompton Mill itself. Long may we all enjoy the great rewards it brings from our hard work."

Ernest enthusiastically raised his glass, but Arthur could endure the torture no longer. He had not touched the drink and tried to organise his jumbled emotions into a semblance of sense.

"Father, I must ask you please to stop this. We all know full well that I have no intention of joining the mill. I have spent the last four years at University and Teaching College that has prepared me for a life helping children to improve *their* lives, while before that even more years myself at Harrow that did nothing more than try to reinforce all its students with the beliefs of the wealthy classes; beliefs that were entirely at odds with my own. I cannot—"

Ernest banged his glass down on the desk and turned on Arthur, a face masked with anger and derision.

"Just close your mouth, brother! How dare you speak to our father in such savage and ungrateful words. Have you no shame? You show now your true colours. You reveal to all how little you care for our family, how you find honest work for a fair reward a disgusting exercise. How you must have hated us for years. How—"

John had recovered himself enough by now to hold both his arms in the air and shout at his sons, not caring that anyone in adjoining rooms would hear him.

"Stop! Both of you! You Arthur, you make me ashamed. I cannot believe that we have harboured such ingratitude in our home and have to hear such scorn poured on the firm that keeps you well fed in a warm and comfortable home and with a good education behind you. Although I doubt the last three years in London have done anything other than teach you to stick a knife into the hearts of your family, of your poor mother, your…" He appeared to have run out of words.

The three men stood facing each other across the large desk, two of whose faces were contorted with rage and one with a mask dragging his whole demeanour down in sorrow and sadness.

A silence followed, broken by Arthur. "Forgive me, but I cannot stay here."

He turned, crossed to the door and let himself out, closing the door quietly behind him. He left his father and brother in an agony of fury, a feeling that they and their life had somehow been stolen from within by a betrayal.

# Chapter Five

John and Ernest stared for a moment at the closed door and then, as if by some unspoken agreement, sank slowly into chairs on opposite sides of the desk, like marionettes being lowered by their strings at the end of a performance. Both found a different spot in the room on which to fix their gaze and sat like that for several minutes. It was Ernest who found his voice first.

"I've never really understood him, you know. I really do believe he lives in some sort of altruistic dream world."

Unable to sit still, he then jumped up and started to pace the floor in front of his father, not pausing in his diatribe to allow John to speak. His father, presently slumped in a chair and staring at the top of his desk, gave no sign of wanting to contribute.

"I think he actually believes what that college has no doubt deluded his mind with." Ernest was now in his stride. "I believe he thinks he is some sort of messenger from the Almighty, who can change the lives of all these ragged, dirty children by teaching them to read and write. He thinks they will then suddenly, by some miracle, burst out into their world, the real world, immediately obtaining riches without any work, have plenty of food on the table for their tribes of children, live in clean houses—"

"Ernest!" John came out of his reverie and slammed his fist on his desktop, causing the ink well to jump and the pen beside it to fall on the floor.

"Ernest! Stop at once. You are making my head hurt... I understand you are angry and you have a right to be. I am angry as well, but really more disappointed than angry. Sit down, my boy, and let's try to think what would be the best thing to do."

"Surely there is no doubt about that, is there, father?" Ernest was unable to hold back his annoyance with his brother. "He bites the hand that feeds him. He pours scorn on all you have done for him and on our family. If he believes he can perform miracles on a teacher's pay, once he has no roof over his head, no dinner waiting for him, no Waterhead Hall, then I say let him try. Cut him off! Let him try it until he comes to his senses. Until he begs you—"

"Please, Ernest, just stop. I can't think with you shouting, loud enough I should think for the whole mill to hear."

John had been hunched forward again, his head in his hands, but now he sat up and Ernest felt that he had mentally shaken himself, as he watched the face that had been, it seemed to him, almost on the point of tears, now clearing and with an obvious effort returning to the look that Ernest had been used to seeing: steely eyed, his mouth fixed in a stubborn line and his chin up. He seemed at last ready to face whatever the world could throw at him and his beloved mill, just as he had done so many times when he had stood up to what appeared to be insurmountable troubles in the past.

Ernest stood facing his father, reminding him of how often as a child he had stood like this in John's study at the Hall, expecting to be punished, only to find a firm hand on his shoulder and words of support, not anger, from this man whom he realised once again was more likely to heal than to hurt.

"Sit down, my boy. Anger will not help this situation."

Ernest pulled up the chair that he had pushed aside and again faced his father across the desk. "I apologise, Father. I realise you must be hurt far more than I am."

"Not at all. Let your anger work for you, not against you. Untamed anger is your enemy, not your helpmate."

John opened a drawer of his desk and produced a box of cigars, offering one to Ernest. Once they had both gone through the process of cutting and lighting, even Ernest felt that the situation could not be as appalling as he had thought at first.

"Cast your mind back, Ernest, to the meeting we had yesterday with William Turnball at the bank. You recall?"

"Yes, naturally. It seemed pretty gloomy to me and it was a surprise to hear Arthur talking so knowledgeably about business just the other night. At this moment, we buy raw cotton from America that gives us six thousand yards of cloth a month, as well as the twist yarn and thread. To do this, the mill has to work without stopping for six days a week."

John tried to bring words of reality back to the situation. "Ernest, I suppose it doesn't take your brother's expensive education to realise what would happen if the banks in the United States collapsed or, God help us, if the southern states tried to break away and a civil war erupted."

"Exactly!" Ernest echoed his father's sentiments, but got no further as John laid his own belief on the table.

"Turnball put all that on the line, maybe to frighten us, maybe even to justify his increased costs. Who knows? But I had a telegraph this morning from a close contact in Liverpool. You remember Alan Buckland?"

Ernest nodded, as a gentleman of solid proportions from Liverpool swam back into his mind.

"Very well," John went on. "His information, just to hand from New York, was positive news that the crisis of the last year with collapsing banks which, indeed, as we well know, did lead to a cotton shortage from the southern states for a few months, but this has now ended. That was very good news and I had to admit we hardly noticed it in any event." He paused and drew on the cigar. "I should apologise not to have told you this sooner, but what with Arthur's outburst I did not—"

"Of course, of course," Ernest could not help interrupting.

"Well, Alan was eager to tell me that there is still a very dark cloud hanging over the land of opportunity on the other side of the ocean. I need time to think more carefully and, naturally, to talk to you in confidence about an idea that has begun to form in my mind; an idea that might just solve our problems if war does come to America."

John appeared to be regaining the good humour he had felt a few hours ago, before he and Ernest met with Arthur. Ernest could actually feel the difference in his father, a new light in his eyes and even the ghost of a smile on his face. John stubbed out his half-smoked cigar and pushed back his chair.

"Ernest, I have a few things to arrange now, if you will excuse me, but I need you to meet me at the Cotton Exchange tomorrow morning at nine o'clock sharp. I shall be down there ahead of you, but I'll meet you under the dome. Tomorrow is Thursday, so it won't be as crowded with merchants as it is on a Tuesday or Friday."

"I will be there, of course, father, but surely you can tell me what this is about. Is it something to do with—"

John cut him off. "No questions now. Just be there tomorrow. Oh, and don't mention this to anyone else, do you understand?"

He gave Ernest no time to reply, as he was already opening the office door and waving his son out.

Arthur meanwhile had already left the mill and walked to the far corner of Frederick Street. There he stopped and glanced up the slope in the direction of the station feeling an overwhelming urge to return home. Immediately, he realised that would involve explaining to Mother, not to mention Enid and Betty, even very possibly Aunt Josephine as well, why he was not at Crompton Mill starting a career there that would occupy him for decades to come and then trying hopelessly to explain to them why he would reject the occupation everyone in the family, and probably every employee of the mill as well, expected him naturally to pursue. They would all assume that as the second son, he would obediently follow in the footsteps of generations of Tissimans and be inordinately grateful for that.

He turned to look in the other direction, past the mill, past the many other mills with belching chimneys receding into the distance Below Town. His mind made up, he turned in that direction and quickened his step, as he made for Nathanial Wilkinson's Methodist chapel.

As he negotiated the narrow streets, he found himself feeling strangely more at home with every step. By the time he reached the simple building with its large plain glass windows, its stone now stained grey or even black in places, its tall double doors similarly painted black and surrounded by a wrought iron railing fence and gate, he felt as though a huge weight was being lifted from his shoulders.

Arthur knew that the door would be open, as it always was during daylight hours and, in any event, the chapel had nothing worth stealing inside or out. He stopped inside the gate and looked across the gravestones; no statues of weeping angels or distraught children here, as he had so often noticed in Anglican churchyards. The simplicity of the place and, once he passed inside, the light from the windows, even on a dull November day, made him feel somehow relieved of the anxiety and guilt that had settled on him in his father's office at the Mill.

The chapel was empty. The plain white walls helped to reflect what light there was across the pine pews and the wooden floor, in need of a good polish. He sat in a pew half way between the door and the table that was the altar here. Time seemed to stop, as he relaxed and closed his eyes, the better to think.

*What had he done? How could he have hurt his father as he had done? How could he be so ungrateful? But how could he possibly throw away what he had learned with such effort and dedication in London and to what he had believed from a young age his life should be dedicated? Surely to guide so many poor children towards a better life was an honourable objective...* He suddenly felt the weariness of the day overcoming him.

He realised he must have been dreaming: something about the mill, but it was empty and silent? He jerked awake with a feeling of shock and then realised that a hand was touching his shoulder.

"Forgive me for disturbing you. Oh, my word! I did not realise. It's surely Mr Arthur Tissiman again, is it not?"

Arthur was immediately wide-awake and well-aware that the hand and the voice were familiar. The person who had woken him sounded unsure. It took him another minute to realise that it was Maggie Wilkinson and then to get groggily to his feet. The young lady in question had taken a few steps back and had her gloved hand held to her mouth, around which Arthur felt sure he could distinguish a smile.

"Miss Wilkinson. I do apologise, I must have fallen asleep and did not hear you come in. It is so quiet and peaceful here; I was far away in my thoughts."

"Please, sir, I can see you were probably deep in prayer and, if I am not mistaken, some grief perhaps?"

Arthur stepped out from the pew. The smile he forced had clearly not disguised his heavy load of worry, which was, he supposed, what he had come into the chapel to share somehow, although with whom he could not have said.

Maggie discovered to her surprise how much she felt Arthur's unease. She was almost sure that when she had stood looking at him for those few moments as he slept, the faint tracks of tears were clear to see on his cheeks. Perhaps it was her forthright nature or her concern for this young man, who seemed more interesting whenever she saw him, that allowed her this insight.

"Mr Tissiman, might I suggest that a little fresh air might revive your spirits, especially as the day looks somewhat brighter than it did?"

She pushed the thought from her mind as to what Agnes would say if she could hear her now, practically propositioning this charming young man or, even worse, what her father's reaction would be if he could hear her, here in the house of God. In fact, she looked around the chapel with a stricken expression on her face as she imagined so clearly his walking down the aisle behind her, roughly placing his hand on her shoulder and swinging her... Maggie gasped, turning around with her hand again to her mouth again, from where a muffled cry emerged.

"Are you quite well, Miss Wilkinson?" Arthur was now the one looking concerned.

"I am perfectly well, thank you, just shadows. I need to get outside into the fresh air."

Maggie almost ran down the aisle to the chapel door with Arthur hurrying after her. He found her leaning against the railings outside, breathing heavily. She pulled herself together as soon as he joined her.

"Perhaps you would be good enough to walk me back to the Manse, if that is not too far out of your way. I feel a little faint, but it will soon pass."

She slipped her hand through Arthur's arm and they walked slowly towards the next crossroad. After a few minutes, Arthur felt he had to explain himself.

"I suspect I may have frightened you, Miss Wilkinson, for which I do apologise." He hurried on. "I have just had an awful shock that should not really have been a shock at all."

The walk from there that ought to have taken five minutes, lasted much longer as their pace slowed and Arthur found himself pouring all his anger and unhappiness out to Maggie, followed by his own surprise at how natural that felt.


The following morning, just before nine o' clock, John Tissiman stood under the magnificent glass dome that crowned the Manchester Cotton Exchange and, for once, a pale winter sun was illuminating the vast trading floor. On a Thursday morning, the exchange was not filled with the usual crowd of mill owners and managers, intent on bargaining as aggressively as possible with prospective buyers, not only from Lancashire, but from other parts of Britain as well, even agents for the colonies. Even so the hall was still far from quiet.

The sound of conversation, often raised voices, rose to the dome from groups of smartly dressed gentlemen, some sitting at round tables, others standing and gesticulating or passing papers that appeared to be of much importance. Some were returning them with a shake of the head.

John pulled out the half hunter from his waistcoat pocket and felt again the irritation of these days having to tilt it into the light to be able to read the time:

five minutes past nine o'clock. Replacing the watch, he turned a slow circle and was surprised to find Ernest, somewhat out of breath, standing in front of him.

"Apologies Father, the train was—"

John abruptly cut his excuse off.

"Not interested, Ernest. Now I want you to meet a friend of mine from Liverpool, whom I mentioned yesterday, as well as an acquaintance of his. They should be in the committee meeting room by now, which I reserved for nine o'clock. So, don't let us keep them waiting any longer."

The Cotton Exchange (13) Committee Room lay at the far end of a wide corridor towards the back of the Exchange building, its double highly polished mahogany doors displaying a brass plate engraved with the title: 'Manchester Cotton Exchange Executive Committee' and underneath in much smaller letters: 'Members only'. Standing by the doors was a tall, rather austere footman dressed in a black tailed coat, black trousers, a grey waistcoat and white bow tie; John recognised his guarding the doors from previous meetings here. The immaculate man looked quizzically at John, at the same time inclining his head.

"Can I be of assistance, sir?"

"John Tissiman, Granger. I have reserved the committee room."

A card was produced from an inside pocket and carefully consulted, as if there might be multiple reservations for the room this morning and hence John Tissiman an intruder.

"Indeed sir. Do I take it that this gentleman is Mr Ernest Tissiman?"

"Yes." John was trying to curb his annoyance at being questioned at all.

"There are two gentlemen awaiting your arrival inside, sir."

With which, he turned and drew both doors fully open to reveal a room of dark wood panelling, a deep red carpet and long wooden shutters concealing all but two of the floor to ceiling windows at the far end of the room, whose lower panels were *obscure* glass that prevented any prying eyes from observing the business of this powerful committee to anyone passing by in the narrow street behind the Exchange.

The doors closed silently behind John and his son. Ernest, who had not been in this privileged space before; he noted the long committee table and its many chairs that stretched away from them down the length of the room towards the windows at the far end. They admitted a strong light into the room.

Overhead were classical chandeliers and on the walls various boards with lists of dates and names.

The two gentlemen who were awaiting their arrival got up from where they had been sitting at the end of the table. The elder held out his hand in greeting and added a smile for John, who now made the introductions, having first warmly shaken the hand of this older, portly gentleman, whom Ernest took to be at least sixty years of age.

"Alan, may I introduce my son Ernest, who, as I explained, is the manager of our Crompton Mill."

As the two men shook hands, Ernest had the distinct impression he had been appraised and found wanting.

"Ernest, this is my business colleague and, I think I may claim also a good friend, Sir Alan Buckland."

"Since I don't know you myself, I am sure I can rely upon your father's good opinion of you." With which words, Sir Alan allowed Ernest a brief handshake. "John assures me of your value to the mill and to our great cotton trade here in Lancashire." Sir Alan made it clear, as he turned away from Ernest that he did not expect a reply.

Waiting a few paces away was the very antithesis of Sir Alan, a young man of slim build and taller than anyone else in the room. His posture was remarkably upright and Ernest felt he would have looked more appropriate in some sort of uniform. His opinion was supported by his carefully trimmed moustache and the tailored cut of his morning dress, with narrow trousers and a cravat with a red and yellow design. The young man in question remained waiting a few paces behind Sir Alan and only when his elder held out his hand in his direction did he step smartly forward.

"John, this is the young officer I wrote to you about. May I introduce Captain George Fitzwilliam of the Fourth Queen's Own Hussars."

"Sir Alan has explained your importance, sir."

Captain Fitzwilliam's handshake was firm, as he also bowed slightly towards John Tissiman, then stepped back and seemed to Ernest to have to resist the need to salute.

Sir Alan then introduced Ernest to the captain, who earned the same strong handshake. He noticed that the officer was tall enough to look down at him and bent slightly at the waist perhaps to emphasise the point.

"Pleased to meet you, sir," was the captain's sole remark before stepping back again into what Ernest felt must be his appropriate place in the order of things.

"Gentlemen, I suggest we sit here at the end of the committee table. Can I arrange refreshment for anyone?" John guided his guests to chairs around the table end and murmurs from each gentleman pointing out that the early hour made any 'refreshment' unnecessary.

Sir Alan glanced at the closed doors behind them. "Is your younger son not joining us, John? I understood he would—"

"No, no...not at the present time anyway." John sounded just a little nervous. "Arthur is attending to business at the mill, but will become part of this discussion, of course, at the appropriate time. So? Shall I start this meeting by reminding all present that whatever is said here is absolutely confidential and must not be shared with anyone else, at least not unless we all agree to do so."

There were words of mumbled agreement and Captain Fitzwilliam bent down to retrieve a leather dispatch case, which he began to open.

"No, captain!" John's admonition was louder than he had intended and the young officer almost dropped the case in surprise. "What I meant to point out, sir, is that we shall not be making any notes of this meeting either. I trust we are all agreed on the importance of secrecy at this time?"

An immediate 'yes' reply followed from Sir Alan. Captain Fitzwilliam looked surprised and put his case back on the floor. "Of course, sir, naturally as you wish."

"Then, gentlemen, let us make a start on a scheme that I dare to suggest could change not only all our fortunes, but could, with the right degree of support, change the fortunes of our country and even the empire. Believe me, I do not exaggerate."


Arthur had, rather than 'attending to business at the mill', was in fact using the time finally to decide that he must face his father again as soon as possible. His intention was honestly to tell him calmly that he could not join him and Ernest in pursuing a career that was anathema to him. At what was an early hour, although he understood that was not so for his father, who had already left for Manchester. Arthur had to settle for the dogcart to take him down to Oldham, determined to be at Crompton Mill at least by the time the workforce

70

arrived. He rehearsed in his head the speech he had practised with Maggie the day before. Arthur had found her so easy to talk to and so understanding of his point of view, not to say positively enthusiastic that, although he had intended simply to walk her back to the Manse after their meeting in the chapel, they had turned around just before reaching the door and walked back up the hill to Alexander Park. By midday, they had walked around the lake several times and finished up at the tearoom that overlooked it.

Over cups of tea and slices of seed cake, the discussion meandered back and forth between them. Maggie, perhaps not surprisingly, was confident that her upbringing in the Methodist Church and her efforts to help to feed and support the poor of the town, made her understanding of Arthur's ideas for the future entirely natural. She refused to believe, as she told him in her forthright manner, that Arthur could ever have seriously considered a life at the 'dreadful place of despair', where his father and brother used 'the downtrodden poor to pay for their lives of luxury'. Arthur became more sure than ever of what he regarded as his philosophy for a meaningful life.

During yesterday morning in Maggie's company, he had felt once again the excitement he and his fellow students had felt in London when eagerly working for the day that they would be responsible for '*lifting the poor and oppressed, their children and families, out of ignorance and into the light of God's grace and benevolence*', as the college chaplain had put it at the end of his last term.

By the time it became obvious how important, not only to himself, but also to Maggie, these ideals were, half Thursday had vanished and, as they walked and sat close together, a feeling spread through both their minds that nothing must be allowed to stop them and others similar to themselves from eventually forcing employers like the Tissimans, in Arthur's own words, 'to see the light of justice and fairness in providing good working conditions, a living wage and universal education'.

They left the Victoria Park Tea Room ready to overthrow the scandal of their age and country with whatever means possible and Maggie, at least, had visions of leading crowds of her poor neighbours in attacking the mills, hurling cobblestones at the windows of the rich and destroying the machines that made slaves of the poor. They had parted outside the park gates, Maggie to descend to the Manse, inspired perhaps by the somewhat unrealistic ideas of a future she now began to believe might be with this inspiring young man, while Arthur was feeling a modicum of guilt that he had enjoyed Maggie's company so much, in spite of her somewhat exaggerated idea of becoming a Victorian destroyer of mill machines, which even he appreciated would result in no looms and hence no jobs.

As he made his way uphill to find Jenks and the carriage, he did, however, decide that he must face up to his father and brother. He determined to be at the Mill on Friday morning and explain clearly and honestly why he had to pursue his ideal of teaching the ragged children of Oldham. He would also agree with them that there was no reason at all for *their* business to put a roof over his head and food in his mouth. He would make his way as best he could, doing what he knew was right for him and allowing whatever God had in mind for him to take its course. That determination remained with him and, to his surprise, made him feel both calm and happy to be doing the right thing.

This feeling of calm allowed him actually to smile as he entered Crompton Mill gates the next morning, just before six o'clock, and walked through the mill's office buildings to knock briskly on his father's door. With no sound from inside, he was about to risk opening the door when Josiah Briggs, the clerk to Mr Ottershaw, the Book Keeper, appeared around the far corner.

"My apologies, sir, but Mr John and, in fact, Mr Ernest also, are not expected at the mill this morning. I will, of course, pass on any urgent message or communication when they arrive, as I am told to expect them this afternoon, sir."

"I see. That is quite satisfactory, Mr…?"

"Briggs, sir, Josiah Briggs. I have the privilege of being the clerk to Mr Ottershaw. Indeed a more reliable and—"

"Yes, thank you, Mr Briggs. I will not wait now, but see my father and brother, no doubt this evening."

"If there is any message or…"

"No, Mr Briggs, there is not any message or anything else. Good day to you."

Arthur left the offices, but not the mill itself. He felt an illogical need at that moment to step into the mill to reassure himself that he was justified in his strong views and the conclusions that he and Maggie had reached yesterday. Nevertheless, he actually found he was having a moment of doubt. Was his father so utterly wrong is his beliefs? Was he on the true moral side himself? Was he exaggerating what these mills represented? In truth, after all, these had been places of employment for the poor since long before the turn of the century.

He walked towards the main entrance to the mill itself, but even twenty yards away, and with the doors closed, the noise from inside was overwhelming, but not as intense as it was a few minutes later when he opened the door to the ground floor with its mass of looms in operation. He could hear no voices over the metallic crashing of the frames and the roar of the steam driven belts on every machine.

He coughed, as he breathed in the tiny particles of lint and within minutes felt the sweat accumulating inside his stiff collar. Not one of the dozens of women labouring to keep the looms running at break neck speed even glanced at him, although his clothes were so at odds with those of the workers here. Just one of the overseers did, indeed, look warily at him, before hastily dragged his eyes back to the looms.

It was a small boy, Arthur guessed aged maybe eight or nine years old, who also failed to pretend not to notice him, as he rolled out from under the nearest loom almost at Arthur's feet; that certainly did arrest his attention.

The child, with an open neck shirt tucked into long trousers that stopped well above his ankles and dirt encrusted bare hands and feet, lay unmoving at Arthur's feet staring up at him, eyes filled with a fear that Arthur would hope never to see again. He automatically reached down to help the lad up, but the boy immediately curled himself into a ball with his arms over his head and lay still and silent amidst the chaos of the mill floor.

The man, whom Arthur took to be a foreman, now looked briefly again at Arthur as he hurried across the floor, bent and, grabbing the boy's arm, hauled him up and then hit him so hard across the face that he staggered and would have fallen if Arthur had not saved him. The boy's right cheek was now red and swollen, but this did not stop him from fighting his way out of Arthur's grasp.

Arthur knew that words were pointless here and he had to allow the foreman to haul the boy away, God knew to what fate. He stood staring at the retreating figures and at the dozens of adults who appeared never to have noticed anything untoward in what now appeared to him to be these almost satanic surroundings and an atmosphere of accepted suffering and enduring poverty. He turned slowly, taking in the whole roaring, sweating, maniacal

73

scene. He then stood still staring at those around him who were absolutely absorbed in their labour.

"What is wrong with you?" he shouted at the mill, but no one could, or wanted, to hear him.

As Arthur left the Mill, he vowed never to return, but to use whatever skills he had to make education the tool to improve these lives.

The only thought now in his head was to walk back to the Manse to talk to Maggie, but common sense prevailed. He realised that he could well embarrass her by being on her doorstep so soon after their last meeting, not to mention setting seeds of worry in Mr Wilkinson's mind that the son from Waterhead Hall was becoming too frequent a visitor to his daughter.

Having hesitated for long enough outside the gates, a place he now could not help but feel was abhorrent, he continued determinedly towards Mumps station. Somewhere in his muddled thoughts was the idea of being at home, being welcome, at least by some members of his family.

By the time he could see the station ahead, he realised just how at odds his thoughts were with a real problem: *How was he supposed to get from here up the moor to Waterhead, a distance, uphill, of more than ten miles? The carriage was not due to come back down until the evening to collect his father and Ernest, while Jenks and the dogcart would be well on the way up to Waterhead by now.*

Cursing himself for his numerous idiocies today, he walked across to the Station Tavern. It being now near the middle of the working day, the saloon bar was deserted of customers.

"What can I get you, sir?"

As Arthur mentally shook himself, he felt that the man with the grubby apron behind the bar must have asked this question of him more than once, but had been ignored; he sounded annoyed.

"My apologies. I was miles away. Could I have some lemonade, please?"

"Lemonade, sir? Was that *with* anything sir?"

Arthur realised that this being a public house he was probably expected to have some sort of alcohol as well, but, in spite of his father's frequent persuasion, he tried to keep away from strong drink.

"No, thank you."

The barman sighed and went in search of his beverage. He returned with a half pint glass of what looked like dull water, but Arthur tried to appear grateful.

"That will be tuppence, sir."

Again, Arthur had no intention of questioning the price and found suitable coins. He then had a sudden thought, although he felt it was almost pointless to ask.

"You seem quiet, this morning. Is there no one else in at the moment?"

"Only in the tap room bar, sir. There's a couple in there from up the moor."

The barman turned away and Arthur, ignoring the glass on the bar, went across this smaller room to the door leading to the much larger public bar. Opening it, he saw, as expected, two young men at the bar with jugs of what he assumed was beer in front of them. With his opening of the door, both turned. One face remained unchanged, but the other produced a gasp that sent beer froth into the air from the glass that had just reached his lips.

"Mr Arthur! My God…er… goodness sir, are you all right sir? What's 'appened?"

"Jenks! Am I glad to see you, although I suspect that the bar of the Station Tavern might not perhaps be your supposed destination?"

Jenks jumped up, pulled off his cap and failed to look anything but embarrassed. Arthur, by this stage, had a smile of both amusement and relief.

"Jenks, you have no idea of the salvation you present to me."

The young groom looked somewhat bemused.

"So we will say no more about where you are now if you simply let me know when you are ready to make your way back to Waterhead, I hope along with a wheeled vehicle of some kind."

"Yes, indeed sir. I was down 'ere, in town like, getting supplies for Ruby, the Cook sir, and then I met Dave 'ere, who was…"

"Jenks, please, there is no need for any explanation. If you can find room for me in the cart, nothing else will ever need to be said. Maybe, just drop me off at the gates to the Hall?"

"Yes, sir. After you, sir. The cart is around in the yard."

The cart was retrieved, Arthur was helped up to the seat beside Jenks and the journey up to the Hall proceeded over the next hour in somewhat strained silence, after Arthur failed to encourage any conversation in his companion. He jumped down just outside the front gates, waited for Jenks and the cart to disappear along the track that would eventually lead to the servant's quarters, stables and kitchens. He then made his way up the drive towards a home that today failed to look as inviting as it used to, not so long ago.

# Chapter Six

Instead of walking up the steps to the front door, Arthur, for no reason he was aware of, walked around to the rear entry, down the steps and through the door that was the servant's entrance. The passage leading to the kitchen was deserted, which made sense as it was not yet time for lunch to be prepared, but even the kitchen contained only Matilda and Janet, the kitchen and scullery maids and, to his surprise, there was none of the usual conversation and bustle going on.

The two girls looked at him with surprise and almost, he felt, trepidation. Any work they might be undertaking seemed to be in slow motion. The doors to the butler's pantry and to the housekeeper's parlour were both closed and silence emanated from within. Arthur found himself slightly concerned and hurried towards the stone stairs that led up to the door that opened onto the ground floor corridor between the dining room and hall. He pushed open the baize lined door and was greeted with silence, not by the usual chatter that would characterise the morning for the ladies of the house.

His mother, Enid, Betty and Aunt Josephine, as well as the servants that had been absent downstairs, were nowhere to be seen or heard up here either. Arthur stood somewhat bemused, until he saw Rose, the parlour maid, running down the main staircase. She stopped abruptly when she realised she was not alone and her hand flew to her mouth.

"Oh! Mr Arthur sir, I didn't realise you was home." She then ran towards the door Arthur had just closed, but stopped with her hand on the handle.

"I'm sorry, sir, I must hurry…you understand? I've got to get more towels and hot water and Doctor Foster will be here any minute and I must…" With which she opened the door and Arthur had a few seconds to see her running down the stone stairs.

*Doctor Foster? What on earth had happened? Why was the house so quiet?*

Arthur stopped trying to solve the unsolvable and hurried up the main staircase himself. When he reached the bedroom landing, he could hear voices from the end of the corridor where Ernest's and Betty's bedrooms were. As he got closer, it was as if there were people inside shouting, but in whispers. When he could hesitate no longer, he went to open the door, but at the same moment, it was thrust outwards almost into his face. There was a muted scream as Enid was revealed inside, looking at him as if some spectre stood on the threshold, not her brother.

"Arthur! What are you doing here? We thought you were at the mill with Ernest and Father and we couldn't…"

She was unable to go any further, as she collapsed against him and pulled him tightly to her, tears now running down her cheeks. Arthur could see into the bedroom, which was a scene of confusion. His mother was half lying across the bed with Betty clasped to her. Aunt Josephine stood against the far wall, a hand to her mouth, holding a crucifix and with a look of horror on her face. Grace Smithson, the Housekeeper, stood at a side table with a bowl of what seemed to be red water and with towels, similarly stained, scattered on the floor. *Blood?* was the thought immediately in his mind.

It was as if the whole tableau were frozen in front of his eyes, but then at once came alive in both sound and action. All eyes turned towards Arthur, all appearing pleading. His mind was so confused that he stood still, shocked and unmoving at the door. Enid pulled herself away and shouted, "Arthur!" into his face. Her brother was forced out of his reverie.

"Enid, for God's sake, what is happening here? Has Betty been attacked?"

He rushed across to the bed and looked down at his mother, who was sobbing against Betty's neck. Aunt Josephine gasped and took a step backwards. Betty herself looked at Arthur through half closed eyes, her skin as pale as porcelain. Smithson wrung out another towel and hurried towards the bed. Betty was unmoving, apart from her eyes, which glanced backwards and forwards across the room. Dorothy seemed now to realise that it was Arthur looking down at them in horror.

"Arthur. Why are you here? Why is Ernest not with you? Where is John?" Then sitting up and turning towards the open door, speaking a little less urgently, "Why is Doctor Foster not here? He should be…"

Arthur, still unsure what was happening, but suspecting the worst, took his mother's hand and spoke gently.

"I'm here, Mother. I'm sure Doctor Foster will be here at any moment. I think Father and Ernest will not know about whatever is happening… Is Betty hurt? Has she been attacked? Or is she sick?… Just tell me so that I can help."

His mother reached up to grasp Arthur's arm and he carefully pulled her upright. If it had not been for the wall, Aunt Josephine would have backed away further, but did no more now than groan.

Dorothy, her face wet with tears and her soaked lace handkerchief still held to her mouth, looked to Arthur to be in a state of despair.

"Arthur, dear, I don't know how to tell you. I need John here! Betty is…was…but…" She seemed to run out of breath, took a gulp of air and struggled on. "She… Oh! I don't know how to tell you." She was interrupted by Enid, while at that moment Arthur heard the sound of men's voices along the corridor.

"Mother, I can hear the doctor coming now," Enid now seemed to be thankfully in charge. "Arthur, stay here with Betty. Aunt Josephine, you need to go to your room now and give the doctor space."

Josephine looked horrified, but Enid went across and guided her firmly towards the door. Just after she rushed from the room, there was a sharp knock at the now open door and Doctor Foster appeared, somewhat breathless. He took in the scene and, as he hurried towards Betty, still unmoving on the bed, he gave instructions to those left in the room.

"Enid, will you kindly take your brother downstairs and wait for me to examine Mrs Elizabeth. Mrs Smithson: gather those soiled cloths and the basin. Come back with hot water and more clean towels. Please close the door behind you. I will send for any further aid should it be necessary. Now, Mrs Tissiman, if you would just move away to give me room. Thank you." Smithson was the last out of the room and softly closed the door behind her.

Arthur had wanted to stay right outside the bedroom door, but Enid persuaded him to accompany her downstairs to the drawing room, where they found the fire lit and a pale winter sun starting to break through the clouds hovering over the moor.

"Enid, for the sake of my sanity, just tell me what is going on, although I suppose I could make a reasonable guess at some sort of injury."

"I understand, but the news isn't good, I'm afraid, as you can imagine, I suppose, from the scene upstairs. This morning, after you had all left for the mill, Betty was still in bed, which is not unusual. Perhaps we should sit down here, by the fire?"

Enid moved to the sofa by the fire and Arthur, after hesitating, joined her. Enid then continued, now speaking as calmly as she could.

"Rose took up her breakfast tray at nine, but she didn't answer Rose's knock. Rose tells me that she called her name several times and then put the tray down and opened the bedroom door just enough to see inside. What she saw was Betty lying across the bed, apparently unconscious."

"Oh, my God! How awful. But she seemed conscious when I was up there just now."

"Yes, but let me finish. Rose also noticed some blood on the sheets. She tried to wake Betty and, in fact, she did come around. She seemed confused to Rose and then started screaming for Mother. Rose thought there must have been an accident and went straight to get Mother."

Enid paused and seemed to be gathering her thoughts, but when her brother started to speak, she held up her hand and continued.

"Just wait. You have to remember that Mother is not at her best when there is some sort of crisis. According to Rose she, Rose, tried to lift Betty up on to the pillows, but then they both saw what was, I suppose, what sounds like a mass of blood in the bed where she was lying... Just let me finish, Arthur, please! ... Mother was hysterical by this time and Rose very sensibly came to find me. I was downstairs having breakfast. Having heard all Rose had to say, I tried to send for Jenks to ride as fast as he could down to Oldham to fetch Doctor Foster, but Jenks was already down in the town by then. You can imagine how I nearly panicked!"

Arthur was looking white with shock by now and that was made worse when he realised he had been with Jenks in Oldham at about that same time, but Enid was brooking no interruption.

"So, I told John Hawthorn, you know, the other stable lad, to saddle a horse and ride as fast as he could to Doctor Foster's house and tell him there was an emergency with Miss Elizabeth and he must come at once. That's what you walked into a while ago."

Arthur moved closer to his sister and drew her into his arms. She seemed then to release the tension that had been building inside her and started to sob against Arthur's shoulder. He held her close and felt tears pricking the back of his own eyes.

"Enid, I am so sorry you had to cope with all this. I don't know what to say. You've been so brave, so *sensible*."

Enid pushed him away to arm's length. "Are you saying I'm not always sensible? What I need, I suppose, is a big, strong brother to care for me! Is that it?"

Before Arthur could reply, she smiled and gently punched his arm, then stood and crossed the room to the tall windows letting in the sunlight that seemed so alien to the awful event they were trying to cope with. Enid wiped her eyes and tucked her handkerchief firmly into her sleeve.

"Now, all we can do is to wait for Doctor Foster to do everything he can and let us know what *we* can do."

Arthur joined her and they stood side by side gazing out of the windows and yet were hardly aware of the glorious winter morning gathering outside.

"What do you think happened?" Arthur asked while still looking towards the now sunlit lawn that he was completely unaware was there. A knock at the door startled them both. Doctor Foster, their family doctor from before either of them had been born, came in, walked across to the fire and put his case down on the table there. Arthur and Enid reluctantly went over to hear what they expected to be terrible news, but hoped would be otherwise.

"I think we had better sit down," Matthew Foster suggested. "Now, first and most important, you need to know that Mrs Elizabeth, has lost a lot of blood, but it has now subsided and she is sleeping. I gave her a sleeping draught to ensure that happened. I have asked Rose to see that your mother went to her own room to rest and have given Rose a mild draught to administer to her; she should sleep for a while anyway. I have also taken the liberty of sending your man, Jenks I believe, to go directly down to Crompton Mill to bring Mr Tissiman and Mr Ernest up here to Woodhead as quickly as possible. I sent a note briefly explaining the situation that was now under control."

"That all sounds very commendable, doctor." Enid, having hardly breathed while he was giving them this account, was now desperate to know more.

"What do you think caused such the large loss of all that blood and will the wound heal without surgery?"

The doctor hesitated and realised that he had not given the young brother and sister the full truth they needed to hear. "No, this was not a wound, at least not in the sense you mean. Your sister-in-law was not exactly wounded or anything of that nature." Clearly, the doctor felt uneasy about explaining his

81

diagnosis, which made his audience far more worried than before. "Mrs Elizabeth appears to have been with child. I would guess for no more than two months. She may well have been unaware of this fact."

"Dear God in heaven," cried Enid, "are you saying she just lost another baby? And not so very long after the first. The loss of that was enough, surely?"

Arthur put his arm around Enid, as fresh tears seemed actually to burst from her eyes. "So, you are telling us that she must have had a miscarriage, is that what it's called?" Arthur asked as calmly as he could. "And that happened when she was all alone this morning. How on earth can we tell Ernest what happened? He will be distraught."

The drawing room door then burst open and Dorothy stood in the doorway. Her hair hung lankly over her face, which was wet with her tears. She had on only a nightdress, bare footed and trying to tear at a lace handkerchief she held between both hands. She gazed around the room and looked surprised at the people she saw through a haze of despair. She let out a long gasp, almost a moan, and slowly, as Arthur would say later, gracefully, sank to the floor.

# Chapter Seven

## December 1860

For the Tissiman family, the Christmas of 1860 was the most miserable in living memory. When Betty's miscarriage occurred, Dorothy had already spent weeks of planning to ensure that the Hall looked even more festive than in previous years: the tree in the hallway was larger than ever, the holly and ivy wreathes trailing down the bannisters of the double flight of stairs and along the landing were greener and more luscious, while the drawing room was so filled with streamers and baubles, holly and ivy and even its own smaller Christmas tree decorated with candles, that guests at the Christmas party were expected to gasp in wonder. The huge tree in the hall had piles of boxes and other mysterious shapes around its base, wrapped in joyous paper and ribbon.

However, when the days of the festival were due to start on Christmas Eve, no member of the family at the Hall felt any joy or goodwill or excitement for another Christmas together, even though there was expected to be more affluence even than last year. The kitchen had baskets of chickens and whole sides of beef. Then there were plum puddings ready for steaming, fresh salmon from the Scottish Highlands, oysters from Kent and enough vegetables, cheeses and breads to make the pantry shelves groan, but this year there was now no sign that this feast was actually being prepared.

Ruby Coal, the cook, and her battalion of kitchen and scullery maids sat around the great kitchen table in virtual silence on the morning of Christmas Eve. Mrs Tissiman had sent for Branson, just two days ago, to inform him that the family would not be celebrating this year. They would all be going to the early church service in Oldham, for which the carriage would be required, and after that the menu should comprise the simplest of food for those who felt able to consume it. The Hall stood in melancholy silence.

There had, of course, been a death, the death of a baby untimely forced from the womb and Dorothy had insisted that the Christmas decorations, trees and wreathes were smothered in black muslin, the curtains drawn and even straw spread on the gravel leading to the front steps to keep quiet the sound of any carriages or horses that might venture up to the Hall to disturb the melancholy and unnatural quiet.

On that desolate Christmas Eve morning, most of the family kept to their rooms once they returned from the early church service. At ten o'clock, Betty remained confined to bed, Ernest was sleeping in his own adjoining room and Dorothy, dressed in mourning black, sat in the largest bedroom looking out with unseeing eyes across the park towards the moors, which reflected the mood with lowering black clouds and downpours of rain from time to time.

At breakfast that morning there had only been John, Arthur and Enid. Aunt Josephine had let it be known that, since she was in deep mourning for the precious baby, she must not be disturbed. She did, however, instruct the kitchen to furnish her with a nourishing breakfast to enable her bear her sadness.

John and two of his children found they had little appetite and even less conversation. Enid did stumble out 'Happy Christmas', to which Arthur smiled his thanks and John stared sternly at his bowl of uneaten porridge.

Throughout the twelve days of Christmas, Arthur mentally wrestled with problems that seemed to him just as gloomy, if not more so, than Betty's miscarriage. Physically, she had recovered well and each time he visited her, she seemed to Arthur to look better and better, with more colour in her cheeks, hair that had resumed its glossy appearance and eyes that began to betray the ghost of a smile on her lips. All this was a happy sign to him of her progress to recovery, but it disappeared whenever Ernest came into the room. Betty changed in an instant at the sight of him. Tears appeared in her eyes and her down curved mouth screamed, "Get out of my room! This is all your fault and I can never forgive you. I don't want you near me: ever."

Ernest tried to bring some reason to bear. He tried to tell her that it was no one's fault. That he did not know she was 'in the family way'; that he loved and needed her, in fact, needed her, but this was all in vain. In spite of the resentment Arthur still felt towards his brother, he could not fail but be saddened by what he heard and saw of Ernest's decline in any desire to fight for his wife and, as the holiday ended and John returned to the mill, which had of course been open every day except Christmas day, he made no effort to join his father there.

Arthur had, over the weeks both before Christmas and just afterwards, made no mention of the ultimatum his father had given him on the day he had walked away from Crompton Mill, vowing never to return. Nor had John mentioned his threat that if Arthur refused the offer of a life of assisting in the management of the mill, he should not expect his comfortable home and living to continue. Arthur was keenly aware that any revisiting of this situation would not only anger both his father and brother, but might even cause his poor mother take her own life in her desperation.

Meanwhile, Waterhead Hall stood as a silent monument to sadness. The servants moved around in silence like automatons although the appropriate work was done as usual. The huge stock of unused Christmas fare was sent to the parish church of St Mary with St Peter for distribution to the poor; needless to say, Nathanial Wilkinson cursed the family for ignoring the 'real poor' living in his chapel's parish.

In fact, Nathanial, before Christmas, has offered Arthur a teaching position at the Methodist Sunday School and lodging with one of his wardens. Arthur was flattered to be asked, but it was a job for one or two days a week and not in schools like those he had trained for while in London.

By the time the year 1861 was ushered in and January was in its second week, Arthur had more of less decided to move to London, where several proper Methodist Schools did exist, and he could shake the dust of Oldham from his feet. Having made up his mind that this was what he felt he needed to do, numerous problems immediately jumped in his way: *would his father cut him off entirely from the family? How would his mother cope with what, to her, would be another disaster? Would he ever see Enid again? Could he even survive in London on a teacher's pay? Finally, the surprisingly important realisation that he might never see Maggie again?*

These thoughts chased each other round and round in his mind for weeks, although those weeks seemed more like months to him. Eventually, on a Sunday in the second week of January, Arthur decided he must share his troubled mind with someone outside the family. The obvious choice was Reverent Wilkinson and then perhaps, hopefully, Maggie. Tomorrow, after his father had taken the carriage to the mill, he would tell Jenks he needed to go into Oldham on business; no one else needed to know.

By ten o'clock on Monday morning, he was knocking on the door of the Manse. It was soon answered by Maggie herself, who looked both surprised and just a little pleased to see him.

"My word! If it isn't Mr Arthur Tissiman himself. I must say I had been worried that you had succumbed to either Typhus or a serious accident or other…things, and before you ask, I had a most pleasant Christmas with my family, although I suspect not quite as grand as the one I am sure you all had up at the Hall."

"Maggie, please stop. I am full of apologies for not having seen you for so long, but believe me, there is a genuine reason. If you felt you could ask me inside, or even walk with me, I will explain. Oh, and I have missed you."

"Well. Arthur, I believe it is a little cold for strolling here below Town, but my mother is in the kitchen, so maybe you would care to join us for a cup of tea?"

Sitting in the warm glow of the kitchen range and with a cup of tea before him on the table, Arthur found that at last he could release his many worries about life in the future. To his surprise, Maggie's mother was very quiet as he talked, but equally sympathetic to his concerns. Even Maggie seemed to have forgiven him for his absence over Christmas and the New Year after he had explained the reason. He eventually realised that he had been talking for far too long and often repeating himself as he poured out the worry, pain and confusion that had plagued his thoughts for so long, as well as the real reason for his absence. He now stopped abruptly as he looked from one to the other of his small audience and suspected that there might be a hint of boredom in their faces.

"I'm so sorry Mrs Wilkinson and, of course, Maggie as well. I have talked far too much and burdened you, I fear, with problems that are entirely my own." He stood up quickly from the table and looked around for his hat and gloves. "I had no right, no right at all to take up your time so selfishly. Please forgive me. And so now I had better leave you in peace."

Both Mrs Wilkinson and Maggie stood up at once and it was Mrs Wilkinson who stepped towards him, as he made his way towards the door and put her hand on his arm.

"Mr Tissiman, both I and my daughter have heard far worse tales of woe, I can assure you. What you have said, albeit that it could have been a little more concise, I very much sympathise with, but wish I could advise you. But only you, sir, can make the decisions over which you have troubled yourself, it seems for so long. I understand from Margaret that you trained as a teacher at a Methodist College in London and so I hope that you will try to listen to what the Lord may be trying to advise you now. I can only ask you to try to find the path that is right both you and for your family."

Arthur smiled for the first time since he had arrived and turned back towards Mrs Wilkinson, but before he could thank her again, Maggie, with a shawl around her shoulders, stepped in front of him and opened the door.

"Let me see you out, Arthur, and wish you well."

The pair left the Manse together and walked a short way towards the chapel before stopping. Rachel Wilkinson could not hear what passed between them as they stood together, but there was a gentle smile on her face as she saw them both looking happier than either had seemed before Arthur arrived.

What she did not know, and what Maggie did not share with her once Arthur strode off up the hill, was that Arthur had told her that he had at last come to a conclusion: he would move to London as soon as possible and find a post in a Methodist school there. He assured Maggie that he would visit her often and suggested, somewhat diffidently, that perhaps in time she might be able to visit him in London, naturally providing her mother could accompany her. What Rachel Wilkinson was too late to see as she went back indoors, was the smile wiped off her daughter's face at this news.

# Chapter Eight

## January 1861: London

It was a chill winter's day in London, Wednesday January 20 1861, when the sun had crept out and by midday, the Mall looked almost spring-like under a clear pale blue sky.

Lord Palmerston's coach was just approaching Buckingham Palace and the gates swung open so that the coachman did not have to slow down. The wheels crunched on the immaculately kept gravel and then drove more slowly under the inner arch to come to a halt in the courtyard, where two footmen awaited its arrival. The coach door was opened and the Prime Minister, dressed in formal morning attire, stepped gingerly down the single step to the paved yard. The inner door was also opened for him and he followed his escort into the Palace, where yet another servant of the royal court took his hat, gloves and winter coat. Following solemn tradition, he walked slowly, slightly limping these days, through two ante rooms, up two shallow flights of stairs, a wide corridor and then halted outside the ornate double doors of the Queen's receiving chamber. The lead footman knocked gently, a formality in reality, since the doors were opened at once from within.

Palmerston proceeded slowly across the broad expanse of carpet and then stopped in front of his monarch. Queen Victoria sat in a winged armchair beneath a large casement that gave a view of the palace garden. Next to her was a small console table and another, presently empty, chair. A sour looking King Charles spaniel sat at her feet. The First Lord of the Treasury, his other title, bowed to the Queen and she then indicated the second chair.

"Please be seated, my lord." Once he had settled his now fairly expansive frame into the chair and was sitting suitably upright, she continued.

"What a fine winter's day it is, my lord, do you not think? When we walked briefly along the arbour with Albert after breakfast, I almost expected to see the wisteria in leaf, but I suspect it is too early yet."

"Indeed, ma'am. My own small garden at Cambridge House looks rather sad at present but I fear is not as finely kept as your splendid retreat from the worrying world here."

"*Worrying* it is indeed, my lord. Albert has been showing me some articles in recent copies of the *Times*, which it seems are, along with his own invaluable notes, preparing us to witness the terrible bloodshed that a civil war in the United States could soon realise."

Palmerston made the mistake of starting to speak, but Her Majesty, never allowing any interruption to a royal proclamation, continued after a brief look of annoyance passed across her face.

"We noted, with some pleasure in November the election of Mr Abraham Lincoln to the Presidency, but one has been alarmed since then to hear that seven of the southern states have seceded from the Union and are now calling themselves, according to the *Times*, the Confederate States of America." Palmerston, aware of making one error already in the audience, kept silent.

"Well, my lord? Can we take it that is true and, if so, what does my government intend to do about it? What will you do to protect the interests of Great Britain and the Empire?" Her piercing gaze now settled squarely on the Prime Minister.

"Naturally, ma'am, you are as ever well informed, as is His Royal Highness. Those states did indeed leave the Union and now have formed what is, in reality, almost another country within the bounds of the United States. I should add that it is the belief of…your government that within a few months, or even weeks, other southern states may join this so-called Confederacy. Your majesty is wise to be concerned for our own interests, of course. These southern states, apart from a few other less important raw materials, supply our cotton industry with almost all our raw cotton, but we have plans…"

The Queen now stopped him before he could add another word.

"Prime Minister, plans are pieces of paper and pieces of paper are not going to stop one of the mainstays of our industry shutting its doors, stilling its looms and bringing starvation to thousands of workers… No! You will listen to your Sovereign. I told you, not so long ago, how upset I was to read that remarkable novel, '*Uncle Tom's Cabin*' (14), which tore at my heart strings. Slavery, sir, is what is at the heart of this, is it not?"

Hesitantly, now a somewhat bowed Palmerston realised he was expected to answer.

"Ma'am, my…your government feels that some discretion is needed here." He hurried on, since the Queen did not speak again. "The mills of Lancashire produce more cotton cloth and thread than France and Germany put together. We export to our Empire and to the world. Cotton has made us richer and more powerful than ever. The government is aware of the threat that the supply of most l raw cotton could well be stopped if the United States government blockades the south." Victoria raised her hand to stop him here.

"Sir, you tell us what we already know, thanks to Albert's outstanding knowledge of, and research into, affairs in America, but one must add again, that to keep human souls in a condition of slavery is an evil practice. Perhaps we should sacrifice our cotton trade and stand beside the government of Mr Lincoln in what will very soon, it seems, be a battle to destroy that evil?"

Palmerston was, at least temporarily, lost for words. His Tory government, but particularly Palmerston himself, had always held very different views on foreign policy from those of Prince Albert and, through his influence, the Queen. The world dominance of the British Empire and hence its wealth, was at the heart of Palmerston's foreign policy.

"Your majesty, I naturally take careful note of the advice that you and the Prince Regent are good enough to furnish me with. However, on this occasion I must point out two important facts. Firstly, we do not know, and will not know for some time, whether Mr Lincoln has any intention to blockade the export of raw cotton from the south and, secondly, if as is most likely in the opinion of the government, if the Republic of the United States wins what is now an inevitable civil war, with all the death and destruction to the south that will bring, he would have no need of the assistance of Britain."

Risking the wrath of the queen, he pressed on, disregarding her starting to speak. "Forgive me, ma'am, but this war is likely to last several years and if the Republic does, indeed, blockade cotton export during that time, we will be the losers. We will suffer untold damage and hardship."

The queen suddenly moved to sit forward in her chair and uttered one word, "No!" She then controlled her obvious anger and continued more calmly. "From what you have said, sir, should we understand that it is the intention of your government, *my* government, to support the Confederacy in a civil war that they will be fighting against the Christian justice that will reside firmly with Mr Lincoln and the United States of America? *And* this, just to supply us with materials simply to make us richer?"

"Ma'am, all I can say is that nothing is yet settled. We are at the mercy of events, and the speed of those events, on the other side of the Atlantic Ocean. Your government will always have the best interests of Britain and our Empire at heart if, or when, a decision needs to be taken. In the meantime, I am authorised to reveal in confidence that before any decision is taken, we are about to review events in America and will be sending gentlemen of standing and intimate experience to conduct that review. Both you, ma'am, and His Royal Highness, will be kept informed of their progress, although naturally the long distances involved will not produce any immediate results."

The Queen sat for several minutes in silence, while she bent to stroke Dash, the second in the line of her spaniels of that name; the dog had been lying asleep beside her chair throughout the less than amicable audience.

"It sounds to me, Prime Minister, as if you believe there is no more to be said. I hope that you are able to see more common sense when you have had the opportunity to consider matters with care and with the advice of these *gentlemen,* on whom you seem to place such importance.... I wish you good day, sir."

Palmerston needed no further reason to delay his departure and so rose, solemnly bowed, took the required few steps backwards, bowed again, turned and left the chamber. He had to admit that the meeting could have gone better, but he doubted the queen was aware of his nickname among those who had tried to thwart him in the past: the hard *Lord Pumice.*

That same afternoon, Arthur would have been found in a hackney cab on his way from Euston Station towards an address which, when it had been given to him by his father two days ago, meant nothing: 27 Bolton Square, London SW. Arthur had, not surprisingly, asked whose address it was and why his father wanted to meet him there.

"I do not understand Father why," Arthur said on that occasion, "if we need to meet, we cannot do so here and now, or if it has to be next week, we could meet at the mill. But I have already told you that I shall not be taking up your offer of a position there and I will be moving to London myself shortly. There is no point in discussing it here, there or even in London."

"Arthur, this has nothing to do with any position at Crompton Mill, nor in fact, has it any real connection with what position. I cannot tell you at this moment why you need to meet me at Bolton Square, but you must take my word for it, as the father who values you. it is vital that you meet me there on Wednesday at two in the afternoon, and you should not be late. Will you take my word of honour for this and oblige me one last time?"

Arthur sighed, as he imagined it was yet another ploy by his father to persuade him to join the management of the Mill. On the other hand, he *was* his father and he had given his solemn word of honour. Even more surprising, he had said he valued him, a word he had not heard from that whiskered mouth in twenty years. A moment of reflection left him with no choice.

"Very well. I will meet you there, but please understand that if this is some underhand attempt—"

"Arthur! I can do no more than assure that what I have said is true. Do I not deserve this small act of respect?"

Arthur had agreed, but with considerable misgivings, that this was the truth, but in his private opinion maybe it was only a version of the truth.

So it was that on this January afternoon that was already growing dim with heavy cloud and the threat of evening soon to be drawing on, Arthur's cab drew up outside a large and imposing town house opposite the gardens in the centre of Bolton Square. He stepped down from the cab, handed the driver his fare and watched as the Hackney clattered away. He turned and looked long and hard at the imposing polished black door at the top of three steps. The number 27 was engraved in the stone column next to a bell pull on the wall. With his every suspicion aroused, he went up the steps and rang the bell, which he could hear echoing inside the building.

A long pause followed and then measured footsteps could be heard. The door was opened by a remarkably tall and thin butler, who looked down on Arthur from a lofty, rather pinched face. "Yes, sir. May I help you?"

Arthur hesitated, unsure exactly how to explain his presence at a house belonging to someone whom he did not know and for a reason, he did not understand.

"Yes, thank you. I am Arthur Tissiman. I have been asked to be here at two o'clock this afternoon by Mr John Tissiman of Oldham? I am not sure…"

The butler stepped back and opened the door fully. "You are expected, sir. If you care to follow me, I will take you to the library."

The hallway was of considerable size, with closed doors at intervals on both sides; at the far end were double doors. An impeccably uniformed maid stood half way down, almost to attention.

"Please give Molly your coat, hat and scarf, sir... Now, please follow me."

Arthur was hugely impressed by a residence far more imposing and grand than Waterhead Hall. They passed a wide staircase, carpeted in red and with carved banister rails. His eyes were also drawn to the portraits that hung between the several doors. All were of military officers, one even shown riding a war horse. The only exception was a large portrait at the head of the staircase. It was of an elegant lady in evening dress with remarkably golden hair and a smile so slight it might not have been a smile at all.

Reaching the double doors, the butler knocked discretely and a voice could be heard from within: "Come!" Both doors were opened by the butler, whom Arthur now noticed was wearing white gloves.

He stepped into the double height chamber. Three walls were covered with bookcases from floor to ceiling, filled with leather bound volumes, some of which showed considerable age. The only interruptions to the flow of books were two sets of double doors. A library ladder attached at the top and with small wheels at the bottom was stranded half way along the left-hand wall.

The far wall opposite the entrance was made up entirely of windows reaching the full height of the room with window seats at the base. Long gold and cream curtains hung beside each one; beyond in the failing light Arthur could see a formal garden surrounded by a high brick wall.

The library had two seating areas. Closest to the doors was a broad table with a few chairs, bronze table lamps with green glass shades and several wooden book rests, at present empty. Several books lay scattered at one end. At the far end of the room, enjoying a huge fireplace, presently flickering with the flames of burning logs, were two leather Chesterfields facing each other across a low table.

Arthur realised that he was still standing just inside the doors, now closed, having gazed around the room with some envy. Why did Waterhead not have a library? Four gentlemen rose from the Chesterfields and Arthur walked slowly towards them; his father was the only person he recognised. In spite of the portraits in the hall, no one here was in uniform and all looked similarly sober in dark suits, waistcoats and white shirts with various subdued coloured stocks. Arthur, although knowing he had nothing to be ashamed of, felt very under-dressed. A tall gentleman with a white neatly trimmed beard, moustache and sideburns came forward to greet Arthur and his military bearing was plain to see. He extended his hand to Arthur and his grip was firm and dry.

"Good afternoon, Mr Tissiman, and thank you for agreeing to join us. I am Regimental Colonel Sir Gerald Wragby of the Queen's 4th Own Royal Hussars. I need hardly introduce your father, of course." John gave Arthur a hardly perceptible smile, but did not speak. The Colonel looked at a younger man of similar bearing to himself. "This is Captain George Fitzwilliam, also of the Queen's Own Royal Hussars." The captain held out his hand and clearly had to restrain himself from clicking his heels; another even firmer handshake.

"I will leave your father to introduce our fourth member," said the colonel.

John Tissiman moved aside to allow a portly gentleman with much more facial hair than the Colonel to hurry forward and rather embarrass Arthur by grasping his hand in both of his and shaking it up and down enthusiastically. He saved John the task of introduction.

"I am most pleased to meet you, Arthur. I hope I may call you Arthur. I met you once when you were just three years old, but I doubt you remember that occasion." Arthur, already confused, gave a small shake of his head. The gentleman continued. "I am a very long time business associate of your father and I am delighted to add also his good friend. Oh, my goodness, I have forgotten to tell you my name." Arthur was instantly reminded of his Mr Pickwick at Manchester station when he arrived last November; the physical resemblance was striking.

"I am Sir Alan Buckland, but please forget all that folderol and call me Alan." There followed a pause while everyone seemed to consider this information.

"While we wait for our final member to join us, may I offer you tea or a drink of some sort?" Colonel Wragby was clearly the host here and Arthur guessed that this might well be his house. There followed a little uncertain muttering until John said, "No tea for me, thank you." He seemed to assume he was speaking for all of them.

Wragby immediately pulled a chord by the window and the butler appeared within seconds. "Jameson, please serve these gentlemen with some of that malt whisky I brought from Scotland. Do all please sit down." He consulted his pocket watch and then checked the clock that hung over the entrance doors. It was half past two.

The whisky was poured and served as a distant doorbell could be heard. Jameson excused himself and returned a few minutes later. He was followed by a figure certainly no stranger to Arthur, although his presence here was more of a shock than a surprise. His brother, Ernest, stood on the threshold and looked equally stunned when he saw Arthur at the far end of the room, holding a glass of what looked like whisky.

# Chapter Nine

## January 1861

A week earlier, and only just after New Year, Colonel Wragby had had a meeting with (15) Lord Sidney Herbert, the Secretary of State for War. Unknown to Arthur, this second meeting followed that in Manchester in November about which Arthur had also been kept in the dark.

## January 2 1861: Office of the Secretary of State for War

"I am grateful that we were able to meet, although it must be a discreet occasion, if you understand me?"

Lord Sidney was sitting behind a huge mahogany desk and even Colonel Wragby felt his own position to be inadequate in comparison with this powerful minister of state, who then continued without pause.

"I understand from Lord Palmerston that you may be in a position to gather for me some, how shall I describe them?: *Discreet gentlemen of your acquaintance?* These gentlemen, who will then travel *incognito* and quietly enter the Confederate southern states to assess the likely effect that a Union blockade will have on those states and that is most likely being put in place as we speak. Such a blockade of the export of southern cotton will undoubtedly have a serious effect on the cotton industry here and will have the same effect, I suspect, on our economy. I also understand that at least one of these gentlemen will be very experienced in the workings of the Lancashire cotton trade and will be aware of what that trade needs in terms of raw cotton on a monthly and annual basis. Am I correct in that assumption?"

Wragby realised that it was now his responsibility to assure Lord Sidney that Ernest Tissiman was, indeed, such a man.

"That is correct, sir. We intend to include this gentleman, whose family has operated one of our largest cotton mills for generations and who now manages that mill himself. He is also a leading figure in the entire Lancashire cotton industry."

"That sounds most satisfactory for a start. May I then ask what the expertise of the other gentlemen will be?"

"Of course. We felt that the leader of this small party should be a serving military officer, whose loyalty, courage and long service must also include the enforcement of absolute secrecy on those serving in this mission: with your agreement, he is a captain in the Queen's Own Royal Hussars (16), well known to me as his Commanding Officer. He is still a relatively young man, has served valiantly in several campaigns abroad *and* has a connection with an officer in South Carolina, now attached to the Confederate army."

"I am aware, Colonel, that you are speaking of Captain George Fitzwilliam and I am assured that he is an acceptable choice to the War Office."

"Thank you, sir. That is valuable confirmation of my own understanding."

Lord Sidney consulted some papers in front of him on the desk before continuing.

"That is two gentlemen you can recommend. What others do you intend to select in what I assume must of necessity should be very small party?"

"I felt, with your agreement sir, that three was all that it will be possible to dispatch and thus retain secure secrecy and allow them some freedom of movement in the Confederacy as war possibly looms."

The Secretary of State stopped Wragby from saying anything more.

"I must emphasise Colonel, that my opinion, made certain by recent events and reports, is that civil war in America is now inevitable and could be but weeks away. I am also sure that will send shares in our cotton industries tumbling and could see the whole trade collapse. I am absolutely certain that this mission is vital to our country and to its continued prosperity. Now please *assure* me that the third member of the party is of equal value to us."

Here Lord Sidney paused and read a paper by his side. The Colonel had no choice but to await whatever else he had to add. After several minutes, Sidney Herbert looked up and then continued.

"Incidentally, while I think of it, you will take from my private secretary today letters for these gentlemen to sign as a guarantee of their understanding that nothing about this mission, in advance or while taking place or once it is complete, must ever be divulged to any unauthorised person and that penalties for breaking that undertaking will be severe."

"Yes, indeed, sir. I had assumed that something of the sort would be required."

"As I indicated earlier, our meeting today and, in fact, this entire matter, must never be mentioned by you to anyone except to myself or the Prime Minister, but I have no doubt of your loyalty to the government and of your complete discretion."

Another pause: "Now, what was I going to ask you? Ah, yes, of course, the third member, who I assume will be responsible for composing reports that will find their way back here by whatever means is available at the time."

*

## January 20 1861

So it was that almost three weeks later, the group of six gentlemen, including the three *Envoys*, as they would now be known, came together for the first time at 27 Bolton Square and with Ernest now holding a much-needed glass of malt whisky. Colonel Wragby asked them all to take their seats again so that the meeting could begin. Ernest was then shocked to discover Arthur coming through the library door and, with some forced discretion, grasped his arm for long enough to allow the others to settle some distance away on the chesterfields.

"Arthur! What the hell are you doing here? Why, in God's name didn't you tell me?"

His brother had no chance to respond as Colonel Wragby was now looking sternly at the two brothers.

"Gentlemen, you were asked to take your seats, so please do so without further delay."

Arthur took the last place on the Chesterfield on one side of the table and thus Ernest had no choice but to cross to the opposite couch. The Colonel then took the single leather chair facing the window and hence made it clear that he would be in charge of whatever was now to happen.

"You will notice in front of you identical documents that, if signed by you, will be your undertaking to act in complete secrecy about this group, about any discussions, decisions or actions you or we may take. Any breaking of your signed undertaking will result in your immediate arrest by the Government's Secret Service."

Arthur was the only one to look aghast at the name of a force he had no idea even existed. Ernest simply raised an eyebrow and smiled. Colonel Wragby continued without pause.

"Please understand that the penalties for breaking the agreement would be severe. Even if you now decide to withdraw from this and further meetings, you will still sign the document and then withdraw immediately. If you do so, you will continue to be bound by the document. You will find a pen and ink on each on the tables. Please now take advantage of these now. No conversation is permitted."

Some of the group, John Tissiman and Sir Alan Buckland in particular, took up a pen and signed at once. Captain Fitzwilliam first looked at the Colonel and received a curt nod; he then also signed. Ernest and Arthur remained as they were, each with a fixed gaze on his brother. Ernest, with a 'very well' took the pen from his father and signed. Arthur was, inevitably, confused and looked from face to face for some sign of encouragement or support; he received none.

"Mr Tissiman?" The Colonel looked pointedly at Arthur. "I have no intention of swaying you and so if you have doubts, please leave the room now, but after signing."

Arthur looked at his father again and was treated to what was intended as an encouraging smile.

"I should register my objection to signing a document that ties me to an involvement I have had no details of and the breaking of it then comes with a serious threat."

No one spoke to offer reassurance and Arthur eventually sighed, sat forward, read the document carefully and then signed. The Colonel stood and gathered all five copies.

"I have previously signed the same document in the presence of the Secretary of State for War," he assured them.

He then crossed to the bookshelves, took the edge of one of the volumes and pulled open a section of false books to reveal a substantial iron door. He withdrew what looked like a watch chain from his waistcoat pocket on the end of which was a key, with which he opened the door to what was clearly a safe. With the documents safely placed inside, he locked the door, closed the false cover of books, returned the key to its lodging and took his seat.

"Gentlemen, it is my duty now to welcome you, on behalf of the Prime Minister, to the first meeting of the Envoys, as you will now be known, and three of you have been selected to undertake a journey to the United States of America in this role. There are, indeed, six of us now sworn to absolute secrecy and may I make it clear that means you communicate with no one outside this group; not with wives, or children and even the best of friends. I did not exaggerate when I said penalties for infringement would be severe. So I suggest a short break, while you all adjust to the situation and I hope start to breathe more easily."

There was a relieved amount of coughing, shuffling of feet and even uncertain words to neighbours. There was a smile or two, but most looked level eyed and ready to hear what was to come next. Colonel Wragby allowed them about five minutes before he brought them to order once more.

"Very well. Some of you had a preliminary meeting in Manchester, which was arranged after the closest consultation with the Prime Minister and the Secretary of State for War. The existence of this meeting today comes as a result of the worries of some of those present there, as well as others in higher office, regarding a dangerous threat to our nation. You will all be aware that Civil War, between the northern and southern United States is, I am assured by my own military sources, likely to become a reality within the next month or two. John and his two sons are here because they represent the cotton trade, in fact one our largest and most profitable manufacturers. The northern states are equipped with naval vessels that will most probably be used to blockade the export of raw cotton from the southern states to England." John and Ernest nodded, but Arthur sat forward and started to speak more loudly than was really necessary.

"Wait! You are misinformed. I am not…"

John struggled to his feet and spoke angrily across the table to his younger son.

"Ernest and I are well aware of what you were going to say. That is not the reason you are here. Now oblige me by sitting still and listening." With a long look into Arthur's eyes, he sat down and Arthur subsided back into his seat, muttering something no one could hear.

"We will come to that in due course," Colonel Wragby said. "For those who do not know them, the Tissiman family operate one of the largest cotton mills in Lancashire and were involved in the brief first meeting in Manchester.

The success of that persuaded Her Majesty's Prime Minister how important this is to our country. Blockade and conflict would most likely cause the closure of most mills, put huge numbers out of work, create wide spread hunger, and most probably civil unrest, here in England. Are we agreed this is potentially very likely?"

John and Ernest Tissiman were swift to express their wholehearted agreement; Arthur simply looked angry.

Colonel Wragby looked pointedly at Sir Alan Buckland. "Sir, may I ask you to explain how you are involved in this complex plan?"

"Yes, Colonel, I certainly will. I have, for the last thirty years run, the shipping business started by my grandfather, Jeremiah, and then expanded even further by Andrew, my father. Buckland and Son are, I can say with certainty, the largest shipping line importing cotton from America. In my grandfather's and father's days, we shipped slaves to the southern states and then for hundreds of years traded them for cotton."

"You sound very proud of that connection, sir." Arthur spoke with sarcasm in his voice.

Sir Alan jumped up and pointed at Arthur. "Yes, *sir,* I am proud of that, of what my forebears did to make England the greatest nation on earth and the richest. Just what is wrong…"

Colonel Wragby hastily held up both hands and then firmly brought the meeting to order with the natural command his voice seemed to have.

"This is not part of what we, as the few engaged in this mission and authorised by our Prime Minister, are required to inspect or discuss. You will both refrain from such disagreeable speech in future." His words brooked no repost from either gentleman. "Please continue, Sir Alan."

"Very well. I apologise for defending my family." He then hurried on before Arthur could interrupt. "My ships' captains are in Charleston and other southern ports most weeks and I have reliable information that the South will rise and defend its new status as a separate and independent country. Don't be surprised if that happens sooner rather than later. When it does, Bucklands will soon afterwards undoubtedly be declared bankrupt and the supply of cotton to hundreds, if not thousands of English mills will cease. Our whole nation will suffer disastrously. England must find a way to stop this happening."

Sir Alan looked enquiringly around the table and Colonel Wragby quickly thanked him.

"Captain Fitzwilliam and I are officers in the Queen's Own Hussars and will officially be stationed in England for the foreseeable future. We are in a position to be aware of events that are not known, thank goodness, to the newspapers nor to the populace as a whole. Captain Fitzwilliam has a connection with an officer in the Confederate army, who had originally been a corporal in the Royal Hussars when Fitzwilliam was a junior officer. George, would you share what you learned before Christmas from your friend in America?"

Captain Fitzwilliam went to stand, but Wragby waved him back into his seat. "We will all hear you better, I think, if you remain seated."

"Very well, sir. Major James Thornbury, as he now is in the Confederacy, can be relied upon for his discretion in this matter. He wrote two long letters to me in November and then December of last year. He wrote of the new president, Abraham Lincoln, and of the president's strong views against slavery and that seems to be one reason why the Confederate states in the south are now breaking away from the union. They are adamant that they must retain slavery so that they can farm huge plantations of cotton with cheap labour and so sell it to us at a good price, or so I understood from Jim. He is my only contact out there. He describes what he calls 'a terrible state of confusion' in the south at present."

"This is very interesting background, Captain," interrupted the Colonel, "but can you tell us briefly what you learned from your Major Thornbury that relates to our present difficulty?"

"My apologies, sir." Captain Fitzwilliam looked a little embarrassed. "He wrote, among other things of an atmosphere in the streets of Washington in the north and Richmond in the south, of outspoken hatred for the other part of the country: for the north by the south and vice versa. The populace was in what he described as a '*mood for blood*' and the certainty that their army would rapidly annihilate the other side. Whether they are Confederate or Federal Union, they wanted what they regarded as their enemy to '*suffer their righteous anger*'. In Charleston, for example, they felt incensed that the north wanted to steal *their* land and make them destitute. While in Washington, they want to teach the south a lesson for daring to defy the Declaration of Independence, enslave the blacks and build their fortunes on their unpaid labour. In fact, in an exact reversal of that, the south believes it is the north which has actually flouted the

Declaration of Independence. I have orders from the War Office to travel with the other two Envoys to the Confederacy in due course."

Fitzwilliam looked around at his silent audience and decided that he had said enough. He sat looking straight ahead. It was John Tissiman who quickly sought to clarify this.

"I'm just a simple cotton mill owner. I've never travelled further than Carlisle in my life, and that was considered a dangerous journey!" There was a ripple of laughter. "*But* I do know the cotton business and I do know that all of us who work in our Lancashire mills earn a good living there and make jobs for thousands and, what's more, help our country and empire to be the greatest on earth."

He paused, looked around and may well have been expecting applause, which was not forthcoming, although several nodded wisely.

"I've listened to all you gentlemen have said and understand that you are, I am sure, wiser in the ways of the world than I am. So, let me be plain and simple, like the man I am. We all need, nay we *must* have, the stuff to make our industry work and earn for the sake of the mill owners, the workers, our land of England and our Empire across the globe. We cannot allow anyone, however righteous they believe they are, to deprive of us that. We *demand,* and I am not ashamed to use that word, that our government does what is needed to ensure we keep that supply coming. I don't pretend to understand military ways, but we have the world's finest navy. If that cannot break any blockade of our supply, then God is no longer in his heaven." To his obvious surprise, there was a polite but genuine ripple of applause from all bar one of the other members.

"Mr Tissiman, thank you for your eloquent contribution and I think I can say on behalf of us all that you have expressed what we all feel."

Colonel Wragby then paused for the murmurs of agreement that greeted this summary, to die away.

"If we have covered as much of the matter as we can, I have a proposal to put to you. It comes directly from Lord Palmerston himself and, if you agree, we will try to put it into immediate effect as quickly as possible. The Secretary of State for War has informed me that the Royal Navy is in a position to break any blockade, given the recent addition to our fleet of two iron or ironclad battle ships, *HMS Prince of Wales and very soon HMS Warrior.* These two join our other heavily armed man-of-war ships, all of which would reduce the ineffectual naval resources of the United States to matchwood in any skirmish at sea. They would only require a week or so of notice to be ready for action and little more than a week under steam power to cross the Atlantic. *But* what we need now is some first-hand proof that the Confederacy wants, and deserves, this assistance from us."

"Hear, hear," came from three of the non-military gentlemen, with only Arthur remaining silent. "The only requirement that Lord Palmerston now insists upon is that we quickly dispatch this group of three Envoys, with Captain Fitzwilliam as overall leader. You three will be charged with reporting from the southern states to ascertain if or when civil war is likely to break out, *if* a blockade is in force already or, as is very likely, what reaction there would be from both sides to British naval intervention. All *we* have to decide is which two of the non-combatants here should be chosen to go with the Captain."

An uneasy silence embraced the gathering. However, it did not take too long for one or two members to begin to chat to neighbours and even cross to the other side of the table to seek out a likely minded member. Ernest was the first to begin such a conversation and, much to the surprise of his brother, it was Arthur he drew aside. Across the room, Sir Alan was chatting to John Tissiman and before long, both could be seen glancing at the pair of brothers whose discussion was growing animated.

Colonel Wragby, inevitably accompanied by Captain Fitzwilliam, withdrew to the far end of the library, where decanters and glasses were still laid out. When both had a drink in their hands, they surveyed those whom they knew would be the other two envoys. Their subsequent conversation was conducted quietly enough not to be heard by the others at the farther end of the room.

"Who would be your choice of companions, George, although I doubt that will be up to you in the end?" asked the Colonel quietly. George Fitzwilliam looked protractedly firstly at Arthur and then Ernest. He also glanced at Sir Alan, but did not linger there.

Hussar Captain Fitzwilliam, experienced in selecting *volunteers* for uncharted excursions into enemy territory, certainly felt a liking for Sir Alan and for his northern ability to look first towards the benefits of any scheme to himself and his family. However, for the captain's liking, the man was too old, as well as showing his fondness for the beer and the beef of old England, to travel on any secret expedition outside his own county. The same went even more so for John Tissiman. He was soon looking intently at Ernest and Arthur.

George Fitzwilliam moved closer to Colonel Wragby and the two spoke quietly, out of the hearing of the others. These unexpected, private conversations did seem to disquiet others not involved.

"The two brothers must be the only possible candidates, I am sure," the Captain said, "and they both have a strong connection with the cotton milling business. I know you have warned me that Arthur Tissiman has recently declared his intention to break away from that business and seek a teaching post, but his previous education actually makes me feel he would actually be an invaluable addition as the author of any reports; to be honest, the only realistic possibility we have."

"And what of his brother?" asked the Colonel.

"Ernest has been managing Lancashire's largest cotton mill for several years, under his father's capable and experienced instruction no doubt. I am certain that the young man's qualifications for this task are unimpeachable. I am sure I can keep what seems some hostility between them under control and thus ensure that they can send back reports that will allow Lord Palmerston and his government to make an informed and correct decision once, or just possibly if, civil war breaks out, as I am personally certain it will."

"While I agree with you," Wragby quickly put in, "I am concerned that the younger brother may not volunteer. I am uncertain what the problem is between him and his brother and, in fact, I suspect with his father as well. We need to find a subtle method of obtaining the willing participation of *both* or this mission will never get beyond this room. The only way that can be achieved, I believe, is with the help of John Tissiman, whom I am sure knows much more about their antipathy than we ever will. I need to speak to him in confidence before this meeting can be allowed to break up."

Colonel Wragby then walked back towards the other four members, while George Fitzwilliam remained as an interested, and somewhat unconvinced, observer. He watched his commanding officer speak quietly to John and then take him gently by the elbow and lead him to a door at the side of the library, through which they both passed, closing it behind them. The remaining members observed the departure with mild surprise and one or two questioned their absence, but with no hope of an explanation. They were left in that state for the best part of half an hour until John Tissiman briefly came back, spoke to Arthur and Ernest and, with what seemed some difficulty, clearly must have persuaded them to follow him out of the library by the same side door.

Another half hour passed and Sir Alan, having helped himself to what was, indeed, a fine malt whisky, was wondering what was going on, an observation to which Captain Fitzwilliam declared he did not have the knowledge to answer. As they were both deciding whether to have another whisky, the side door opened and John Tissiman hurried out followed by his two sons and finally by Colonel Wragby, who asked everyone if they would kindly sit down again, as he had some final information to impart.

What passed in Colonel Wragby's study in the next few minutes would determine whether the Envoys were going to report from the United States of America, or not.

Before his two sons came back into the library, John had shared with Colonel Wragby two important pieces of information, namely: Ernest had recently suffered a severe attack of 'illness of the mind', as had Arthur, but for very different reasons. Ernest had not been able to cope with the miscarriage of the baby he had not known even existed and, as a result, his wife had blamed him, although John pointed out that he felt that was unreasonable. Ernest and Elizabeth were now, hopefully only temporarily, estranged, but John felt the proposed challenging journey to America would indeed be most welcome to Ernest at this time. He also emphasised what Colonel Wragby already knew, that Ernest was the most able member of the group to represent the understanding, and hence survival of, the English cotton trade.

As far as Arthur was concerned, he had, as he had already told Wragby, fallen out with both his father and his brother and had declined, in no uncertain terms, to enter the family milling business in order to teach what Ernest had described as 'the poor children of London to read and write'. John desperately did not want Arthur to move to London and suffer what he was sure would be poverty there, but he had been unable to persuade him otherwise. He was convinced that if Colonel Wragby would stress that the Prime Minister specifically had insisted that one member of the group of Envoys must have the level of university education that Arthur had and thus the knowledge, intellect and ability to compose the type of report of their visit that the government would heed. This he was sure would persuade Arthur that a delay of a few weeks before the start of his teaching career would be a small price to pay for the gratitude of his country.

The result of the sometimes-heated discussion that followed resulted in an agreement, although John remained unsure how it would materialise in practise.

Once the six gentlemen were seated together again, Gerald Wragby addressed them for the last time.

"You will be pleased to hear that it has been agreed that Ernest and Arthur Tissiman should both represent us, alongside Captain Fitzwilliam, in this vital and totally confidential journey on board the *HMS Prince of Wales.* They will land at Sabine Pass on the border of Texas and Louisiana, the only port presently beyond the reach of the growing, but not yet water-tight blockade. Ernest and Arthur, if you will kindly wait here for a short time, Captain Fitzwilliam will explain what you will need to bring with you for your expedition. I wish the three of you God speed and await your reports with eagerness. On behalf of Lord Palmerston, I thank you all for agreeing to serve your queen, country and empire at this time of great danger."

Having ended what he now felt was a rather too formal an address to the three Envoys he asked them to adjourn to his study for their briefing; to John and Sir Arthur, he wished a speedy journey via nearby Euston Station and on to Lancashire.

# Chapter Ten

**February 1861**

In late February and following a briefing at the Naval Yard at Liverpool, the three Envoys joined *HMS Prince of Wales* for the crossing to the Sabine Pass, the Confederate-chosen landing place for them on the coast of Texas, right on the border with Louisiana. They saw no sign of any threatened blockade on the passage, since the Captain of the *Prince of Wales* had orders to avoid any contact and sailed well south-east of the Atlantic coast and far enough due south to navigate between Florida and Cuba and then into the Gulf of Mexico. Once there, he headed north-west to meet the American coast at Sabine Pass.

The passage across the Atlantic took twenty-five days and they finally anchored at their destination on March 22. Ernest had admitted in Liverpool to being very nervous about making such a long and potentially uncomfortable journey across a huge expanse of ocean, although their vessel was, as Arthur had assured him, a very modern ship of the line. Neither of the brothers had been to sea in their lives, but Arthur seemed to regard the prospect of the voyage with equanimity, while Ernest's nervousness expressed itself in frequent bouts of seasickness.

The *Prince of Wales* was much larger than they had expected. It was encased in iron, powered by both steam and sail and carried nearly seven hundred crewmembers and was more than two hundred feet in length, with three decks.

Arthur had tried to reassure his brother that: "*This is no rowing boat and not at all like the sailing ships-of-the-line that were at Trafalgar,*" but Ernest insisted the whole voyage was given over to: '*a dangerous ship and, what is more, guaranteed to give those who sail on it life-threatening sickness of the stomach*'.

The *Prince of Wales*, England's premiere man-of-war, joined a large fleet, although nowhere near Trafalgar, of existing mainly sail powered ships, while it would soon be a fleet to include the ultra-modern ironclad *HMS Warrior* as well.

Nevertheless, crossing the Atlantic in February at a top speed of just in excess of twenty miles an hour, was certainly no pleasure cruise. They encountered all too regular storms and, with a range of less than three thousand miles under steam, had to rely on sail for several hundred of those miles.

Even George Fitzwilliam, who had been transported by ship many times in his career to campaigns outside England, suffered seasickness, but not nearly as often nor as violently as the unfortunate Ernest. Eventually arriving in the Gulf of Mexico, they were treated to more friendly seas, but all three were exhausted by the time the coast of Texas came into sight just after dawn on February 23.

Before the moment came to disembark, George had insisted that they must stop addressing him by his army rank, since they were equals on this mission and should stick to first names, although when absolutely necessary they should use their true surnames; no one west of Liverpool could have an idea who they were.

The three Envoys were dressed in civilian clothes that gave an impression that they were all middle-class gentlemen of some affluence and had considerable experience of the cotton trade. The only person who knew who they really were and what was the purpose of their mission was George's contact, Jim Thornbury, whom they expected to have travelled from his home in Beaufort County, Virginia, to meet them on their arrival in Texas.

The sky was just growing lighter as the Texas-Louisiana coast was seen on the starboard bow, about a mile distant. None of the officers on board had visited Sabine Pass before, but George had assumed it would be a small port on a flat coastline. However, as they steamed slowly towards the shore it became clear that a fairly wide river mouth lay ahead and where *HMS Prince of Wales* appeared to be heading. A junior lieutenant, unknown so far to the group, stopped when he saw them staring at the approaching river mouth.

"I suspect you may not have any knowledge of this part of the world gentlemen, so perhaps you will allow me to help you?"

"Absolutely, if that's no trouble," said George and shook hands with the young man, whose name was Lieutenant Dickens and who now seemed delighted to show off his seafaring knowledge.

"I was allowed to study the maps prior to our arrival, so I can tell you that ahead is the Sabine River, which flows out of Sabine Lake, a few miles to the north. What you cannot see from here, beyond that bend in the far distance, is Fort Griffith and further up from that is Fort Sabine. Both are Confederate forts, although not in the English sense of a fort or castle, I believe. There are log houses, huts and so forth with a stockade and a small artillery battery. The problem for *Prince of Wales* is that the river has shallows and mud banks, so we, I mean the senior officers, have informed the crew that we will anchor offshore about half a mile up the river." Here he hesitated, unsure if any more information was wanted. "I hope I have been of assistance, sir."

It was clearly George he had been addressing and it was he who shook his informant's hand again, which was all that was needed for the younger man hurriedly to depart. From where they stood on the starboard side of the deck, they were able to observe their entry into the river mouth and the banks at once seemed to close in on such a huge vessel. The engine must have been cut to its slowest speed and the ship was now travelling at a snail's pace, while gradually moving closer to the starboard bank.

At that moment, they heard the engine stop and were now drifting very slowly towards the shore, about a hundred yards away. There were shouts of command from both fore and aft, followed by two loud splashes, which they realised were the anchors being dropped. This caused the *Prince of Wales*, which was more or less stationary just before this happened, to halt with a mild jerk and then settle gently to rest.

The riverbank before them was about ten feet high, with luxuriant trees, bushes and undergrowth as far as they could see along the river in both directions. Arthur, looking to the north, spotted about half a mile upstream what could have been a landslip in the bank and he pointed it out to the others. Ernest agreed it was some sort of collapse of the bank, but George pulled a small telescope from an inside pocket, which the brothers had not seen before.

"No, I don't think it's a landslip," he said, "You can see what looks like a wide path cut into the earth making a more gradual ascent to the top of the bank. Not what you would call a road, but maybe a dirt track. Here, look for yourselves." Ernest was the first to take the telescope, and then passed it to Arthur. They both agreed with George's assumption.

"That must mean," said Ernest, "that we will need to be rowed across there and then take the track to the fort, although I'm not sure how far away it is, but that should be the plan, don't you think?"

Before Arthur could agree, they were interrupted by Commander Pierce, who told then, "Step lively and fetch all your belongings from below so you are ready to go ashore."

As they obediently went below, a long boat was lowered over the starboard side.

The three Envoys gathered their luggage in the form of sturdy leather satchels, just large enough to contain a few clothes and a revolver with fifty rounds of ammunition. Arthur also had charge of several folders of paper and pencils, pens and ink. George had been given responsibility for the bulk of the money they carried, mostly in the form of gold sovereigns and half sovereigns, but they also expected several hundred dollars to be awaiting them ashore, courtesy of a convoluted stipend, via several messengers from the British Ambassador in Washington DC. Most importantly of all was the letter they carried from Lord Palmerston, secreted about George's person that introduced them to whoever it might concern in the Confederacy in the future.

Messages had already been sent to the Confederate Government now in place in Richmond, Virginia and under the command of Jefferson Davis, appointed as President of the Confederacy on February 18. Ernest had already expressed his somewhat peeved annoyance that he alone had no specific task any longer: George was what Ernest called 'effectively in command of himself alone', while Arthur was to use his university and college education to write reports, which he felt would be somewhat undemanding of his university degree.

The three of them now waited on the deck, ready with their belongings at their feet, when Commander Pierce, whom they had come to know and rather liked on the voyage, stood ready to take his place in the long boat immediately below him. A landing net made of rope squares was dropped and eight able seamen and a lieutenant belayed down the net and into the boat at what seemed amazing speed and dexterity. The eight sat with oars raised upright out of the water and the young lieutenant had command of the tiller. Commander Pierce then looked meaningfully at the three non-sailors.

"Gentlemen, time to go, unless you have another destination in mind? Just follow me: drop your satchels down into the boat, then *very carefully* climb over the rail and work your way down. You can see that one of the lads there is standing, ready to steady you, or rescue you when you drop into the water."

Like the seamen before him, the Commander, in full uniform, went down the net like a monkey, sat in the stern of the boat and looked up with a smile on his face.

"This must be the most enjoyable moment for him of this whole damned trip," Ernest growled, but he was the first over the side. George immediately followed Ernest, who had surprised himself by reaching the boat, rather than landing in the water.

"You've got to go now, Arthur. I'll be just here to catch you if you miss your footing," George tried to assure Arthur, who was suddenly assailed by fear of making a fool of himself in front of a dozen others; he looked around and also discovered a group of sailors standing on deck and trying to conceal their hilarity at this land-lubber.

He gritted his teeth and forced himself to step over the rail and find a foothold on the top rung of the net, but his hands seemed to have a will of their own and were now firmly fixed around the rail, with no apparent intention of letting go.

"Come along Arthur, we haven't got all day," his helpful brother shouted up at him.

Arthur closed his eyes and found a dim picture of Maggie's face looking up at him. She would have done this with ease, he knew. So, keeping his eyes closed he let go with one hand, moved one foot down to the next rope and, admittedly slowly, reached the side of the boat, now rising and falling on the swell. In the end, he half fell, half jumped into the boat and landed across both George and Ernest, who roughly pushed him off, so that he had to pick himself up off the bottom of the boat and squeeze himself onto a seat next to George.

The ropes holding the boat to the side of the ship were pulled up and as the longboat drifted away from the starboard side, oars were lowered, a brusque command given by the lieutenant and they were rowing smartly towards what they had already assumed must be the track that would lead them into the Confederacy.

As they approached water so shallow that they could see the mud just below the surface, the rowers increased speed and, at the last moment before the keel hit the mud, raised the oars; the longboat ground to a halt, firmly fixed. Commander Pierce was first to jump down onto dry land and George, Ernest and finally Arthur joined him. The crew of the longboat got out and pulled it further up onto the dry earth. Two of them stayed with the boat and the remainder, led by Commander Pierce and the lieutenant, joined the trio of Envoys as they walked up the slope and joined the fairly wide dirt track ahead of them that eventually curved out of sight.. On their right, a small lighthouse could be seen on the far Louisiana shore, while on both sides, the greenery was dense with what Commander Pierce informed them were mangroves dipping their toes in the river.

They rounded the bend in the track, still following the River Sabine and after about twenty minutes saw a collection of log buildings, both large and small, a scattering of tents, all surrounded by a stockade of logs about six or seven feet high. The track ended at a gate into the stockade, presently open. As they came closer, they saw the barrels of cannon protruding through gaps in the stockade facing the river.

Their party was about fifty yards away when a group of men carrying rifles marched in double time out of the gate and stopped, blocking the track. They were dressed in grey uniforms and some sort of forage caps, although no one outfit was exactly the same as another, due they guessed to some personal decoration or material of different shades; some wore trousers and jackets that were closer to brown than to grey. The rifles they carried George thought looked very much like English Enfield rifles, but were somewhat different in design. What they assumed was an officer then stepped forward with a drawn sword and commanded the English party to halt and explain their business.

Commander Pierce walked the short distance to confront the Confederate officer. "These able seamen, my lieutenant and myself, Commander Pierce, are from the English man-of-war *HMS Prince of Wales*, presently anchored around the bend in the Sabine Pass, along with its crew of seven hundred men and one hundred and twenty cannon and artillery pieces. We are here to see the three gentlemen beside me in safety to Fort Griffin. If your commander, General Magruder of Fort Sabine is here as we expected, you should take us to him at once; he has been expecting these important visitors for at least the last week."

"You will wait here, sir, and I will seek some advice from the commander." The officer sheathed his sword and spoke to his men.

"You will all wait here and see to it that none of these gentlemen comes any closer for the time being."

He then walked quickly back through the gate and the soldiers, immediately aimed the rifles they were carrying at the midriffs of the ship's party.

The ten minutes that passed seemed considerably longer to three of the gentlemen, anxiously regarding the rifles with fixed bayonets pointing at them, but since Commander Pierce did not say a word, they followed his lead. Eventually the Confederate officer returned and spoke to his small party of soldiers.

"At ease men, this party is expected." Rifles were, in some cases, shouldered, while one or two carried them more casually.

"The Commander has ordered me to escort you into the fort, where he is waiting to receive you, sir."

He then turned and shooed his men to the side with a wave of his hand. The party from the *Prince of Wales* followed him through the stockade gate and into the fort. Commander Pierce ordered his lieutenant to wait outside with the six able seamen, who were clearly fascinated by the sight of their first Confederate soldiers.

The group of Confederates moved away without further orders and the four men from the *Prince of Wales* followed their officer into a large building, constructed of rough logs. The room they entered was populated by a few other Confederate officers, all of whom were dressed in better presented uniforms and had side arms on their belts. Their interest in the party passing through was obvious, but the only sign of that was the cessation of all conversation.

Their accompanying Confederate officer knocked on a door at the far end of the room, immediately opened it and stood aside. Commander Pierce preceded the other three into a small room that seemed to serve as an office. A very tall, thin officer with a long moustache stood behind a desk. He was dressed in a smart Confederate officer's uniform with a considerable amount of gold brocade and tassels on the jacket. On the desk lay a broad brimmed hat, a pair of kid gloves and a sword. Commander Pierce somewhat uncertainly saluted him and received a very brief, but similar, response.

"I am General Magruder and I command Fort Sabine up river and this small fort as well. I also command the Jeff Davis Texas Guards in the Sabine area. We received a document informing us of your intended arrival a month ago and notice of the reason for your brief visit. I understand that these three English gentlemen are here to assist the Confederacy in some way, not revealed to me.

My duty would appear to be getting you on the railroad to New Bridge up state on the east side of the border with Louisiana."

George now took over the conversation. "That is correct sir and we are most grateful for any assistance you can give us. I am Captain George Fitzwilliam and these two gentlemen, brothers in fact, are Ernest and Arthur Tissiman."

The General made no attempt to move from behind his desk nor to shake any hands. He picked up a paper lying on the desk and carefully read it, although George assumed he must have previously read it when he received it. He ran his finger along two or three of the lines of script, which were not possible to view as he held the paper close to his face, as if his eyesight might be very poor.

"Yes, that is the information here. I have been instructed by a *higher* authority not to question you further."

There followed a lengthy pause while he studied the rest of the document. The four Englishmen in front of him could not think of anything useful to say and so remained silent. "You will stay at Fort Sabine tonight and travel there now by wagon. I will ride ahead of you. It is not a long journey. Tomorrow, you will be accompanied to the railhead and await the first train north to New Bridge. I am told you are fully equipped for this and other journeys that will be long and, I regret, not particularly comfortable. Lieutenant Dowling, who is waiting for you outside, will also go with you to Fort Sabine." There was another lengthy pause, into which Ernest felt he should step.

"We thank you, sir, for your help in this matter. We look forward to seeing more of the Confederacy on our journey to the east. May I ask if a Major Thornbury is here? We were told to expect him." The General looked non-plussed by the question and Ernest felt he also had run out of relevant words.

"I have been told nothing of a Major Thornbury. Kindly close the door as you leave," said the General, slightly irritably, and sat down at the desk, pulling the same document back before him and looking earnestly down at it again.

# Chapter Eleven

## March/April 1861: The Confederate States (17)

The journey that followed was, indeed, most definitely '*not particularly comfortable*', as George diplomatically put it, nor was it in any way speedy, but tedious with frequent long waits for trains to arrive and, eventually, depart. They had, so George reckoned, hundreds of miles of Confederate states yet to cross in order even to reach their first important destination: Louisiana. They would then cross the states of Mississippi, Alabama, Georgia and eventually hope to reach South Carolina. Everywhere they went were signs of impending war. Trains crammed with men, some in uniform and some not, and refusing to take civilian passengers. The small towns *en route* were frequently showing signs of action far off in the future, or so they optimistically hoped.

They waited for a train at New Bridge for nearly ten hours, which proved to be a *short* waiting time. From there far worse was a journey not possible by train, as no line existed. They sat most uncomfortably on a wagon piled with timber and going at what must have been its usual snail-like crawl along narrow, winding country roads, filled with huge potholes and, not unusually, fallen trees to block the route left by Union sympathisers. This was made worse by other wagons carrying war materials forcing them off the road under the auspices of at least four or five soldiers on board. This part of the journey lasted they guessed for the best part of eighty miles until Jackson, Mississippi.

To get to Jackson involved crossing the vast Mississippi River at Vicksburg about twenty miles before Jackson city. Vicksburg was destined to suffer a huge siege much later in the war, in which thousands were killed or wounded on both sides. Today only Confederate soldiers could be seen in the area.

However, to ride a stern paddle wheel steamer for several miles down the Mississippi was a pleasant break that they all needed. The tedious problem they encountered along all the railroads was a hazard that would also be a major disadvantage to the Confederacy when or if war eventually began. Every town of any size to be called such was traditionally a break in the railroad. This was to give an advantage to taverns, hotels and shops, since passengers had to alight, cross the town and, almost inevitably, wait at least twenty-four hours for a train running out of the town in the right direction. They were also hence often forced into stays overnight; *through lines* did not seem to exist in the south. There were also stops for changes in the gauge of the rails; one train stopped and one on the wider rails eventually continued until it, too, stopped to make the change back to yet another locomotive, now on narrower gauge again. In due course, this would involve lengthy delays to the movement of troops, which meant that they might well fail to arrive at a battle that was already pushing outnumbered Confederate regiments towards a potential defeat.

The Envoy's destination, which seen from a dockside in Liverpool appeared to be months away, now seemed closer at last. Charleston seemed far away and then it was on to Beaufort County in Virginia, which was not far from Richmond, itself about 400 miles inland and north from Charleston. Their destination could then, in theory at any rate, be reached by railroad.

"We seem to be discovering that the people of the south don't often travel far from home," Ernest observed three weeks into what seemed to be an unending journey.

This obvious problem, along with a lot of other information about the South, they gathered once again from George, who seemed to know far more helpful knowledge of this country than the two brothers had been trusted with. After more than three weeks of Confederate rail travel, not to mention numerous road detours and constant delays waiting for trains, they finally reached Charleston in early April.

The weather was becoming much warmer than their English bodies were used to. The scenery they had passed by had also changed, often dramatically and more or less from day to day: the flat river plains of the Mississippi, blue shaded mountains seen in the distance in Alabama and Georgia, but most noticeably the huge areas under cultivation, which they learned were called plantations. These were often very large farms owned by wealthy families, which were what the south generally regarded as *aristocracy*. The plantations, spreading as far as the eye could see for mile after mile, were studded with cotton bushes, in March and April not yet ready to harvest. When they guessed they might be about an hour from Charleston, Ernest raised the question that was on all their minds.

"George, can you just remind us exactly what we are hoping to learn in Charleston? Seeing a country that doesn't seem really close to being at war, I can't imagine what Charleston could have for us actually to report on."

George looked surprised to be asked. "What you see is exactly what I hoped you would have expected to see, I suppose. For you two surely it is all about the export of cotton and would a blockade be put in place to shut the ports. I assume most of the cotton you buy from the confederate states comes via Charleston on ships belonging to Sir Alan. So I would have *thought* we would need to get to the harbour and see what the situation is with a Union blockade: is it in force yet? That's the question surely? If not, is the blockade ready to be put in place? If in place how strong does it look? Is it possible that the Union might even have mined these harbours? Just use your eyes and ears and record all the information you can get hold of."

"And what will you be doing, George? I doubt you will be looking at bales of cotton."

"True. I need to get as close as I can to the fortress in the bay there, which is manned by Union forces in a strongly Confederate town. My information in London suggested it could well be where a pre-emptive strike could be launched by the Confederacy that just might light the fuse of war. Also, I need to see what I can learn about the strength and readiness of the Confederate army. More than anything, our government wants to know if they look as if they could win a war against the Union and especially if they manage to keep the ports open without our help."

When they arrived in Charleston, they were not prepared for the Victorian charm, not to say beauty, of this large town and its Atlantic seaport, one of the major southern ports for the export of cotton to England.

Once out of the railroad depot, they found themselves in a town that seemed never to have experienced an Industrial Revolution. There were streets lined with both large and small colonial houses, many with white picket fences to the front, often lush trees and gardens fronting the roads and with Spanish Moss hanging down from the tree branches. Magnolias just coming into bloom were a common sight. The roads themselves were only paved in the central areas of the town, while those serving streets of houses further out were dusty with earth and gravel surfaces. There was no sign of any heavy industry, as would be found in towns of a similar size in England.

As they wandered with no real plan, now in the late morning, they discovered streets and squares full of numerous citizens in clothes that were fashionable in England ten or twenty years ago. In some parts of the city, even larger colonial mansions existed than nearer the rail depot, most surrounded by acres of lawns and carefully tended gardens. Carriages, broughams, wagons and gentlemen on horseback lent an atmosphere of a life in a controlled hurry. They noticed many black women, dressed much more simply than the white population and soon realised that they must be domestic servants; in fact, they eventually would have to accept that they must in reality be slaves.

These women often had charge of white children, far better turned out than they were themselves. Black faces were becoming common as the day progressed, including what they learned were called *car men* driving wagons, but also the passenger trolley cars pulled along the streets by horses, as well as acting as porters, carrying a wide variety of heavy loads. It became obvious to the Envoys that the black slave population was regarded by the white population as inferior creatures put on earth to do their bidding.

They had all been aware that slavery still existed in the United States and had done for more than a century. What they had not known was that it was not just restricted to field workers on plantations, producing the cotton that was the life blood of the mills of Oldham. Their opinions of the idea of enslavement of black human beings varied between members of the trio: Arthur, who had studied the history both of slavery in the past in England and today in America, expressed his strongly held view that it was morally appalling and should be abolished as it had been at home just before he was born. He dismissed the argument, loudly put forward by Ernest, that the cotton mills of England needed slavery if they were to continue production. Ernest had what he called a 'more realistic' view based on the survival of his family's cotton trade, where abolition of slavery at the cotton's source would raise the price of cotton so much that it would cripple the trade in England.

George was the only member of the group who had seen slavery in action when he served in other theatres of war, including most recently the Crimea. He simply felt, but did not consider it worthwhile to argue about, that it was an inevitable part of the human condition and always had been and always would be. None of them had yet seen slaves in large numbers working in plantation fields, where they were obliged to toil at the whim of their masters, who owned and controlled them absolutely, in most cases from birth to death.

As the three of them walked into the central area of Charleston they saw more colonial-style buildings: a fine city hall, the huge Huguenot Protestant Church and the Old Exchange and Provost Dungeon on Broad Street that was already more than one hundred years old. They stopped at an eating-place shaded by giant oaks and with customers that were all white; it would have been described as a 'luxurious restaurant' in Manchester. They ate a sort of fish soup, called chowder, and drank local beer.

They were struck from the outset by the gentility of all Charleston's citizens, a kind of politeness that seemed to create a natural friendliness towards others in a way that all three of them felt had begun to disappear in England many years ago. It was George who noticed that people of all ages had a kind of natural nobility, hard to describe, but once mentioned that was impossible to ignore.

"I believe," George said, as they were finishing their luncheon, "that the natures of these Charlestonians, if that is how they name themselves, must come from a strong belief in a history that owes its qualities, I am sure, to their English ancestry and their unabashed love and loyalty of the south and all it stands for, entirely distinct from the rest of these, so called United States."

"You sound as if you are ready to join their ranks, George," Ernest said with a smile and sound slap on the back.

They reluctantly left the restaurant as the afternoon changed from warm to positively hot. They intended to make for the docks and hoped to see cotton bales intended for England being shipped. They asked for directions and were told they could walk or take a trolley car. Their decision to walk, in order to see as much as they could on the way, was regretted an hour later by all. The day was far warmer than they had expected and as they moved away from the city proper towards the sea, jackets were abandoned and the three Englishmen experienced the unusual feeling of sweat sticking their shirts to their backs. Eventually they came to a natural anchorage, sheltered by a peninsular and with a large fortress on an island in the bay. They then found the harbour proper, which comprised a large area of quays piled with a huge variety of cargo, most of it bales of cotton, but with no ships awaiting loading. A short way further on were numerous individual wharves, signed with the names of private owners or businesses and similarly laden with goods, but, now it seemed, with no means of shipping goods out.

George managed to stop what seemed to be a gentleman coming out of one of these wharves and asked why goods were not being shipped.

"I guess you gents don't live here. Am I right? I guess you'll be damned foreigners or you wouldn't be askin'. Am I right?" Ernest was quick to respond, for once ahead of George.

"Yes, sir, you are correct. We are visiting from England and represent the cotton industry there. Our family mill, close to Manchester, has bought your cotton for generations and we are here to try to discover how, if a war were to break out, the government in the north could enforce a blockade of this and perhaps other harbours? Our cotton mills and the English government would be extremely unhappy if that happened."

"By God, sir, that is a fine and dandy thing to hear."

The well-dressed gentleman then slapped Ernest on the back and grabbed his hand and shook it violently.

"And I guess you other gents will be English, too?"

When that was confirmed, Arthur and George received the same exuberant welcome.

"I'm gonna take you to the tavern over the other side of the wharves there and you'll be my guests for a measure of our finest ale."

There was no question of refusal and the gentleman, who revealed his name as Joshua Davis – '*No relation I'm afraid to old Jeff*' – set off at some speed across the docks to a small tavern, where a number of what looked like dock workers, but all white skinned, stood drinking around the few occupied tables and benches. They noticed that not a single black face was present, although they saw many of what they took to be slaves, standing in a group around the harbour itself and obviously guarded by two white men swinging wicked looking wooden clubs.

Mr Davis, having set tankards of beer in front of all three, raised a toast to 'Old Dixie', which none of the trio understood. The somewhat one-sided conversation lasted for some considerable time, from which they learned that a virtual blockade was already in place, although no shot had been fired by either side. The export of cotton bales to England and other goods, such as lumber, rice, tobacco and furs, from American ports were equally at a virtual stand-still. Their host wanted to take them to meet other businessmen like himself, but they excused themselves with the half-truth that they had to get to the railroad depot. They left their host with more handshakes and were sworn to make sure their English government knew what Charleston and the whole Confederacy hoped for. Mr Davis's final word stayed in their minds for a long time: *'I pray Our friends in England will come to our aid pretty damned soon and stop this bloody ruinous blockade'!*

"We must have missed news of all this while we were travelling," said Ernest once they were out of earshot. "If this blockade is already stopping trade in some places, what on earth will it be like if a war starts?"

"You sound as though you're certain it will start," George pointed out.

"Just remember what we've seen so far in a short time. Can you doubt for a moment that this country is on the very brink of civil war and that it is much closer that we expected back in England?"

Arthur looked back at the docks crammed with bales of cotton going nowhere.

"Of course, you're right, Ernest. This is all going to blow up before many more months pass and, while we have seen what it must already be doing to our cotton trade, we have no way of getting even this small amount of information back to London at any time soon. *The Prince of Wales* was supposed to come into harbour here in about two months' time to take dispatches to London. Add to that another two or three weeks to get to Liverpool and by then, this war will have started, of that I'm sure."

George looked back at the docks as they began their return walk to Charleston town. He eventually broke an uneasy silence that had settled over them.

"I must admit it all seems to be happening faster than we expected, but I think we have to continue on to the Haywards at Beaufort County, since we are expected there some time in April and then we can see what they can tell us. They are likely, I think, to have more reliable information. Daniel is in command of a division of cavalry and will know what Jefferson Davis and the Confederate government are planning. After that, I'm trying to work out how we get information back to London, although I do have an idea about that."

"Is this something else you can't share with us?" asked Ernest, obviously annoyed. "And who is Daniel, if I may ask, since we have heard nothing about Beaufort County or the Haywards, except that it would be a good place from which to travel into the borders of the Union before war breaks out?"

George looked at them with a steady gaze that showed no emotion, but the brothers could sense he was either annoyed or worried.

"I apologise if I have been secretive, but I assure you I have no choice. I have instructions from the Secretary of State for War, who has the ultimate say in what orders are issued to me as a serving officer. I am also officially in charge of this expedition. I do not withhold any information that I am not instructed to keep private and, for the time being at least, everything to do with where we go and what we do from Charleston onwards, I am prohibited from sharing. I have no choice but to say that you must trust me. We are in a dangerous place and we can only survive if we respect the orders we are *all* under."

Neither Ernest nor Arthur felt much reassured by what seemed to be a well-rehearsed speech. They were both unsure about trusting George blindly, but there was at present no choice. Arthur voiced his own opinion.

"Very well, George, but it does sound s bit military in tone. I think we both appreciate the danger we could find ourselves in by falling out over something like this, but we would ask you to assure us that you will never withhold anything that does not come under the military orders you have now told us about."

George had no problem with giving this assurance and the three of them continued through the outskirts and into the town. A short while later, they turned into a square, surrounded by warehouses and were surprised to be unable to find any way through a crowd so large and so boisterous that filled it to bursting. They could just see that in the centre of the square was a stone platform with a few steps up to it, but that did not seem to account for such a gathering, mostly of men but with a few well to do women as well. Unable to get through the crowd in the square, they agreed to try to find another route back to the town centre, but just as they took the first few steps to leave and to walk back towards the harbour, the crowd grew quieter as a man in a long coat climbed the steps to the platform and held his hands aloft to request quiet, which he gradually received.

"Gentlemen! Gentlemen! Order please. You have seen on the notice the order of today's sale and I have some very fine lots for you and at a very fine price I'll be bound."

This provoked cries from the crowd of 'Get on with it!'; 'We ain't got all day mister!'; 'Just get the goods on show you charlatan!' and several others, but quietened again by the raised arms of what seemed to be the auctioneer, who now looked behind him to the doorway of a warehouse and yelled, "Let's have them out here now!"

George was already sure he knew a slave auction when he saw one, but the brothers had expected actual goods, not people.

An overseer, a thickset white man holding the handle of a whip, came through the open doorway leading a line of either terrified or simply resigned black slaves roped together, barefooted and naked. The line included young and old, men and women and, at the end of the line several children. Ernest and Arthur were stunned into silence, but unable to look away.

The overseer undid the rope from the young man at the head of the line and pushed him up onto the platform, where he stood erect and gazed out over the crowd with a look of disdain on his face.

"This fine young buck is just eighteen years old and used to hard work in the cotton fields. See the hardness of those muscles."

At a nod from him, the overseer punched the young man in the stomach and received simply a look of pity. The auctioneer's assistant although older, smaller and clearly weaker than the slave, knew he was safe from any attack and so grasped the man's head and forced his jaws open to reveal a good set of teeth.

The auctioneer boasted, "He has all his own teeth, as you can see, and is well trained by the previous owner… Now what am I bid."

There was a shout of 'Two dollars'! That caused a flurry of bidding and a new owner who paid five dollars, which he gave to the auctioneer and dragged the young man off to a wagon waiting at the rear of the crowd.

The auction proceeded at a good pace. Two much older men were described as 'still good for cleaning the shit pits in the slave cabins, weeding the crop or maybe domestic work in the house…and they don't eat much, neither'!

Following these, next driven on to the platform were two good looking girls, naked like the rest, but trying to cover themselves with their hands; That was quickly stopped by a hard slap to both sides of the face of the young woman now first in the line.

They were described as, "Just maybe fifteen, in fine shape and obedient. They are used to field work, but also some *work* in the master's house, if you know what I mean!"

They went for fifteen dollars and twenty dollars respectively.

After all the adults had been sold, the four children were arranged in a line on the platform. They looked to Arthur to be aged from about five to maybe ten years old, but were described simply as: "Young bodies ready for training and hard work, wherever you want them. Don't worry, they don't come attached to any family, so you'd be free to train and use them how you like."

The oldest went for three dollars, the youngest for twenty-five cents.

As another line was brought out, the three Envoys had had enough and turned away, pushed through the now thinning crowd and walked back in the direction of the town. Arthur felt physically sick with disgust and was only prevented from going back and beating the overseer with his own whip by Ernest and George seizing an arm each and dragging him into a narrow street where they were no longer visible.

By the time they reached the City Hall in its square surrounded by live oaks, shading the white painted benches for local gentle folk to relax in the shade, Arthur had stopped struggling and venting his furious opinion of the barbaric trade and his older brother was able to sit him on a bench between himself and George to treat him to what he called 'the realistic view'.

"We are in the South, Arthur, and on a mission dangerous enough as it is without you getting us lynched by virtually any white man in the town who would be delighted to put a noose around our necks. We're here to report all we see, not to start a riot that would see us dead and hence useless to our country and our business."

Arthur had not said a word as this diatribe was delivered with its speaker's face close to his own.

George continued, "You will not put our lives at risk and will bloody well remember this or I will personally drown you in the Ashley River."

As the afternoon was now cooling and the streets becoming busier. The three went in search of some accommodation for the few days that they had decided they should stay in Charleston and really try to get an idea of what this most Confederate of towns thought about war: whether the Confederates could win such a great trial of strength, whether the blockade was about to tighten further and whether the Confederacy would be able to harness its undoubted patriotism and belief in its army in order to come out of such a conflict having succeeded in setting their new country free from the Union and free to carry on its profitable businesses unhindered by being forced to end slavery.

They found a small hotel several streets north of Broad Street that was pleased to have three *'such charming English gentlemen'* gracing their hotel. The daily rate seemed reasonable and they soon discovered that the food was good, if sometimes unusual. The next morning was April 8 and they were about to have their first taste of what a war, and especially a civil war, might actually be like.

# Chapter Twelve

## April 1861 Charleston and Fort Sumpter

After the shock of seeing human beings sold like animals, but with less care than even those creatures receive, Arthur found it impossible at first to sleep. He tossed and turned, sweating in the claustrophobic night air. At some time after midnight, Ernest could stand the disruption to his own sleep no longer and left the bedroom to try to find a bench or chair in the open air, where he might stand a chance of getting at least some sleep before dawn.

Whether it was Ernest's unquiet departure or simply his own exhaustion, but Arthur then sank into a deep and worried period of sleep in the bedroom. He dreamt of Maggie, but Maggie through a swirling mist in a run-down street. He thought, *She seemed to be angry with me?* and, *worse, was convulsed with hysterical tears. No words came from her, although her mouth gave the appearance of speaking.* As Arthur felt himself reaching out for her, he came suddenly awake. It was still dark and it took him several minutes to come to terms with where he was and the reality that he had only been dreaming. This left him in a state of desperation, realising that he had never really said goodbye to her, never explained to her where he was going or why. Worse still, he had never found the courage to tell her that he loved her, even though it had taken this journey so far away from Oldham, for him to realise this was true.

As the sky became that strange shade of black, almost a deep purple, which it took on occasionally as dawn was still well over the horizon in the southern states, he went back to sleep. He did not dream. He did not hear Ernest come back to bed at about four o'clock, having also been unable to find anywhere else to sleep comfortably for long.

Both brothers were woken on the morning of April 8. It was still at that moment as darkness was giving way to the new day. What woke them both was the sudden sound of the extraordinary noise of a very considerable number of men's voices and then shouted commands just below their window. Arthur was the first to open the shutters onto the balcony that overlooked a square. What he saw and heard below them was a shock, especially after the generally peaceful atmosphere of the day before.

Looking down, he saw dozens of men, mostly he reckoned in their fifties and sixties, and many even white-haired grandfathers. They were dressed in various attempts at uniform, or parts of the uniform, but Arthur could clearly recognise it as being of the Confederacy colours. Most carried guns of some sort, although more often than not these were shotguns and even examples of old flintlocks. Others, perhaps those better off, carried rifles, although not the most modern types, while a few had to make do with pistols and swords. Officers, a little more completely uniformed, were trying to persuade the mob into orderly lines, but generally had to have recourse to screaming orders at deaf ears.

Ernest had by now realised that some sort of military commotion was going on outside and had joined Arthur, shortly followed by George, who had come from his room at the back of the hotel.

"It must be some sort of local guard," said George, boasting a little more knowledge of such things. "They look a ragtag bunch. I wouldn't fancy getting any sort of order out of that lot!"

"Why do you think they're out here at this hour? It's only just getting light," Ernest queried.

"I suspect they haven't been called out in response to some sort of rumour of a Union threat. There are always a bunch of such rumours, usually false, when war or battle is in the air. I've seen it before when something serious is coming closer, in India for example it was very common."

The hundred or so men were by now in some semblance of lines and were standing still, if not to attention. The next command, hard to hear exactly, must have been to march, because the lines turned and tramped out of the square in the direction of the harbour.

In the quiet that followed, the three Envoys on the balcony, realising there was nothing else to see, moved inside. It was decided that they might as well get dressed and go down to see if they could find out if anything of interest was, in fact, going on in the normally quiet streets of Charleston. Only yesterday, the owner of the hotel had impressed upon them when they arrived, that the town wanted no part in a war and hoped, even expected, that no conflict would upset their peaceful way of life here.

By the time they reached the front entrance of the hotel, having taken a hastily composed breakfast that the hotel had laid out on one table in dining room, where they were told that it was all they had at this early hour. They found Mr Dobbs, the owner, also standing just outside the front door looking at nothing in particular in the now empty square.

"I suspect that the home guard must have disturbed you gentlemen and I do apologise for that."

"Not at all," said Ernest, "but what was it all about? We understand that some sort of trouble, maybe even a fight, is in the wind, but has something actually happened?"

"Well, sir, in a way I suppose it has, but it's all rumour you understand. A week or so before you arrived, a lot of people here had heard that the Union garrison at Fort Sumpter, out there in the harbour, was going to withdraw and go back up north. After all, Charleston and South Carolina are in the south, in what is now, I suppose, the new Confederacy. So, the men out there on the island would be a bit out of their own territory. It would make sense if they just marched away and left us in peace."

"Is that likely to happen?" asked Arthur.

"To tell the truth, sir, I couldn't say. Citizens are saying so many different things. Only the day before yesterday I was told that Fort Commander Anderson had been told by Abe Lincoln not to surrender *and* that there was a ship on its way from New York with fresh supplies for the fort, so they wouldn't have to ever give up Fort Sumpter. I said to Mrs Dobbs that maybe she should go and stay with her aunt down in Savannah, but she said it was all nonsense and would just blow over, just the same as that rumour about Jud Wilkins stabbing that boy from the Marshall family last month – he reckoned the lad was about to sign up for them Yankees. It was all a mess of lies."

George took the opportunity of a pause to start to move slowly away from the hotel. He called back over his shoulder to Mr Dobbs.

"Thank you, Mr Dobbs, for your well-informed news, but we have to meet up with friends near City Hall, so we will see you this evening."

Ernest and Arthur took the hint and they now all strode off at a brisk pace towards City Hall, but once out of sight, changed direction towards the harbour, to see if anything at all *was* going on.

What they found as they reached the peninsular was very little of any note. Fort Sumpter sat, as yesterday, on its artificial island of rubble and the Union flag was clearly to be seen fluttering in the breeze above the high fortress walls that encircled most of the small island. In front of them at the seaward end of the island was an old emplacement for guns that had been there, it seemed, as defence against invaders from the sea, but it was in a poor state, unmanned and the canons looked unlikely to be in a condition to be fired.

Being careful not to seem particularly interested, they enquired of a several passers-by and also dock workers, as yesterday doing very little in the way of work, if they had seen anything worrying, but the answers were all either, 'Don't know what you'm on about', or, suspiciously, 'Mind your own damned business'!

They spent the day wandering the town trying to seek out news of any sort, but heard only rumour. Rumour that circulated from some ladies in the north of the town whom they found packing all the belongings they could carry into a coach with the intention of driving further south, 'away from this foolish fighting'. Then later, in contrast, speaking to a group of hauliers, also with no work in hand, who were trying to find out how to join a Confederate regiment to fight the 'bloody Yankees', 'teach them a lesson' and 'give them a bloody nose'.

As the day moved towards evening, crowds of onlookers gathered along the harbour sides, eager to see what would happen next and hoping that the Yankees were about to be forced to surrender. George had disappeared some time before, but Ernest and Arthur eventually went back to the hotel, ate supper, and discussed the very little they had learned, then retired to bed, assuming George would find his way back when he was good and ready.

The next morning, April 9, the whole town was in uproar. George reappeared from upstairs as the brothers appeared in the square, again filled with citizens of Charleston trying to find out what was happening, some already having definitely decided to leave the town. As well, there were columns of soldiers in Confederate uniforms marching through in the direction of the harbour. People seemed to be in too much of a hurry to speak to strangers, but it was not hard to pick up conversations, often shouted to friends or neighbours separated by others going in the opposite direction.

It seemed that a General Beauregard, a senior Confederate officer, was marching into the town with 'thousands' of men, who were heading for all sides of the harbour, on both the Ashley River as well as the Cooper River banks. Horse-drawn rigs pulled artillery pieces in the same direction.

One young man, gripping a confederate cap and much the worse for the drink he must have been consuming since sun up, was shouting to the world in general, "He's gonna put a circle of fire around Sumpter! Oh yes, he is! Praise be to God!"

They eventually reached the tip of the peninsular, where they had been yesterday, but by now the gun emplacements there were equipped with several newer artillery pieces and manned by Confederate gunners trying to make sense of the boxes of shells being delivered by wagons. The three Englishmen stopped to take in all the action, but were quickly told to: "Get the fuck out of here before you get thrown in the stockade!" A rifle aimed at their heads made rapid departure the wisest option.

Within a few hours, it became impossible to stay anywhere near the harbour as Confederate troops forced the crowds back at gun point, although the onlookers still remained in force a few hundred yards away. To the two brothers, but apparently not so to George, it was as if the crowds had come for a show at a theatre or music hall; an exciting afternoon of entertainment was promised. George shook his head in despair and explained that it had, until recently, been common in Europe for civilians to gather to watch battles in progress and that seemed to be happening here.

Looking across at both the northeast and northwest river banks, the same hectic activity could be seen. It became clear that the little island in the middle of the harbour was now the bull's eye of a target for more than a dozen batteries of guns and hundreds, maybe thousands, of confederate soldiers under the command of a general whose very aristocratic name they learned was properly Pierre Gustave Toutant Beauregard, but Charleston citizens much enjoyed his nickname of 'the Little Napoleon'.

Apart from his impressive name, it was Arthur who was told by a fellow guest at the hotel that evening that the Commander of the Fort for the Union was Robert Anderson who, in the 1830s had been an instructor to Beauregard at West Point.

"Such are the unbelievable coincidences of war," said Arthur, when retailing this gem of information to the other two: "Because, my friends, this is going to be a war and a mighty bloody one as well; of that I am now sure."

Rumour was spreading like wild fire as they made their laboured way back to the hotel. Newspapers were being printed and distributed free of charge, with the next edition a few hours later headlining a different *true account*. Ernest picked one up from the road and read that the Union ship, the *Baltic,* sent to bring supplies to the fort, had been sunk before reaching the harbour, while within the hour it was declared that the ship had reached Sumpter unharmed. What was true was that the harbour was already littered with Union mines while, further out, were the wrecks of ships sunk by Union soldiers trying to break out of the blockade.

When the Envoys reached the hotel, it was to the sound of singing from a crowd gathered beneath a balcony. A fat, well-dressed man of some fifty odd years was waving from the balcony to the crowd below him, who were serenading him with patriotic southern songs and shouting his name again and again: "Roger Pryor! Roger Pryor! Champion Pryor!" (18) They learned that he was a congressman from Virginia and a rabid proponent of *Free Dixie*.

Sleep that night was impossible as the crowds never stopped their celebrating, singing and shouting for the death and destruction of the Union. Soon after five the following morning Arthur was out in front of the hotel and was soon joined by Ernest and George. Within the hour signal guns were fired to call up all reserves in the town, although columns of men in grey Confederate uniforms could already be seen on all sides, heading for the harbour batteries, no doubt in response to yet more rumour that the *Baltic* had arrived and delivered desperately needed ammunition and food to the fort.

The Englishmen found it hard to keep track of time as the tenth merged into April 11. When George, trying to rest in the hotel already full to bursting point, heard that a Confederate long boat under a white flag was to be sent in the next hour to the fort to demand Anderson's surrender or face the consequences of an apocalyptic bombardment, he made for the harbour as quickly as was possible; but with the crowds of both civilians and soldiers, it was over an hour before he could even see the waters of the harbour, with Fort Sumpter helpless at its centre.

He knew he was watching history being made when he saw a small boat with four or five soldiers on board, a large white flag at the stern and the Confederate Stars & Bars flag flying beside it. It made slow progress, but neither side fired a shot. George pulled out his small telescope and could make out a Confederate Officer stepping onto a jetty under the fortress wall. He was met by a Union officer and something was handed over.

The Confederate officer retuned to the boat still tied to the jetty. George began to fear that they might be fired at as they sat there, but over an hour later, the same Union officer came back out, spoke to his Confederate counterpart, saluted and returned through the huge doors set in the twenty-foot-high wall, which were then slammed shut. The longboat made its way back to the far side of the harbour.

The rest of the day was, to his surprise, without any real information as to what was happening. Single news sheets were spread around the town, either boasting that the 'coward Anderson' would surrender the next day at dawn, or, with just as much certainty, that the Rebs 'would destroy the fort by canon fire the next day and leave it a mass of smouldering rubble by nightfall'.

Along with the citizens of Charleston, the five and a half thousand Confederate troops now under the command of General Beauregard around the fortress could apparently do no more than watch. Meanwhile, the eighty-seven Union soldiers, including some musicians unused to bearing arms, and the three English Envoys, held their breath as the quiet of the day moved into night.

In spite of his best efforts to find out what was going on and whether Fort Sumpter would surrender or endure the barrage, George could discover nothing. He tried to reach Confederate officers manning the artillery batteries, but was turned away and warned of arrest if he persisted. No one in Charleston enjoyed much sleep again that night. In fact, Ernest, the last of the Envoys to lie down on his bed, fully clothed, had just dozed off when he heard a single shell burst in the direction of the harbour and then a barrage of gunfire echoed across the water as it reached its target of the fort.

He woke so suddenly that he thought the explosions were in his dreams, but quickly realised it was reality. He pulled his watch from his waistcoat pocket and held it to the light coming through the shutters from the street; it was 4.40am on April 12 1861. Ernest was among the first of the trio to hear the opening shots fired in the American Civil War: a barrage from Fort Johnson on James Island aimed at Fort Sumpter.

# Chapter Thirteen

**April 12 1861**

As Arthur was to discover much later, that first shot of the Civil War was in reality fired by a southerner determined to uphold his rights and damn the Yankees: Abel Doubleday, whose hand lit the fuse on the cannon that launched the first grenade that burst over Fort Sumpter had signalled that the barrage could now begin and was thus assured a place in the history of the American Civil War.

At that moment, crowds throughout Charleston, as soon as news spread that the fort was under siege from a Confederate force, broke into wild cheering that resounded throughout the town. Major Anderson, who was, in fact, himself a slave owner, had ditched his personal life-long belief in the value of their labour and had recently pledged his loyalty to the Union.

In the following hour or so when he was faced more than once by a Confederate demand that he surrender, Anderson had courageously, or possibly foolishly, refused to consider such an act, but had quietly informed the Union officer, who was waiting for his decision on the jetty at Fort Sumpter, that if his force did not receive supplies of food, water and gun powder, he would, in fact quite possibly be forced to surrender by midday on April 15.

The cannon fire and all the deadly barrages Fort Sumpter would experience from April 12 came from fifteen batteries scattered around the harbour and its peninsular shores. The cannons were mostly smooth bore and fired solid metal rounds. The batteries were protected by walls of sandbags, although the return fire the Confederates had been told to expect hardly materialised. The fifty cannons, now focussed on the fort, fired with hardly a pause for over thirty hours and used in excess of three thousand three hundred cannon balls. At night, as the fuses of the shells burned, they drew red lines in the sky towards their target.

Anderson had forty-eight guns in the fort, but only twenty-one of these were operational, placed on the lower casements of the outer fortress walls. They were only thirty-two or forty-two pounders, generally less powerful than those in the hands of the Confederacy. Anderson decided not to fire nearly as much as he could have done because he did not want to be accused of '*starting a war*'.

The Union soldiers had eaten a breakfast of salt pork and water just before the barrage began. They manned their guns, but were told to fire only intermittently to preserve powder, which was very limited. In the harbour itself, the Confederates had picket boats looking out for the expected Union relief fleet; if spotted, blue rockets were to be launched.

The fortress was well protected by high, five-foot-thick stone and brick walls and then with an inner casement wall. There were stone ceilings between the two walls protecting the rooms beneath them, used for storage and barracks when the fort was fully manned. The Union flag with its thirty-three stars was flown from a giant flagpole in the centre of the fort parade ground, the size and height of a good-sized pine tree.

By midday on April 12, the Confederate fire had become better focussed and much more accurate. They were also heating cannon balls on fires by each gun emplacement. Called 'hot shot', this was aimed at the wooden buildings inside the fort, which caused fires very effectively.

It was during the first hours of the barrage that George came across a Confederate major, who had, by incredible coincidence, served with the Royal Hussars ten years before as an American observer in India; such military coincidences were by no means unusual in the British army that served with men by the thousand in three continents.

The coincidental soldier smuggled George into the battery embrasure on the tip of the peninsular that commanded the central arc of the harbour facing the fort. From there, with the aid of his telescope, he was able to observe the relentless bombardment for more than two days, during which time he hardly slept or even ate.

He was a witness able clearly to see the walls of the fort being pummelled and the rooves beginning to collapse, followed by the inner walls. The wooden barracks caught fire and many injuries must have been sustained by flying masonry debris, which rained into the central parade ground.

The following day, April 13, heavy rain prevented more fires breaking out, but did not prevent the defenders being able to see a Union supply fleet stalled several miles beyond the harbour entrance. This was Captain Fox's relief expedition. They had sailed from Sandy Hook, near New York, well before the shooting started. There was the war ship *Pawnee*, the cutter *Harriet Lane* and further out at sea the larger *Baltic* commanded by Captain Fox himself. George was aware that all these ships were powered only by sail.

Fox was unable to get near to the entrance to the harbour, due to stormy seas outside and the barrage around Fort Sumpter. He was desperately frustrated at being marooned too far away to assist the garrison, but was hopefully awaiting the *Pocahontas*, a much larger ship, that he believed could force its way in, but it failed to arrive that day nor in the days yet to come. When Fox was told the Union flag had been 'lowered', he assumed that it was all over. It was not; the flagpole had been felled by incoming shot.

The barrage had rained cannon balls and huge chunks of stone and brick on the eighty-five defending Union soldiers, as well as the civilian workers, who had been reinforcing the fort. This continued day and night from dawn on the twelfth to the morning of April 14. By that time Anderson and his exhausted, often wounded men, could hardly stay awake, let alone defend the fort. George actually saw, at around midday, the flagstaff within the fort, hit by cannon fire and collapse, taking the flag with it, which was what Fox had mistakenly taken for the surrender of the fort.

The Confederate troops had, from time to time during the conflict, genuinely cheered for their Unionist enemy's courage. Whether the besieged Union men realised they were cheering them, rather than cheering themselves, seemed to George doubtful. This roaring cheer that echoed across the harbour when the flag was felled, was repeated and repeated for several minutes and was followed at one-thirty in the afternoon by shouted orders across the Confederate bastions to '*cease fire*'.

So many people were now crowded around the harbour, often actually under the guns and in danger of being felled by them, that one Confederate gunner actually aimed his cannon over their heads in frustration and managed to scare a few hundred out of the way. George was beside the major who received the order from a messenger on horseback to cease-fire and understood that there was an assumption that Anderson had surrendered.

Within twenty minutes, a boat under the flag of truce was dispatched to the fort. However, just prior to that a Confederate man named Colonel Wigfall had, without orders, crossed to the fort alone in a small rowing boat. He managed then to climb around the walls to an embrasure and looked in at an astonished Union gunner. Wigfall had a white flag tied to his sword and demanded to be taken to Major Anderson. To his delight this was done and he was able to address the fort's commanding officer in person.

*"Major Anderson, I come from General Beauregard. It is time to put a stop to this ill-conceived attempt at defence. Will you evacuate?"* The Major actually agreed on conditions already sent to General Beauregard, but was confused when Beauregard's official envoys then arrived with similar demands soon afterwards.

The silence across not only the harbour, but also well into Charleston itself, was an eerie feeling so suddenly experienced after such a protracted period of ear shattering sound, as well as the sight and smell of such an intense barrage. George was told that Beauregard's most senior officer had gone in the boat with instructions to demand an immediate surrender.

As hours passed with no official news, although the ceasefire held, the rumour of surrender had spread through Charleston like a forest fire and citizens began to push forward behind the gun batteries. People were leaning out of house windows with views of the harbour and many were even up on the rooves.

By two o'clock, George could make out, through the gaps now blown in occasional places in the fortress walls, the movement of men in the central parade ground but, beyond that, nothing was obvious apart from the uncanny silence of the guns. Later in the afternoon, the Confederate longboat returned, but no news reached George's ears, nor apparently did it reach anyone else's around the harbour. Rumour again: *General Beauregard was considering surrender terms.*

As darkness fell, George decided to return to the hotel to try to find his two companions. It took him several hours to make that journey through throngs of people, mostly emotional with glee, others with fear that the Union fleet seen earlier was now in the harbour and must have reinforced Sumpter after dark last night.

There was no sign of either Arthur or Ernest when he reached the hotel. He eventually made his way indoors, appropriated a bottle of brandy and found his bedroom thankfully empty. He collapsed fully clothed onto his bed without even opening the bottle.

He was woken to broad daylight by Ernest shaking him and asking if he was injured. "You look awful! What happened? We've searched everywhere, except that wasn't really effective with such riotous crowds… Well, where were you?"

George now became aware that he could still hear the barrage, which he seemed to remember had ceased, but his memory was muddled with sleep. He had become so used to it for so long that it took an effort to realise that he was no longer sheltering behind the sandbags of the gun emplacement. He was by now sitting up, but unsure what was real and what he might have imagined, or even dreamt.

"Come on, George. What happened? We didn't see anything, just heard roars like thunder as if the world was coming to an end: for days!"

George, who did indeed look pale and drawn, as well as aching in every joint, managed with some effort to reply.

"I just need to wash and eat something. I've lived off hard tack for a couple of days. Let me get myself together and then I'll have a report for Arthur to write down that will shake even those dull lords in London. That is, if it ever gets back to them. Go on; I'll meet you downstairs. Oh, and I suppose Arthur is safe and not injured?"

"He certainly is," replied Ernest, "but I feel I should remind you that we are appointed Envoys and you seem to have been in the thick of some alarming action yourself, which I don't think you were intended to be involved with at all."

"Nonsense! I was doing exactly what we were charged to do: observe and report."

The best part of an hour later, George, having eaten anything that was set in front of him, however basic or even stale it was, told Arthur, who had only just joined them, to get out the journal and then began to dictate his experiences. It took another hour and a half to do so and by that time, the brothers were considerably impressed by their Captain of Hussars. George seemed to have recovered most of his energy once he had relayed all he could remember.

"Now," he said, as Arthur packed away all his secretarial tools, "we need to get down to the harbour and see what's going on."

At that moment, the barrage, that George had genuinely heard, gradually came to a halt and he shook his head violently to make sure he had not gone deaf.

"At last! A truce of some sort might be in place. What time is it?" Arthur pulled out his watch and announced it was just after one thirty.

The truce did hold, at least for the time being. George was in no position to share any reliable information since he had left the harbour and hence the trio decided to remain where they were for the time being or at least until anything significant happened. In fact, there was no cannon fire that afternoon or night, nor into the following morning. Apart from the ever-present rumour-mongering, there was no indication as to why there had been what was guessed to be only a truce, not a cessation of action.

Charleston seemed restless. People had grown to discount rumour at last, but were back on edge again, thinking that cannon fire might soon rock the town once more. Surely, the Union garrison must surrender soon or all die in the attempt. It was clear to anyone close to the harbour that the Union relief fleet had made no attempt to enter the waters there and had, it seemed, drifted even further away. There were now numerous citizens in boats on the waters of the harbour, although mostly nervous of getting anywhere near the fort.

The morning of April 15 dawned. Although smoke blew from the fortress, all appeared quiet. In reality and unknown as yet to the onlookers, Anderson had agreed to surrender at a meeting on the fourteenth, but on condition that his small force could leave unhindered, with its flag flying and keeping its weapons.

One Union private, Daniel Hough, had been killed, whether by Confederate fire or accident was unknown; on the Confederate shore, one casualty was also recorded: a horse. Frustrated by lack of knowledge and boredom the English Envoys had left the square outside the hotel by mid-morning and, on forcing their way through even larger crowds now gathered on the peaceful area around the harbour and after a laborious and long-winded walk, they soon heard that Major Anderson had indeed surrendered. They gathered that no one, except the Confederate's senior officers, knew when he might emerge and exactly how. Would the Union troops be dragged out with hands bound and hustled off to some place of imprisonment? Would they all, as some eager Rebs yelled for blood, be taken out and shot on the quayside? Surely, they would not be allowed simply to march away as if nothing had happened?

Arthur, as on previous days, dared not make any notes while he was in public view; he would certainly have been taken as a spy for the Union if he had. So he watched and tried to absorb every detail. At about three o'clock in the afternoon, after a quiet morning, rifle shots were heard inside the fort.

At first, many assumed it was some sort of suicide pact, but the shots were regular every few seconds and, if anyone had counted them, it would have been obvious that a fifty-shot salute was being fired. It was, in truth, in honour of the Union flag, now taken off its broken staff and folded ready for carriage. It was perhaps also for Private Hough, who had been buried inside the fortress compound. While all this was happening, the Confederate command had apparently given permission for a steamer to navigate from the Union fleet to the jetty of the fort. At four o'clock, the battered gates of Fort Sumpter were opened at last.

Major Anderson was the first to step out at the head of his now ragged garrison of eighty-four men. Anderson was in his dress uniform, which he had done his best to make presentable, with his sword at his side and the folded Union flag under his arm. His men marched with knapsacks and rolled blankets on their backs and with rifles held at the slope. Their small band played 'Rally 'Round the Flag' among other rallying favourites. Arthur and his colleagues stood in the crowd that had been almost silent as the gates were opened. However, as the garrison marched out along the jetty, a cheer started to form in the mouths of some of the crowd, which then swelled across the entire harbour and even a few hats were thrown into the air. The Confederate batteries also fired their empty cannon in a salute. George was in no doubt that they were not cheering the surrender, but the bravery of the enemy.

The small, injured and exhausted Union force made its way out to the Union steamer *Ysabel*, now secured at the end of the jetty and when fully loaded it headed for New York, via Sandy Hook.

It was George who, once the steamer was out of sight, spoke first.

"I suspect that may be the last time that either Confederate or Unionist will cheer the bravery of their enemy now that this bloody war has started. I am certain that a cheer will not be heard again until one side or the other lies bleeding to death on some American battlefield."

With the Union force on its way back to New York, or maybe Washington DC, the town of Charleston returned to some of its former peace and quiet. No damage had been done anywhere, except to Fort Sumpter and that now quickly became a tourist attraction. Governors of several neighbouring states, including Governor Pickles of Carolina, made their way to see the incredible sight of a huge Union fort demolished by their Confederate army. As well, there were local mayors and generals, or would-be generals, in the Confederate army; Wade Hampton was one of these. He was a large plantation and slave owner in South Carolina and rose to the rank of Lieutenant General of cavalry soon after the war proper started.

The next day the three Englishmen went back to the harbour and found several boats willing, for an extortionate fee, to row them out to Fort Sumpter. Once there, they found they were not alone. Affluent citizens of the town were posing on guns and ruined walls to have their photographs taken. Tall-hatted Governors walked sternly around the ruins and pronounced the achievement of the Confederate force under Beauregard to be '*wonderful*', '*remarkable*' and a '*taste of the short war to come, in which we shall undoubtedly trounce the Yankee and drive him from our land for ever*'.

George, Ernest and Arthur posed on an existing fortress roof with a view over the harbour. Ernest commandeered a six-foot long ramrod, lying on the ground, to pose with and, at their willingness to pay extra, the photographer moved them until the Confederate flag could be seen on the end of the jetty and two of the fort's thirty-two pounder guns were in the foreground. George parted with three dollars and the agreement to collect the photograph the next day, when a further two dollars would be required.

They saw the burned-out barracks and the remnants of the powder store that was so dangerously close to the fire, but had been saved by the rain. They stood by fifteen cannons in the courtyard that had never even been moved to firing positions, as well as the piles of rubble from collapsed walls. They stood together in the sally port, the still-standing porticoed entrance from the courtyard to the fort's interior, and tried to imagine what Major Anderson must have felt when he realised that surrender was inevitable.

Beside the ruined officer's quarters, they stood by the broken flagpole that had held the Union flag. Ernest found an abandoned knapsack lying against a pile of rubble. It contained the essentials a Union private had needed for battle: tinderbox, tobacco, a pair of nearly new boots, a Union cap with the insignia of the Maryland Volunteers on it and a pair of knitted socks, still in their tissue paper from, in all probability, an anxious mother, grandmother or aunt. George shook his head at Ernest when he picked up the knapsack and prepared to carry it away.

"That is looting, Ernest, and is seriously frowned upon by the British army. Just drop it." (18a)

Ernest obliged, but back in the town much later, showed the others the cap badge that had remained in his pocket.

They returned to a Charleston town sobered by what they had seen. Ernest, ever the optimist, declared his belief that the Confederacy would surely now win any war with the North and that he doubted they would need any assistance from the British parliament or the Royal Navy. George shook his head in despair; he had seen war so often before throughout his army career and knew that sort of uninformed guesswork was destined to be badly mistaken in reality.

Back in the hotel, now a much calmer place than it had been for the last five days, they gathered in Ernest's bedroom. The decision was taken that Arthur should complete his account that evening, collect the photograph tomorrow and then they should try to make the railroad journey as far north as they could get and try, if possible, to reach Richmond, which they estimated was at least four hundred miles distant from Charleston. Once there, they hoped somehow to travel by road to Beaufort County.

George admitted that he had no real idea of how far that was from Richmond nor what the roads were like, nor even if any transport could be found. However, they all agreed that they would then, in all likelihood, be in Richmond, the Confederate capital, or close to it, and well into Virginia, where George's sources in London had been confident the serious conflict would start.

# Chapter Fourteen

## April/May 1861: Beaufort County, Virginia

Boarding a train at Charleston the next day was to prove the easiest part of the journey yet to come, since very few citizens were heading north, where fighting was expected to begin before long. However, there were considerable numbers of Confederate soldiers who seemed to be quite joyous to be travelling north on a Richmond train, although special trains had been laid on for most of them. A few short conversations with those in uniform now waiting at the depot revealed that they were eager to fight the Yankees and were making for assembly camps outside Richmond, Virginia.

The journey towards the Confederate capital was slowed considerably by more and more of these military trains, causing delays to civilian transport as they struggled northwards. They were first of all carried west towards Augusta, Georgia, which seemed the wrong direction to strangers like themselves. However, by late afternoon, and having changed trains on to a northbound line, they were moving steadily, but slowly, north towards the final destination of the line, which was Washington DC; the Envoys did not intend to go that far. The train eventually stopped late that night sixty miles short of Washington DC, the Union capital, but no connection to Richmond would be possible until the next day.

War was strongly in the air and wherever they stopped, there was evidence of military movements. The interminable journey so far, like the previous one from Texas to Charleston, had allowed for little food or rest, since the trains rarely stopped close to civilisation. Their night was spent at an inn of basic comfort and the next day, the second of their journey through three southern states, they were able to travel west to Richmond, where they arrived in the early afternoon.

Exhausted, hungry and travel stained, they arrived at the railroad depot, which was a building of some size and grandeur. The streets appeared well maintained and the whole place had an atmosphere, rather like Charleston but much larger, nevertheless with a similarity to the way of life of yesteryear. Yet again they were all struck, as they had been in Charleston, by a city and a people whose ancestors, not so very long ago, had made the perilous journey from England to the New World to start a whole new life and build new generations. It seemed to the Envoys that somewhere deep in the southern psyche was a flavour of Old England, manners that were now gradually becoming outmoded in their homeland, as well as a sense of the history of their new land that they honoured above all else; they just called it Dixie, probably after a railway line called the Mason-Dixon. Again, like the English, they clung to their rights even into the jaws of death.

As they walked away from the depot, hoping to find some decent accommodation, they soon found themselves beside the wide James River and then, in what they took to be the centre of the city, a fine Capitol building, where now the new Congress and House of Representatives would meet to administer the Confederacy. A short distance away on Clay Street they found the White House of the Confederacy, where the President, Jefferson (Jeff) Davis, lived and worked. Until recently, they learned, Montgomery was the capital, but the President had favoured Richmond.

They passed a huge slave market, not in use that day, a hospital and, in the distance, where a tall smokestack gushed black smoke into the air, from what they later learned was the Tredegar Iron Works. This produced artillery, munitions and even iron plating for the Confederacy's only ironclad ship, the *CSS Virginia*. They did understand, however, from a less than patriotic gentleman, that the Iron Works was in truth the one and only such manufactory in the south.

Eventually, as the afternoon wore on, they found a quieter, leafier part of the town and a small *Gentleman's Hotel* that had just two rooms available. Ernest and Arthur drew the short straw again and finished up in one, rather cramped room that did, at least, have two separate beds. As they walked back into the town centre looking for somewhere to eat supper, they passed a grand church, St John's, and a remarkable Egyptian style building, the home of the School of Medicine. They finished up close to the river again, but were surprised to see, not warehouses for cotton, but for tobacco. The meal they had

144

near there was, in fact, pretty good, but, as Arthur had said, they were so hungry they would have been grateful for stale bread and water. They collapsed into none too comfortable beds by nine o'clock and slept until the noise of passers-by in the street below woke them soon after eight o'clock the next morning.

Having revived themselves with both sleep and breakfast, they returned to George's bedroom to review what they had to report so far and how they might find transport to Beaufort County, which they had ascertained was about eighty miles north-west of Richmond in the general direction of Washington and Alexandria.

"As far as getting to Beaufort County is concerned," said George, "I have already been to the rail depot this morning and there is a train from here to Frederiksberg, which is forty miles north of here. After that, all I could gather from various people at the depot was that we need to aim for a town called Culpepper and by then we should be *in* Beaufort County. There is only one road to Culpepper and, according to my informants, it is twenty miles from the railhead at Frederiksberg, but it could well be forty miles judging from the vague notion of distance the porter at the station had."

"So, assuming there are trains running to this Frederiksberg and that we can get on one, we could be there today?" questioned Ernest.

"Your guess is as good as mine," replied George, "but it must be worth a try. We won't know anything for certain about reaching Culpepper until we get off the train."

Another train journey was not the most popular prospect, but they realised there was no alternative. Before they left for the depot, Arthur read out his written reports so far and George agreed that they seemed to describe well the cotton trade out of Charleston and the time before Sumpter where the situation was now that the harbour was probably mined. There was hearsay about how many Union warships were blockading the Atlantic and Gulf coasts between Virginia and Texas, since Charlestonians had seen nothing, apart from the Union ships that had tried to relieve Fort Sumpter. Hearsay was that the whole Atlantic coast was blockaded and no cotton had moved out for some time.

George seemed pleased with how Arthur had described the atmosphere of the coming war and what local Confederates felt so strongly about the military preparedness they had seen.

The only problem with the growing number of pages in the reports was the question of how they would be able to get the information back to London, but George seemed hopeful that once they reached the Cotton Hall plantation, Daniel Hayward's local power and influence might be able to find some sort of solution. Ernest expressed some serious doubt that this would exist in the '*back of beyond*'.

By mid-morning, they were at Richmond depot and found a train going to Frederiksberg in two hours' time. Having learned the need to take food and water supplies with them, George purchased all they needed for the next couple of days. They reached Frederiksberg while it was still daylight, which meant finding some sort of hotel or, better still, a lodging house for the night, since George was starting to remind Arthur of Ebenezer Scrooge in his concern that their funds must be 'more carefully preserved'.

Frederiksberg was another town that seemed not to have progressed with time in the last fifty years. Fortunately, its elegant buildings included several small hotels that did not seriously rob them for a night's lodging and a hearty breakfast.

The next day, with the weather now showing a kindly face suitable for the beginning of May, they started their search for transport to Culpepper by asking the owner of the hotel, whose name was shown in Italic script on the hotel's sign to be: *Mr Samuel Grimes*. He turned out to be a kindly gentleman, who had a fondness for the English, since his great grandfather had made passage to America from Liverpool in the late eighteenth century. He started by warning them that the roads from Frederiksberg were not in the finest condition and, with a large number of 'young gentlemen, not from the best of homes, on the lookout for unsuspecting persons to take advantage of'; they would be better not to travel after dark.

Still not getting as far as advice on *how* they might travel, his stories of woe continued with warnings of the number of soldiers using the roads, both on foot, horseback and in wagons. This seemed to mean that they needed to be very careful to keep out of the way of such persons. Ernest had reminded him at this point that they badly needed to find a carrier or even a regular coach of some sort to take them to Culpepper and then on into Beaufort County and Cotton Hall.

At last, Mr Grimes admitted he knew of a reliable and confidential local carrier, who might be persuaded, for a price, to put his waggon and a driver at their disposal. Ernest then pressed him to understand that it was urgent that they get to Culpepper and, after some persuasion in the form of three dollars changed hands, they were escorted to a livery stable on a street behind the hotel. The whole drawn out process was repeated there with what turned out to be Mr Grimes's cousin and, again with payment being reluctantly accepted, they were to present themselves the next morning. "No later than seven o'clock, since this most awkward journey would take up a good part of the day, not to mention the wagon having to return without a fare, which must be compensated for."

The next morning, well in time for departure, the three English passengers were at the stables, carrying all their possessions and well wrapped up for a long day in an open wagon. With the full payment handed over and a lad of no more than sixteen in charge of the rig and its two horses, they rumbled north-west out of Frederiksberg on an unmade country road, frequently with potholes of considerable size and constant ruts rattling their transport, but in what they hoped was the direction of Culpepper. The lad holding the reins was obviously unused to partaking in any form of conversation.

Mr Grimes was not mistaken in his warning of Confederate soldiers using the road, but their numbers were far greater than even George had expected: wagons carrying all forms of war materiel, as well as gun carriages and columns of marching men in the grey of the Confederacy. Officers galloped past them, often it seemed in a great hurry, while smaller groups of young men in their farm clothes, some carrying shotguns, pushed forward, cheering as they came across each batch of soldiers; George suspected the farm lads were would-be volunteers for a fight.

The very uncomfortable journey, taken at a slow but regular pace by their young coachman, lasted from soon after seven in the morning, with numerous stops, until they entered the small, scattered farming community of Culpepper at just before five in the afternoon. They were dropped in the so-called 'main' street, stepping directly into its muddy surface, and watched the waggon turn swiftly around and disappear far faster than it progressed on the outward journey.

Across the street was what looked as if it might be a tavern and they made their way across the street and through its open door. Inside were some empty tables and chairs and a rough-hewn bar along one wall; the room was completely empty.

George called out, "Good day!" and, when no one appeared, moved closer to the bar and shouted it again. To their surprise a tall, thin man, dressed in a spotless, perfect Confederate officer's uniform appeared through a door at the side of the bar. He wore a carefully barbered golden beard, sideburns and matching long hair almost to his shoulders. Once out of the shadow of the low ceiling at the back of the room, the sabre hanging in its scabbard at his side could not fail to draw their attention, as he touched his hat in greeting.

"Good day, gentlemen. I'm Captain Phillips of the Beaufort Virginia Volunteers. How may I be of service?"

George inevitably warmed to another officer of his own rank and stepped forward immediately with his hand held out.

"My pleasure to meet a fellow officer, sir. I am Captain George Fitzwilliam of the Queen's Royal Hussars."

The two officers shook hands firmly and George introduced the two brothers, although with no explanation of their rank or position.

Captain Phillips, without hesitation, insisted they join him for 'a glass of the finest Virginia bourbon', which could hardly be refused and did cause Arthur, the least used to strong drink, to splutter as it hit the back of his throat. Several glasses later and they were sharing stories of each of their backgrounds, as well as the English trio's need to reach Cotton Hall plantation in Prince William parish, which they hoped was not too far way, as they were expected there by a Mr Daniel Hayward.

"Damn it, that is true fortune that you've found already in our great Confederacy. Dan Hayward is my wife's cousin and his son, Paul, is the major commanding our gallant Beaufort Virginia Volunteers. The righteous hand of the Lord surely led you here to my tavern on this day!"

He went on to explain that Cotton Hall was a mere ten miles distant and that he had ridden from there just that morning.

"I trust you gentlemen are from the fabled stable of fine English horsemen and, if so, it would be an honour to lend you horses so that you can ride with me to Cotton Hall, which should ensure you are there for dinner tonight. Is that convenient to you gentlemen?"

Both Ernest and Arthur had had riding lessons more than ten years earlier, but had never had occasion to ride since then. However, George was already delighted with the prospect of dinner and a proper bed and did not even bother to ask if the brothers were happy to join the expedition. Captain Phillips excused himself to make preparations and to send 'a lad' post haste to Cotton Hall to warn them of the imminent arrival of the English gentlemen they were expecting.

The subsequent ride along trails and also through open country and woods was, as Arthur later described it, "Exhilarating, once I started to get used to the size of my horse and the speed we now seemed to be moving."

By the time Cotton Hall was in sight, the two brothers were laughing with the pleasure and relief of not being confined to trains, coaches and waggons any more. They stopped on a small rise in the ground so that Captain Phillips could point out the regal nature of Cotton Hall itself. Beyond the scattering of Spanish Oaks, hung with moss as they had seen in Charleston, were other broad-leafed trees spread across the acres of grassland that dropped gradually down to a small river. Standing a half mile or so away, on the other side of the stream, was the magnificent white columned mansion that was Cotton Hall.

# Chapter Fifteen

**May 1861**

Cotton Hall made the fine old houses they had seen in Charleston look small and insignificant by comparison. The central portion of the building, probably a hundred and fifty feet long, had tall Ionic columns reaching to the top of the second story and then what they realised must be the entrance portico that protruded from the front ground floor of the mansion. Those two floors also comprised two equally long wings, one on each side of the elegant central portion, which Arthur suspected was older than the two wings. The second floor, probably featuring bedrooms, had a balcony that ran its full length with large French windows, now wide open and fine white curtains could be seen moving in the gentle breeze. Above that was a third floor with smaller windows and finally a fine rust red tiled roof.

The two wings had been built at right angles to each side of the main mansion and stretched back towards the low hill behind this huge and ornate building. Cotton Hall was painted a pale cream with lemon yellow balcony railings and paintwork. The clearly wealthy family that lived there also enjoyed a covered veranda along the full length of the ground floor, with sofas and rocking chairs scattered in its shade.

Standing several yards away from the entrance doors was a tall flagpole flying the Confederate 'stars and bars' flag and another beside it featuring a flag with two birds: an eagle and above it a dove. A river ran several hundred yards in front of the house, meandering through the trees and grassland for about half a mile before passing the front of the mansion and then disappearing into the woodland to the Hall's far side.

A broad, dusty driveway wound from the country road just below the gentle hill where the Envoys now sat astride their mounts admiring the view of the grand estate. A broad white stone bridge could be seen taking the driveway across the river. Behind this truly magnificent home, the land gently rose again to form a green backdrop of what looked like a large orchard of some sort on its slopes.

"Just like yourselves, most people seeing Cotton Hall for the first time can only look and wonder at it in silence," Captain Phillips proudly announced as if he owned it himself and then pointed to the flagstaff.

"The second flag is that of the family, the Haywards," the Confederate captain hastily explained. "The eagle shows what could be the avenging beak and sharp claws if you cross him, while the dove is the symbol of their respect and loyalty to all friends of Dixie."

"Cotton Hall is indeed admirable, but it isn't named as I had expected a grand southern mansion to be," commented Arthur, "but then I suppose it tells the world where their wealth comes from."

"You're right, sir, but in the days of the Hayward grandfather and his father, who built the house, it was originally called Four Oaks, but Dan's father, Nathanial Hayward, expanded the plantation by more than a further thousand acres, making it the largest cotton plantation hereabouts. So he changed the name. You can't see the plantation from here, but it's just over that rise back there, behind the house. I reckon Dan will be more than happy to show you while you're here."

"It's so peaceful, so very…different," observed Ernest as he gazed across the pristine landscape to the perfection of a house that looked so dramatically at odds with Manchester, Oldham and even many other not eve the vast country estates in England.

Nathan turned his horse back onto the road, ready to move off.

"Well, I guess we'd better be moving. The sun is beginning to drop over there in the west and, if I know anything about the Hayward family hospitality, they will want you to enjoy a hot bath and change into some clean clothes before they welcome you to a proper southern dinner. Follow me down there to the bridge and then we'll head up the carriage drive."

As the three of them followed the captain, they noticed that the sun, that had been so hot all day, was now noticeably lower in the sky to their left and close to touching the higher ground behind Cotton Hall.

Once they reached level ground and crossed the bridge into the property, a white horse ridden by a young man dressed in pale blue trousers and an open necked, brilliantly white shirt exploded from the far side of the house and came racing towards them with a cloud of dust billowing behind him. The Envoys all anticipated an attack, but were quick to realise that the very opposite was true.

Captain Phillips pulled his own horse to an abrupt stop and the others followed suit. As the young man skidded his mount to a halt in front of them, the dust cloud mercifully drifting to the side to reveal not only a sweating horse, but a remarkably handsome young man, clean shaven with tousled red hair. He had finished his remarkable arrival next to Captain Phillips, who was laughing out loud, as he clapped him on the back.

"Hey, Paul! These here folks I reckon you and your Pa was expecting. At least I hope you was, 'cause if not they may be Union spies and then I reckon I'd have no choice but to run 'em through right here and now."

This was followed by another roar of laughter and a grin on the face of the young horseman, who wheeled his mount around and managed to shake the hands of the three, somewhat startled, Englishmen.

"Gentlemen, please excuse my rather un-English arrival, but you sure are welcome. I'm Paul, Paul Hayward, and my Pa's Daniel. Me and Pa was wondering what had happened to you. We was told you'd be here about a week ago, but you obviously didn't fall into the hands of the damned Yankees, so all's well, eh? Come and meet the family and enjoy the comforts of Cotton Hall, at least for the few days before we're all shot to hell."

With that he pulled his horse sharply around and set off up the driveway at a much more leisurely pace than exhibited in his dramatic arrival. He led them around to the back of the house, to an array of at least a dozen stables, as well as coach barns and fenced fields where groups of horses where placidly grazing the grass.

Three young black men, dressed in what the Envoys assumed was the Hayward groom's uniform, ran out, took the reins and held their horses still. As the young black men led their mounts away towards the stables, Paul ushered the guests through a side entrance, along a broad corridor with a polished wood floor and into an enormous entrance hall.

The double front doors they had seen from outside were now open and opposite them in the hall was a magnificent double staircase leading up, after two turns, to a wide balcony that ran across the hall below, with archways to right and left that the visitors assumed must lead to bedrooms.

Waiting for them was another black servant, whom Arthur realised, now all too easily, must be another slave dressed in a uniform of the same colour as the grooms, but with knee britches, a waistcoat, shirt and neckerchief. He stood like a statue at the foot of the stairs, staring into space.

"I'll go find Pa, if you just wait there a moment…" but before Paul could set off on a hunt for the master of the house, another set of tall polished wood double doors on the right of the hall were pushed open and a rather portly, short gentleman hurried out. To the surprise of the three guests, he was dressed in a startlingly fine Confederate uniform, perfectly tailored to accommodate his rotund form. The tight-fitting trousers were, of course, in Confederate grey, while his officer's jacket had a shining double row of brass buttons and a high, stiff collar with gold filigrees in the shape of oak leaves and branches. Across his breast was a wide yellow silk sash, with a bow on his hip, while on his shoulders were epaulets with gold tassels dropping from them. The broad leather belt around his waist held a scabbard, decorated again in gold, from which the handle of a sword protruded, with a tassel hanging from it. His feet were in fine black leather boots. Arthur was surprised he was not wearing spurs and carrying cavalry gauntlets. He could also not help noticing how very hot he appeared to be.

They later learned from Paul that he was wearing the uniform of a Confederate general, self-appointed, worn to impress his visitors. He had been hastily eased into it as soon as the family heard from Culpepper that the Envoys were on their way.

As he came towards them, with both hands held out, he obviously could not decide whether to smile in welcome or look grave as was befitting a general soon to be off to war. The result was somewhere between the two, with a smile that flickered off and on against a more serious expression.

"Welcome! Welcome at last to Cotton Hall. Welcome to Virginia and the home of the free Confederacy. Welcome to our English friends who come to represent their Lord and…errr… Government."

As each of these sentiments was expressed, he moved his firm, rather active, handshake from one to another of the Englishmen.

"You find us soon to be in a state of deadly conflict, but I am confident that you," a glance around to check the numbers, "you three will help us to ensure that the mighty army of Dixie will, within a few weeks, annihilate that evil man in the White House in Washington and destroy his jumped-up little army. Yes! That's what I say."

Having somewhat stunned his audience by these patriotic sentiments, Daniel Hayward became silent and transferred his gaze to his son, who quickly took the hint that his father's welcome speech was now over.

"Thank you, Pa. I'm sure our English friends are now assured of our good intentions in this great adventure… May I suggest gentlemen that you follow Jacob," he indicated the silent figure at the foot of the stairs, "and he will take you to your bedrooms and make sure you have everything you need for your comfort. You will find clothes that might be more suitable for our weather and hot baths will be ready for you. Anything else you need please tell Jacob and it will be found for you at once. Perhaps in an hour or so, we may have the honour of welcoming you to meet the rest of the family on the veranda and then join us for a simple southern supper."

When no one appeared to be sure whether to move or not, Daniel snapped his fingers at Jacob, who sprang to attention and turned to face the staircase; Paul, opening his arms as if guiding a flock of sheep, ushered the three Englishmen in the direction Jacob was now taking as he slowly mounted the staircase.

The three Envoys, still rather over-awed by the mansion and its surroundings, were shown into bedrooms far more magnificent than any of them had entered either at home or as guests anywhere before. Awaiting Arthur's arrival, although he assumed also the other two, were sets of comfortable, if a little old fashioned, clothes in what appeared to be a suitable size, laid out upon a large double bed, which had a red silk cover over fine white cotton sheets. The gentle breeze from the hill across the river ruffled the damask curtains covering the open French doors, outside which was the balcony and beyond that a perfect pastoral landscape. Adjoining each of their rooms was a sumptuous bathroom, with a gleaming copper bathtub, although there was no sign of taps on the bath or the wash bowl nearby. A large porcelain bowl with a seat and lid stood on the floor in the far corner, with a partly open screen and was obviously intended as a lavatory; it was, he was pleased to note, spotlessly clean.

Before he could question how he was to wash, or even bathe, there was a knock on the door which, when opened, revealed a young black girl in a long, plain dress with a scarf concealing her hair. She was carrying a sizeable copper jug in each hand, each of steaming hot water. As Arthur opened the door, she curtsied, looked steadily at the floor and mumbled something which sounded like, "I be bringin' de water fors you sah."

Behind her were two boys with even larger jugs of hot water. Without looking up, they then went quickly into the bathroom and emptied the jugs into the tub. They immediately left, leaving the young girl behind. She crossed the bathroom and opened a cupboard, from which she took a spotlessly large white towel and draped it over the rim of the tub. Still not looking at Arthur, she curtsied again and hurried from the room, closing the door quietly behind her. *More slaves:* this was at the forefront of Arthur's mind and the impression he had received was that they were cowed in his presence. He instinctively thought, *but surely, I am no better a person than they are?*

It was growing dark when Arthur ventured into the corridor and almost ran into Ernest and George coming the other way. Like Arthur, both were dressed in the clothes left for them and, in Arthur's eyes, both now looked like recently polished, well-dressed young gentlemen; he hoped he looked the same.

"It's very quiet, don't you think," Ernest said in what was close to a whisper.

"I think the family must all be some way away downstairs. In fact, I could have sworn a few minutes ago I could hear voices outside, but I couldn't see anyone," replied George in his normal, rather brusque voice.

Ernest' second tour seemed more to make him more at home here than the other two and he strode off down the corridor towards the distant stairs. "Come on. I could eat a horse…but I hope that's not on the menu."

As they descended the last flight of stairs, they saw that the front doors were wide open and were flanked by two more middle aged men, whom they realised must also be slaves, very much in the image of Jacob. As they crossed the hall, a hubbub of distant voices outside became clearer. As they stepped over the threshold, both footmen, if that was their title, bowed. This caused the three young men to stop in embarrassment, while Arthur murmured, "Good evening." This was met with a steady stare in the direction of the glow of light they could now all see spreading along the veranda on their right.

The party, from which the sound of both men's and women's voices merged into a chorus from people enjoying themselves, was at the far end of the veranda. Lanterns and even candelabra hung all along its length. As they approached, Paul strode out to meet them. He was dressed now, as were the Englishmen in their borrowed attire, more formally than they had been when they arrived. Paul's cream shirt had a wide cravat at the throat and his twill, fawn trousers were decorated at the waist with a blue sash.

He shook hands very firmly all around, grasping theirs, to their surprise, with his other hand as well.

"I hope you found everything to your liking upstairs. I trust the house slaves treated you well and with respect. They can be remiss at times and can need firmly reminding."

The brothers were unable to find any immediate reply, but George stepped in. "Everything was, of course, absolute perfection. Thank you. We all feel so much better for a bath and fresh clothes."

"Excellent!" Paul said, clapping his hands together.

He then guided them towards the far end of the veranda, where the previous gabble of conversation stuttered to an end as the five people seated on sofas and rockers all stared at the visitors, some with smiles and a couple with looks of earnest enquiry. Paul made himself responsible for the introductions. The gentlemen, two of whom the visitors had already met, were already standing. Captain Phillips seemed in an even better mood than earlier, perhaps due to the goblet in his hand, while Daniel Hayward, contrary to their previous meeting with him in his general's finery, had an expression almost of surprise, as if they were so insignificant that he had to rack his memory to recall who these strangers were.

"Mother, Father…well everyone here," Paul said with obvious pleasure in his voice. "These are our most welcome English visitors, who have travelled all the way from England over treacherous seas to be with us here at Cotton Hall. The rather upright, military gentleman is George Fitzwilliam." George's face twitched, rather than smiled. "The other two are brothers, Ernest and Arthur Tissiman; Ernest is the one trying to grow a moustache!"

While Arthur and George smiled broadly at Ernest's recent attempt to look like the Prince Regent, while the man himself couldn't help stroking the decoration above his top lip and for once looked embarrassed. Daniel Hayward shook hands again with all three and then sat down again with a loud sigh. Nathaniel Phillips, who preferred to be known as Nat, simply said, "Good to see y'all clean. Hardly recognised ya!"

Paul then ushered them to where three ladies reclined on the plump cushions of a pair of cane sofas. All three wore long, multiple layered dresses in various pale shades, although it seemed that colours closest to white were favoured. Ernest had in mind the word *flounced*, which he hoped he would remember to use in the description he hoped to be able to give when, or perhaps if, he eventually returned home.

One particularly gorgeous creature, in Ernest's eyes, also had on a wide brimmed white hat with a deep red ribbon, while the older lady had a lace cap and fingerless lace gloves.

Paul introduced them first to his mother.

"Gentlemen, may I introduce you to my darlin' mother: Mrs Catherine-Louise Hayward."

The lady in question remained seated, but held out the back of her hand, which George realised was to be kissed and hence Ernest and Arthur followed suit.

"This is my beautiful sister, Anne-Louise."

Since he had named the beauty Ernest had already noticed with interest, he stepped forward first and kissed her coquettishly held out hand and smiled into her eyes at the same time. Her response was to bring up the fan that had been on her lap, as if she were shy, which Ernest strongly doubted was the case. It was noticeable that both the Hayward ladies had hair that they would have described as auburn, although less flatteringly it would have been called red.

Finally, Paul turned to a young lady with dark, almost black, hair. Unlike Paul's sister, this was not in ringlets, but straight and fell down her back, beyond his line of sight.

"Finally, the young lady I am honoured to be engaged to be married to: Miss Charlotte Hotchkiss."

This young lady, swung her legs off the sofa and rose to extend a delicate pale hand to each of the English gentlemen and added, once all three had stooped to kiss the proffered soft, cool hand and stood grouped around her: "I am so pleased to meet such fine foreign gentlemen, who have come so far to meet my Paul's family. I trust you will enjoy your stay."

Her accent was even stronger in its southern lilt than Paul's own family. With remarkable confidence, she then sat down again and smiled up at her handsome fiancé.

Another servant, as Arthur at least tried to think of them, then passed around a tray of chilled glasses of champagne and gradually the three foreign visitors were able to talk more openly to the gathering of family and friends. As the sky turned truly dark with a mass of stars lighting the heavens above Cotton

Hall, the party were invited to move indoors to a grand dining room that would have easily seated three times their number and whose tall French doors along one side of the room, were all open to the cooling night air. Regarding the spread of food before them, some of which was not instantly recognisable to those not born in Virginia, it was Nat Phillips who exclaimed, "This is surely a fine southern feast! I hope that even you strangers will find it as delicious as we locals surely will."

The dishes and chargers of food were placed along the table by a battery of servants and included boiled crabs and oysters from Chesapeake Bay, cold ham and beans from the plantation, as well as suckling pig, fried chicken and what were described as 'biscuits', but were more like small English scones. There was also crayfish from the river outside, peach cobbler from the plantation orchard, along with sugared fruits, including apples, pears, peaches, apricots and berries and, served throughout the meal, imported wines, such as champagne, claret and hock.

Once the meal was over, the ladies withdrew to the smaller sitting room of which the mansion had three of various sizes and uses. Here they were served coffee and sweetmeats, while the gentlemen enjoyed port and brandy with their cigars, except, of course, for Arthur, who did not smoke and only drank enough to be polite.

After what Arthur discretely described back in their rooms as an 'overblown feast to demonstrate wealth', entertainment was provided by the two young ladies, who were happy to demonstrate their musical skills at the pianoforte and also, joined by Paul and Nat, some patriotic songs of the Confederacy.

The English trio found the stairs more difficult to climb than they had that afternoon and all collapsed into the most comfortable beds they had enjoyed for many months. They slept untroubled by dreams that under more sober circumstances might well have plagued them with nightmares of death and mutilation, the whistle and explosion of cannon and rifle fire and the screams of the wounded and dying, while the innumerable dead lay unburied on a battlefield.

# Chapter Sixteen

The next morning, with at least one of their number still with a sore head, they discovered that the plan for the day was to show off the plantation: how it was worked and how the cotton, that would eventually find its way to the Lancashire mills, was produced. This was announced, after another lavish meal for breakfast, by Daniel, who was no longer dressed in his military finery, but in high, black boots with white trousers, a billowing white cotton shirt tucked in a wide black belt and a cravat under a beautifully embroidered waistcoat; his wide brimmed straw hat was held at the ready by Jacob.

"Paul and I hope you will honour our plantation by allowing us to show you how your cotton is farmed and picked, separating fibre from seeds and then pressed into bales to be sold to your English cotton mills. I am told that Mr Ernest manages such a mill in Oldford, England. Is that not so, sir?"

Ernest was pleased to be asked, but could see his brother was clearly worried by the incorrect name of their town by the esteemed head of the house. However, he stumbled on, without exactly remarking on the mistaken name.

"Indeed, sir, we buy most of our cotton from these southern states and it is then transported across the Atlantic and finally by rail to *Oldham* where our mill is situated." He suspected his emphasis on their town's name might simply go unnoticed.

"Naturally," Daniel Heyward added as he rose from the table, his chair hurriedly pulled back by another black servant. Neither Ernest nor Arthur had yet to come to terms with the words *slave* or, even worse *nigger*, now firmly in their own minds. The latter description of a slave, frequently used by their masters was, at least to Arthur, genuinely derogatory and inhuman.

"Naturally," Daniel repeated as two of his guests seemed lost in thought, "We hope that Captain Fitzwilliam will also join us."

"Honoured, sir," was his only reply, as George got up from the table and joined Daniel and Paul, as well as Ernest and Arthur, who were, somewhat hesitantly, starting to follow the two Haywards out into the hall, having been advised to hand their jackets to another black footman.

"You will find suitable headgear over there, which you will need in the open fields at this time of year," advised Paul, who was hurrying to catch up with his father, already striding towards a door at the other side of the hall. The party came out beyond the stables and were led by father and son on a paved lane that wound up the gently rising ground behind the mansion.

Once at the top and now able to see Cotton Hall from above, they also looked out over an expanse of fields that stretched, it seemed, almost to the horizon. The fields, as far as the eye could see, were covered in what appeared to be bushes covered with green leaves and some white buds showing on a few of them; Ernest knew full well that rather than buds turning to petals, these would become fluffy balls of fibre, rather than flowers. Only Ernest of the three English guests already knew very well how cotton fibre grew and was eventually exported to Oldham and the Manchester market.

As they stood looking down at the peaceful pastoral scene and feeling the sun already hot upon their faces and bare arms, Daniel was already fully into the role of a teacher addressing a class of ignorant Englishmen.

"You will see that the cotton bushes are covered at present in leaves and some flower buds, which produce the fibre and seeds of the plant. You will also see that every field has water channels running through and around it. These are fed from our Powarnee River. You can perhaps make out in the distance our niggers already labouring in the fields. At this time of year, that means them working as long as there is any daylight and in a few months, if the moon is full, as it will be soon, at night as well."

Arthur was shading his eyes as they were facing east into an already blazing sun. "Am I right in thinking that your workers are actually slaves, sir?"

Daniel chuckled. "Absolutely, Mr Arthur. Our niggers, and we have more than four hundred here at Cotton Hall, are the reason we can sell you cotton at such reasonable prices! Some would say that makes them a necessary evil, but I say there is no evil involved here. Indeed, it is a positive good; good for them and good for us. Without us white folks giving these niggers homes and food and clothing and looking after them just as if they were our own children, they would be dying of starvation and disease. We give them these rewards for their labour and, I can tell you, they surely appreciate that."

He started to walk down the far side of the hill, but turned suddenly, so that Arthur, close on his heels, collided with him and apologised for his clumsiness. Daniel's mouth had changed from one with a broad smile to a hard grim line in once showing off his plantation.

"Don't you go gettin' any of your holier than thou English ideas here, Mr Arthur. They are not welcome and they are surely not true!" With which he stomped off with Paul at his side leaving the others having to run to catch up.

It proved a long walk down the hillside and then, having eventually reached the cover of trees, to follow a trail towards the fields they had seen from above. The path eventually opened out into a wide, open space surrounded by what looked more like huts than houses. These encircled the open area, leaving bare land in the centre and between the dozens of huts. These varied in size and design. Some were of a single storey, some had two stories; some had chimneys, most had wooden doors, now open, and some with wooden shutters covering empty window spaces.

Once they had reached the middle of the compound, they could see that the earthen ground stretched inside as the floor of the huts. There were several places in the open that were obviously used for cooking, with stones as surrounds in some cases, although with no fires at present. Some had blackened cooking pots beside or hanging over where the heat would be. The place was eerily quiet, no sign of man, woman or child.

"These are some of the slave huts, where our nigger families have rooves over their heads and cooking fires for their meals. There is an irrigation channel, not far away for water." Paul had now taken up the narrative and was giving the impression of a salesman selling some fine house, or maybe a particularly strong slave, which is what resounded in Arthur's mind.

"Everyone is working, of course, since it must be about nine o'clock and in another three hours, they will be allowed to take a few minutes for a drink and whatever they have brought with them to eat."

"What time did they start to work this morning?" asked Arthur.

Paul pulled out a gold half hunter to assure himself that it was really nine o'clock. "They start in the fields by six o'clock now that the days are drawing out and the sun is warm."

Arthur, murmuring to Ernest, said, "That's already three hours in this sun without a break and another three to come," he hesitated, "although I suppose that is more or less what you insist on at your mill, is it not?"

Ernest had no time to reply, as Paul started to move off towards the wider path that led out of the slave village. Before they reached the first field, however, all three Englishmen were struck by an appalling smell off to their left which they guessed must be coming from some sort of manure. It caused the brothers, although no less hardy than George, to cough and cover their noses against the foul scent, pulling kerchiefs from their sleeves.

Paul could not fail to see their reaction and replied with a hearty laugh.

"Don't worry none about that! They have to shit somewhere and there's a pit a way over there for that. We'll soon move away from their stink."

Although the trees still hid the fields, they began to hear voices singing, which Ernest later called a '*dirge*'. Arthur quickly disabused him of his condemnation.

"I actually think, Ernest, although I cannot hear any precise words, that the song is soulful and rather melodious and quite possibly Christian in its theme, although I admit very different from what we hear in church or sing around the piano at home."

The sound of the singing grew gradually louder until they came out of the trees and stood on the edge of a huge field, filled with cotton bushes grown up to about waist height and covered with the leaves they had seen from the hill. Between the rows of bushes were lines of black *field hands* hoeing up the weeds, while women and children from, they guessed, maybe four or five years old upwards to perhaps ten or twelve years old, were feeling amongst the leaves and branches, throwing whatever it was they found into sacks or baskets on their backs.

They could not ignore the fact that many of the women had slings of cloth hanging around their necks, inside which babies could just be made out. They also noticed that some of what they had arbitrarily called men were in truth really children themselves, just old enough to wield a hoe. Then there were men whose age was hard to assess. All of these slaves were singing, although the songs were quiet and often repetitive as far as Ernest was apparently concerned.

Daniel and Paul had not stopped at the edge of the field, but the other three were left mesmerised by a sight so foreign to their eyes. Arthur could not help thinking that it certainly looked very different, but wondered if it was, in fact, so far removed from the workers labouring in Crompton Mill. Neither Ernest nor George showed any particular emotion, which reinforced exactly what

Arthur had been thinking about Oldham, and he also could not help wondering, *Maybe it's not so very different from George's British army as well?*

Daniel stopped when he realised that several of his party were not following his lead and this forced both Haywards to turn and wait for them to catch up.

"You will notice, I am sure," Paul now continued, as if he had never paused, "that all our nigger field workers look contented in their labour and require no coercion to encourage them. Even our children and babies are happy to be out in God's clean open air."

George spoke for the first time that morning, having so far seemed to absorb every new sight and sound without comment.

"The man dressed rather better than those labouring? The one in the jacket and hat? What's his role in all this?"

Daniel immediately spoke up, before Paul could answer. "Oh, that man? That's…er…not sure of his name, we have several like him. He's an overseer. His job is to make sure that the work is done properly, nothing missed… You must know the sort of thing at that mill of yours?"

"I just wondered what the crop he's carrying was really for. Or am I mistaken in thinking it's actually a whip?" George continued quietly.

At that moment, his question was answered as the overseer raising what could now be seen as a bullwhip, which he cracked again and again over the heads of the slaves. As shouts continued so the whip was suddenly targeted on a young woman. She made no sound that George could hear, but dropped to the ground like a felled sapling. The whip struck her again and again, as she struggled to get up, eventually being bodily lifted upright by the strong young man next to her. The overseer turned his attention at once to him and George could clearly hear the smack of whip leather on flesh, but the youth did not fall nor cry out, simply stepped back into the line and carried on with the task of using a wooden stake to make holes for the young cotton bushes, which were being planted by the next in the line of humanity moving across the muddy field.

Daniel seemed lost for the right words and Paul stepped in.

"Just for reinforcement. Occasionally, there might be a lazy nigger who needs to be reminded that his roof and food don't come free; they have to work to repay our generosity."

The tour of the plantation continued forward, through several fields, again with frequent commentary by Daniel and with occasional assistance from his son. They learned that the fields at this time of year were being replanted with cotton saplings that would grow fast in the summer heat and produce a crop later in the year; late summer and autumn would see the start of the harvest in the busiest of all seasons.

Soon after midday, they arrived at a group of large barns, many open sided, but all presently empty, except for great piles of sacking that they were told would eventually hold the harvested and pressed cotton fibres. In the same area, they saw a very large machine of some sort, which featured a huge corkscrew-like spindle about ten feet high in the centre of a wood box structure. Connected to the top of the spindle were two long, flexible arms that drooped down almost to the ground, not quite touching a path in the grass, making a in a worn circle around the machine. Paul quickly explained that his father, while in charge of most of the plantation, had left the more modern machinery to him.

"This excellent aid to cotton production won't be in use until the harvest starts to come in. Donkeys are harnessed to each arm, with nigger boys on their backs; they drive them at a steady pace round and round all day long. The cotton fibres, which have been stripped of their seeds, are then fed in at the top and the rollers inside compress them; the pressed cotton comes out gradually at the side there and is carried to be baled."

"You said the fibres were stripped of seeds. I suppose that is done by hand and must be a very lengthy and exhausting process I guess?" Ernest, as throughout the expedition, was the most interested in the process that got the cotton from the bush to the bales that eventually arrived at Crompton Mill.

Paul smiled happily at the question. "You are right in a way. It *used* to be done by hand and thank God, we had even more slaves to do it in those days. For the last forty years, our plantation has had two of Mr Witney's Cotton Gins. Come with me and I'll show you. They're in that barn at the moment."

Paul led them across a yard and into one of the other barns. At one side was a tarpaulin covering a large object that seemed to be standing on a huge and very solid looking sort of table. With the cover removed, Paul revealed two boxes about four feet long and two or three feet high. At one end was an opening and on one side an iron wheel was attached.

"This amazing machine can strip raw cotton of all its seeds and other scraps that shouldn't be there. As the wheel attached to the side turns the saw-toothed combs inside, they draw the raw cotton in and then push it out clean and ready to bale. It can produce enough cotton in a day to be pressed and then fill dozens of bales."

"That must surely mean," said Arthur with some enthusiasm, "that these days you need far fewer...er...field hands than you did before."

"No, sir!" Paul quickly corrected him. "The cotton gin just means the niggers we have can now do other tasks: harvesting, pressing, packing, which, in turn means we can produce more cotton from the enlarged plantation. The gins are getting far larger these days than Mr Witney's original invention and will, I reckon, one day get much bigger still and may be used in the actual fields, rather than here in the barn."

Arthur tried to conceal his disgust that the machine, that should make workers lives easier, was actually just moving them from one manual task to another. He turned away, pretending to look across the huge yard to the pressing machine they had seen earlier. He then walked the short distance to the edge of the nearest field, expecting to find the *field workers*, as he preferred to think of the slaves, sitting in the shade with bottles of drink and the equivalent of the 'snap' that all Crompton Mill workers brought to work.

What he actually saw were numerous huddles of slaves already moving back into the fields. He checked his pocket watch: it was ten past twelve, meaning they had worked for six hours and had now had a break of about ten or fifteen minutes. What shocked him, however, was the sight of an overseer, easy now for him to pick out, thrashing an old woman who had apparently fallen to the ground. He was shouting at her, although Arthur could not make out what he said each time the whip came down on her back and shoulders. What had seemed a riding crop, actually had two or three feet of a leather strap attached to the end. The other slaves, both men and women, looked away from the woman on the ground and walked past. Arthur stood in shock for several minutes and then realised that she made no sound, simply covered her head with her hands.

As he came out of his shocked stupor, he was about to run to her aid, in his mind already beating the overseer to the ground. As he took the first step, a firm had gripped his arm from behind, with a strength that prevented him from any movement forwards. George's mouth was then against his ear. His raw whisper made Arthur try to swing around and drag himself away.

"Arthur, stop! Stop now or I will throw you to the ground."

Arthur continued to struggle to be free, but George was at least six inches taller, probably a stone heavier and, more significant he now realised, a very fit and powerful soldier.

Arthur finally managed to swing around towards him, but George then gripped his other arm as well and pulled him up against his body, both his arms locked behind Arthur's back. To an onlooker, it would seem they were hugging each other.

"Don't fuck with me, Arthur, or I'll have to kick your legs from under you as well."

There was a pause as both men drew breath and Arthur realised there was no way he could break the grip, which was still not released.

"If you raced over there and, God help us, assaulted that cretin, we would all be in the shit. No way would we ever send any report home and probably we'd disappear into some convenient shallow grave... *Do you understand*?"

Arthur slumped against him and George partially slackened his grip as they now faced each other, almost nose to nose. George, who was looking towards the barns, saw that Paul had noticed them and was walking slowly in their direction.

"We were just congratulating each other on our luck at being made so welcome with all this information here. It will be so useful in promoting the cause of..."

Paul was close enough now to hear some of what George had just said. "Hey? Are you two gentlemen finished with the...hugging, I suppose I should call it? Glad you're so pleased with how we get your cotton ready."

George had a rictus grin on his face by now and Arthur turned to face Paul with a not very convincing smile just touching his lips. He muttered something that was fortunately unintelligible to Paul.

"Well, I guess we could all do with some luncheon, so if you come with me, we'll join Father and Ernest in the shade of the barn and see what the kitchen has prepared for us."

George walked next to Paul, as they crossed the yard. Arthur allowed a separation to open and could see the two talking, perhaps rather too seriously he felt. As they entered the cool shade under the high roof of the farthest barn,

Arthur felt he should not be surprised by what he saw before him, but he could not help himself.

A table was laid with a pristine white cloth and comfortable chairs arranged around it, as well as china, glass and silverware, which held a rich variety of cold foods, from ham to seafood, game, salads and bowls set in ice full of summer fruits: strawberries, peaches, oranges and even what he took to be ice cream. Bottles of what looked like champagne, rested on more ice in coolers.

Sitting in front of what the family regarded as a picnic, Arthur felt suddenly isolated. The thought of the unpleasant truth that just a short distance away were hundreds of human beings held in what he now had to acknowledge was savage slavery and who had been allowed a drink of water and probably scraps of food, while he sat in front of a veritable feast for just five people; it made him feel sick. He knew he would be unable to touch the food laid out in such selfish excess. He stood up and, with the excuse that he felt affected by the heat, left the table and walked outside.

Meanwhile father and son, but also Ernest and George, seemed in good spirits and the conversation was mostly about the successful plantation and the need that England had for their fine quality cotton. Nothing, it was agreed on all sides, must be allowed to interfere with its continued transportation to England and especially to Crompton Mill in Oldham.

In the barn, Arthur had felt as if he were alone in a bubble, floating above the more than amply stocked tables and the sounds of most of those present content to be enjoying a pleasant lunch in the shade and all was well with their world. He knew now that he had nothing in common with any of them, nothing said here that he could agree with.

He decided that he had seen enough for one day and started on the trek back to Cotton Hall. He tried to ignore the sight of slaves in the fields and hurried forward until he reached the shelter of the trees. He did then feel genuinely overwhelmed by the heat of the afternoon sun and slowed his pace. As he approached the slave village, assuming it would still be deserted, he was surprised to hear voices just ahead of him.

He nervously approached the collection of huts, worried what his reception might be, but there seemed no choice other than to walk through the village to gain the path leading back to Cotton Hall. Having reached the rear of the first huts, voices, although not loud, sounded more numerous. He turned the final corner and stood on the edge of the open space in the middle of the village. A group of women, maybe a dozen or more, were sitting on the ground in the shade cast by a two-storey hut. As soon as he was spotted, the group fell silent and suspicious eyes stared at the white stranger.

Arthur walked slowly forward; it was either that or return to the barn, which he knew he most certainly did not want to do. As he took a few paces forward he realised that most of the women were either holding a baby, or in some cases two, and with what must have been ten or more toddlers playing in the dust around them. He started to walk more purposefully again, although it inevitably meant he would pass closer to the group. He tried to overcome his nervousness.

*Why was he so unsure of himself? Surely, these women would do him no harm? Or would they take advantage of his being alone and take revenge for those whom men like him had abused for so many decades?*

"Good afternoon." He spoke louder than he had intended and realised, too late, how blunt, practically rude, he sounded. Then to his utter surprise, the women all scrambled up, gathering babies into their arms and stood staring at him in what he took to be fear. "Please, I mean you no harm." He hesitated, concern for his safety now recurring. *Once they realise I'm no threat and a foreigner as well,* he thought, but he was only too aware of how ridiculous this was, pulled himself together and walked more slowly towards the group. He stopped a few yards in front of them and smiled.

"I am from a land far across the ocean, an English man." This sounded patronising and as if he were addressing a crowd of young children. "I do not know very much about your country, but I mean you no harm, I promise."

He found he could think of nothing else to say and then looked again at their young children. "You have some very beautiful babies… You must all have quite a lot of other children."

From the back of the group, an elderly, white haired woman pushed her way forward. She was stooped and walked with the help of a rough stick. She stopped when she was just in front of the others.

"If't please ya sah, we'm jus' minders for t'others. Not jus' our own babbies. You please don' tell massa that we was here restin'. We no wan' a beatin'."

Her expression was pleading, while the other women retained close to blank expressions.

Arthur found their words difficult to understand perfectly, but the gist was clear. They seemed afraid of him, certainly not aggressive. He could think of nothing else to say, although there were many hundreds he ought to say. As he stood uncertain of how to extricate himself and be on his way, he noticed that several of them suddenly looked over his left shoulder and immediately all eyes were focussed there.

Arthur slowly turned. In the doorway of the nearest hut, a tall figure stood in the semi-dark shade. The man, since man he clearly was, turned slowly, so he could now make out the figure better. The man's age was difficult to tell, but he was as tall as Arthur, but much thinner, almost emaciated; even his feet were bare. Arthur noticed his eyes. Deep, dark pools, were fixed on him, but it was impossible to concentrate on anything when he saw that around his neck was an iron collar, out of which, at intervals, protruded arms of iron, bent upwards at the ends. Arthur's next thought was: *how can he ever lie down?*

The man seemed aware that everyone's eyes were upon him. He then, totally unexpectedly, smiled broadly, but the smile never reached his eyes; the ghost of the smile lay cold as the grave on his lips. Arthur was rooted to the spot and none of the women had moved either, nor remarkably had the children. Those who could walk stood clinging to the nearest skirt.

The man, his skin almost as dark as the shade in which he still stood, retained the rictus smile still unmoving. He then took a few steps out of the doorway until he was in the sunlight. He then performed an almost majestic half a pirouette, stopping with his back to the audience before, after a few minutes, he continued around to stop again facing Arthur. The moment Arthur had seen his back, he let out a sound between a gasp and a cry. From neck to waist, his skin was lacerated with bloody stripes, criss-crossing each other so that the skin between was forced to lift its corners against them. The man stared at Arthur with his smile still in place. After another minute, gracefully as a dancer, he returned to the doorway and disappeared into the gloom inside.

Arthur could not immediately formulate any words. Clearly, the man had been beaten or, more likely, whipped in the most brutal, sadistic fashion. His mind was demanding: *Why? What had he done? How could anything warrant this? Who had done it? Why were these women doing nothing?* But none of these thoughts were translated into words. He looked in astonishment at the women and the still obviously frightened children.

Just one word then burst out of him, directed at the only humans in sight, but perhaps also at the loving God in whom he had believed for most of his life: "*Why!*"

# Chapter Seventeen

## June 1861: Cotton Hall, Beaufort County

Weeks had slipped by as the three Englishmen, without really being aware of time passing, succumbed unresisting to the slow, leisurely life and the hot sun of the Cotton Hall plantation. Ernest was learning more each day about the details of production of cotton that would soon be harvested and sent, or possibly not sent, on its way to the Atlantic ports, destined for Liverpool. He optimistically hoped that one day this first-hand knowledge might benefit Crompton Mill. Meanwhile George spent most of his time questioning anyone he could persuade to give him information about the blockade that, rumour had it, was already in place and preventing southern ports from exporting cotton to England, or anywhere else.

Daniel Hayward, patriarch of the great plantation, had mentioned to George that he was a Democrat member of the Confederate Congress, although the present state of '*almost war*' had prevented his being in Richmond for some time past. However, he was able to communicate with the Congress Chairman via the telegraph office in Culpepper and had pretty much up to date news from friends and colleagues in the Confederate capital. The cables that Nat was entrusted to take to and from Culpepper soon confirmed that Charleston's port was now definitely closed to the export of cotton, just as George had seen for himself, while Savannah and several other Atlantic and Gulf ports were becoming increasingly difficult for even smugglers to operate from them.

Arthur became more and more withdrawn and downcast as the increasing heat of June beat down on Cotton Hall. Having failed to make Ernest or George understand that slavery was 'immoral for a Christian man', Arthur, by the middle of the month, refused to discuss the matter at all with anyone, especially his two companions, both of whom now insisted it was a necessary evil if the British cotton trade were to survive and that inevitably included Crompton

Mill. He had then, in a dramatic, almost symbolic act, handed Ernest all his reports, papers and any evidence. He could not be responsible any longer for trying to be objective in what he saw and recorded for eventual passage to the government in London.

It was at the beginning of the third week in June that cables from Richmond began to increase in volume, with news that Union troops were, firstly, preparing to march south into Virginia and secondly, on the heels of this, that President Jeff Davis had warned his countrymen that the Confederacy only had 'a little army' and was short of equipment, men and supplies. The tone of these cables persuaded both the Haywards and their English guests that, regardless of an actual declaration of war, the Union was now moving regardless into the jaws of a war that might well suffocate the Confederate states soon after its birth.

On June 22, a day threatened with thunder storms in Beaufort County, a cable arrived telling them that William Russell, the war correspondent of the *London Times*, had been in the north for some weeks, including time in New York and Washington, and was expected to arrive in Richmond within the next few days. Included in a stream of cables over those days was a quotation attributed to Abraham Lincoln himself: (19) *"The Times" is perhaps the most important thing in the world."* And another comment that the Union President, *"Of course would feel sore if it [the Times] turns against him."*

Another cable, rushed by Nat to Cotton Hall the same day, read: '*Mr William Russell has written that he is coming south to see with his own eyes how affairs stand there, before the two sections come to open rupture*'.

Even Arthur was drawn into the eager anticipation of seeing these cables, especially those that confirmed that William Russell was regarded here as: (20) '*The most respected reporter of the Times of London, having excited the nation before with his fine war correspondence*'.

"The way I read these reports," Arthur said that evening, "is that Abe Lincoln must be desperate to have Russell reporting favourably about the Union's limited expectation of success, but by his coming to Richmond Jeff Davis now had his great opportunity. If Mr Russell writes that England must have its cotton supplies and, since that is being denied by Lincoln, England could well suffer ruin...then Davis could have the tiger by the tail."

The three Envoys, now joined by Paul, were on the veranda awaiting each message Nat brought them from Culpepper at break neck speed during that afternoon and evening. An excited Daniel was there as well as the news arrived with agonisingly long periods of time between each cable. As night descended, it was Daniel who turned to the trio and to Paul, with his hand on the collection of messages now lying on the table before them. It seemed that Daniel was optimistic about what he had read so far.

"It seems to me," he said, "that, as a Congressman for West Virginia, I should ensure that Mr Russell is made aware of the risk that his country faces, and that we face also, if our cotton trade with Britain is strangled. I think I will have to travel to Richmond as soon as it is light tomorrow and use the (20) powerful influence that I naturally have with Jeff Davis to give the *London Times* a true account of the danger its readers now face."

Ernest looked more concerned than either Arthur or George.

"That is all very well, but surely time is now short and any report by Mr Russell will take at least two weeks to reach London and that is if storms and the speed of ships are on his side."

"You're behind the times Ernest," Paul interrupted any further exchange of views. "You probably know that the Trans-Atlantic cable that was opened for use three years ago, did indeed fail within a short time."

"Exactly," Ernest spoke urgently, no doubt to emphasise his knowledge of the news that would now mean anything they, as Envoys, needed to get to London in a very short time would be forced to take weeks, rather than days. He continued to emphasise that. The knowledge he now had was surely accurate. "That is what I said and what will undoubtedly......"

Paul was, by then, too impatient to allow Ernest to continue.

"*But* what you could not know is that the cable was repaired just two months ago and the new *American* cable now has established the connection via Newfoundland and Ireland, from there London and, in its turn, is connected to dozens of cable offices throughout the country here, including Richmond!"

Paul looked in triumph at his audience and as the value of this news dawned on the rest of the small group, George laughed out loud.

"That not only means that Russell's report will possibly get to London inside a day, but, even more important, it could mean that, with the right person speaking for us," and here he looked meaningfully at Daniel, "we could get our up-to-date report to the War Office in London in time for our Government to have the latest news and our considered views within a day or so." Both he and Ernest looked expectantly at Paul and Daniel before speaking a few moments later. Is possible that England might then act to protect our trade with you as a result, don't you think?"

Daniel held up his hand in a calming gesture. "I understand and appreciate your enthusiasm and even possible assistance in our cause, as well as your own cause Ernest... *But* I am not sure I can represent West Virginia and the honesty of the cause of the Confederacy *and* the needs of Britain's economy at the same time."

No one spoke for a few minutes. Paul looked at his father and shrugged his shoulders. Ernest looked first at George and then at Arthur with his eyebrows questioningly raised. It was George who seemed to feel the need to make a decision.

"May I suggest, Daniel, that I accompany you to Richmond. I am a serving officer in Her Majesty's army and would, if nothing else, perhaps prove a useful escort to you on the journey in these dangerous times. Then, if you keep me at your side, perhaps as your assistant, I can talk to Mr Russell, one Englishman to another, and hopefully persuade him that the report I shall have with me urgently needs to be conveyed to the Secretary of State for War, Lord Sidney Herbert. No patriotic Englishman could refuse such a request on behalf of his queen and country."

Daniel Hayward, embracing his role as Congressman, now assumed a serious expression. He looked from one to the other, started to say something, but then stopped. No one felt it appropriate to interrupt his thoughts. Eventually he did speak.

"Gentlemen, I hear everything you say and my heart is with you, of course, but I must think carefully on this, if you will permit me a little time. Remember that I must put my responsibility to the Confederate State first, although I do see how possibly our two nations could well be equally served. I am going to take a short stroll down to the river, so that I can consider what I should do. I will not be too long."

Congressman Daniel Hayward, his hands linked behind his back, then walked along the veranda, down the steps on to the grass and disappeared out of the lights in the direction of the river, which on this quiet night could just be heard in the distance. Unsure what to do the others eventually gravitated to the nearest group of chairs, although Paul quickly realised that a drink might be required and turned to the open doors into the house to arrange it. A few minutes later, crystal glasses, a bowl of ice and a decanter of southern rye whiskey were brought out and placed on the table by a silent black house slave. It was more than half an hour later that the master of Cotton Hall could be seen approaching them across the grass from the direction of the river, a serious expression on his face.

The four young men, who had been unable to find anything of interest to talk about once Daniel had disappeared from sight earlier, now nervously stood up, all of them concerned by the expression on his face. He did not speak at first, but sat down and helped himself to a glass of whiskey, which he downed in one.

"Sit down all of you, for God's sake," he muttered.

Once they had hastily obeyed, there were then another few moments of silence.

"I have thought through all this as carefully as I can, given what I know of the few facts available," Daniel spoke slowly, much to the annoyance of his audience. He then continued in the same serious tone. "I understand how important it is, not just to those who, like me, depend on the money our cotton earns, but also vital to my homeland, my Confederate South, which has only recently made itself a legitimate country and faces a bloody infancy. I appreciate how important this is to England, the country my grandfather fought against for our freedom less than a century ago." He paused, but no one seemed inclined to interrupt.

"Cotton is the key," he continued. "The Confederacy needs to grow cotton to sell to England and so to earn the dollars we need to survive, by which I mean *my* country and *my* family. You Englishmen need the cotton to keep coming for the same reason. I hate the idea of war with men who were so recently my fellow countrymen. I, we," he waved a hand at Paul, "have a nephew, who we have not seen for many years, but who lives in Pennsylvania. I have no idea how to contact him now. Will he be our enemy when war begins, as it must, in a few weeks? Could I, or could you Paul, face the horror of meeting him on some battlefield and putting a bullet through his brain or he through mine or yours?"

Daniel sighed loudly and waved a hand in front of his face, as if to swat away mosquitos. Eventually, having poured himself another drink and swallowed a mouthful, and then stared at each expectant face before he continued.

"Perhaps you can see how terrible this is for an old man like me. I have weighed the alternatives and come down on the side, as always, of my family and my country and *my friends.*"

At this, there were no actual words spoken by his attentive audience, but grunts, smiles and, from, Ernest a long release of breath, as if he had been holding it for a long time. Daniel held his hand up to ensure no one interrupted him now.

"As I said, I shall travel to Richmond tomorrow and, if he is still willing to accompany me, I will take Captain Fitzwilliam with me, to represent the voice of the British government. I would normally take you Paul, but I cannot leave the family and our other guests without a man to take decisions here in these dangerous days, so Paul you will stay here as the head of the family in my absence. Can I take it that this is agreeable to you all?"

George was the first to find his voice. "Thank you, sir, for the honour you do me, in fact that you do all three of us in agreeing to allow me to take our country's needs to enlighten Mr Russell about our observations here and to ask him to convey our report to the British War Office, along with his newspaper article to the *London Times*. The time saved could well be essential to both our countries."

Daniel had been watching his son's expression ever since he had delivered his judgement and Paul now shifted his gaze to a point in the dark distance, then returned his father's expectant look.

"I accept, of course Pa, what you have decided and I will do my best not to fail you should war come upon us here before you return, but you must understand that if the Beaufort and West Virginia Volunteers are called on to fight in the next few weeks, then I must join them. I hope and pray that will not be the case. In fact if your mission, George, is a success, we may avoid shedding Yankee blood at all, which would be a pity in my opinion."

"Arthur, Ernest," George said, "I shall need our full reports to take with me tomorrow and the recommendation that the way to stop a war erupting, to stop cotton from lying rotting on so many quay sides and harbours here in the south, is for our government to demand an end to the blockades and, if that is resisted, to send her majesty's navy to enforce it. Can you do that?"

"Yes, I don't doubt it may be done," Arthur quickly replied, "but it is Ernest who now has charge of the papers, so I doubt it is he who will get much sleep tonight. I wish him well in the task of ensuring the reports are complete and accurate." A brief look passed between the two brothers as Arthur finished speaking.

The four young men made their various apologies for taking to their rooms so early, said 'good night' to Daniel and set about the tasks they needed to complete before the Virginia Congressman and the English Captain set off at dawn the next day, the seventh of July, on a journey that could prove a turning point in the history of both their countries.

# Chapter Eighteen

## Richmond, Virginia; July 1861

For both Daniel and George, the journey to Culpepper by coach and four, followed by a first-class carriage on the train to Richmond was surprisingly pleasant and undisturbed. They passed through territory they had both seen before, in Daniel's case many times, but now denuded, as far as they could tell, of the majority of its male population between the ages of about fifteen and sixty years old.

They arrived at (21) Richmond rail depot, which George again judged to be rather fine, without incident or delay in the late afternoon of the next day. George could still not help smiling at the huge smoke stacks of two other American locomotives waiting in the depot to depart. He was reminded of a serious and boring concert he was obliged to attend in London many years before. What stood on the front of each locomotive looked uncannily like giant euphonium musical instruments turned upside down. Even the dour George now grinned broadly. Although he could not have failed to have felt surrounded by considerable movements of Confederate troops on his earlier journey north, but going south on this day, there was a noticeable absence of troops travelling either north or south.

They were met outside the station by a beautifully turned-out carriage and four greys belonging to Ian Cameron, (21a) the Democrat Congressional Leader, who had come to meet them himself. Having been introduced to George, the elderly, white haired and bearded gentleman was obviously eager to explain the details of meetings he had arranged for the following days. Once they were on board, he leant forward from his seat opposite Daniel.

"I cannot tell you how pleased I am to see you Daniel and I know your fellow members of Congress, at least those who have braved getting up here earlier in February and March on roads clogged with soldiers, will I am certain also welcome you. Now, apart from a gathering of those members of Congress tomorrow, I have also met Mr Russell and, after I had explained what valuable information Captain Fitzwilliam is expected to be bringing with him, he has kindly agreed to meet with you both at midday tomorrow in my office at the Capitol. I do understand that the Captain also has a favour to ask him to do with sharing the telegraph facility of the Capital, but I will leave you, Captain Fitzwilliam, to talk to him yourself about that."

George could not fail to be impressed by hearing that so much had already been organised and this made him optimistic about a favourable outcome. The carriage was now trotting down streets which George felt he had seen before, but on the previous journey, which seemed a lifetime ago. He glimpsed the James River, initially between swaths of warehouses and then good-looking terraces of houses, while finally, as the May Bridge across the James came into sight on his right, there above them opposite was the Confederate State Capitol in all its dazzling white splendour, although builders seemed to be in charge of the almost completed building.

After the fairly short journey from the station, the carriage rounded Capitol Square and stopped outside the Richmond Hotel.

"I have booked you as guests of the Confederate Government in our finest hotel for as long as you need to stay. Please ensure all your expenses are put down to myself."

Ivan Cameron was clearly proud of the facilities of their new capital city and even accompanied them into the hotel to ensure they had the very best rooms available.

The next day, not wishing to be late for their appointment, Daniel and George walked from Capital Square the short distance to the Capitol itself just after half past eleven. The exterior of the building was impressive and seemed to reign over Richmond from the small hill on which it stood. Once inside the opulence continued in the open space below the rotunda.

"My word," exclaimed George as they stood beneath the centre of the dome, albeit still only covering part of the parabola of space available, "this is almost as awe inspiring as St Pauls in London, although that was completed a few hundred years ago."

Daniel glanced up. "I suppose I've got used to it, but nowadays, I have nightmares about the Yankees getting close enough to shell it and reduce it to rubble. Then all the craftsmanship and years of work could be gone in a few hours…the potential horrors of the coming war are just too terrible to contemplate."

Daniel, who seemed to be in somewhat of a hurry, briefly took George in to see the Congress chamber; George was surprised at its being so different from the arrangement of the House of Commons in England. Daniel then led the way to the Congress Leader's office, which was in one of the two wings that 'flew' out from the rotunda. He pulled out his pocket watch and waiting until exactly midday, knocked on the door through which they heard a faint 'Come in' beyond its highly polished wood.

The office they entered was certainly grand and could easily have been in a government building in London: panelling, window frames and doors that George guessed must all be of walnut, as well as a mighty desk of a darker wood. Ivan Cameron sat in one of the leather easy chairs placed around a table in front of his desk, but got up as soon as Daniel and George entered and closed the door behind them. The gentleman sitting in another similar chair remained seated.

"You are both very welcome," Congress Leader Cameron said and warmly shook the hands of both men. He then turned towards the other gentleman, whose face held a dour, almost supercilious, expression.

"May I introduce you to Mr William Russell, whose fame as a war reporter on the *London Times* I am sure goes before him."

The gentleman concerned eased himself up and waited for the two new arrivals to cross to where he stood. Russell was a portly, but pleasant looking gentleman. He was dressed, observing him as George now did from the top downwards, in a sort of military cap of dark material with a peak, which he apparently did not feel the need to take off indoors. This was followed by a long buttoned and belted jacket, reaching just below his waist and then tight dun-coloured trousers tucked in to knee high, black boots. He had a dark beard and moustache and fairly long hair to match. George took the few steps towards the celebrity and shook his hand; he was surprised how strong his grip was.

"Naturally, I know all about your career as a newspaper man, sir," he said, "and I have read many of your war reports in the *Times*. I was myself in the Crimea six years ago and took part in the siege of Sevastopol. Sadly, I was wounded there and returned to England, where, as you can see, I recovered."

George paused for the laugh he thought inevitable, but when none came, he continued.

"I was then privileged to be able to read most of your previous reports on the war and was impressed by how they conveyed the genuine atmosphere and truth of events."

Russell had still not spoken and Daniel then shook his hand and made a few obvious remarks about the great man's career. Cameron invited them all to sit down and offered coffee, but this was declined. Mr Cameron clearly felt the need to use the short time they had in as succinct a manner as possible and so brought George's reminiscences quickly to a close.

"Knowing how precious your time here is, Mr Russell, may I suggest that Captain Fitzwilliam explains why he is here to meet you, a meeting which both I and Congressman Hayward believe is of the utmost importance to all of us."

William Russell waved his hand at George, presumably to encourage him to speak. George sat forward on the edge of his chair and fixed his attention entirely on the man who could quite possibly, although unaware of it, alter the course of the forthcoming war, not with a sword, but with the stroke of a pen.

"I and two other English gentlemen, who are presently at Mr Hayward's plantation and who have an intimate knowledge of the cotton industry in Lancashire, have been given the great responsibility by Lord Palmerston, and also Lord Sidney Herbert, to observe closely the state of the Confederacy in preparing for a civil war, a conflict which they certainly hope will not manifest itself. We have seen at first hand the present lamentable condition of the export of cotton from the Confederacy to England. We have found that already ports like Charleston are blockaded and cannot export a single fibre of cotton. This is also increasingly true in other ports along the Atlantic and Gulf coasts of the Confederacy. Bales of cotton are lying uselessly on quay sides and harbours while England is being starved of cotton, of which I am sure you are aware."

At last, Russell appeared to be interested and, instead of being slumped in his chair in silence, he now sat up and was clearly listening with interest.

"And what, Captain, do you believe the real effect of this blockade will have on the cotton mills of Lancashire?"

"The result, sir, if the blockade is a ring of iron entirely cutting off the Confederate State from England and the world, will be disaster for our cotton trade. I will repeat what the Prime Minister has already told his ministers and that is that the mills will gradually, over perhaps four or five months or less, run out of cotton. That will mean that they will be forced to close, no doubt become bankrupt, and tens of thousands of workers, employed in hundreds, if not thousands, of mills will be laid off and face starvation. The economy of our country would be so severely damaged that it would take decades to recover, far longer than the collapse of the South Sea Bubble (22). A further result may well be that the government then has insufficient money to keep our army and navy up to strength as a force that is at present the finest and strongest in the world. I must add that this information is completely confidential and must not be repeated at present."

Russell had, during this heart-felt explanation, taken out a notebook and pencil and was making lengthy entries in it. George, surprised still to have the floor, was delighted to be able to continue.

"I have already noticed," he said, "in the short time I have been here, that southern people are well bred, courteous and hospitable, as are Mr Cameron and Mr Hayward, *but* are they brave, strong, self-sacrificing and genuinely willing to kill and be killed, not simply to be courteous and so on? What do you, sir, now believe are the chances of the Confederacy actually winning this war, very likely against their own brothers, sons, cousins, nephews or even fathers? I apologise to Mr Hayward for questioning their army's will and strength, but it must....."

Ivan Cameron was quick to jump in and provide the answer, possibly feeling that Daniel was likely to exaggerate the strength and God-given rights of the Confederate army.

"We are a smaller and less industrial nation than our late brothers in the north, but we are far more united than they are. They will come to the fight in the belief that they cannot be beaten and any war will last months and not years. *They are wrong.* Our state is totally united, as is our army; the north is not. It is likely, Mr Russell, that very shortly you will still be in Virginia to see the opening battles of this war. I and every other southerner, whether in uniform, or loyally supporting our boys at home, are convinced that we will have the victory we deserve. After all the talk, we will fight to support the sentiments of the Declaration of Independence itself. We will drive the Yankees back into the north and take their capital. We will claim the freedom we won last century. When that happens, you will be able to write in your newspaper that Dixie... I mean of course the Confederate States, are alive, well and free."

Daniel shouted, "Hear, hear!" and clapped his hands at this. Russell continued writing for a few minutes and no one dared to interrupt him or stop his then speaking.

"If it is your hope that England will declare war on the Union, I suspect you will be disappointed," were the first words of the Great War correspondent of the Times. He held up his hand to stop anyone from denying this possibility. "Equally, as Captain Fitzwilliam and his two colleagues must know by now, I assume from conversations with some gentlemen in our government in London, that England must do something to ensure our cotton industry can continue without disturbance and not just sit on our hands. You have described the growing strength of a blockade of ports, but you may find the reality of war on land equally hard to resist."

"Our report to the Secretary of State for War," George was now in danger of falling off his chair as he edged even further forward, "will no doubt agree with your view, but surely England has other options than declaring all-out war?"

"Then your report needs to make clear what you, as witnesses to these calamitous events, believe our Prime Minister and his Secretary of State for War should do."

Daniel at last found a lull that allowed him to join the conversation.

"Both our nations have the same needs: one to sell, one to buy, unlimited amounts of cotton. All that stops this in the Union's navy, which from what I have seen of them in the past in and around the waters to the east, is mostly made up of out of date sailing vessels, including war ships. I thought that England had the world's most powerful fleet and ruled the seas; am I mistaken?"

"No, Daniel," George swiftly assured him, "you are not mistaken. Our iron hulled war ships like *HMS Prince of Wales* and the *HMS Warrior* have no equals here or anywhere else on earth."

"In which case," Russell now stepped briskly in, "perhaps the English navy could demand the removal of the blockade, as it is damaging our country, not officially at war with the Union, although bear in mind that England is already in what is deemed as '*a state of belligerency with the Union*'(23). Hence, England is just one-half step away from actually being at war with that State. If the threat of British naval action is disregarded, I have no doubt our government would be obliged to enforce it, as we have done before elsewhere, with shot and shell."

Ivan Cameron, Daniel Hayward and George Fitzwilliam now looked at each other, first questioningly and then with positive smiles.

"That is exactly what we have outlined in our report," said George.

"In which case," replied Russell, "we are in agreement. Your observations seem to me to be accurate, at least in as far as you have been able to determine. I shall, no doubt, compose a piece to be sent to the *London Times* forthwith that will reflect what I am allowed to report you have told me and with my comments upon it. I do not doubt that all members of Parliament will have an opportunity to read it in the a few days' time." Russell put his notebook away and started to rise.

George realised that he had only a few precious moments to persuade him to do them, or rather England, a favour before he disappeared.

"If I may take another few moments of your time, Mr Russell?"

The journalist, who had already taken a couple of steps towards the door, hesitated long enough for George to rise and stand beside him, as he turned his back to the still closed door.

"I am sure we believe that your war report in the *London Times* will undoubtedly help both England and the Confederacy to continue trading and, perhaps even to bring the war, which we are on the brink of, to a hasty conclusion, *but* it is vital that the full report of all we have observed and concluded during the months we have been here, must somehow get to London more quickly than by a slow-moving ship."

"Yes?" was the only reply.

"Things are moving faster here than we, or I think anyone in the government in London, ever anticipated. It seems from all we hear and see that a battle is very close to being joined and that will start a civil war that will, of course, be a disaster for both sides in the conflict *and* it is quite likely to be a disaster for England as well..." George's voice trailed off, as he looked steadily down at Russell.

The *Times* reporter seemed to be becoming impatient with George's long-winded speeches and interrupted him.

"Captain Fitzwilliam, I am aware of all this and now have to write a report to *The London Times,* for which I am paid. So if you will, excuse me..."

Russell was clearly set on leaving the office but George placed a hand on his arm.

"I must apologise. Just a few moments, are all I need and then we have to throw ourselves on your generosity to help your country."

Russell gently removed the hand and said, "Just as much time as it takes me to walk through this door. That is all the time I have available, sir."

George spoke firmly and very quickly. "It is urgent that our government reads now, before any hostilities start in earnest, what we have observed here over the last three months. Will you please take our report and telegraph it to the War Office for the urgent and personal attention of Lord Sidney Herbert and thus help to save our cotton industry?"

William Russell had already turned, reached for the door handle and started to open it. George knew that Russell had already gained access by his formidable connections to the telegraph in the residence of Jeff Davis, the only such service in Richmond. He stopped as George finished speaking and then turned back to his fellow countryman, who now stood staring at him, it seemed holding his breath. Russell tightened the belt on his jacket and then focussed his deep brown eyes on George for a few moments of silence.

"Very well, sir. I cannot refuse your request as one patriotic Englishman to another, even though I shall still continue to report this coming conflict without fear or favour. If you will give me the report,(34) I will try to do as you ask."

George let out a long breath, but Russel stopped him from speaking again. George held out his hand and shook Russell's hand warmly. "I cannot tell you how much—"

"If you meet me in the lobby of the Richmond hotel in two hours with your report in a sealed envelope, I will see that it is telegraphed from here this afternoon to London by a secure hand. It should be with Lord Sidney during the day after tomorrow. If a reply is necessary, it may be sent to me here via the Richmond Hotel, but I shall not be here myself after midday tomorrow. Tomorrow afternoon, I shall be leaving to go north to Manassas."

With that, he opened the door and left, walking swiftly away down the corridor towards the central space beneath the rotunda, now in dazzlingly full of sunlight.

George and Daniel carried out Russel's instructions, having first added to their report the strong recommendation that the Lords Palmerston and Herbert should consider very carefully England's options in the light of their report and particularly what they had observed at first hand, that could represent the means to allow the export of cotton to continue through the coming fury. George, after much soul searching, did not include in the report a page that Arthur had written outlining his horror of the 'E*vil of slavery in the Confederacy*', since he felt obliged to include nothing that could cause his government to hesitate in the action that seemed so vital.

George did not get to meet Jeff Davis, as he had hoped, although in the next two days Daniel had several lengthy meetings with Ivan Cameron, as well as the congressmen who were still present in Richmond.

Having done all that George and Daniel felt it was possible to achieve, they made the return journey to Cotton Hall. Unlike their fairly smooth coach and train travel towards Richmond, the return took nearly two days. This was caused by the great escalation in the number of troops moving from Richmond, where numerous battalions, groups of volunteers and even regiments had gathered from all over Virginia; all were set on travelling north, by any means possible, since it seemed that Richmond itself did not yet need defending. This meant that their train, also crammed with soldiers, had no choice but to wait for other trains erratically moving ahead of them. As far as they could gather, all the traffic seemed destined to pass through Culpepper on the way to a town called Manassas.

# Chapter Nineteen

**July 1861**

By the time they made the return journey to Cotton Hall, it was to a scene that George described as '*chaotic*', although Daniel immediately saw it as '*preparation for a fight…at last*'.

As soon as their coach crested the last hill and they could look down on the plantation, they no longer saw the placid grassland with its grand live oaks, but a large military camp, which now devoured the land sloping down to the river, including its bridge and several new fords built across the water as well. The ramshackle camp then spread right up to the mansion and way beyond it to both right and left. Bell tents had been erected, campfires were burning, piles of arms and ammunition were scattered and field guns were drawn up hundreds of yards beyond the horse lines in the distance.

A cloud of dust hung over the whole area, caused by the feet of the many hundreds of men in Confederate uniforms, or at least an approximation of uniforms. Arising from the camp came a melee of noise: shouted orders, the clatter of field guns being moved, the voices of so many men in a confined area, as well as nervous horse lines and riders galloping both into and out of the camp in what seemed an haphazard fashion.

Although Daniel seemed surprisingly delighted with the prospect of a military camp covering his beloved plantation gardens, George had his telescope out and saw what Daniel certainly did not see: soldiers running apparently aimlessly in different directions, others lounging outside tents, uniforms half on, with caps and jackets on the ground, rifles lying out of reach and field guns scattered in no particular order, while limbers were over half a mile away; hence his muttered summary: '*a mess of chaos*'.

Daniel obviously wanted to get down into the camp at once and ordered the coach to proceed down the hill at full speed. However, they had to wait to cross the bridge for some time, as it was not only the home to groups of men sitting on the sidewalls smoking and drinking, but also crates in untidy piles blocking the way.

General Daniel Hayward descended from the coach as quickly as he was able and started to shout orders to those on the bridge. Unfortunately, most did not appear to know who he was and he had to yell orders at an officer on the other side of the river, who did eventually acknowledge him. It became clear that it would take some considerable time to clear a way, so Daniel and George walked into the camp, receiving some odd looks, as they were not in uniform. Once inside the large area of the camp, George could see more clearly how disorganised it was. He determined that, once they reached Cotton Hall itself, he would need to have a serious discussion with Daniel, but more importantly with Paul and, if he were present, Captain Nat Phillips as well.

They eventually arrived at the mansion, dusty, sweaty and dirty from the walk through the camp. Daniel suggested George should sit in his study while he went to find Paul. George had only just eased himself into a comfortable chair when Arthur and Ernest burst into the room. George was relieved to see them but looked perturbed at their outbursts of words tripping over each other, while they attempted to tell him what had happened. Eventually, George persuaded them to sit down with him and explain calmly how such dramatic changes had occurred in just a few days.

After what seemed a very long time, he was able to sew together their often excited, often worrying stories of what had occurred there since he and Daniel left for Richmond less than a week ago. He heard how a command had come from Richmond soon after they left that all the local volunteer brigades, as well as the regular platoons and regiments of the Confederate army, should mobilise at once, make their way with urgency to their headquarters, or agreed mobilisation stations, and then prepare to advance towards Manassas.

Apart from that there was only, as ever, rumour, which was more rife than ever. Paul had triggered the mobilisation of the Beaufort County Volunteers and he and Nat Phillips had left just yesterday with the first five hundred men to entrain at Culpepper for Manassas Junction. In normal times, this would have involved a quick march to Culpepper of no more than a day and then the rail journey just fifty miles to Manassas; they all agreed that with the chaos on the railways, which George and Daniel had seen, they were unlikely to reach Manassas Junction for several days. Paul had left a letter for his father to explain what he hoped Daniel could arrange for the rest of the local force of at least six hundred at Cotton Hall.

While the brothers were trying to tell George what they knew, Daniel had arrived and was given Paul's letter, which he opened and read, a deep frown on his forehead. Having read it through quickly and then again much more slowly, he walked across the room, ignoring his three guests and gazed fixedly out of the long window at the camp and its haze of dust and noise. He eventually turned to face the three, now silent, young men.

"It's probably best if I just read you Paul's letter," he said in a quiet, controlled voice, before turning away and walking off to be alone with his son's letter.

*"Dear Pa, I've had to rush off – Beaufort County calls. I know you're not going to be pleased with what you come across around Cotton Hall, but Nat and I took about half of the men off north as soon as we received the news that every able bodied man who loved Dixie was needed. We must have about 500 with us. They all have weapons and uniforms of some sort, but with the short notice we had, some had to make do with what they had at home. Pa – it's time for our great Confederate state to show the bloody Yankees what we're made of and give them a good hiding! We reckon we'll be in a battle any day now – somewhere near Manassas. I left a major in charge there – he's called Justin Scott – he needs to understand that you are the General of the Volunteers, so I beg you, Pa, put everything else aside and drill them until they bleed! They must march out of there no later than July 14. You can get to Culpepper OK, but try to get Scott to do anything necessary to get them on a train to Manassas Junction, whatever that takes. I will be at the army Head Quarters, wherever it is set up. God bless you, Pa.*

*"PS: You need to look after Ma and Ann-Louise. Maybe you ought to keep some men back, just in case – and keep an eye on them niggers – they don't need to know anything. Make damn sure that Jason and the others are armed and not afraid to use force to keep them in their place.*

*Your loving son, Paul. God bless Dixie!"*

Daniel looked confused by the letter and took to pacing between the window and where the others now stood, silent and unsure what to do. After two turns, he stopped in front of them.

"I should go with them, shouldn't I? I'm the ranking officer. I owe it to my men... What should I do first?"

It was Arthur who, surprisingly, took the lead now.

"Sir, I think you owe it to your family and your plantation to stand firm here. Do what Paul has asked and get that unruly mess of men down there sorted out. They obviously need discipline and a sense of duty. Use this Major Scott, but impress on him that you are in command. Maybe the time has come to put your uniform on? You've got just a few days, so go to it and then be ready here when Paul and the Volunteers return victorious."

George said immediately, "Daniel, may I offer my services as well? I have trained hundreds, if not thousands, of common soldiers in my time. Let me lend you my expertise and between the three of us, that is Major Scott and yourself as well, we can have them ready to march; I'd say by the fourteenth without a doubt."

Daniel's rather frightened expression now gradually changed to relief and he clapped George on his arm, seized his hand and shook it.

"You're right. Of course you are. That's it... Uniform!"

He hurried to the door, pulled it open and yelled, "Jacob! Jacob, come here at once!"

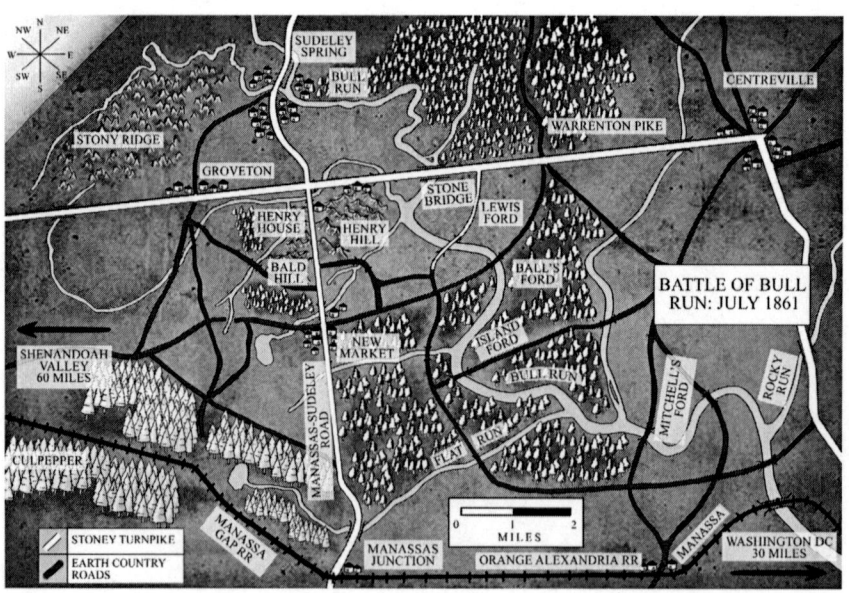

In Washington, Abraham Lincoln was watching columns of Union soldiers marching down Pennsylvania Avenue in the direction that would lead them, in less than thirty miles, out of Pennsylvania and into Confederate West Virginia. (24) Those who were there to observe the Union president at this moment would later recall that his expression was not one that reflected his pride and optimism in his men, but rather one of '*sober reflection*', perhaps even tinged with sadness. Lincoln would have seen, albeit with mingled sadness and hope, well-armed, fully uniformed Union soldiers marching with the cheerful certainty of victory to the tunes of the numerous military bands and with the sunlight glinting off their bayonets. Mounted officers rode alongside, while at the rear was an incredibly lengthy wagon train of supplies, along with numerous pieces of field artillery attached to their limbers and drawn by teams of sweating horses.

General McDowell was now in command of this army, since General Robert E Lee had declined the offer a few months ago of overall command of the Union's forces and rather vowed his loyalty to his home state; he now rode as a general in the Confederate force, one of thousands of examples of men, who had once been his associates, friends or relations, perhaps who had trained in military academies together, but who now found their loyalties torn in the decision to fight for their *country,* but that would now mean a decision as to which their country was: the Federal Union or the seceded Confederacy?

General McDowell had devised a plan for the speedy defeat of the Confederacy, which he christened the 'Anaconda Plan', named after the huge snake that slowly strangles its victim in its serpentine coils, rather than inflicting the speedy, poisonous bite of death. He was perhaps unaware that some confederate states still rallied around the Gadsden flag, depicting a coiled rattlesnake with the warning 'Do not tread on me'.

McDowell's intention was to direct the Union's several armies south and west, encircle the Confederacy's smaller army and slowly strangle it, while no doubt yelling 'Forward to Richmond!' Unfortunately for McDowell and the Union, General Beauregard, last seen pounding the small Union force at Fort Sumpter, had numerous spies in the Union and especially in Washington. Such Union plans were easily discovered and passed to Richmond. To make matters worse, the northern press seemed to have no difficulty in also establishing what McDowell's plans were and then publishing them for all to read. In the end, the commanding General's plan, now virtually public property, was rejected by President Lincoln as being likely to take far too long in the '*strangulation*' process and which would also not appeal to the public in the north, who wanted a swift, and preferably bloody, victory.

The south was, in the days around early to mid-July, equally uncertain of the future. Plans were drawn up by Generals Beauregard and Lee that President Davis warned were *'too premature'* and would require *'many alterations'* and hence no real plan existed here at all.

So it was that, by the time Paul Hayward had gathered his five hundred Beaufort County Volunteers in a semblance of order on July 18, after marching three miles from Manassas Junction to north of the Flat Run tributary of Bull Run, he was just two miles south of the very recently established Head Quarters of the Confederacy. There the Confederate commanders were in a state of confusion over the basic information needed for a battle, just as were those of the Union commanders off to their northeast.

Paul was, not surprisingly, aware that this battle would be fought in their home district of Prince William, which he hoped would make his men even more eager to whip the Yankees, who had dared invade the very homes and land of the Confederate army's families and friends.

By Saturday July 20, the Confederacy had brought about twenty-two thousand men from Richmond to a spot near the town of Manassas in West Virginia, where the small river Flat Run ran and also where beside the Bull Run river there were already three to five thousand more men gathered from elsewhere in the state of Virginia. The Union force, rather slowly making its way the thirty-one miles from Washington, was thought to have almost thirty-four thousand men and boasted another ten thousand in reserve further to the east of Manassas with a General Patterson.

Paul Hayward and his five hundred men were commanded to turn east at New Market, pass below the Confederate Headquarters and join what would become a *'formidable'* force of soldiers along the western bank of the Bull Run. However, Paul, who had no knowledge whatever of the area covered with fields in some places, woods and scrub in others, mistakenly finished up somewhat south of the intended position, at Mitchell's Ford on the Bull Run a mile south of the south-eastern end of the main Confederate line itself. There they joined two other smaller groups that rejoiced in the names of the Clinch Rifles and the Lincoln Killers on Friday (24a).

Both Paul and Nat were shocked by the confusion that they found around the ford. Many of the Confederate soldiers were in bits and pieces of uniform, some had no uniform at all, while probably a minority, many of these being part of the Beauforts, were in a complete uniform. They possessed a variety of guns, mostly a mixture of types of rifles of varying age and a few old flintlocks, but a good number with bayonets. There was no artillery nearby, although they were aware of larger units less than two miles to the northeast who did possess field guns and cannons. Paul and Nat did their best to organise their men, but they were outranked by officers in the other groups and it was a ragged line that settled down on the riverbank facing east that afternoon.

There was no question that most of the men, now on the brink of what was probably the first real fight of their lives, were scared shitless in spite of plenty of bravado, including shouts across the water of 'Come over here, Yanks, and get yer arses bloodied' and 'We'm goin' to kill you all and then that damned Abe Lincoln' among many other slanders. This was probably false courage, since so far they had neither seen nor heard a single Union soldier and visibility today was pretty good; they could see across the Bull Run, over the bushes and scrub on the other side and as far as the green fields opposite.

Paul kept looking behind them in the hope that the Beauforts, under Major Scott left at Cotton Hall, would find them before the battle started, but he remained disappointed: there was no sign of them. As the sun left the sky, campfires were lit and water boiled, useful only to those who had coffee or maybe even some meat in their knapsacks. They could never have imagined that very soon they would be under fire and desperate for any sort of water as their mouths turned to dust in the heat of battle.

# Chapter Twenty

Paul Hayward was certainly not the only Confederate officer gathered along Bull Run, who even by the next day had scant idea where the Union army was and when, or if, they would arrive where a Confederate force was waiting for them.

The Union column was, in fact, travelling at a snail's pace, party hampered by the huge, slow wagon train that was carrying their entire store of supplies, munitions and food, since nothing had been moved forward in advance. The column of Union soldiers was several miles long and could not advance any faster than the wagons for fear of having its supplies left behind.

When the head of the column left Washington, the tail was not in place or even ready to join the column on the other side of the capital city. A large number of Union soldiers had very little or no training. Many were neither hardened fighters nor prepared to march all day across country in the heat and humidity of July. The result was that groups of men stopped frequently or even lay exhausted on the ground; others broke away from the column to collect berries or to find water, of which there was little. One soldier noted in his dairy that *'the number of Union soldiers with their lips stained red or purple from berries is remarkable'*.

In both Confederate and Union armies, uniforms varied and many wore grey in the Union army and blue in the Confederate. As a result, General McDowell ordered that the union flag be displayed at frequent intervals on the march and he intended to do the same in the forthcoming battle; confusing friend with foe was likely to be a major issue when the fight was joined. (23) General Beauregard called it a *'battle of amateurs'*, but told his officers that *'we are now face to face with weapons, instead of words'*.

As the sun came up on Saturday the twentieth on the *'unordered mess'* that was the overnight camp for the Beauforts and the other two groups of Confederates at Mitchell's Ford on the Bull Run. Officers there tried to restore some order by commanding the men to tidy up their uniforms, clean and load their weapons and have bayonets at the ready. Some did as they were told, but others went down to the river for water to boil and hence fires were lit in the dim light of dawn. Paul was the only officer to send pickets across the ford to spy out the land ahead. The Lincoln Killers laughed at his order and told the Beauforts that there were 'No Yankees 'tween this little brown river and Washington'.

Paul was concerned that he had no idea where Major Scott and the rest of his force were, since surely they should be in the area by now. He was tempted to ride to the Confederate Headquarters, where he had expected them to be waiting for him. By midday, his patience ran out and he sent a junior officer to ride the two and a half miles to Manassas Junction to try to discover where they actually were. He was to hear nothing of either the messenger or Major Scott for the rest of that day.

With nothing to do, most of the force by the ford was content to sit or lie in whatever shade they could find as the day became hot and sunny again. Their only defence was in the hands of a dozen of Paul's Beaufort Volunteers now on the other side of the river.

It was late afternoon and the heat was beginning to go out of the day, when two of the pickets raced out of the scrub on the far side of the Bull Run and splashed across the ford. They were followed closely by the other ten men, all of them shouting incoherently since their comrades were too far away to understand them. As they came closer, the rest of the men could at last hear them and scrambled to their feet.

*"Them Yankees is comin'."*

*"There's hundreds just across them fields."*

*"They got guns and bayonets at the ready."*

*"We better skedaddle our arses. Right now!"*

There were about seven hundred Confederates in the area around Mitchell's ford. Some grabbed their guns at once; some just left them on the ground and ran away. Most stood looking nervously across Bull Run, while several dozen were now running away from the river. However, Paul and Ned were there before them and, to their credit, were joined by several officers from the other groups. Paul fired several shots in the air and commanded them, *"Stop now! Are you cowards frightened of a few filthy Yankees? Stop or I'll put a bullet in every deserter, God help me if I don't!"* Unsupported by the majority, the potential deserters did stop and turn back.

Officers grudgingly got them under cover on the eastern side of the ford. Fires were stamped out and bayonets fixed. Within a few minutes, the sound of an advancing force could be heard. The Confederate volunteers awaiting them were by then positioned for two or three hundred yards along their side of the river.

Officers took positions scattered among their men. *"Load and be ready to fire on command!"* was the order that passed along the line. Flashes of blue uniforms could now be distinguished ahead of them, advancing through the trees and scrub. The Confederates had the advantage of lying down and were much less visible. Quieter orders of *'Hold your fire!'* were passed.

It was clear to Paul that this was a scavenger group, probably sent ahead to find a place to cross the river. The main force would certainly come down the Warrenden Turnpike to cross the only bridge across Bull Run, which was further to the north. Groups like the one slowly coming at them, but possibly not yet aware that they were there, would be looking for ways to cross the river in order to take the Confederate line from behind.

A group of Union soldiers suddenly broke through the scrub and reeds on the far bank, upriver from the ford; many others could now be seen behind them on the eastern side of the ford. The order to *'Fire!'* was given by an officer to Paul's left. He and others now repeated the command up and down the line.

The Union soldiers reaching the river first were obviously taken by surprise and took numerous casualties from rifle fire, which was far from accurate, but the Confederates were close enough for this not to matter too much. The surprise for these Confederates, mostly still lying prone on the ground, was that their initial fear gave way to what soldiers both before and after would recognise as 'blood-lust' or the excitement of seeing bullets striking their enemies in limbs, heads and chests and bright red blood appearing on the bodies of the despised. So excited were the Confederates, although none of them had fought in a real battle before, that someone down the line screamed with delight. The scream was copied and mixed with yells. The *Rebel Yell* was quite possibly born here at Bull Run.

The Union soldiers initially received a hard blow out of the blue, but most of the force dropped down behind any cover they could find and started to return fire. It was a terrifying shock to the totally uninitiated to see the man next to him scream as a bullet drove through his chest, or the man just feet away die silently with a look of shock on his face as a hole appeared in his forehead. The haphazard exchange of fire continued for a short while, but the Union soldiers soon establish order in their ranks. Some found enough cover to keep the Confederates busy, while others were sent both upstream and down in an effort to get across the river somehow and roll up the small Confederate force, which was now beginning to take heavy losses.

Paul, along with other officers, realised that the nearest woodland they could retreat to was two or three hundred yards back from the river. Their men were effectively pinned down in almost open ground, only protected by the taller reeds and bushes in some areas. Ned took the sole decision to run, not back to the woodland but fifty yards to his left and just back from the river, where a small copse of trees surrounded closely by scrub could provide some cover. He then sprinted from there, bent almost double, behind the Confederate line upstream, a line that now showed gaps where the bodies of the dead and wounded lay. A stray Union bullet clipped his shoulder, causing him to stagger, but he carried on into the fuller cover of the wood further north and disappeared from view. Paul suspected he had almost certainly fallen.

In fact, Nat was still on his feet, but hidden from view. He worked his way back to the river close to the top end of the Confederate line. Paul did not see him again that day, but as the rifle fire continued during the late afternoon, sporadically from both sides, an officer from the Clinch Rifles, who were trying to hold their position at the far end of their line, crawled down to him.

He had to shout into the man's ear in order to be heard above the sound of gunfire.

"Your Cap'in Nat says the way at the end of the line has cover back into the tress. If we can hold them off 'till it's dark, he says we can retreat that way. We might get away with it."

Hours dragged by. Paul, looked at the clouds of smoke rising from the exploding gunpowder of the cartridges and could understand what Nat meant; how he had got a message along the line he had no idea. He pulled his watch from his jacket and saw to his surprise that it was eight pm. He could not believe that four hours had passed on this dusty and now bloody piece of riverbank, but he was also convinced that they must be running short of ammunition by now. The officer from the Clinch Rifles was still crouched next to him and he noticed that he had a neckerchief wound around his head with blood oozing through it above his right ear.

"What's your name?"

The reply was spoken hoarsely: "Jones, sir. Lieutenant Jack Jones of the Clinch Rifles."

"Lieutenant Jones, do you reckon you can make it back up the line?"

"Got here, didn't I? Easier goin' back."

"Try to get to Captain Phillips, but tell any officer you see on the way as well. Tell them to be ready to retreat in an hour. Hold on till then, but save ammunition if they can. Leave a small vanguard behind to keep up the fire and tell those soldiers to get the hell out as soon as the line has moved. We'll regroup once we get into that woodland back there. Got that?"

"Yes, sir." He tried to give a salute, which was near impossible as he tried to shelter from the fire still coming from the other bank. "I'll sure make it sir."

With that, he disappeared into the smoke and the uproar of battle around a shallow river crossing that some of them would eventually learn was called 'Mitchell's Ford' on the Bull Run River.

# Chapter Twenty-One

## July 18–21 1861: The Battle of Bull Run

The farmhouse chosen, or perhaps more realistically found by chance, was considered by General Beauregard to be suitable as the Confederate High Command Headquarters for battle at Bull Run (The Union called it *Manassas*). It was about three miles north-west of Mitchell's Ford and a mile back from the Bull Run River. The three-mile-long Confederate line on the west bank was made up of some five thousand men. On the evening of Friday July 19/20, General Beauregard was established in the farmhouse with his most senior officers, but with no General Johnston, who had, in fact, already arrived by rail at Manassas Junction and was now moving, along with his cavalry squadrons, rapidly towards the stone bridge located on the Warrenton Turnpike, stopping briefly when it was too dark to move the two final miles.

Beauregard stood with a large map of the Manassas area on a table in front of him and a group of senior commanders around the old farmhouse table. He was satisfied that his line of defence, and hopefully of eventual attack, was securely in place along the Bull Run from Ball's Ford, four miles upriver from Island Ford, to just short of the stone bridge carrying the Warrenden Turnpike across the river.

General Johnston's reserve division of eleven thousand men was being held seven miles south of the Headquarters on the other side of the Orange and Alexandria Rail Road. Johnston was supported there by General Jackson and they were ready to pour these reserves due north from Manassas, largely across-country, when advised they were needed. Communication with this and other Confederate divisions, battalions and regiments, over anything but short distances, was by horse messenger, but this was less than reliable once battle was joined. What Beauregard did not know was that Johnston was already at the stone bridge by early on the morning of Saturday 20.

To the north-east on the Confederate west bank of Bull Run, just short of the stone bridge and the Turnpike, were the Confederate batteries of artillery, facing both the Warrenden Turnpike and, in the opposite direction, the hamlet of Groveton.

Beauregard moved his hand across these positions without comment and those watching him thought it expedient to keep silent also. Eventually he looked up.

(25) "Our men are badly armed and are suffering from the inefficiency of the Quartermasters' and Commissary Departments," he announced bluntly.

A colonel on the fringe of the group started to speak, probably in defence of the slandered departments, but only got as far as; "Sir, I really must…" before he was silenced by Beauregard's glare and his quietly controlled voice.

*(25a) "I do not say that they will not do well enough when battle is joined, since they have not tired themselves nor damaged our organisation by a long march, as has the Union army."* He continued, *"I have also sent a request to the ladies of Richmond to contribute coloured scarves for the men to wear pinned to their jackets, to ensure that we can tell friend from foe."*

At that moment, a fairly young confederate officer pushed the farmhouse door open and with an expression of great urgency that could not be misunderstood, stepped directly up to the table. He was dressed in a uniform of which very few around the table, if any, had seen the like before: his grey cape was lined in red, across his jacket was a wide yellow sash and on his head a cocked hat with an ostrich plume in it; in his button hole was a red flower. He saluted Beauregard and appeared breathless when he spoke.

"My apologies, sir, for this unexpected intrusion. I am Lieutenant Colonel James Stuart and I come with a message from General Johnston. General McDowell and what is said to be a large Union force is only twenty miles to our northeast, but is travelling towards us at a snail's pace. Our spy network in Washington is proving most worthwhile and we do not expect them to show their faces this side of Centreville before tomorrow. General Johnston sends his greeting and expects to be at the stone bridge, with his cavalry by then, which is why he sent me post haste with *my* cavalry unit."

"That is good news; colonel and General Johnston's presence, as well as his men, will be very welcome."

(26) James Stuart, known to those who fought with him as Jeb Stuart, spoke again quickly.

"There is other news I bring, sir

It concerns *Brigadier General Jackson, who was at Harper's Ferry just two weeks ago. When he arrived there, he found no Union force, but just officials of the Baltimore and Ohio Railroad in charge of large numbers of Union locomotives and rail cars. General Jackson had a considerable force with him and could not be prevented from confiscating all the wheeled vehicles he could get his hands on."* Shouts of pleasure at that news came from most officers in the room. *"He actually took over forty locomotives and nearly three hundred railcars, but…"* which word stopped further cheering, *"most of these finished up wrecked in the struggle and either driven or thrown into the river."* No cheers now, just a glum silence. *"However, he was able to haul fourteen locomotives and just a few boxcars overland using horses. They are now at Strasburg on the Manassas Gap Railroad. They should be here within forty-eight hours, ready to operate under your command."*

"Thank you for your excellent news, Lieutenant Colonel Stuart. I suggest you go and organise your cavalry to be ready for battle, which we believe will erupt here within the next two days. Although a skirmish has been reported at Mitchell's Ford; to our south, but no further news has yet arrived." Beauregard's hand moved to cover the area. "Also our forward pickets some way forward along the turnpike are hearing from our men dressed as farmers further forward, that McDowell and his straggling column are still at least two days away from joining a fight here."

Another Confederate colonel, who had been studying the map closely, was moving his finger slowly down the turnpike, through Fairfax Court House and up what was indicated as a climb to Centreville. From there the road dropped down into the valley of the Bull Run and eventually to the stone bridge over the river.

With his finger still on Centreville, he then asked, "Do we have any estimate of the size of the Union army that must by now be somewhere between Fairfax and Centreville?" Beauregard, looked around his dozen or so officers, as if for an accurate answer; there was none.

"Colonel…er?"

"Graves, sir," was the reply.

"Well, Colonel Graves, we have no accurate measurement of an army that we have never seen and that has been assembled in Washington very quickly and marched very slowly. We have five thousand men drawn up along the Bull

Run for six or so miles, rested, fed and watered and ready for a fight. We have reinforcements on their way from both south and northeast. We *suspect*, and I emphasise that word, that our previously fraternal enemy may have a slightly larger force, but they will be exhausted, hungry, thirsty and hence less prepared than we are for the fight. I hope that answers your question sir."

Colonel Graves felt he had somehow been reprimanded and said no more.

Friday July 19 rolled into Saturday July 20 with no further reports of any action or movement of the enemy. However, unknown to the Confederate generals in the Head Quarters, the force of volunteers from Virginia's Beaufort County, Clinch Rifles and Lincoln Killers now numbering over eight hundred, had already left Mitchell's Ford and joined the Confederate line along the bank of Bull Run. They had left behind their dead at Mitchell's Ford, hoping that the walking wounded would eventually make their way north and west to join the rest of Confederate army nearer Bull Run. They were counting themselves fortunate that they had not been pursued by the Union skirmishers as they retreated. By Saturday morning, they had joined the tail end of the Confederate line along the river, although they discovered only meagre rations among the soldiers already there and they were not prepared to share.

The messenger that Paul Hayward had sent to Confederate Headquarters had obviously not been able to find the place and hence no senior officer had news of Major Phillips or Hayward and the remainder of the Beaufort Volunteers.

The rest of the group from Mitchell's Ford were relieved to be able to rest in the company of the large confederate army along the river and from there gazed at the distant white roadway cutting down the far hill, part of the quiet, green countryside.

Most were unaware that Centreville lay over the hill out of sight, but, believing that a 'massive' Union army was coming over that crest at any time, fear was the only emotion at the forefront of their minds. With nothing to do now that the lucky escape from the ford for many of their number was over, imaginations in the Beauforts ran riot: images of their own death and that of their comrades, as artillery fire could be imagined decimating their ranks; the crackle and roar of thousands of muskets and rifles sending mini balls and bullets into the bodies of those now quietly waiting in the sunshine within sight of the calm, brown waters of the river.

Daniel Hayward, to his overwhelming frustration, knew nothing of what was happening a few miles north of the town of Manassas. He felt trapped at Cotton Hall with nothing to do, with no information about his son and with apparently now no means of getting any news.

"For Christ's sake! Why am I tortured like this? The fucking telegraph down, my son probably lying dead on some field... the bodies of the valiant Beauforts being picked over by some damned Yankees and I stand here completely helpless," he screamed to the wind now rising across the river, as he stood at the front of his veranda at Cotton Hall, Daniel turned and began to beat his head against the wall. His three English guests heard his shouts and came running out through the doors of the mansion. They stopped short of a pathetic figure, now with blood dripping down his face, mingled with the tears he was shedding. Arthur moved quietly and slowly forward, putting a gentle hand on his shoulder and turning him slowly around. Daniel looked years older than he had just that morning, now bent and desperately trying to find a kerchief; Arthur quickly supplied his own.

"Come and sit down, sir. Here, let me just mop those scratches."

Ernest and George joined them once Daniel had collapsed into a cane chair, his head in his hands. He looked up as the three sat down beside him.

"I understand how awful this must be for you sir," George said in a firm, sensible and unemotional voice, "but I think you know full well that there has not yet been enough time for any fighting even to begin and it may not even happen at all."

Daniel waved his arms as if swatting mosquitos, while whispering, "No, no, no..." continuously. George, however, was not to be put off.

"You know that I am a soldier and have been for almost as long as I can remember. I have seen more battles and more bloodshed of good men than I want to remember. Believe me, I know how these great trials of soldiers of all nations are conducted. Paul and his men will so far undoubtedly not be close to battle. Both parties will be humming and hawing about who is where, when their reserves might arrive, where the enemy may be and no one knows any of that. I reckon the Union will still be thinking about what to do once they hear of your boys being on the march. I would not be surprised to learn in a few days' time that Lincoln's men never even left Washington."

George's calm words seemed to reassure Daniel, who was now sitting up and mopping at the bruise now showing on his forehead, still oozing a little blood. They all lapsed into a melancholy silence in spite of George's attempt to find some comfort. A couple of hundred yards in front on the mansion the camp was now a relatively peaceful place. The scars of doused fires were obvious, as well as occupied tents still standing with others piled up awaiting news of a possible hurried move. A shortened horse line and the voices of the fifty or so men left behind to guard the plantation gave the impression of a place holding its breath; no news was the worry on all minds. The telegraph at Culpepper had been reported as out of action by a sergeant who had ridden over yesterday morning to pick up any messages. The three young men on the veranda were secretly just as worried as Daniel, but for his sake had tried for the past few days not to show it.

Last night, after everyone had finally decided there was no point in waiting up any longer, they had met in George's room to discuss what they should do now. "We're sitting here with no idea what is happening at Manassas – if anything. For all we know the Union army has blasted its way through there and is heading this way," Ernest could not help allowing his worries to surface.

"We're sitting ducks just waiting here. We should move out now and go south. We've got fifty or so men who can keep us safe…"

George stopped him. "That's coward's talk and, not only that, but completely unreasoned. You don't know—"

Ernest, who had been sitting on a bed, jumped up and grabbed George by his shirt front. "Who the hell are you calling a coward? You know nothing more than we do, mister soldier! You bloody hypocrite!"

George, standing nearly six inches taller, forced his right arm under Ernest's chin and flicked him away as if he were a fly. Ernest staggered back and fell to the floor. If his look focussed on George could have killed, the captain would have died on the spot.

Arthur eventually calmed them down and returned them to what had started out as an attempt to decide what they should do now that war seemed to be imminent and practically on their doorstep. Inevitably, it was George who was experienced enough to bring common sense to bear. He outlined what he suspected the situation might be at Manassas, after which he went on, as if never interrupted …

"…*and* I think we should remember what we were actually sent here to do: to report on the state of the south, the Confederacy, as we see it and, most important, how the export of cotton is being forcibly strangled, which we have already reported via the telegraph to London, or so we at least hope it has already been telegraphed. Now we have to report on what the outbreak of a civil war will mean for the south and if the export of our desperately needed cotton could possibly be resumed. The answer to that will now lie on battlefields and the movement of great armies. We have to see this for ourselves. We have no choice."

"I hate to say it, but I agree," Arthur spoke immediately. "I agree we have no choice. We have sworn to carry out this mission as a patriotic duty. Ernest and I are not, God knows, soldiers as you are, but the future of our own family, as well as our country, will be decided on *this* side of the Atlantic."

Ernest did not say a word, but slumped back on the bed, his eyes on the floor.

"What do you think, Ernest?" Arthur asked.

Ernest looked at his younger brother, a look that was both unhappy and questioning and let a pause develop, which eventually seemed to create the will to speak more calmly.

"I have a wife at home, who has just lost another child. I wish I were at home now and not here in this awful place…but I am realistic enough to know that cannot be… So I will follow you, admittedly without much enthusiasm. I suppose I will do my best not to let my country down."

By the time they sat with Daniel the next morning, trying to console him, their decision had been made: they would travel north towards Manassas immediately and continue with the mission they had been set and determined to advise Daniel, as strongly as they could, to be prepared to move south if things looked likely to turn against the Confederacy.

They would try to persuade him that in the meantime he should utilise the soldiers he had at Cotton Hall to take on picket duty around the plantation. They also asked that he ordered someone to ride to Culpepper daily to see if the telegraph was working. George's real concern, not expressed to anyone, was that there might already be some sort of Union action at Manassas Junction that had cut the telegraph lines.

The three of them left Cotton Hall at midday, July 18, to ride to Culpepper and hoped to find passage on a train to Manassas from there. They were loath to leave Daniel with no real guaranteed support, but agreed they had no choice. They took all the supplies they could manage and a soldier from the camp to bring their horses back to the plantation.

It was Arthur who, before they left, quietly took Daniel aside and tried to warn him to consider carefully what he proposed to do with the slaves if a Union force were reported to be moving their way. Such a situation would be very dangerous for him and the family and Arthur expressed his heart felt hope that he would immediately free every slave at such a moment. Not surprisingly, he received no response, other than a shrug.

As the small party crossed the river and started up the slope beyond, every one of the trio was fearful of what the next few days, and very likely the next few months, would bring and whether they would live to take a ship back to Liverpool and home.

# Chapter Twenty-Two

**Friday July 19 1861**

The two brothers, along with Captain George Fitzwilliam, arrived at Manassas Junction on Friday afternoon, July 19 and found the place in uproar; or was it simply ordered chaos? They had followed another train into the station, very much like the one they had managed to squeeze on board, but this one was filled with hundreds of Confederate soldiers. Like the Beauforts they had seen at the camp at Cotton Hall. These young farm hands were dressed in a medley of uniforms, but most had similar brightly coloured kerchiefs pinned to their belts or jackets. On the journey, they had learned that the men were in various regiments that made up the battalion commanded by a General Jackson. As the Envoys now stood in the dust and noise of the rail yard and its surrounding trampled fields, they were impressed by the sight of so many thousands of armed men being gathered into columns by officers.

George had pushed his way through the throng to speak to an officer he guessed was a captain like himself. When he returned, he had to shout to make himself heard.

"I have no idea how the hell we are going to get anywhere near where that officer told me there's expected to be a battle. Apparently, it's all several miles up some river he called the Bull Run."

Ernest, coughing and then spitting onto the ground as dust swirled into his mouth, had, like his companions, absolutely no idea even in which direction this battle might be. His voice was still roughened by the grit still in his mouth. "Let's get out of this mass of bodies and try to discover what's happening."

Following Ernest, they began to make their desperately slow way towards the nearest piece of farmland just west of the Manassas road that seemed less crammed with men, many of whom they had already noticed, as they pushed their way forward, were closer in age to boys than men. Ernest reckoned that the enormous crowd of Confederates on the eastern side of the road must be covering fields for all of ten acres. As they looked back, they observed that what had at the start been a ragged mass of soldiers was now transforming into orderly regiments as they were corralled into columns, facing towards what George's compass indicated was the north-east.

Another few hundred yards and they found themselves on a country road, just as dusty as Manassas Junction, but with far fewer soldiers, most of whom were sitting on the banks along the side of the road or in adjoining fields. By now, evening was coming on and dark clouds had blotted out the sun, which to their relief caused the temperature to drop, but might well promise rain.

"We aren't going to be able to walk to Bull Run tonight, although these men seem to think this road will lead there eventually," said George, who had again assumed the role of decision maker, but to which neither Ernest nor Arthur now bothered to object. They both felt that in the face of a possible battle, he would be the one most likely to guide them away from life threatening danger, or so at least they hoped.

"I suggest we need to find somewhere to shelter for tonight, since it looks like it will rain fairly soon," George continued. "We'll walk for the next hour or so and then look for a barn or some such where we can shelter. If not, we'll just have to sleep under a hedge and it wouldn't be the first time I've had to do that when waiting for a battle to start, I can assure you."

Ernest started to protest, uselessly since George was already out of earshot, accompanied by Arthur, both already disappearing towards the next bend. Over an hour later, it was getting really dark under threatening skies. By the time they spotted a partly collapsed barn in a field about a hundred yards off the road, the rain had begun to fall. Ernest had ceased any attempt to complain and joined the others as they carefully approached the ancient building.

The end wall facing towards the road had entirely collapsed, along with part of the roof that now lay on the floor in piles of stone and tiles covered by tufts of grass and weeds. Neither brother stood in George's way as he slowly worked his way forward into the building under what was left of the roof. Arthur and Ernest did their best to remain concealed as they watched him disappear into the gloom. Minutes later, he was back to assure them that it was safe to move into whatever cover they could find, as the persistent rain now fell. Darkness proper quickly began to blot out the landscape around them, as did much heavier rain that followed. With difficulty, they managed to find a small area in the far corner that was more or less dry. All they had with them was what was left in two water flasks, since they had already eaten their meagre meal, which had been packed at Cotton Hall. Ernest again led the complaints and groans as water dripped through holes in the roof, but eventually they curled up on what must have been straw a very long while ago and, to their surprise, did eventually manage to get some short bursts of sleep as the hours of darkness passed.

Ernest was woken by sunlight shining through the gaps in the roof and consulting his pocket watch, found it was just after five in the morning. He could see it was going to be a really sunny Sunday and the words that flashed through his mind were: '*A fine day for killing*'.

By the time the three young men, who had started this journey looking fairly smart and well groomed, joined the road again, they looked haggard and exhausted, sporting two day's growth of beards and desperate for a drink of any sort. To make it worse, they had found it hard to get their aching joints moving once they were awake. By now, it was well into the morning of Sunday July 21.

They had been on the road for no more than half an hour when they heard the crunch of waggon wheels (27) approaching rapidly from behind, accompanied by loud voices and choruses of laughter. As they stood aside, anticipating a military convoy, what they actually saw was the first of a straggling, extensive group of carriages stretching out of sight and with many more to be heard beyond the bend. The stunned Envoys were forced off the road by the carriages, all of them clearly belonging to wealthy people and filled with finely dressed southern ladies and gentlemen. The gentlemen generally were wearing top hats and suits suitable for a holiday morning, while the ladies were fashionably clad in pale summer dresses, with equally fashionable hats and parasols to protect themselves from the sun that was now growing hot.

As several more open carriages passed the trio who, to the well to do passengers, must have appeared to be rough workmen, many of the gentlemen whooped a greeting and toasted them with glasses held high; the ladies smiled and waved. There seemed now to be at least twenty such carriages and broughams that had passed them and disappeared in a cloud of dust.

"What in God's name was all that about?" shouted Ernest over the noise of the last departing carriage, leaving them huddled against the bankside. However, before they could collect their astonished wits, another similar group could be heard and then swept around the bend. Unlike the first instalment of what seemed to be wealth totally out of place, the leading carriage of this group slowed and stopped a few yards beyond the three Englishmen. Others behind were then forced to do the same, which caused an uproar among coachmen and gentlemen drivers hauling on the reins and causing at least one splendid white horse to rear, which in turn resulted in the screams of the ladies on board.

One of the gentlemen in the first open brougham stood up and raised his hat in greeting to the English trio.

"My word, sirs, you look a sorry sight, I must say. My sister here," he indicated a middle-aged matron dressed in purple with a face of similar colour as she perspired under her parasol, "just warned us all that you might be Union spies, dressed up to look like workmen! But I can see now that you're perhaps even gentlemen yourselves, maybe fallen on hard times? Might that be the case?"

He then turned and told one of the other two gentlemen on board to pour a glass of champagne for each of these poor wayfarers. The stunned Englishmen in the road had not yet found suitable words that could fit this extremely unworldly situation, but one or two gentlemen on board began to step down into the road and more glasses of champagne were produced. For the three Envoys, who had not drunk anything since their water canteens had been emptied several hours earlier, champagne was perhaps not the best drink to be given now, but all three swallowed the first glass eagerly and happily accepted another.

Eventually, Arthur felt able to ask, "What in heaven's name are you all doing here? We've been told there may be a battle very soon up ahead a few miles. You should turn around at once and get back to safety as quickly as you can."

A group of some dozen gentlemen were now gathered around them and laughed delightedly.

"You, sir, I reckon to be an Englishman, unless I am much mistaken," said one of the group dressed in morning trousers, but with a Confederate officer's jacket. There followed cries of 'You bet!' and 'God save the Queen' from the others, who had evidently been enjoying the alcohol for several hours, secured in hampers strapped to the rear of the carriages.

George, in his best English officer's voice, now felt the need to respond, although he was certain he must, look ridiculous, as if a part of a theatrical production, rather than standing on a dusty roadside in West Virginia as a bloody battle threatened this side of the horizon.

"We are, indeed Englishmen, sir. I am an officer in Her Majesty's Royal Hussars and these gentlemen are important businessmen from the cotton mills in England."

This was immediately met with woops of congratulation and hands had to be shaken with the growing number of civilians on the Manassas to Sudely Road. Since there was now a substantial blockage of carriages stretching back for some distance, although no one would have been so rude as to object to this, the three Envoys were invited to join the leading carriages, which would apparently whisk them towards the Bull Run.

Once the now rather large gathering of southern gentry was on the move again, George, who was with Arthur in a carriage just back from the front of the party now advancing on Bull Run, asked whether they were really intending to reach Bull Run in order to see a battle. He added that he had observed this phenomenon in one or two battles in Europe that he had fought in, but he had no idea it could happen here, where it seemed to him that brother could well be fighting brother, as the appreciative audience watched.

A Senator in his carriage, which was particularly well-appointed with two coachmen up front and two footmen riding on the back, tried to put George straight on this matter.

"Well, sir, I have no knowledge of what happens way over there in Europe, but we, as loyal sons of Dixie and Confederates to the core, agreed we could not allow our brave boys to go out and kill them Yankees without showing them our support. We aim to be there today, or maybe tomorrow, to cheer them on; yes sir!" He then dropped his voice to a conspiratorial whisper, "Naturally, we shall ensure that the ladies do not see the actual bloodshed, but most of that will be out of sight as the damned Union cowards run away with their tails between their legs, as I'm certain sure will be the case!"

Ernest looked at his brother, possibly hoping he might offer a suitable rejoinder, but one glance at Arthur's disgusted expression assured him that he alone must bear the burden.

"May I ask then, how you know that there will be a battle at all at this Bull Run River? We have only heard stories and rumours of the start of a war and it sure doesn't look to be near here."

The Senator, for West Virginia, as George now learned he was, produced a bottle of brandy and filled the captain's empty glass.

"Your health, sir," he paused, as they both appreciated what was a fine French brandy. He then continued his instruction to George.

"As a Senator in Jeff Davis's Confederate government, you may be assured that I am privy to the most up to date information. If you intend also to watch this fight, you will see the first serious blow that we in the south will strike against the dictator Lincoln. We already shocked them at Charleston, but we were magnanimous to them there so they had a chance to walk away from what would have been a damned mighty beating! Mark my words, this battle will drive the Yankees back to Washington and then sweep them into the sea from there. Our boys will be," a quick glance at the ladies and a more hushed voice, "up their arses as we beat them back, as they so well deserve. Then they can surrender and apologise for being so bloody false and pretending to be superior to the gentlemen and ladies of the old south!"

This speech, and a few more shared glasses of what seemed to be an endless supply of wine and brandy, saw the cavalcade pass through New Market, where locals who had not seen any need to evacuate the town cheered them to the echo. A mile or so further on, to their right they could then catch sight of a large farmhouse on land that led down into a small valley, which some, like the Senator, were pleased to inform anyone who would listen, was indeed the valley of the Bull Run River. It seemed by unspoken agreement that they all selected this green and gently sloping ground as the site for their picnics and watch the fun..

There were already numerous carriages, broughams and gigs, as well as tethered horses, now scattered across the open landscape when these additional members of the southern audience arrived. The new arrivals began to direct their servants to find suitable spots for elaborate picnics that also ensured a clear view of Bull Run in the distance and the land around. Blankets were spread; the more ostentatious had chairs unloaded, while others remained in their carriages for a better view from a slightly elevated position. It resembled nothing so much as a Fourth of July picnic, with happy voices, corks popping and splendid fare being laid out.

Gentlemen equipped with field glasses looking to the east saw woodland across the view in the north, but could just pick out the profiles of batteries of artillery there. To the east, in front of them across fields with a few stands of woodland, was the faint line of the Bull Run River and the sight in the far distance of tiny figures, being part of what must be thousands upon thousands of Confederate soldiers. It was, all agreed, a perfect spot to enjoy the spectacle of a real battle, almost certainly never seen before by any of the spectators, while feeling safe behind the great army of '*our boys*' down there in the distance. As the morning began to grow hotter, the silver calls of bugles could be heard and the galloping of cavalry moving towards what the gentlemen assured their ladies was to be the battlefield.

# Chapter Twenty-Three

**Saturday July 20 1861**

The picnickers, happy and confident (27) with both the alcohol and cold cuts, as well as extravagant salads they were enjoying with the righteous self-assurance that they were about to see at first hand the historical sight of the now hated army of Abe Lincoln's Union being slaughtered in front of their very eyes, while observing those who managed to survive running for the hills like the cowards they were; or so their hearts assured them. What they could not see were the regiments of McDowell's Federal army, those at least in the first two miles formed up into compact military columns, slowly advancing down the road from Centreville, bayonets reflecting the sunshine, just a couple of miles from the other side of the Bull Run. They could not yet hear the sound of the many bands accompanying the Union fighting force, blaring out popular marching tunes. (28) One Union soldier looking up the hill was to describe the great column as: '*Like a bristling monster lifting itself by a slow, wavy motion*'.

The men on the march were confident, well turned out and well-armed, bragging of the death and destruction they would bring to the 'Dixie lovers' today. Full of patriotism and pride, they looked forward to bringing back souvenirs to show their families at home: Confederate buttons and caps, or maybe even an ear or a scalp from one of the unholy enemy(29) It was only after the battle was over that one surviving Union soldier, named Virgil Chestnut, remembered that before he left home to join the army, his wife, Mary, had prayed, "*This is our first ever battle summer; please God, it is our first and our last.*" A hope that was doomed to be very far from the truth.

General McDowell had already put the first part of his plan of action into force the day before, by sending a small force to attack the fords on the lower Bull Run and so to persuade General Beauregard and the other Confederate generals that he was going to attack there. As Paul Hayward had already discovered in the spilled blood of so many of his men, this was a feint and the Union force faded away once they had killed dozens and scared the rest of those untried Dixie boys half to death.

What McDowell actually intended was to push his main force north and east of the river, cross the Warrenton Pike, but not attempt to take the stone bridge to cross the river, which he believed the Rebels had mined. He had no intention of a head-on attack, but would come around behind them from the north at Sudely Springs. That would leave the bulk of their army stranded along the Bull Run, waiting for an attack that would never come.

A South Carolina colonel, Nathan Evans was on the Confederate side of the bridge across Bull Run with just eleven hundred men in two small regiments and some cavalry. If McDowell's plan worked then Evans, or Shanks as his friends knew him, would face several thousand Union troops alone.

Meanwhile, at the Confederate farmhouse headquarters Beauregard was faced with the arrival of General Joe Johnston, who outranked him and now took over command. Johnston had outstripped McDowell and reached the stone bridge an hour or two before the Union's advance columns. His small force was dispatched towards Groveton, while the General rode southeast to the Confederate headquarters.

Johnston had brought with him that day, but now split off on his southern flank, General Thomas Jackson and his large force of reserves, which would assemble close to Manassas Junction and await the call to join the fray.

The Confederate headquarters, was already in a state of confusion, partly caused by the change of leadership, but also by the muddled and ill conveyed orders to several regiments being manoeuvred either late in reaching their planned destination or even, in some cases, marched to the wrong point of the compass before the first shot was fired.

The main Union force, that had looked so spectacular as it marched through Centreville then fell once more into the ill-discipline of their march from Washington; men started to straggle, to stop for water or berries, or maybe even as fear struck them once they cleared Centreville and looked down the long slope from their developing camp towards what would be the battlefield. The march became slow and disjointed. At the head of the giant column were four regiments from New England, commanded by Colonel Burnside, accompanied by the governor of Rhode Island, who had assured Burnside that

215

it was natural for one of his importance to be with his troops to encourage them. However, it was not to be the men of the Union column who fired the first shots that started the real war that day.

Union General Tyler had earlier moved his small battalion of men and their few cannons away from the general advance and west towards the Bull Run River. They met no opposition in the fields below the stone bridge and were able to set up their artillery with the intention of blasting the unsuspecting Rebels, now half a mile across the water. The intended surprise cannonade did, in fact, turn out to be a rather tame affair, resulting in no casualties, but simply warning the Confederate line to be ready for a genuine attack from beyond the far bank.

Confederate Captain Alexander, positioned well north of the stone bridge (30), was woken from just an hour's sleep by a few shells that landed near the tents of his men. His own tent suffered holes where the shrapnel tore the canvas. Alexander was so incensed that he sent a signal to Colonel Nathan Evans, closer to the bridge, warning him that he might become the victim of a Union move to outflank him. Evans reacted by moving a detachment of men and two field guns north of the turnpike facing east and was ready and waiting for any serious Union attempt to outflank his Dixie boys.

As the Union column came into sight, advancing down the turnpike from Centreville, crossing the small bridge across the Cub Run, a tributary of Bull Run to the east, Captain Alexander gave the order to open fire. After what had been several minor skirmishes on that hot Saturday and Sunday, the real war had now eventually burst into life.

The thirty-four thousand men of the Union army had marched in not the most disciplined order from Washington and the Shenandoah Valley, with many groups of men having deserted their columns on the way to find food and drink, but most had eventually been hounded back into line. The army had been on their feet for over ten hours through that morning and the previous night and were by now seriously tired and hungry.

Once the head of the column from Washington could see down into the Bull Run Valley, they felt the shock of observing their enemy in large numbers both beyond the river, but also the batteries of artillery beyond that. They were ordered into line abreast, two ranks deep and four regiments wide. This attempt at order turned out to be both haphazard and slow.

The Rebels under Nathan Evans's command opened fire, as did most of the eight thousand on the Confederate far bank of Bull Run. A hail of bullets made a horrifying whistling noise, at first over the heads of the men at the front of the blue clad line, but then they quickly began to find their targets in the bodies of horrified Union soldiers, who were still looking in disbelief at the Rebs now so close to them.

The Union front lines lurched forward to lie flat on the grass and returned fire from there. Shells from the Confederate batteries, commanded by Captains Pickett and Griffin, began to find their marks also. Many of General McDowell's men found short-lived shelter behind haystacks and wooden barns, but the artillery quickly found accurate distances and the fields were soon covered in swirling dried grass and wooden smithereens. The Rebel rifle and musket fire filled the air around the Union men like the screaming of banshees and within half an hour, the battlefield had erupted into a picture of hell on earth as shot and shell hammered the Union force. However, the Confederates at last also began to receive the blows of death and destruction with equal viciousness.

Huge clouds of smoke and dust began to fill the sky as McDowell's Union army struggled to fight its way towards the rear, the north, of the Rebel's strong position beyond the river. The Confederate commanders, Generals Beauregard and Johnston, actually still on the northern battlefield, dispatched regiments to move north across the turnpike to meet what they realised by now was a Union move to head north and then west to attack them on two fronts: directly down the turnpike and across the stone bridge, but also to make the one hundred and eighty degree turn and come at them from the north as well.

McDowell himself had a force of some ten thousand, commanded by General Sherman, on its way directly from Maryland to the north to support the bulk of the numerous regiments that would avoid the stone bridge and swing north and west, although McDowell himself maintained his command from near the rear, rather than at the front where some might have expected to find him.

Communication was, a few hours into the battle, becoming either chaotic or impossible. Large numbers of brigades and regiments were on the move. The rail fences of farms proved more of an obstacle than anyone could have expected. Many Union soldiers died simply trying to cross them and either falling to break bones, even necks or, as they climbed over the fences, presenting easy targets for the Confederate sharpshooters.

McDowell, along with the rest of the Union command some distance to the west, had no idea that a very large Confederate force of reinforcements, under the command of General Jackson, was already halfway to Bull Run from their positions at Manassas Junction and the railhead a mile beyond that on the way to Alexandria. [*This was the first time that United States armies would use railways for the transport of soldiers and the speed of movement confused many officers on both sides, who had previously moved their men on foot or in horse-drawn waggons.*]

Jackson's two-pronged Confederate advance marched easily up the valley between the Bull Run and New Market across reasonably flat fields and farms; General Johnston lead one prong, comprising the cavalry, north and well in advance of Jackson's infantry, the other prong passing Confederate HQ. They would soon halt behind the Confederate batteries facing their weapons towards the Union advance across the turnpike, west of the stone bridge. Here the rebels were ready to take on the Union army, which would concentrate virtually its whole force on the north and not across the Bull Run.

What was, by early afternoon, a very substantial group of spectators just north of New Market, had spread their picnics on the grass of fields around half a mile off the road and somewhat east of the Confederate headquarters. They had been enjoying the sights of distant action nearly two miles away along the Bull Run and, beyond that in the far distance more difficult to distinguish fields and woods around the turnpike. There were frequent cheers from the gentlemen and gasps from ladies as they shielded their eyes whenever they saw and heard progressively more frequent rifle and musket fire and the spurts of smoke that now made a haze along the river. To louder gasps, that interrupted the even the most hardened in enjoying their meal, they saw shells exploding over two miles to the north-east, near what they surmised to be the Warrenton Turnpike. The confused noise of battle was far enough away not to unsettle them, but the excitement was palpable. Many gentlemen were obliged to assure the more fragile ladies that they were quite safe with them and they only had to look to the distant sights and sounds to realise that their boys were already mercilessly thrashing the Yankees.

Unfortunately for these cultured southern gentry, the self-satisfaction was not to last. By the hottest part of the afternoon, with the battle still raging to the north and east, but at a '*safe*' distance, their attention was drawn, not north, but south. There was a rise in the ground in that direction, not quite enough to be called a hill. A noise that was almost like the sound of a roaring river in the distance, which was growing louder, while most of the spectators now faced that way with some concern, but no idea what they were hearing. Servants were sent to climb up on carriages to see if anything could be seen. As the noise grew louder, a coachman perched on the top of one coach shouted that there were '*soldiers*' coming over the rise to the southeast. In a few minutes, all the gentlemen were on their feet, while most ladies were either reduced to screams muffled in kerchiefs or hurrying as best they could to their carriages.

At first, some were able to distinguish the head of a column of marching men possibly in grey, but it couldn't, please God, possibly be blue, could it?

The force, of whatever colour, could be distinguished as twenty or thirty abreast and was now steadily advancing down the slope about a mile away. What added to the feeling of panic amongst the spectators was not only the sight but, frightening as that was, the suspicion of another, slightly narrower, column that was also heading it seemed directly towards where they had, until very recently, been enjoying an afternoon of excitement, enhanced by a rich meal and fine wines.

What these well-heeled citizens had not yet realised was that what they were actually seeing were the two prongs of the Confederate reserve force commanded by General Jackson. The column, churning up a cloud of dust as they advanced, was now less than a mile away and moving quickly. Panic overtaking a large and unprepared crowd is a dangerous state of affairs and a terrifying thing to observe.

Meanwhile, on the edge of the field closest to the road, Ernest, and even Arthur, had been enjoying the delightful generosity of the southern gentry and were starting, with the help of a great many glasses of wine, to forget there was a battle going on not more than a couple of miles away. George, although fascinated by what might seem to be an illusion of a picnic in the midst of battle, was by now well aware of their precarious position. He moved closer to Ernest and Arthur and, in a quiet voice told them, in no uncertain terms, that it was time to move. Arthur wanted to warn those around him, but George was insistent that would cause panic and they needed to be on their way before that happened, as it surely would. They had told the coach in which they had driven them from Manassas Junction, to wait further along the road edge and they were much relieved, once they got close enough, to see that it was still there.

George told the coachman to drive them north and take the first turning he saw on the left, that being to the west and away from the battle raging ahead in the north and east. Ernest, shocked by this, shouted that they must go south, away from this 'field of hell on earth'. George turned around, his face only inches from Ernest.

"I know what I'm doing! I have commanded a division in just this situation and you can trust me when I say that, as the battle moves towards its height, you want to be close to the winning side. So close your mouth and get in the coach!"

Since George gave him less than a minute to make up his mind, Ernest grudgingly complied, after which George yelled to the coachman to do as he had commanded. Ernest muttered to himself about the chaos of the one-time picnic and the coach set off north. They drove along it for maybe a couple of miles before George gave the order to stop. The sound of battle was much quieter here and there was no sign of soldiers of either colour nearby.

On the picnic site itself the screams of the sensitive, and generally spoiled, ladies grew louder with every minute. Gentlemen were shouting confusing commands to get their women into carriages and servants to hurry and pack up the picnics, while others were ordered on pain of death to get horses into the shafts to take them away from the nightmare that was almost upon them. Unseemly sights now followed, where some gentlemen, who seemed to have abandoned that title, forced their way into any convenient transport and tried to thrash the horses to get back to the road faster than was actually possible. Many ladies, now badly dishevelled, hatless and with tears of fear and frustration running down their cheeks, stood helpless as their carriages disappeared without them. Many of these conveyances, however, either under the command of a more gallant gentleman or, in some cases, with just a coachman, were observed pulling any ladies nearby into their carriages, which were driven at such speed and with such a state of fear, that many either crashed into each other or caused others to be flung over, with their passengers spilling onto the ground.

There were voices, impossible now to hear clearly, shouting that the soldiers, only about half a mile away, were 'Our boys!', but since they were making no attempt to alter course, this was of no consolation. Some carriages had now made it as far as the road and were racing away in more clouds of dust towards Manassas; they were the lucky ones.

The front of the Confederate column was heading unwaveringly towards the melee of overturned coaches, screaming horses thrashing about horribly injured, trapped in the shafts, and men and women running aimlessly in all directions. Many bodies were now lying on the ground, whether alive or dead being unknown. No one suffering in the cloud of dust that had once been a peaceful picnic could have had any idea whether the column would simply march over them or, by some divine intervention, avoid them.

In fact, officers at the head of the column had eventually realised the danger to their men was more significant than the safety a group of insane civilians. They were under half a mile away when orders were shouted and, supported by bugle calls, almost at the last minute the column, which had clearly been drilled sufficiently on obedience to a command, marched sharply to their right and, having then narrowly avoided the mass of civilians, horses and carriages, renewed their march in a north-easterly direction. It was unlikely that anyone still caught up in the disaster was really aware of just how close they all came to being trampled to death underfoot. The soldiers, who were able to see the remains of a now destroyed picnic, on the whole simply laughed at their plight, although some kind souls did have the charity to look shocked at the scene of devastation they were passing.

North of the turnpike the Confederate battery, which Evans had now rushed from its original position facing the Union regiments across the stone bridge, was now joined by other batteries commanded by Colonel Bartow and Major General Bee However, at the same time the wing of one-half of the Union army commanded by General Sherman was arriving from Shenandoah. Sherman, ignoring his late arrival, was intent on out-manoeuvring the Confederates and moved south towards the turnpike as fast as he could, supposing he could surprise the Rebels by hitting them from the rear.

However, he was the one to be surprised. The Confederate batteries that he had not realised were now in front of him were, shockingly, now facing his way and began to pound his advance. To add to that unknown factor came the roar of shells starting to explode on his advance party from their rear as well as ahead: Colonels Evans and Bartow, also General Bee, had already set up firing positions there and opened fire on him from behind, to the north.

General Sherman immediately diverted two small regiments from the main advance to deal with these impudent artillery men, but Colonel Evans' own infantry regiment met them head-on and managed to hold them back from reaching the guns. Sherman's so far untested force was now trapped between artillery attacks from both his front and rear. He was taking considerable numbers of dead and wounded, while he still tried to advance and take the batteries of Pickett and Griffin to his front in the south.

By four in the afternoon the battle of Bull Run, which the Union had from the first called *Manassas*, was at a crucial stage. The entire Union army was now concentrating on advancing, not across Bull Run itself, but having circled around the turnpike and crossing the river to the west, were now hell bent on breaking the Confederate army now largely based in the area between the river and Bald Hill on the western side of the Manassas-Sudely Road. The land they occupied was mostly farmland, fields with scattered trees and copses and also small farmhouses and buildings. General Jackson's Confederate reserve force, having spoiled a good picnic en route, was rapidly moving up to join the rear of the Confederate batteries, commanded by Pickett and Griffins. They were, by four in the afternoon mopping up the Union troops on Bald Hill and were now climbing up towards the plateau known as Henry Hill, named after the estate of Henry House nearby.

The battle, although no one knew that at the time, would be decided on that plateau in the afternoon and evening of July 21 1862; the struggle on Bald Hill had been short lived. Certainly no one, of however high a rank, could have envisaged what that victory would mean in the days and months that were to follow.

Below Henry Hill, by little more than a mile, the Confederate Headquarters, Wilmer Maclean's farmhouse, had stood for several hours like a rock in a gushing stream of advancing Confederate soldiers, although by now most had gathered to the north beyond it and below the hill.

General Johnston, based at those Headquarters, was trying to understand the state of the battle through messengers arriving, or in many cases failing to arrive, from the various commanders in the field. He was in belligerent mood, alternately pacing the floor, glowering at the maps his junior officers were trying to keep up to date and peering through his telescope which, much to his anger, showed little except smoke and often a mass of men in the distance, where he could not tell friend from foe.

He now shouted to Beauregard in frustration, 'The battle is over *there*'! waving a hand towards Henry Hill, 'I am going there'.

Beauregard had just completed dispatching the order to move all the remaining men who had waited along the bank of the Bull Run after the brief exchange of fire at the start of the battle, to move with all haste north to reinforce Thomas Jackson's force under Henry Hill and onto Bald Hill. Beauregard was more cautious than Johnston and now hesitated as to whether he should join him, but his commanding officer was already in the saddle and riding north with a small contingent of other officers, so he stayed where he was.

Although there was now undeniably a very large combined Confederate force trying to move up Henry Hill to the plateau at the top, there were equal numbers from Jackson's supporting column fighting their way, also north, but between the now largely silent batteries set up by Captains Pickett and Griffin on the north and west edge of the plateau. The Union army, nominally still commanded by General McDowell, although Sherman was also leading the very large Union reserve force and was also arriving successfully into the heart of the battle proper, albeit faster in some areas than others. He was fighting his way through the existing Confederate batteries that were still firing, making for Henry Hill from the north side. Fierce fighting, long inevitable, was now beginning in earnest and covering all of Henry Hill.

The Confederate army, which the Union labelled as *rebels,* were by then still trying to fight their way to the top, intent on pushing the Union boys away from the plateau and then to have the advantage of height over their enemy.

The entire hill was by now a tangled mass of men in both grey and blue, firing round after round into each other's ranks. The noise was deafening, the smoke of powder often blinding and now, as the Rebs struggled up and over the brow, the sight of dead and dying fellow Confederates, which they were literally *wading* through, was horrifying. Bayonets were fixed and slowly became the principal weapon of both attack and defence. Those Confederates still fighting around Colonel Francis Bartow found themselves being gradually pushed back and falling over the bodies of their own dead. Bartow himself seized a flag, the rebel battel flag of crossed stars and bars, and yelled at the top of his voice, "*General Beauregard says you must hold this place. Georgians, I appeal to you to hold on!*" A Union shell at that moment exploded close to

General Beauregard; his horse was killed in an instant, but the general remarkably survived unhurt.

Of the six thousand Confederates still struggling up Henry Hill, half had lost all leadership, their officers either dead or wounded beyond ability to fight further. This caused terrible confusion and the fight often now constituted of simple self-defence: the instinct just to try to stay alive. The brigades of both Thomas Jackson's Virginians and Wade Hampton's South Carolinians were remarkably still in line and fighting furiously. They were among the growing numbers of Confederate soldiers now again over the edge of the top of the plateau and on to flatter ground.

Brigadier General Bee, having failed to receive any command to either stay or go from his original position near the stone bridge, when the fighting moved west, made a unilateral decision to move his men south-west and found himself close to General Jackson in the furnace of battle on Henry Hill. (31) He shouted to Jackson, "*General, they are beating us back.*"

Jackson looked at him, cool as ever, and simply replied, "*Sir, we will give them the bayonet.*"

Barnard Bee then turned his horse to face the mass of disorganised stragglers and pointing his sword towards Jackson's brigade, stood in his stirrups and shouted, "*Look! There is Jackson standing like a stonewall. Rally behind the Virginians,*" It was a name that stuck with General Jackson, who became known as 'Stonewall Jackson'.

Bee himself was killed very shortly afterwards, but the soldiers, who had been on the verge of retreat, were inspired by both generals and responded, driving the Union mass back with shot and bayonet. It was a moment which swayed the battle

The exhausted, and often dispirited, Union men were slowly driven back down the northern slope. This was helped by Jackson yet again shouting to the muddled force around him: *'Yell like the furies',* another occasion when the Rebel Yell may perhaps have been born. Thomas Jackson's place in history was confirmed that day, as was the other phrase depicting him as *Old blue light*, which referred to his startlingly blue eyes, which it was said could be seen even through the heat and smoke of battle.

The union army on Henry Hill was now pushed more quickly back and down the slope. They were not only badly mauled, with over five thousand of them killed that day, but had lost the lust for victory and now, more importantly, *believed* they were beaten. A mass retreat began across both the north and south of the Warrenton Turnpike. The whooping Confederate force to north, south and now west of the vast majority of the Union army, or what was left of it, ruthlessly pursued them like dogs rounding up sheep. Those soldiers of the Union, who had remained north of the stone bridge as the principal conflict raged, were swiftly swept up in the horror of the massive and rapidly moving retreat.

Lincoln's once optimistic soldiers were now pushed out of the Bull Run valley and then gradually up the incline towards Centreville as the rain became torrential. The camp, only so recently set up on the edge of the town, was trampled by thousands of men, some whole and many, many more wounded, grinding it under foot into the mud. The retreat now became a rout as any semblance of a rear-guard action disappeared into the mud and blood under foot. Union officers tried to stop their men deserting, but these would-be deserters soon discovered that throwing down their weapons made running easier. Officers drew their pistols and told them to halt or they would be shot, which had little or no effect, even as they fired into the air. Thousands of soldiers, knowing they were beaten, and now moving northeast as fast as they could, were as impossible to stop as a raging river in full flood.

To make matters worse, by six in the evening the rain became persistent and the remains of a once proud and gloriously turned-out Union army, exhausted by defeat, was trying to plod through mud and growing darkness. As they left the battlefield behind, in no order of any sort, but just the survival of the fittest, they passed teams of surgeons beside the road, where tables had been erected and occasionally tents.

These resembled the halls of hell. Some of the wounded who had not simply been left behind on the battlefield, had crawled or been carried to these stations during the day. The surgeons themselves were stripped to the waist and splattered with blood. They used saws and long knives which, once a man was forcibly held down on the table, were used to cut off frightfully mangled limbs; these were thrown into piles on the ground. The screams of the living wounded caused those still able to walk to move even faster

It was at this point in the retreat that the Confederate command unknowingly followed (32) Stonewall Jackson's advice in a previous conflict: *'Once you get 'em running, keep at 'em. That way a small force can defeat a large one'*. Whether Generals Beauregard and Johnston were aware of Jackson's epithet, or whether they were themselves aware of the hand of history on their shoulders, is not known.

# Chapter Twenty-Four

**Sunday July 21 1861**

The Envoys had, much to George's disgust, spent the remainder of the Saturday night and much of Sunday, once they had left the chaotic picnic site, some distance from the battle; in fact, about two miles along the narrow country road that led from the north-south Sudley road west of Bull Run. They had finally stopped at Five Forks, where their road was joined at a dusty, deserted junction with four other lanes. They were now two or three miles to the west of what had already become the *Battle of Bull Run*.

George was torn between his soldierly desire to get closer to the action of the battle and what he felt was his duty to protect his two companions, who had never even been in the same country as a battle in their lives, let alone almost dragged into the action. The muted sounds of fighting with occasional clouds of smoke and dust were the distant reminders throughout the day of the mayhem of a battle largely being fought out of their sight.

Both brothers tried to keep quiet about the ever-increasing sense of fear they felt that the fighting would soon inevitably reach them. Since George showed impatience at not being able to move closer to the sites of gory death, their self-esteem forced them, somewhat half-heartedly, to try to appear independent on his presence. Nevertheless, the Captain of Hussars stayed at his post with them all of a day that seemed to them to be never ending.

By the early evening, the sounds of battle had virtually ceased as far as they were concerned and what occasional evidence there was that the Battle of Bull Run had been fought in the fields to their north-east was equally in the far distance.

Their coachman had disappeared without his coach during the previous night and they took the decision to use the coach, with Arthur nervously put in charge of the two well-rested horses. They did also agree to proceed with caution, as George had emphasised, to seek to discover if the Union had, indeed, retreated, which the quiet of the ruined countryside ahead of them seemed to suggest might be the case. It could also mean the absolute opposite.

Careful reconnaissance gradually revealed the increasingly obvious truth that the Union army had indeed fled the field, which was now held by a small force of Confederate soldiers, left to ensure there was no surprise return of the enemy. The Envoys learned from high spirited Confederates on their route that the remainder of the army of the Bull Run victors had by then consolidated into a pursuit force, which was so close behind the Yankees who were obliged to sacrifice hundreds of men as prisoners in their vain attempt to slow the Confederate chase and somehow allow them to make for what they prayed was some sort of safety once they reached Washington.

In fact, both armies were also equally hampered by what was left of the Union's civilian supporters, who had left Washington that morning to enjoy the sight of a battle, which they had expected to allow them to witness the rebels being soundly whipped. By the time it started to grow dark, this second crowd of picnickers, most of whom had been unable to leave the field ahead of the retreating army, were now spread across the roads and the surrounding fields on the route east towards Centreville, Fairfax Courthouse and beyond. With their carriages frequently overturned or utterly wrecked, many of the Union civilians were either lying as mangled corpses or seriously injured. In their own pain and terror, they heard the all too frequent and distressing cries for help of large numbers who had been trampled or flung aside firstly by panicking Union soldiers and then by the pursuing Confederates.

As Lincoln's grand Army of the Potomac staggered the twenty-five miles towards Washington in pitch darkness and steady rain, many of walking wounded not already left behind simply lay down in the mud in exhaustion waiting to die. General McDowell had been able to hold back a small number of his regiments, which had advanced onto the Confederate rear at the height of the battle, but these too were now leaving the battlefield of Bull Run behind. The general organised a reasonably orderly, but very hasty, retreat to the north to try to save as many of his men as he could. McDowell was stunned to receive overnight, as he sought refuge on the way to temporary safety in the Shenandoah valley, an exhausted messenger from General Scott, who had been left in charge in Washington with several reserve regiments.

The cable told him simply, *"We are not discouraged."* Scott himself was at that time desperately trying to find enough men to defend Washington from the Confederates now chasing the shattered remnants of the Union army heading inexorably in his direction. Meanwhile, that Confederate army, in the high spirits of victory, had sent cavalry ahead of their infantry to harry the Yankees, to kill all they could, to take a large number of prisoners, the first of this war, and to drive the rest through Washington and ideally "into the sea far beyond".

In fact, rumour being as rife as ever, it had convinced the terrified and fleeing Union army that the rebel cavalry were all astride black horses and riding like ruthless Cossacks. Horrified cries could be heard throughout the rout of: *"Black horse cavalry coming!"*

The only thing that caused the Confederates to move less quickly than they should have done was their lack of training in the business of battle. There was much confusion delaying their advance and it took the far better skills of their officers to keep them motivated. There were also delays for some as they stopped to capture dozens of field guns, caissons and ammunition, small arms, blankets, waggons and ambulances, all abandoned by the defeated.

The Envoys had decided, as soon as they saw the rout that was the Union army, that they should follow the victorious Confederates and try to make for Washington DC. Arthur, at last finding that he had not entirely forgotten his childhood's enforced riding lessons, guided their coach with firm hands to meld with the rear of the Confederate force leaving Bull Run and hence was not involved in the advancing regiments further ahead, which were now engaged in the aggressive pursuit of the Union army.

Not surprisingly, the Envoy's presence in the dark downpour was not questioned, although George was ready to establish both their nationality and their mission to the Confederacy if necessary; he sat on the box of the coach with Arthur, while Ernest was relegated to sit inside.

Although the evening and night of the relatively short, but often chaotic journey was dramatically quieter that the battle itself, the Envoys made only slow and frequently halting progress, which meant that by midnight they were mixed with the last Confederate soldiers to leave Bull Run and were forced to make frequent stops by the denser numbers in front. However, this allowed them to catch occasional snatches of sleep inside the coach.

It was during one such short lived halt that Arthur, searching for something to trigger a conversation, asked George, "Did you see the report that was in one newspaper I read, about the Union senator who, before this bloody conflict began, had confidently foretold that there would never be a war and no more blood would be shed than he could mop up with his pocket handkerchief?"

"I certainly did," replied a grim-faced George, "but I reckon he would have needed one hell of a lot of handkerchiefs today if he had been at Bull Run." Both enjoyed a few moments of bitter laughter in the midst of a scene that reminded Arthur of descriptions of hell in Dante's *Inferno* that he had been obliged to study at school. He found it hard to believe that it had become a reality before his very eyes.

By the time the first remnants of the crushed Union army reached the outskirts of Washington, dawn revealed their filthy state causing (33) one of General Scott's soldiers to remark, as he had no choice but to join the column in its retreat: *"Just look at these foul men, covered in mud, soaked through with rain and with the vapour of steam rising over them."* Then he, like the rest of General Scott's so-called defence force of the capital, continued north with the miles long column he had just derided. The thousands from Manassas and now thousands more awaiting them in Washington continued their desperate flight right through Washington and out the other side.

During this retreat, maybe a quarter of the Army of the Potomac, or even a half by some reckoning, continued in some vague semblance of order out of Washington during Monday July 22. The remainder simply evaporated into the city and the drenched countryside beyond. These were labelled as 'skedaddlers', men who had had quite enough, often throwing aside their weapons and dragging their weary and often wounded bodies east, west or north to try to reach home before the Rebs caught them and shot them out of hand.

Although George and the brothers were with the last of the Confederate army leaving Bull Run, they were aware that ahead of them by many miles was the far larger force now chasing the Union onward on what was to be a gruesome journey, although for tens of thousands of men in grey it was the glorious proof that God was on their side and ensuring that: 'The land of Dixie was always and inevitably destined to prove to Abe Lincoln, that traitor to the Constitution, that the Union was never going to be allowed to force the South into being part of their United States'(Anonymous Confederate officer)

The Union forces had put several miles between themselves and their pursuers by the time the miserable dawn arrived. This was due to the fact that the Confederate regiments in the forefront of the pursuit were exhausted by that time. Washington was now many miles behind them, but as the rain ceased and the day brightened the Confederate command called a halt, as they reached the farmlands of Pennsylvania.

The senior Confederate generals gathered in a deserted farmhouse, while a large part of the Army of West Virginia came to a halt in the city to eat, drink and attempt get some sleep. The pursuit regiments, which had now left that part of the force well behind, bivouacked in fields and woods around the newly established Confederate Field Headquarters. The more fortunate senior officers' requisitioned barns, farmhouses and village homes from the Union owners, who had fled before them like herded cattle and were now homeless, scattered somewhere ahead.

The Envoys could not have known it but, like the Army of the Confederacy, William Russell would also be in Washington the next day, having seen enough of the Battle at Bull Run to sketch out the bones of a report to the *Times of London*, before he left the battlefield well ahead of the victors and the defeated. He had told George when they met in Richmond that Washington was his next destination, although that seemed to the captain of Hussars a lifetime ago, a time when they had all assumed Washington DC would still be the Union capital when they arrived there.

(34) Russell's first telegraphed report to his newspaper went off that evening and read: *'The inmates of the White House were today in a state of the utmost trepidation and are packing their bags. So short has been the Union, that those men who saw it rise, will now live to see it fall'*.

His report went on to describe the utter defeat of the Union army, its rag tag retreat and, at the last minute before it was telegraphed via Newfoundland, then to Ireland and so to London, he was able to include the news that President Lincoln and his government had also *skedaddled* by train to Philadelphia, Pennsylvania, to set up a temporary command headquarters there, far to the north east of the Confederate army.

Another telegraph also went out that night from President Davis in Richmond to General Johnston: *"Your little army, often derided, met with the grand army of the Union and destroyed them today."*

What he did not reported in *The Times* a few days later was the hypocrisy that allowed a shrewd businessman from the south to buy up the land where the battle had been fought in order to turn it into a profitable tourist attraction.

Arthur had driven the coach through most of that night, although, as he would later admit, it was at times erratically, as either the road ahead became blocked, was dramatically uneven with huge ruts from the wagons ahead or when he unintentionally dozed off and the horses came to a stop of their own accord. On occasion, they were forced to halt when firing far ahead was heard or a troop of cavalry galloped through the mass of men on foot. On one occasion, such a cavalry squadron had Jeb Stuart, now raised in rank to General, riding as the lead and wildly cheered as he was recognised in his splendid uniform, although now mud and blood stained.

Eventually in the dim small hours before dawn, Ernest hung out of the window and offered to drive. Arthur was half-asleep again and grudgingly accepted, taking his brother's place inside and immediately falling asleep.

By the time dawn broke and they could at last see Washington in the distance, the sky at last cleared of rain clouds. They were then forced to stop behind the large stationary mass of halted Confederate soldiers that stretched forward as far as the eye could see. George, who had managed to stay awake all night, stepped down from the now battered coach and was joined by Ernest.

They both looked mud spattered and exhausted as they leant against one of the rear wheels. As they did so, there was a groan and then a loud crack of splintering wood that came from the coach's rear axle. They rapidly stepped away from what sounded like the death knell of the vehicle that had served them remarkably well for the last few days. At that moment, the rear wheel fell forward, having been split from its support, and the whole vehicle crashed sideways and backwards until the body was resting on the mud that had once been a road. This roused Arthur from sleep and his head appeared through the lopsided window to see what had happened. The other two helped him down. They surveyed the coach with the resignation that it would travel no further. As they managed with the last of their strength to extricate the horses from the shafts, the soldiers behind them pushed past the coach that would travel no further. Arthur, holding both sets of reins, demanded what he was supposed to do with the poor animals now.

"You have no choice, unless you want to lead them through this heaving crowd as far as the White House and leave them there!"

Ernest spoke loudly enough for his brother to hear him above the noise of hundreds of men's voices, most of whom appeared to be enjoying the need to stop, but equally still seemed full of the optimistic words about the battle, maybe even a war now won, as well as the prospect of seeing their homes again before too long, which to them now seemed a real possibility. Arthur reluctantly let go of the reins, although the pathetic beasts just stood where they were, their heads drooping to the ground.

After they had very slowly and with considerable difficulty forced their way to the edge of the roadway, they struggled for some distance further on and then, frustrated by the blockages of the huge crowd of grey uniforms, turned up a side street, now empty of any of its former residents. It was then that Arthur asked a question that neither of the other two had had in mind since they had arrived at Manassas Junction, which seemed weeks ago.

"Do you think there is any way we could find out what's happened to Paul?"

Ernest laughed loudly and sarcastically. "Is that supposed to be a joke? Look around you, Arthur. Do you see any notices with neat lists of the casualties of a battle that has barely finished and in a city crammed with thousands of Confederate soldiers determined, it seems to me, to chase their enemy to destruction? Well…do you?"

Arthur replied simply, "Oh, for God's sake, Ernest! I just thought George might have some idea of what happens when…"

George had to laugh himself then, although there was a hint of understanding in his tone.

"No, Arthur, no idea really. All I can suggest now is that we at least get ourselves away from here and try to make it to the White House. I doubt the Union government will still be occupying the building, but it's a symbol of power and the Confederates could well have some sort of command post there already."

Unable to think of any better alternative they set off in what they guessed was at least the right direction. They were surprised as they trudged east that the streets were largely empty, but then in contrast in some cases, filled with Washington citizens they assumed must be true Unionists and supporters of Abe Lincoln. Men, women and even children were loading all manner of carts, waggons and any other wheeled vehicles they could find to hold their furniture and prized possessions prior to an attempt to flee the city.

Within the next two hours that it took them to locate the White House, they joined a stream of such vehicles, laden with goods and people, heading north-east, presumably in the direction of Philadelphia, where they might hope they would be safer than in their erstwhile calm and civilised capital city. Although this journey still revealed what must be thousands of Washingtonians leaving the city in fear for their lives, it also led them past some large buildings, including churches, libraries and hotels, all of which stood with open doors and, outside which considerable numbers of wounded men were sitting or lying on the roadways and pavements; soldiers dressed largely in grey, but with blue tunics and caps scattered among the horribly wounded, hoping to find some relief for their battle wounds from some Christian souls, who might be prepared to disregard the blue uniform. So far there seemed to be no attempt from the Confederate command to seize Washington's thousands of non-military citizens and put them in prison camps, not even the severely wounded Union soldiers looking for mercy in the hastily set up, so called hospitals.

Ernest was the only one of the trio who decided to look inside the doors of a large church. What he saw was a much bigger version of the surgeon's stations near the battlefield: what looked like hundreds of sorely wounded men lying in aisles and between pews, while in other areas the pews had been torn out to make room for tables for the surgeons to work on. The air was putrid with the smell of blood, the floor covered with patches and pools of blackened red, while torn limbs lay in buckets. There were also women here, who often seemed to have once been well dressed, but were now bloody as they worked as volunteer nurses. Ernest returned from the scene within a few minutes and, on his way back to the street had to stop and vomit violently into some flowerbeds.

What was also now obvious to all of them was that there were no Confederate troops attempting to wreak havoc and death amongst these fleeing refugees; they were left alone to leave the city. The army command had clearly decided that these newly homeless souls were not intent on anything except finding a safe place, a place where no grey uniformed soldiers ruled the land; it would not be found for many, many miles, but the Confederacy had no facilities to incarcerate these tragic souls.

The Envoys soon came across some open grassland, which had once they guessed been a park, but was now home to what must have been perhaps a hundred or more abandoned field guns and cannons. These and their horseless caissons and limbers, as well as scattered piles of ammunition, lay around with no Union soldiers to guard them. Beyond the widely scattered military leavings, they spotted what looked to be an area of orchard and, realising how hungry they were, hurried in that direction, only to find the trees stripped bare of fruit. Their empty stomachs would seem to be destined to wait even longer to receive nourishment, although later they did find water pumps in the streets in the poorer districts that allowed them at least to slake their thirst.

It was well into the afternoon by the time they reached the Capitol. It did not appear as they had expected: all the ornate fencing had been beaten down, most doors were hanging open and many windows and window frames were broken. The gardens around Lincoln's Capitol building and office were trampled into mud; it looked as if a herd of cows or horses had passed that way, rather than an orderly army.

Once they walked closer, however, they realised that, regardless of the state of the building, there were plenty of people in and around the huge Capitol. Outside what seemed the only serviceable entrance stood disparate groups of non-military men, some of whom looked extremely concerned, while others uncertain whether to go in or not. Bored coachmen were sitting at the front of several coaches, which were mostly not in the best of condition, holding the reins of two, or even four horses.

There was no one to prevent their walking up to these coaches and, as they did so in an attempt to find some news, another such coach was driven rapidly in from the road and pulled up closer than the others to the open entrance doors of the famous building. Natural curiosity made the trio disregard the other carriages and walk over to see why the new arrival seemed in such a hurry. Before they were close enough to look inside, a well-built gentleman alighted and George quickly realised who it was, with his high black boots, long jacket and military looking hat, crowning his long hair and bearded face. With the rather full body and under average height, there was no mistaking William Russell, the *London Times* reporter whom he had met in Richmond.

"My God!" he now exclaimed. "Am I dreaming or is that Mr Russell?"

Neither of the brothers had any idea what Russel looked like and there was no time for any discussion as George led the way across to where the reporter was loudly instructing his coachman to wait for him. He did not even glance at the three young men and unless someone had spoken, he would surely have walked straight past them.

"Mr Russell!" called George. William Russell looked surprised, but turned, gazing at the three young men of dubious appearance, dried mud over their trousers and the rest of their clothes looking as if they had slept in them, which indeed they had.

"Do I know you? I have urgent business here and cannot be delayed." Russel went to walk past the trio, but George stepped closer and held out his hand.

"Captain George Fitzwilliam, sir. I had the honour to meet you in the Confederate Senate in Richmond, not so long ago."

Russell now focused his attention on George.

"I do believe you are in the right. I recall you sir and I think you were with Senator Hayward, if I am not mistaken. How on earth…? I mean, why are you here and how did you get here? There's been a battle not so far away, you know."

"Yes, sir, we do indeed know. We were there, as I think you must have been yourself."

"Indeed, captain, indeed I was and I think only my lengthy experience of the trials of war, and maybe a little luck, enabled me to get away from that place unharmed."

"We are delighted to see that you are still in good health."

"Yes…yes, I am. Now I have to get inside to find out who is in charge here. Good luck in your endeavours, whatever they are. Now you must excuse me."

George looked at Ernest and Arthur and then, as Russell began to walk away in some urgency, he reached out and held his arm for a moment.

"Sir, might we ask if we could accompany you? I think we have some information that will be very important to your realistic reports, as well as to our own country, but we have no idea who to talk to. I am confident that your contacts, with your fame going before you, might enable us to locate the right person, if only we could get inside."

Russell smiled and spoke as he turned again towards the entrance. "If *you* can accompany me?" He paused for several moments. "Very well. I don't see why not. You are, after all, fellow Englishmen."

Here he turned his attention to the damaged building.

"There is, I understand, very little organisation here at present, but, although I am sure I can see that you are able to find someone who may be able to help you, I must then desert you. Follow me and don't dawdle."

He set off rapidly even before he finished speaking and the three had to run to catch up with him.

Having negotiated two Confederate soldiers at the door, who clearly knew that William Russell was a man of importance, he guided his charges towards a group of men on the far side of what seemed to be some sort of antechamber. The group he approached consisted of both Confederate officers and non-uniformed gentlemen gathered around what, judging by the gold braid on his grey uniform, must be a senior Confederate officer. Those around him were listening to what he was saying, but also were often interrupting him with questions. The officer was trying to answer a string of such questions, as well as some demands; he was undoubtedly having difficulty in controlling his temper.

Standing on the outside of the group, George and the brothers looked at their surroundings: the contents of the large room, being chairs, tables and cabinets, which they guessed had once been placed neatly around the room, but were now either broken, badly damaged or simply overturned and flung back against the walls. George was only too aware that their chances of getting any information at all, either about casualties or what was happening beyond the city, were very slim, since he was certain the Confederates were even now focussing all their energies on destroying the rest of the Union army before they could escape very far.

# Chapter Twenty-Five

It was George who then took command of the situation, as he so often did these days, and using his height and confident demeanour, he marched to the front of the group. There he smartly saluted the gilded officer and introduced himself, silencing the other, surprised gentlemen.

"Captain George Fitzgerald, sir, of Her Majesty Queen Victoria's Royal Hussars. Whom, may I ask, have I the honour of addressing?"

The officer concerned was obviously impressed, although equally taken by surprise by the confident approach.

"Well, sir... I am Colonel Charles Alexander and have the honour of belonging to General Johnston's Confederate army, late victors at Bull Run."

George then reached inside his jacket and produced a slightly crumpled paper, which he handed to the Colonel.

"This document, Colonel, is from the desk of the British Prime Minister, Lord Palmerston, and gives myself and my two companions here, safe passage to travel to the American states on an extremely important and urgent mission."

George paused, as Colonel Alexander looked questioningly at him. The Envoy then went on, "May I suggest, sir, that we find a less crowded and public place, so that you can read it in full and I can then explain our mission to the Confederacy in more detail?"

The Colonel still looked a little taken aback, but opened the paper and must have seen at once its title:

'*Her Majesty's Government of Great Britain and Ireland*' (and also the following): '*Prime Minister, the Viscount, Lord Palmerston... '.*

He folded the paper again, quietly instructed them to 'come' and walked through the crowd, who had been trying, and failing, to listen to the conversation. Colonel Alexander strode towards a door set in the far wall of the hall. George, Ernest and Arthur quickly followed in his wake.

They found themselves not, as expected in an office or similar room, but in what was essentially a large cupboard that contained stacked brooms, cleaning materials and haphazard heaps of papers. Not fazed by this, Colonel Alexander leant against a pile of closed boxes and opened the paper again. This time he read it carefully, before looking up and letting his gaze rest briefly on each of the Englishmen before him.

"So, would it be fair of me to understand that you have been sent by Lord Palmerston, that would seem to have been several months ago, to discover whether a blockade is in place to stop cotton being exported to your country from the Confederacy. Is that correct?"

"Yes sir, at least in general terms, but—"

George was cut short and the colonel continued, now slowly pacing between the boxes and a wall.

"The answer to that is simply that, as I suspect you already know, the blockade of the Atlantic ports was in place two months ago and now has the south sealed in tight. Does that answer your Lord Palmerston's question?"

Before replying, George cracked open the door to the hall to make sure that there was no one outside within hearing distance and then firmly closed it again. He did his best to explain the situation in as brief a way as possible.

"You are correct, sir, and we indeed did discover this and telegraphed a report to the Prime Minister several weeks ago. That was done with the help of Mr William Russell of the *London Times*. However, there is more to our presence here than that. Firstly, can I ask whether what I am about to reveal will only be passed by you to a higher authority in the Confederate army or government, assuming that you believe it to be of importance and of vital concern to both our governments? Also that it is kept exclusively between you and that member of your army or government."

Colonel Alexander hesitated for several minutes, again pacing as he gave the matter some thought. Eventually he did reply.

"As you can see the Confederacy's far from being in command of affairs here at present, but we are nevertheless firmly established in Washington. President Jefferson is still in Richmond, but has given responsibility for a provisional forward government department here under the command of a general of our army, whom I cannot name for obvious reasons at present. You may take it that the general concerned is now in regular touch with the President by telegraph, which has been restored, or rather, I should say, cobbled together. What you may tell me now will be passed by me to that general and, at his discretion, may go on to Richmond. If you are happy that I should go ahead on that basis, then I will do so. If not, then I do not think I will be able to help you further."

"May I have a moment to consult with these two other gentlemen, sir?" asked George.

"Yes, but I have very little time and none at all unless this is genuinely of real importance to my government."

George and the two brothers went as far back as they could in the confines of the cupboard and whispered together for a few minutes. After a short interval, they then came back to stand with the colonel. George continued as their spokesman.

"All three of us feel that we can trust your discretion as a colonel in the Confederate army. What I tell you now can be taken as coming directly from both Lord Palmerston and from Lord Sidney Herbert, the British Minister for War. If we are able to report to them, as it is our intention now to do, that the Confederacy appears to be in a position to be optimistic about a military victory on land in this very sad conflict, *but* has little sea power to break the blockade, then the British government may well be prepared to send, having asked for and received the agreement of our parliament, sufficient ships of our naval fleet to break the blockade on the Atlantic seaboard and eventually beyond. My government would hope that the mere sight of British warships will cause the blockade to be withdrawn, but if not, parliament will have been asked to agree to a limited use of force to effect a withdrawal of all Union ships, failing which the British fleet will, reluctantly, open fire. If your president and government can agree to this, authorising us to telegraph their agreement to London or by doing so directly themselves, then you can expect to receive a positive response."

The colonel nodded and said, "I certainly understand and I will do everything I can to get your message to President Davis as quickly as is possible. Under the circumstances at the moment this may take some time. I suggest you remain in Washington for the time being. If it is at all possible, you should try to visit me here after midday from tomorrow until such time as a reply is received. I would expect, to have news for you within a few days. I should add that I suspect President Davis will telegraph your Prime Minister himself but will, of course, need to confirm your particulars firstly with that gentleman."

George thanked him for his agreement to pass on the information he had just received and said that either he or one of the two Tissiman brothers would report to the Capitol each day for as long as necessary. All three then shook hands with Colonel Alexander and left the building, their first intention being to try to find somewhere to stay, although they realised that could well be a problem with thousands of Confederate officers looking for some sort of accommodation.

They walked nearly a mile from the Capitol in their search before they eventually found a place to lay their heads. It was a small inn near the train depot now in the hands of a Confederate sympathiser and had the most basic facilities. Pleased to escape the previous rodent infested barn of a lodging, they reached their rendezvous well before midday on each of the following two days, but with no result. In fact, they were not even able to speak to Colonel Alexander, but had to make do with seeing him hurry by, looking in their direction and shaking his head

On the third day, they decided to turn up even earlier than usual and were in the anteroom to the ground floor of the White House before nine in the morning. The room was treated more like a corridor now with officers of various ranks often running between one doorway and another holding papers or leather satchels. It took them nearly an hour before Ernest managed to attract the attention of a young lieutenant willing, even pleased, to share some positive news of the situation of the Confederate forces. As soon as Ernest located George not too far away, he pushed his way through the throng. George looked frustrated and told Ernest that he had been unable to get any information at all.

"Then you'll be pleased to know that I do have news," said Ernest, trying to disguise his delight in knowing something that the captain did not and went on: "A young officer was in a rush like everyone else, but had time to tell me that the Confederate army under the command of the Generals Robert E Lee and General Jackson, who is now apparently known as *Stonewall*, has pursued what was left of the Union force halted sixty miles north. The rump of the Union army is now apparently led by a General George Meade, who has at last found another place to stop, about twenty miles ahead of his pursuers and is attempting to fortify the area. It's at a place pretty well in the wilds, west of Baltimore. Anyway, the Confederate generals have also halted and are not expected to advance further for some time, as they now need to draw the army together in good order and consolidate their position." George could not help looking pleased with the news.

"That's the sort of news we need to get on the wire back to London," he said with the trace of a rare smile on his face. "Mind you, that's assuming our report of the battle at Bull Run has been telegraphed to London. The ragged retreat of the Union will be of even greater interest I suspect."

George was certainly pleased by the news, but also concerned about how little they really knew.

"It's fortuitous that you learned so much," he went on, "*but* without knowing whether the Confederacy will accept Lord Palmerston's offer or even whether it was sent to Richmond, let alone a reply received. So we are definitely stuck here for the time being."

Neither George nor Ernest could think of anything else to say that might solve their dilemma in the immediate future and so they tried to pick out Arthur in the crowd, since there had been no sign of him for over an hour. In the next few minutes, it was Arthur who found them. He trotted through the knots of gentlemen and was spotted by Ernest, just a few yards away.

"Ah, at last! There he is," said Ernest, "but, I say, who's that just behind him? I could swear it's, what's his name: Phillips by God! Captain Nat, surely?"

By that time, Arthur had stopped in front of them and the man Ernest had rightly identified as Captain Nathaniel Phillips of the Beaufort Virginia Volunteers, supposedly dead on a Bull Run field, was beside him.

"It seems anything is possible in this crazy place," said an out of breath Arthur and Captain Phillips simply managed a forced smile that was more like a grimace. It was impossible for the other two not to notice that the tall officer's left sleeve was pinned across his chest, while the jacket itself was blood stained.

Nathaniel remained silent and grim faced and Arthur realised he was not about to speak and so explained the situation himself, as best he could from what he had apparently already learned of the Union retreat.

"As you may know, I fought at Bull Run with the Beaufort Volunteers and, as you can see, I thank God I survived—" Arthur started to sympathise, but he was interrupted by Nat.

"No need to sweeten it up. I was shot from the side and the bullet smashed my arm rather alarmingly and took a chunk out of my side as well…maybe I'll talk about it one day, but not now."

An awkward silence followed and none of them could think how to say anything appropriate. George eventually suggested they should go outside and find a place where they could talk, away from the crowd. Nat followed them slowly and when they reached the muddy area outside, held his right arm over his eyes to keep the sun out, as if it were blinding him. They found one of the few unbroken benches left in the park. Nat, refusing Arthur's offered hand, half fell awkwardly on to the bench with a groan of pain.

George tried to find words to express how he felt, but got only as far as, "I, we are all so very—"

Nat waved his one good arm and in a loud, angry voice commanded him, "Just stop! I don't want your sympathy. I'm alive or at least some of me is. You should be mourning all the boys who are now lying dead around Bull Run or up on that bloody hill. They fought like demons and what did they get for that? A general's thanks? A useless medal? Nothing, absolutely nothing. Their bodies lie ripped open up there!"

There were tears in his eyes by now and he tried to wipe them away on his sleeve.

"We don't know what to say. We know…" Ernest was quickly silenced.

"You know nothing, you two brothers come from some big house in England. Maybe George knows… But the worst is… I did all I could to keep him safe…he wouldn't listen."

The others waited in silence, although they now suspected what this survivor was trying to tell them must refer to Paul, not George..

"I went up the line to get the boys moving away from the attack… The volleys of bullets were never ending. I told Paul to keep down and head for the trees when I'd told the others not to go yet…he never came back!"

Nat Phillips, in their memory the high-spirited captain always ready to accept a challenge and laugh about it, was now slumped forward, quiet groans shaking his body. Arthur, sitting next to him, put what he intended to be a comforting hand on his shoulder, but it was roughly shaken off.

After a few minutes, the sobs eventually stopped, but Nat's head was still down in what they supposed was an agony of mind and body. George looked at Ernest and then Arthur; minutes passed. George asked himself, *why do I always seem to be expected to take a lead?* He sighed and got up from the bench, stood in front of Nathaniel and crouched down. He spoke quietly.

"Nat, are you sure that Paul is dead? I understand if you can't answer at the moment, but…"

Nat raised his clearly pained face and looked into George's eyes. He spoke quietly, in fact almost a whisper that the others could not hear.

"I didn't see him die. I was hundreds of yards away by then…It was one of our boys told me. He was right next to Paul…"

There was a long pause, as he got control again.

"He was next to Paul and the bullets were flying all around us like mosquitos over a swamp… He said the captain went to stand up to tell the boys to retreat at once to the trees. Then he threw his arms up in the air and looked down at his chest, kinda surprised like…and then just slid to the ground, didn't say a word. I reckon that's sort of definite, don't you?"

"Well, maybe," said George, standing up, but then leant down again, "and I don't want to get anyone's hopes up, but I know that strong gentlemen like yourself and many others, have still managed to come through such awful events. So I suppose we may still hear some positive news from one of the Beauforts who might know roughly where he fell."

## July 14 1861: The Atlantic Ocean

Seven days prior to the English trio observing the first furious shots of the Civil War at Bull Run, almost two hundred miles to the southeast of Washington and twenty miles offshore in the Atlantic, an incident occurred that was to have a considerable influence on the outcome of the next stage of the war.

(35) On July 14 1861, the British mail packet *RMS Augusta* had left Norfolk, Virginia, officially a port blockaded by the Union, believing that the Union was completely unaware of its intended destination and the passengers that they had taken on board: two Confederate diplomats, John Murray Mason and John Slidell.

The Confederate government had spent many weeks previously in telegraphic contact with Lord Palmerston's government in London. They had discovered that Britain was not unsympathetic to the Confederate cause, although they hoped this was more than a matter of principal, but realistically, they knew full well that the main consideration of the British was to maintain the supply of raw cotton, which was now threatened by the Union blockade. Mason and Slidell intended to meet with the British Prime Minister and the Secretary of State for War in London. The message they would deliver from President Davis was that the Confederacy needed the intervention of British naval power to remove the blockade and open up the seas to the export of cotton from the southern states once more. The diplomats were also strongly to suggest that, while this just might be enough to force the Union to recognise the Confederacy, the threat of military intervention would also be of great value in itself; to this end, the British government had, as early as March 1861, reinforced British troops already in Canada, who by July 1861 were on standby to move south if need be. They had now had invaluable cables from the Envoys, which verified and supported the hoped-for Confederate plea carried by the diplomats.

On the July day that the *RMS Augusta* had taken the two diplomats on board and sailed out into the Atlantic, the Union government was far too involved with impending war to have its departure at the forefront of their minds. However, they had already given an order to the blockading Union ships that the ship just might attempt to break the blockade; the order was to seize the diplomats, as contraband to the lawful blockade and to use any force necessary should this happen. However, since the Confederate navy was well-known to be both smaller and weaker than that of the Union, no problem had been foreseen. Nevertheless, just the previous year the United States military had had its naval budget seriously reduced. One Union senator even went so far as to affirm that: '*There is no longer any need for a navy at all*'.

So it was really by chance that the *USS Jacinto* was already in the general area that ships from Norfolk would normally follow in order to set course for Britain. The captain of the *Jacinto* was called on deck at midday on the fourteenth and the approaching British mail packet was pointed out a mile away. The *Jacinto* altered course and sailed across the bows of the *Augusta,* which was hailed to heave-to immediately or the *Jacinto* would legally open fire.

Captain Charles Wilkes on the deck of the *Augusta,* an unarmed mail ship, had no choice but to comply. He was boarded by a party of armed sailors and an officer from the *Jacinto.* He was presented with a written demand to hand over the contraband of the two Confederate diplomats that they had evidence were on board. The captain was hence accused of breaking '*the lawful blockade of the government of the United States of America'*. Mason and Slidell were reluctantly handed over, roughly persuaded into a longboat, along with a note from Captain Wilkes on the *Augusta* that stated: *"Her Majesty's government will be informed of this illegal act of piracy."*

It took the *Augusta* nine days, with a fortuitously strong following wind, to land at Liverpool and to contact the authorities in London. Lord Sidney Herbert, Secretary of State for War, received the information first and contacted Lord Palmerston immediately. Captain Wilkes was rushed to London and provided details of what became known as '*the Augusta Affair'*.

Lord Palmerston had, in the months leading up to the probability of war, favoured keeping Britain neutral in any conflict. He had considered a change of mind during the formation of the trio of Envoys whom he had, a little reluctantly, sent to the southern states in the persons of George Fitzwilliam and the two brothers.

After that, he had openly moved towards the Confederate position and condemned Lincoln and the Union for having '*pandered to the democratic mob*' in their aggressive demands that the south should not be allowed to secede. He also concurred with the Confederates that secession now meant '*the meaning of freedom.*

Lord Lyon, the British ambassador to the United States, had complained in early 1861 that the Union now enjoyed '*making political capital*' at Britain's expense and was '*well-disposed to play the old game*': meaning *that of gaining popularity abroad by displaying violence to those at home who displeased it.*

On July 30 1860, Lord Palmerston sent a note via Lord Lyon, to be conveyed '*with urgency* to *Mr Abraham Lincoln, President of the United States of America, Washington DC'*. In this brief, but strongly worded note, he complained of: *"The piracy perpetrated against RMS Augusta in the Atlantic Ocean, the illegal seizure of gentlemen in the protection of the British Empire and the armed infringement of international waters."* He went on to make clear that, *"The British Empire thus now claims the right in legality to protect, if necessary with deadly force, any vessel that is in the future threatened or attacked by the naval ships of the United States of America when entering or leaving any port on the eastern seaboard of the said United States."* The note was formally signed: *"I have the honour to be, with high consideration, sir, your obedient servant, Henry John Templeton, Third Viscount Palmerston GCB, PC, FRS: Prime Minister of Great Britain."*

Lord Lyon was well aware that Lincoln was no longer in Washington, but he had no idea as to where the Union president had fled. Hence, the letter of protest was doomed never to be delivered and resided in a dusty drawer for many years.

# Chapter Twenty-Six

**London: July 31 1861**

At eleven o'clock, Lord Stanley Herbert was in conference with Lord Palmerston in No.10 Downing Street, with instructions that they were not to be disturbed under any circumstances. A telegraphic message had been received from Jefferson Davis, the Confederate president, late the previous night. Lord Herbert now had it in his hand and was slowly reading it for the second time. The message read as follows:

*To: Her Majesty's Prime Minister of Great Britain and Ireland in London:*

*From Mr Jefferson Davis, President of the Sovereign Confederate States of America in Richmond, Virginia.*

*Sir, I have received two days ago a communication, via Confederate Colonel Alexander in Washington, from your Envoys in Washington DC. I understand that you have arranged the presence there of persons known as your Envoys, three English gentlemen, one a Captain of the Queen's Royal Hussars, sent on your instructions several months ago to report on the state of the southern states and particularly on their ability to export raw cotton and how that has been affected by the Union blockade of southern ports. They have recently, I understand, reported to you. The blockade, especially of the Atlantic ports, is still forcing the closure of all those ports and hence stopping their cotton exports. Confederate forces have now driven the Union army right through Washington and what is left of that force is possibly preparing for battle in Pennsylvania or states even more northerly, conceivably in the next few months.*

*The Union army is in turmoil and has suffered enormous losses. I expect that my Confederate Army will dispose of them within a few months. I understand that you are prepared to listen to a fervent request from myself and my government that Great Britain use her naval power now to break the blockade and allow your supply of cotton to resume after many months of no supply at all. This will undoubtedly shorten the war further and allow the Confederacy to enjoy a peaceful future as an independent and sovereign country here in North America.*

*We look to you now, Prime Minister, in our hour of need, to give support for us and your own cotton industry, so that this appallingly vicious civil war can be concluded and all Americans can enjoy the freedom promised by the Declaration of Independence to live their lives, as they believe to be their right and as defined in our Declaration.*

*We are, sir, your obedient servants: President Jefferson Finis Davis and Vice President Alexander H Stephens.*

"Well?" Palmerston was eager to hear the opinion of his Secretary of State for War before revealing his own view, but what he got was a question:

"Do you believe we have a strong enough position in Parliament to ensure any military action we might decide to take will pass a vote in both Commons and Lords?"

Palmerston paused, since the question, at least at this stage, was unexpected.

"I think you are as aware as I am that our strength is, as it has been for some time, more than adequate. So are you saying that you agree with the request and would expect a Parliamentary vote to support it?"

"Prime Minister, although I am your Secretary of State for War, I am most cognisant of the already desperate condition of our cotton mills in Lancashire. I have seen the estimates of unemployed workers after just a few more months and that the majority of mills now have no raw cotton at all. Mills are being declared bankrupt almost daily. If we do nothing, the war in America is likely to drag on for years, in spite of the reported Confederate successes recently. Our cotton industry and economy will undoubtedly suffer even more massive harm."

There was another long pause, while Lord Sidney took out a large handkerchief and loudly blew his nose. Palmerston decided that at this juncture, it was expedient not to interrupt him.

"However," Lord Sidney went on, "I have also listened to the demands from President Lincoln that Britain must not and should not become involved militarily in a war within the confines of the United States of America... Although I agree that the word 'United' is beginning to appear a serious exaggeration."

Another pause, this time to take a drink of water from the glass on the table in front of him.. "Have you considered what the *Times* is calling the *Augusta Affair* of a few weeks ago?"

Palmerston nodded and changed his position in his chair to relieve the frequent pain he had in his back these days. "I have, as you know, been involved in the investigation and questioning of Captain Wilkes, as well as our letter of protest to Mr Lincoln, whom I understand is no longer lodged in the White House in Washington. I believe, as of course do all our ministers, that this was an act of piracy. Are you suggesting we should now punish the Union for this act?"

"Yes, I think that is exactly what I am suggesting."

"Let me send for some tea, while we consider this further."

The outcome was that the two gentlemen, who had in the past, both been supporters of many policies, but equally also violently objecting to others, agreed to have a Bill urgently prepared to lay before Parliament within the next five days. This was because it was now Friday and the matter demanded settlement before the weekend after next.

The Bill laid before a packed house on the Friday afternoon was to allow Great Britain to send a letter to the American Union ambassador in London giving the Union seven days in which to recall the fleet blockading the ports of the Confederacy. Also that the Union fleet had carried out an act of piracy against Great Britain, her Empire, her Queen and Empress of India. The Bill then spelled out the inevitable outcome, that being that the British navy, a far more powerful sea power than the Union could ever have set on the seas, would then reserve the right to enforce the removal of the blockade.

However, on the day after his meeting with Lord Palmerston, the Secretary of State for War issued instructions that *HMS Price of Wales,* with the Admiral of the Fleet on board, was to depart as soon as she was primed for the voyage, along with ten other warships. The fleet was, once across the Atlantic, ordered to spread out and drop anchor fifteen miles off the east coast of the Confederate states. The final lines of the orders spelled out what alternative action was to follow the withdrawal, or refused withdrawal, of the Union blockading ships.

On the following Thursday morning, the day before the debate and vote on the Bill to enable the British navy to enforce the removal of the blockade of the ports of the Confederate states, Lord Palmerston received a demand, since a royal demand was rarely a request, to attend the Queen at Windsor Castle at twelve noon that day. This was an unusual place to hold an audience, but Lord Palmerston was ever aware in such circumstances that he did not occupy the favoured place in the Queen's heart that had been filled twenty years before by Lord Melbourne, Victoria's well-known favourite, although nowadays rarely spoken of in public, but known to her as 'her Lord M'; Palmerston did not have his privileges.

This audience involved a much longer carriage journey than to Buckingham Palace and, on a windy and overcast day, not a particularly pleasant one. Unlike an arrival at the Palace, he then had to negotiate a flight of stairs within the rather cold stone building, draughty and cool even on a summer's day. After the usual process of reaching the royal presence, no doubt purposely arranged to show any commoner how important the Queen was, Lord Palmerston found himself ushered into a large drawing room, with a view of a misty Great Park beyond the long windows.

As Victoria gave him permission to sit, he hoped he had not shown his surprise not to see the Prince Consort, who nowadays always accompanied his wife at audiences. Lord Palmerston could not help noticing that Victoria looked somewhat plumper these days; he wondered if she might eventually grow almost as wide as she was tall. The beginning of a laugh escaped his mouth, which he hoped he had camouflaged with a cough.

"Your majesty, it is as ever a pleasure to be invited to an audience with you. Since I was not aware of any scheduled meeting, I much regret that I have nothing prepared."

He noticed in the ensuing silence that the queen looked especially stern and made no effort to reply.

"I trust His Royal Highness is well," Palmerston quietly added.

This question seemed to cause Her Majesty to sigh deeply, as if in pain.

"Prime Minister, we had expected that you would be aware that His Royal Highness was taken unwell yet again after our visit to the Prince of Wales's training camp in the north. This, we fear, expedited the shock to his constitution last year, when he heroically saved his carriage from colliding with a poor wagoner's cart..." Palmerston tried to speak and so to express his deepest concern, but the Queen continued to speak over his lame efforts.

"However, you may be sure he takes an interest in the unfortunate situation in America and especially the *Augusta Affair*, as the popular press has dubbed it."

"That is naturally of great comfort to your government, ma'am. May I be so bold as to ask how I can be of assistance to you today?"

The Queen regarded him in silence, rather as if he were a troublesome pest that had wandered into her royal presence. Eventually, she sighed again.

"We regret that you are already about to *do* something about which we are surprised not to have been appraised in advance."

"Ma'am, I regret I am not at all aware to what you refer."

"Prime Minister, we have had to learn from another source about the Bill that you are, we believe, about to *force* through Parliament tomorrow. We refer, of course, to the act of war you are proposing against the United States of America... Is that correct?"

Palmerston had only seconds to consider an answer, but having suspected this might be the reason for his presence at the palace that morning, he responded as if it were, of course, no surprise.

"Ma'am, the Bill that will be laid before Parliament tomorrow naturally requires to be voted for or against and *may* then become law as an Act of Parliament. If the vote is in favour, obtaining a majority in the commons and also passing the Lords, then Great Britain will *not* be proposing an act of war."

Here he was cut off by one, rather loud, royal command: "Stop!"

The Queen then paused to regain her majestic voice, rather than that of a martial commander.

"We cannot imagine, Prime Minister, what else you would call an attack on the navy of the United States by the war ships of this country, of which we are the supreme head. We are aware of the event that the newspapers are pleased to call the *Augusta Affair* and you should know full well that we have sympathy with the United States legally blockading the southern states, which are responsible for the horrors of slavery, which we have read about in *Uncle Tom's Cabin*. We are fully aware that slave owners have attacked and forced labour from their own countrymen with no provocation for many lifetimes."

Palmerston began to answer, but got no further than 'Ma'am...' before his unamused monarch stopped him again.

252

"Prime Minister, you know our opinion of the dreadful practise of enslaving one's fellow human beings and we will not let the name of your Queen and Empress be linked with your support of that regime."

Palmerston was becoming rapidly frustrated by the obstinate impression being given, namely that the Queen, not Parliament, ruled the country. He was not prepared to go as far as to tell her this bluntly to her face since he feared she might then even order the Yeomen of the Guard to throw him into the dungeons of the Tower of London, even though he knew that thought was, in reality, nonsense of course.

"Ma'am, I am most grateful for your valuable insight into a problem with which we have wrestled for some time, knowing as we do that our cotton industry in Lancashire is dying and is thus threatening our country's whole economy. Your insightful view will certainly be made clear to those with responsibility before the Bill is presented to the Commons. You may rest assured of my ever-present belief in the value of your majesty's views, which are always based upon the good of your country and Empire. I am sure that my ministers in the Liberal government will give full weight to what you have said so graciously today."

Victoria turned in her chair with an expression, which Palmerston would later confide to none but his closest ministers, was that of a young sulking girl. When he looked as if he were ready to dare to speak once more, she deliberately turned and stared out of the window; he could not possibly address the back of his monarch's head. He had to wait several minutes for her to turn her stern gaze back in his direction.

"We have heard what you have said, Prime Minister, and can only rely, we trust correctly, on your loyalty to the crown and to your being a gentleman, that you will undertake appropriate action in the light of our responsible objections." The last word was spoken with a firm nod of the head. "I feel we have made our requirement of you quite clear. You may return to your," she hesitated, searching for final words, "your responsibilities."

The Prime Minister rose, straightened his back, causing a lance of pain, bowed, took several paces backwards, bowed again and left the royal presence.

Once back in Downing Street, he sent for Sidney Herbert. He explained to him the content of his meeting with the Queen that morning. The Secretary of State for War was, however, in realistic mood and said as much.

"I am not obliged, as I fear you are, to appear to bow to the opinions of our monarch and to those of her German husband. I agree that no harm in fact has been done, nor I am certain that we need to broadcast those views to the Commons. The passage of the Bill tomorrow should remain unimpaired."

"I should remind you," Palmerston said rather pedantically, "that I alone can decide when the content of an audience of the Queen is privileged to myself and hence neither ministers nor the Commons should be involved in the contents of today's audience. So the only thing that will stop this Bill's passage is if we do not get the anticipated majority in the Commons, and later the Lords, tomorrow evening. I expect my whole cabinet to be active between now and then to ensure that the vote is solidly in favour of this righteous Bill. I ask you to make that expectation clearly known to all ministers today."

## Friday July 31, 3pm: The House of Commons

*A Bill: To enable the government of the United Kingdom of Great Britain and Ireland, in the person of the Secretary of State for War, immediately to dispatch as many warships to the coast of the United States of America as are considered necessary by Her Majesty's Government, in order to prevent any ships of the Union States of America from preventing the rightful free passage of any other shipping, arriving or leaving any or all ports on the coast of the Union States of America for the purposes of trade, export or import of goods or passengers. The Bill to permit enforcement of this right by any means as now seen fit by appropriate authority given by the Parliament of the United Kingdom and Ireland, whether by peaceful means or by enforcement, using any powers or naval force considered expedient.*

This Bill was laid before the House of Commons on the afternoon of July 31, 1861, moved by the Baron Sidney Herbert of Lea MP, the Secretary of State for War. The Liberal MPs filled the government benches, a three-line whip having been imposed. There was a considerable amount of shouting back and forth between government and opposition benches throughout the debate which followed and Mr. Speaker was required to call for 'Order!' more frequently than he recalled ever having to do before.

Lord Sidney spoke for the Bill eloquently, emphasising the importance of the measure to the British cotton industry and the country's economy. (36) The leader of the opposition, the Conservative Benjamin Disraeli, who in spite of the noise often of almost deafening proportions, spoke forcefully against the motion. His primary argument, which enraged numerous northern MPs of both parties, was that the *'so-called collapse of the cotton industry'* was an *'appalling exaggeration of the facts'*. He also declared his party's support for the United States and its president, Mr Abraham Lincoln. He brushed aside reports that the army of the Union had been brought to its knees and was on the verge of surrender as a *'disgraceful untruth propagated by the London Times newspaper and the Liberal government'*.

His final words were ironically an attack on Lord Palmerston's earlier fame for aggressive solutions and was greeted by cheers from the opposition: *"We all know that the right honourable gentleman, the Prime Minister, has too often attempted to solve every embarrassing situation abroad by sending in his gunboats!"*

This was followed by numerous Liberal MPs and even Ministers jumping to their feet and yelling abuse at the opposition benches. At this point, the Speaker threatened to clear the House.

After three hours of furious debate, a vote was called for. As members began to leave the chamber in order to vote, one Conservative MP, Cecil Carmichael, attempted to punch a Liberal MP, George Arthur Harrison; a fight was only prevented from breaking out by other members forcefully dragging the pair apart.

The vote took over an hour to complete and upon their return members continued to be even more vocal until the Speaker was able to create some order and demand that the number of votes be declared: *"The ayes to the right: three hundred and thirty. The noes to the left: three hundred and twenty-six. The ayes have it."*

With a majority of only four the Opposition called loudly for a "Voice Vote", which caused insults shouted from either side and from Disraeli the loud accusation of "Fixed Vote! Fixed Vote! Fixed Vote1" while others demanded "A ballot, that's what we want!", "Ballot!" Ballot"! As it became a little calmer, Cecil Carmichael rose again and at that the chamber was quieter.

"Mr Speaker. I and my party demand another ballot to such a close vote. If not I shall resign" he sat down to cheers and boos and Mr Speaker hammered the desk with his fist. A semi silence followed.

"I rule that a vote was given by ballot and a majority obtained. That stands." He then left the chamber accompanied by his acolytes. That was how Hansard reported a majority in favour of the motion.

*The Times* the following morning printed a report of the previous day's business in the Houses of Commons and Lords, including Palmerston's final remark: *"So: this House approves the motion and the intention of the Right Honourable Secretary of State for War immediately to send warships to international waters off the coast of the Carolinas and there to enforce free passage for all ships entering or leaving the ports of the United States of America."*


"A majority of four and a damned close-run thing!" The Prime Minister, sitting behind his desk in his office in Number Ten, couldn't help adding a smile to his pronouncement, in spite of the recent memory of the *'appallingly rowdy Commons'*.

"Nevertheless, the vote approves the Bill, which will now, as speedily as possible, become an Act and that is effectively a fait accompli; the Lords will do as they usually do and go with a Liberal Government," the Secretary of State for War, sitting on the other side of the desk happily replied. He continued, "The fleet, under the command of the Admiral of the Fleet, Sir John West, is expected to be in position off the American coast within the next week, since it was already almost half way across the Atlantic when the vote was taken."

"Very well. That piece of information should not be broadcast and we should telegraph President Davis in Richmond immediately, informing him of the agreement of Parliament to an Act giving Great Britain the right to demand the cessation of the naval blockade against the Confederacy and to enforce that cessation with any or all power at the command of the Admiral of the Fleet. It must also be clear that this is not to be construed as an act of war, but an act of *self-defence*. I am unsure whether President Lincoln, whom I understand has indeed recently been forced out of Washington and has set up his capital in Pennsylvania, is even in a position to receive a telegraphic message. Similarly, our ambassador to what may still be called the United States, is clearly not receiving any form of communication; at present it is even impossible to discover where Mr Lincoln actually is."

"May I suggest," Sir Sidney put in hastily, "that you are *seen* to be trying to telegraph Mr Lincoln, but if that proves impossible, perhaps we could contact the *London Times* to ascertain if their man, Mr William Russell, is in a position to advise about his location and if a telegraphic message could be expected to reach Mr Lincoln or not."

"Yes, I will do that, but we do not want any delay to our fleet and so I will also telegraph the Envoys to ask their view of Mr Lincoln's whereabouts. That means, I believe, that the telegraph to President Davis must go at once and those to Mr Lincoln, *The Times and the Envoys*. What are Admiral West's orders once he is in position?"

"Since it was always bound to be impossible for him to receive messages at sea and the country off which he lies is in a state of war, he will commence action against the Union blockade at dawn on August 6, if he has received no contrary message by then, which would be equally *difficult*, of course."

Since the under-sea telegraph cable, via Ireland and Canada, was still operational to New York and, as of August 1, still intact to Washington and to Richmond, the message to President Davis was satisfactorily despatched from London and received in Richmond after only forty-eight hours of delay en-route; President Davis had it in his hand before August 6. The attempt to contact President Lincoln was, however, unsuccessful.

The *London Times* Editor, John Thadeus Delane, informed the Prime Minister that William Russel had been in Washington until recently, but was now out of reach somewhere to the north; equally, no message was said to be impossible to the Envoys, who had left Washington. The cable that arrived in Washington itself was, of course, received by the Confederate command there and was actually also passed to President Davis, for his information, several months later.

# Chapter Twenty-Seven

**August 6 1861: Atlantic Ocean, 15 Miles off the Coast of The Carolinas**

It was almost noon and a hot sun was overhead the calm waters of the Atlantic; as a result ten anchored British war ships rocked gently in the light swell. On board, *HMS Prince of Wales* Admiral Sir John West stood with four of his most senior officers on the top deck, holding a telescope to his right eye.

"What time have you, Commodore?"

"Midday, sir, less perhaps a few minutes," replied Commodore William Shaw, who had served in the Royal Navy now for over twenty-five years.

"Take a look to port. I believe that is the *Warrior.* Would you concur and estimate her distance?"

Commodore Shaw and the officer standing with him, Captain Smith, carefully adjusted the focus of their telescopes. It was the Commodore, next in rank on the ship to the Admiral, who confirmed the ship in question was, indeed, *HMS Warrior,* the newest ship in the fleet and only commissioned earlier that year. She was larger than the *Prince of Wales*, another of the new breed of ironclads and, while powered by a powerful trunk steam engine, also had sails, if conditions allowed them to be raised. The *Prince of Wales* had a smaller steam engine and two masts rigged with sail.

"I estimate she is lying about ten miles off the port side, sir."

Admiral West then crossed the deck to the starboard quarter with his officers hurrying behind him. Looking across the gentle swell on that side, he asked the same questions, although he supposed this time was that the warship in the distance was *HMS Drake.*

Commodore Shaw again gave the confirmation of the ship to starboard and a similar distance was estimated. In fact, the ten ships of the fleet, five to starboard and five to port, were spread out and sea-anchored over a distance of over one hundred miles, but always just within sight of another ship of the line, to enable flag messages to be passed.

"Very well," said the Admiral, apparently satisfied with the position of the fleet. "Captain Smith, you will signal to both *Warrior* and *Drake*. *Warrior* is to move southwest, as are the ships in her squadron, and take up the positions in their orders, while *Drake* is to move north east with her squadron also as ordered. Once in position, they are to move towards the coast and look for Union blockaders. *Prince of Wales* will make a similar passage. Orders issued are then to be followed."

"Sir!" Captain Smith strode off to pass the command to the Signal warrant officer.

"Commander," the Admiral reminded his next in command, "I confirm the issued orders, of which you are aware. *Warrior* and *Drake* have the same orders and will now weigh anchor and move with all speed due west. Gun crews are to prepare for action, which could come at any time. I shall be in my cabin, but require all commissioned officers to assemble in the wardroom in one hour's time."

Captain Smith saluted smartly and disappeared towards the aft to relay the orders to engineers and anchor crews. The other officers on the deck saluted while Admiral West returned the salute and walked quickly aft to make his way towards the two, well-furnished cabins he occupied, one as a day cabin and one for use at night.

It was several hours later that *Prince of Wales* started to receive flag signals from various warships in the fleet, relayed to them along the line. Some ships had already come across Union blockaders and had signalled them to turn and make speed for their homeport. Signals, due to being reliant solely on flags, were often delayed, but so far, the results were that two British ships, the *Warrior* and the *Drake* had received no flag reply from the Union ships they had signalled, other than shots that had fallen short. Both captains had then signalled the flagship that they had immediately opened fire. The *Warrior* had severely damaged its target, which had sunk, while the *Drake* had experienced less resistance and only one volley of six shells had been needed, causing light damage, before the Union cutter they had encountered had turned tail and fled.

Admiral West was pleased with these positive signals, but knew that they had only just started a campaign of attrition that could take days, if not weeks, if it were to be completed.

## August 7 1861: Washington DC, the Capitol

George Fitzwilliam and the two Tissimans s had attended the Capitol that morning, as they did every morning, hoping to receive a message, although whether that would come from Daniel Hayward at Cotton Hall, the Confederate Government in Richmond or even from their contacts in London, they had no idea. In fact, as time had slowly passed in what was now a relatively peaceful city under Confederate occupation, they had grown increasingly frustrated that the war seemed to have passed them by.

Ernest complained, "I feel we could be left to die here of boredom or simply old age. We have no idea what is going on beyond Washington in any direction. Even if we manage to track down an officer at the White House, they all give the clear impression they would like to avoid us. They seem never to have any news, no information and find us an embarrassment. Why's that do you think?" Receiving no reply, just shrugs, he added, "I think it's because we've fulfilled our purpose."

"Maybe you're right," said Arthur, "There's no sign now of Colonel Alexander and any enquiry I've tried to make about Mr Russell, or even where the Union or Confederate armies are now, is met with blank faces and either a shake of the head or just, 'No idea'."

George looked as disconsolate as the other two. "Yes, we've all hit a brick wall, and I don't understand why, unless, as you said, they've got all they can out of us and now wish we'd just go home."

They decided that there was no point in uselessly wandering around the ever-busy reception hallway and that they might as well find somewhere to eat, although their funds were not looking as healthy as they once had. They were pushing their way towards the entrance when what they took to be a young lieutenant grabbed hold of George's arm.

"I sure am sorry to come on to you like this sir, but are you, by any chance Captain Fitzwilliam from England?"

George swung around, as if he had been attacked, until he saw the uniform and a very apologetic lieutenant, who looked no more than eighteen years old.

"Yes, I am Captain Fitzwilliam and these two gentlemen are both Mr Tissimans. We are all from England. What can we do for you?"

"Well, sir, I've been sent to try to find you, I mean all of you, by General Johnston. I have to tell you, I suppose I mean to *request* you, to come with me to see the General. I mean to say, that is, if you would be able to—"

George interrupted his confusion at this point. "Indeed lieutenant. We are happy to follow you wherever you need to conduct us. I suggest you lead on."

They were hurriedly led out of the antechamber, through guarded double doors and down a long, wide passage. The lieutenant nervously looked behind him every few steps to make sure they were still there. The passage had several windows along its length, many either broken or cracked. The lieutenant stopped at a door just before the passage ended. He looked at the door and then back at his three charges and at last hesitantly knocked and, receiving no response, put his ear to the door, which at that moment was opened from within, causing the young man to stumble over the threshold. He regained his nerve and his footing to announce, "The English Captain for General Johnston, sir."

George, closely followed by Ernest and Arthur, walked past him, turned to say a brief 'Thank you', and then stood just inside the room, aware that the door had been quickly closed behind them. They had entered a small office, already occupied by two Confederate officers standing next to a desk in the corner. They appeared to George to be fairly high ranking, but he had not yet been able to grasp exactly how to recognise all military Confederate ranks from their uniforms, which seemed to have so many different forms of design.

Sitting at the desk, which was littered with papers, maps and several pens, was another officer. He was, George guessed, in his fifties, or possibly older. His hair had receded well back from his forehead, but was neatly trimmed, as was his small, pointed beard and narrow moustache. His grey Confederate jacket had a high collar with the stars on it that must have indicated his general's rank. On this presumption, George came to attention and saluted. "Captain George Fitzwilliam, sir, of Her Majesty's Royal Hussars."

Ernest and Arthur could think of nothing to do or say and so simply stood looking around the room, rather than stare at the man whose strong military aura seemed to make all others in the room seem smaller. The general, if that was, in fact, who he was, signed a document in front of him and then rose from the desk, walked around it and stopped in front of the three young men.

"I am General Joseph Johnston, gentlemen, and obliged to you for coming to see me." He turned and spoke to one of the officers who still stood beside the desk.

"Major, would you both leave us now. I will call when I need you next." They both saluted and left the room.

"Pull up chairs, gentlemen, I need to talk to you."

They each located a chair in various parts of the room and pulled them up to the desk, where General Johnston now sat once again. He opened a drawer and took out a paper that looked as if it had telegraphic message strips glued on to it.

"I have today received this cable from Sir…" he looked closely for the name on the cable, "Lord Herbert of Lea, who is, as I am sure you know, your Secretary of State for War in London. In this, he asks that the Confederate command here facilitate you travelling north into Pennsylvania, so that you may report to him, and your Prime Minister, Lord…ah…" his finger now ran along the lines of print until he found the second name, "Palmerston, about the situation that now exists between the Confederate and Union forces."

George looked surprised, to say the least, while Arthur raised an eyebrow and Ernest spoke almost accusingly. "We are surprised, sir, that we have received no such communication ourselves from London, especially as we were assured we could now be reached here, via your good offices."

General Johnston gave Ernest the long, direct and silent stare that had reduced many an officer in the Confederate ranks to look away in embarrassment in the past. Ernest refused to be intimidated by a mere American soldier and stared straight back.

"I know nothing about that," Johnston replied, "especially as I was requested to contact you as quickly as possible, having received the cable." He then waved aside George's attempt at a response, and continued with a question.

"Have you heard about the incident that was christened the Augusta affair in the *London Times*?"

There was pause as the three looked at each other and the general received only shrugs or shaken heads in reply.

"It seems from your expressions that you have not. Briefly, a Union warship recently stopped a British merchantman off Carolina, seized two Confederate politicians, who were on board bound for England. Your government, regarding this as act of piracy, has now sent a fleet to break the blockade of our Confederate ports."

The shock of such news could be easily read on the faces of the general's audience, but he gave them no chance to speak. "The result is that we have heard from Charleston that a brief engagement ensued between a strong British naval force and far less powerful Union ships, many of which were either sunk or disabled, while the rest turned tail and sailed north. Your Prime Minister has said, we have been told, that while (37) this is not an act of war in support of the Confederacy, he has also, as a precaution, ordered British army reinforcements to proceed to Canada, where your existing troops are already mustering on the border with the Union."

George spoke as soon as Johnston gave him an opportunity to do so. "Does this mean that the war is over, sir? Has the Union surrendered? Or is Britain really actually at war as well?"

Johnston laughed. "No, captain. That is in the hands of God and, of course, the success and courage of our rapidly advancing army. To date, it would seem that the damned Yankees are licking their wounds and gathering every regiment that remains intact well to the north of here, and congregating in the fields and hills north and west of Baltimore."

"Not wishing to ask you anything that would breach any confidences of war, sir," George, ever the soldier, now asked, "but have your Confederate forces pursued the Union there, or are—"

"Come, come, captain! I cannot reveal such details at present, even to a representative of Great Britain, who we now regard as a friend, if not yet an ally."

"I apologise for suggesting you reveal any plans, of course. I think we were all wondering exactly where and when you would be able to assist us to get to a position to report to our government the state of affairs now, at what seems to be a turning point in this unfortunate conflict."

# Chapter Twenty-Eight

**September 1861**

It was early September by the time George, Ernest and Arthur were allowed to leave Washington, but no longer alone and now not in any doubt as to where they were going and why. They were a party of fourteen, once they were accompanied by ten seasoned Confederate infantrymen and a Major James Meredith. They had been assured by General Johnston that the Confederacy would cover the costs for the expedition, which would allow them to see for themselves what was very much hoped, by the Confederate Command would be the last chapter of this Civil War.

On their way to the rail depot of the Baltimore and Ohio Rail Company in Washington, they saw what a few weeks could achieve in terms of change in the old Union capital. Several Confederate battalions were already firmly settled into camps in and around the city, many in what were clearly new, or at least cleaned, uniforms. Artillery batteries were set up on the northern and western outskirts and work had even started to repair some of the buildings that now housed command headquarters, supply warehouses and offices for the Confederate army, and hospitals as well as more suitable accommodation for the Confederate Headquarters in Washington.

The train they boarded on that bright autumn morning also contained in its fifteen carriages further reinforcements for the large Confederate force now establishing itself between Hanover and the small town of Gettysburg. They had to change trains before reaching Hanover Junction, with its long, narrow station building, with somewhat out of place columns supporting the overhang over the platform, the rails being at the same level, and with several large windows in the station building. Their journey had covered about sixty miles and had been more than five hours of stop-start travel from Washington. The junction was, in fact, only a small station in a small settlement amongst the low wooded hills and more open ground that spread north-west about fifteen or twenty miles towards Gettysburg.

All the way from the smaller town of Westminster, they had seen large numbers of Confederate troops on the move northwest, as well as some large army encampments. Alighting at Hanover Junction into the melee of detraining soldiers, they were greeted by the sight of what seemed to be a whole army as far as they could see, parts moving west, while other parts were joining two huge troop camps. Artillery of a wide variety of shapes and sizes was being drawn by dozens of horse teams attached to casements and the wheeled artillery pieces themselves. Even in an area that still appeared at least partly green, clouds of dust rolled over the various regiments and war materiel on the move, the air filled with shouted orders and numerous military bands striking up patriotic tunes as they marched. One such was previously a Union anthem, but that had quickly become adopted by the Confederacy: yet again *Rally 'Round the Flag*.

The three Englishmen who, several months ago, had seen a ferocious part of the battle at Bull Run, were now overawed by the sheer size of the army which filled their whole field of view, large numbers moving between the rows of tents in the camps, others gathered around feeding stations or attending to long lines of tethered horses, while groups of cavalry were part of the stream of men for ever moving away into the distance.

Major Meredith had halted his small party behind the station, where there was just enough room to stand without being run down by either jostling cavalry horses or lumbering pieces of field artillery that stopped for no man. The major had then disappeared towards a sizeable farmhouse with a stream of officers of various ranks constantly either entering or leaving the building with a real urgency of movement. The ten soldiers whom they left behind at the station, broke ranks as soon as Meredith strode off; they then began smoking and making the most of the temporary lack of disciplined orders.

"We've seen a lot of military might since we left Texas, which seems a lifetime ago, but this sea of men and weapons is something else," Ernest said, as he gazed around them at what seemed the whole armed strength of the Confederacy of the South in this one place.

Arthur, too, looked mesmerised by what filled the landscape from horizon to horizon, as he turned slowly around to take in the full spectacle.

"I just hope that the Major will come back with some idea of our part in all this and what exactly is planned for us." He paused and then in a somewhat exasperated voice asked, "Where's the army of the Union, or what's left of it? Do you think they've been reinforced and hidden somewhere and, more importantly, what the hell is going to happen now?"

His questions were destined to remain unanswered as they waited for over half an hour for Major Meredith to reappear. George eventually saw him as he pushed his way out of the farmhouse and then dodged across what was now a crowded highway between there and Hanover Junction station, where he reached his small band of soldiers, flapping his hat against his uniform to remove some of the dust. The ten infantrymen reluctantly came to attention, cigarettes having been squeezed out and placed in convenient pockets; rifles were then picked up from their resting places against the station wall and a semblance of order restored.

George, deciding that he alone could empathise with the major, was pleased that Meredith quickly crossed to speak to him, although all three Envoys were actually standing together. They then had no choice but to try to follow his constantly diverted progress through the mob of soldiery. He also managed at the same time to explain what he had been privy to in the Confederate farmhouse.

"It's pretty crowded in there, I can tell you! Anyway, I came in on a briefing for officers by General Beauregard himself and it seems that we shall soon have an overwhelming force of at least thirty thousand men between here and Gettysburg, which is some distance to the west. This army, the army of the Northern Confederacy, has been boosted by thousands of new recruits from the south, anxious to be in at the death of the Union. Numbers are still growing, here and also with the second army, the army of the Southern Confederacy, based in part around the Shenandoah and Ohio valleys and forming a rough arc to the west of Washington, from Culpepper in the south to Frederick in the north *to fully protect the city*."

As they made slow progress through the confused mass of men, Major Meredith, apparently able to disregard the crush, continued his debriefing for the Envoys.

"Scouting divisions north of here have reported that the Union army appears to be losing soldiers to desertion every day, but they should apparently not be written off entirely. The scouts report that they have set up defences

266

southwest of Gettysburg with trenches, wood spike fencing, artillery widely spread and numerous encampments of troops. They guess there may be as many as many as fifteen to twenty thousand men spread out over several miles."

"Did the General say anything about any other Union forces elsewhere than here?" asked George, who noticed that Ernest was scribbling rapidly in his notebook.

"He was somewhat unwilling to be drawn on that, except to warn that he was aware of reports that are, he admitted, possibly unreliable, but the Union regiments which were not a Bull Run, or escaped from there to the west, as well as units that remained between there and the Mississippi, could still be active. General Stuart was of the view that these outlying regiments were undoubtedly now scattered and had almost certainly lost a lot of men to desertion. So, by my reckoning, we can't be real sure what size their army might be until we force them into a fight."

"Can I just ask, as it is more relevant to us," asked Ernest, his pencil poised, "what the plans are for Captain Fitzwilliam, my brother and myself? We need to compile a report to go by cable to our government in London and although what you have just told us will form an important part of our thoughts, I feel we need to get closer to the action which it seems likely is going to take place at some time in the distance in the next few weeks. We also need to get an idea of the Union strength and their plans from here on."

"Yes indeed, sir," the major quickly responded, "My orders, following the briefing, are to attach you to the rear guard, under the command of General Longstreet. His regiments are presently a few miles to the north-west of us here. It will entail travelling on foot and I fear, since I understand that two of you gentlemen are unacquainted with military marching speeds and duration, this may prove somewhat uncomfortable."

Ernest looked furious at such a suggestion, but a nudge from his brother kept him from speaking his mind.

The major continued, "I will still do my best to try to find some horse transport for you, but, as you can see, this could be difficult at the moment."

Ernest let his irritation at being judged too weak, or maybe just too English, to make it on foot for just a few miles, be reflected in his tone of voice.

"We shall need to have access to a telegraph station, if we are to keep our Prime Minister and Secretary of State for War informed of events here in the next weeks. Where do you think the nearest such telegraph station may be where ever we are going now?"

"As I understand it that would have to be here at Hanover Junction. There's a telegraph station here that is now manned at all times by the army and that links to Washington."

Ernest had a fleeting vision of being able to requisition a horse when such cables needed to be sent, but the vision evaporated as soon as they started the walk towards the north west along with columns of infantry and their mounted officers, while divisions of cavalry trotted past them and gun carriages and waggons loaded with ammunition, boxes and sacks of supplies threw up even more dust that drifted into their mouths and eyes. Ernest resigned himself to several hours of uncomfortable foot slogging through the hot afternoon, but tried to persuade himself that this was his patriotic duty to his Queen and country. However, the alternative of getting some Confederate cavalry officer to undertake the responsibility of taking charge of their cables, did now enter his mind.

Two hours later, Ernest's patriotism was being stretched. Not only did they suffer dust and constant periods of being forced off the track by troops and supplies moving much faster, but also by the steadily rising ground that slowed them further, even more than their simply being unused to walking on such rough tracks for hours at a time. Eventually, Major Meredith was persuaded to stop for a chance to quench their thirst from canteens carried by the soldiers and by the major, who seemed happy to share his supply. As they moved off the track to shelter from the heat under a small group of trees, whose leaves were now brilliant with shades of autumn, a coach could be heard approaching at speed and throwing up clouds of dust as the soldier at the reins encouraged the sweating horses to gallop at top speed; the figure of a single man could just be distinguished inside.

George was closest to it and shouted, "Hey! I'm sure that was Russell inside there. I'd know that head and hat anywhere."

The carriage and its possibly identified passenger were already well past them by the time Ernest and Arthur turned to look. "That damned man always seems to be treated as if he was royalty," remarked Ernest.

"Fate seems determined that Mr Russell dogs our footsteps wherever we go," said Arthur, although Ernest, believing nothing he did not see for himself, simply added, "That's *if* that was William Russell and I don't see how you could possible identify anyone inside a coach at speed and covered with billows of dust."

It was late afternoon by the time Major Meredith lead his small group into the huge Confederate army camp that had been set up on open ground, while beyond the tents the land dropped gradually away down a gentle slope to the north. Below the farthest edge of the camp, at the bottom of the downward slope, was fairly flat land, with fields interspersed with scattered trees and occasional dense copses. Farm buildings could be glimpsed and the Baltimore turnpike, which they were told would eventually, after many miles, lead to the presently invisible town of Gettysburg; it ran from south to north about a mile to their east.

By six o'clock, it was becoming cool and the sun, still occasionally to be seen between clouds rushing in from the west, served only to illuminate the scene, rather than warm it. Meredith directed his soldiers to report to a Lieutenant on the outskirts of the camp, while he led his three English charges towards a farmhouse on the eastern flank. This was constructed, as were most farm buildings they had seen elsewhere, of timber boards with a brick chimneystack.

"This old, but fairly solid farmhouse is the where General Longstreet is to be found," Meredith explained. "He's in command of the reserve rear guard, which is made up of the ten thousand men who are based here and in the smaller second camp half a mile to the south. As we are unlikely to need a rear guard, they will, in fact, become reinforcements for the battle that now must surely come at some time in the near future."

He stopped just short of the farmhouse, which had several sentries posted to ensure no one who did not have authorised business was able to approach the general. Meredith was saluted by one of the sentries and quickly admitted to the building.

As the Envoys waited outside, they took the chance to look more carefully at the camp, which stretched out of site on three sides to north, east and west. They walked as far as the top end of the camp and were able to look down the slope at what now had the appearance of a canvas city spread before them. What must have been a thousand tents, some bell and some oblong, were set up in regular lines like streets, with occasional open spaces where larger tents could be seen. Most of the tents they could see had open fires outside them, over which hung steaming cauldrons or spits with small-skinned animals roasting over them.

With no set pattern of size, they also spotted numerous much larger tents that had wooden rooves and chimneys. A number of the smaller tents, especially those grouped together, also had evergreen branches arranged over the tops as an additional roof, which they learned later kept them cooler in hot weather and supposedly helped to prevent disease. Small, rough tables could be seen outside many with men sitting around, some playing cards, some cleaning rifles, while others sat on the ground with mugs of some e sort of drink; they discovered that many had basic coffee grinders to help to produce hot black coffee. Rifles were pitched like tepees in front of many of the tents. They also suspected that most of those seated in this area were not officers. What they assumed was washing hung over the ridgepoles of many tents to dry. There was a permanent sound of men's voices with shouts, laughter and raucous swearing filling the air, along with the smoke of the many fires.

Officer's tents were generally, it seemed, larger with wooden frameworks and outside, as well as tables, were chairs, often with wooden frames with canvas hung from these to provide more comfortable seating, very similar to an English deck chair. The occasional sound of music came from what appeared to be small groups of bandsmen entertaining their fellows. Tobacco smoke arose from every occupied living area, since cigars, cigarettes and clay pipes abounded, as they seemed to in every army. Arthur pointed out one large tent just a hundred yards away, where there were stacks of hundreds of loaves. The man who seemed in charge was clearly a civilian and was weighing trays of a dozen loaves at a time with scales.

Further on, a small waggon was stacked with news sheets being sold by another civilian. Ernest was especially intrigued, but somewhat mystified, by the heaps of bread, until George explained that bread was the staple diet of all armies he knew of and that it was issued to soldiers by weight. Behind them and beyond the rear edge of the camp, they had already passed many dozens of empty covered waggons, whose horses were nearby in long lines tethered to stout ropes slung between posts.

"Have you noticed the man just across there," asked George, "the one sitting on that pile of logs, but who is obviously not a soldier?"

The other two focussed on a bearded man wearing a broad brimmed hat, long brown jacket and knee length boots. He had a large open book resting on one knee and looked as if he was writing in it.

"What on earth is he doing?" asked Ernest. "Surely, he's not supposed to be openly jotting down information in a military camp that is preparing for action."

George seemed to have seen someone like him before. "I think you'll find that he's not writing, but drawing. I've seen the likes of him in the Crimea. He and probably several fellows, are artists who draw scenes of battle or, like this, the living conditions of soldiers, and sell them to newspapers, or they may even be employed by them, the same as is Mr Russell. They travel with an army, live with them and eat with them. They also risk their lives with them, since whomever the enemy happens to be at the time is quite likely to take them for members of the opposing force. I know from personal experience that Mr Russell was so close to the fighting at Sebastopol that on one occasion, he was flung in the air by an exploding shell but, very fortunately for him, suffering only cuts bruises."

They eventually walked back, hoping to find the major, but he had still not reappeared. They found a place to sit on the ground with their backs to a fence that partially protected them from a cold wind that was beginning to chill them, as well as swaying the trees that were scattered throughout the camp.

This was where Major Meredith found them after his lengthy wait to speak with General Longstreet. He explained that a tent had been set aside for them and although claiming it was his *duty* to show them to their quarters, it was clear by now that he would be pleased to be relieved of his responsibility to them and he clearly wanted to get on with his real duties as an officer.

The trio had walked only a short distance when, turning sharply after a copse of trees they saw what must have been hundreds of pieces of field artillery and cannons neatly lined up with their caissons behind them, obviously ready to be taken forward in the case of action.

The tent Meredith then took them to, one of the bell-shaped examples, was just two lines across and a hundred yards down into a camp *street*; this even had a name board nailed to a post: *Long Street*. Arthur laughed out loud, as he pointed it out.

The major explained that they would be amongst a regiment of soldiers from Tennessee and apologised for the fact that they were not in more salubrious accommodation.

As they made their way down the tent line, they were not only closely inspected by men relaxing outside their own tents in the quickly cooling evening air, but comments were fired towards them as they passed, including many unflatteringly noting their dress, their *swanky* accents and also questioning: '*What the hell these pale townies doin' here?*', as well as: '*I reckon boys, them's Yankees and with an officer!*' and: '*Maybe they's prisoners?*'

When they reached the only empty tent in the line so far, they noticed that there was just one stool outside, one leg shorter than the other two, while inside were relics of the last occupants: two filthy blankets, what looked like a bar of orange soap, a grey forage cap with a bullet hole in it, and an old album with a broken spine, open to show two photographs of ragged children and an elderly man and woman.

"My apologies for this, gentlemen," Major Meredith said again without much conviction as he looked around. "I will do my best to get you some bed rolls and blankets and see if any chairs can be found. You are to eat in the officer's mess of the Kentucky Mountain Boys, which is down the end there." He waved his hand in the direction of the far end of the line.

"General Longstreet requires you to report to his headquarters after you've eaten. Ask for Colonel Grey. He will brief you there." He turned away and marched back up the line and disappeared from view.

The rest of the evening was an experience that none of them would readily forget. Having decided that food was a priority, they made their way to a long wooden hut that had a board over the entrance, on which *OFFICERS* was written in red paint.

Inside the 'canteen', dozens of men whom they presumed to be Tennessee officers in various styles of uniform, albeit mostly grey in colour, were conducting conversations that, more often than not, required to be shouted to be heard. There were some women as well as a few soldiers of non-officer rank who served the officers plates of food, as well as mugs and tankards of drink.

Since no one questioned who the Englishmen were, they decided, after some hesitation, that it would be better to queue for food at the long counter, rather than sit and wait at one of the long tables, where there was probably little chance of being served. Behind the service counter was the hot, steamy and rather chaotic kitchen. The meal consisted of meat and potato stew, bread and tin mugs of ale. They found enough space to sit at one crowded table, but were ignored by those already there. They did, however, note with somewhat jealous glances that there were also wine bottles circulating, but no sign of where they might be obtained. It was two weeks before they discovered that the waggons selling newspapers also had a side-line in '*The finest quality wine this side of Hanover Junction, just $2*'.

They were surprised at the presence of so many other women in the room, whom they decided were definitely not there in the role of cooks or waiters. These sat amongst the men, with whom some were openly flirting, while others sat next to officers with whom they seemed to have some connection. They later learned that in front line regiments like these, wives often accompanied their soldier husbands, while others acted as paid servants, cooks, laundresses and, not apparently a shock to George, some who were prostitutes.

What, however, was another surprise to Arthur and Ernest in the camp as a whole, but not apparently to George, who had seen it often on campaigns abroad, was the presence of numerous children. George confirmed that many of the families of private soldiers on campaign had no one at home who could feed their children, while in the camps food and lodging were free.

They were pleased to get out into the open air, albeit noticeably colder by now, and get away from the tobacco smoke drifting across every table in the canteen and mingled with the steam from the kitchen cauldrons to fill the atmosphere.

They were pleased to discover on their return that their tent had been cleared out and three bedrolls and blankets heaped on some sort of, possibly waterproof, ground sheet. There was also an oil lantern, a small table and three chairs, which could perhaps be folded, that looked as if they had suffered in several previous campaigns. With a meal inside them and at least some basic accommodation to come back to, they continued on towards General Longstreet's headquarters. They kept their satchels of personal belongings with them, being nervous that they might disappear in their absence.

Having persuaded the sentries at the headquarters, located in the far corner of the camp, that they were expected by Colonel Grey, they were admitted to the farmhouse. This boasted a large room, which looked as if several interior walls had been roughly knocked down to allow an area suitable for meetings.

Oil lanterns provided some light for the meeting room. The ceilings were quite low, while the only furniture in the room consisted of a large kitchen table, covered with maps and other papers, an array of unmatched chairs and what must once have been a kitchen store cupboard, but which now had no doors and was overflowing with books and more papers.

Colonel Grey, a relatively young man for his rank, was leaning over the table studying a map, but was made aware of their presence by the sentry. The Colonel was dressed in the traditional long grey Confederate coat, with gold braiding on sleeves and neck. He had a small, well-clipped beard and moustache, while his most noticeable feature was an extremely crooked nose that had obviously been badly broken and not set back at its rightful angle. He took them through one of the other doors into an adjoining room that looked as if it might have been a parlour before the Confederate army commandeered the house. The colonel took an oil lamp from a shelf and lit it with a silver-coloured metal match safe from his pocket.

George saluted the colonel and introduced both himself and his two companions. With no furniture other than two old and very dilapidated easy chairs, they were forced to stand uneasily in front of the colonel, who explained that he was an adjutant to General Longstreet, who was elsewhere at the present time, but he had been briefed by the General about their role and objectives on behalf of the British government.

"The General has issued orders that we should at all times attempt to keep you in places of safety, while ensuring that you are able to report as much as possible on the bravery and patriotic spirit of the Confederate army. Also he feels sure you will want to advise your English government of the victories you will soon witness and which are driving the Union towards their ignominious defeat."

He paused and for some inexplicable reason looked up at the low ceiling. "Perhaps you might also wish to add how you have seen evidence that the intervention of your navy has already shortened the war and no doubt saved thousands of lives."

"I have no doubt," George said, trying to be as diplomatic as possible under the circumstances, "that you and your men will help us to observe all the evidence you have outlined."

The Colonel looked a little confused by his answer, but continued according to whatever script he had been given.

"Yes...precisely. I have been instructed to give you some information about our present situation."

Here he paused again, as if he had forgotten what came next and looked around the room as if he were expecting to spot a clue.

"I am sorry that I cannot offer you seating...so, to continue: the bulk of the Confederate army is now some distance away, perhaps twenty miles closer to the town of Gettysburg than the reserve camp here and is a very strong force indeed. In fact, it is almost sixty-five thousand strong and spread over several miles to the south and east of the town of Gettysburg. The Union General Meade has dug in about twenty miles to our north with whatever Union force he can assemble." The colonel seemed to have gained confidence now and continued more fluently.

"We are unsure of exactly what the strength of the enemy is, since we are aware that quite large numbers of the men they commanded two months ago have been killed, wounded or simply fled for home; numbers are hard to come by."

He paused for long enough to glance down at one of the papers on the desk.

"We believe that there are probably pockets of Union troops well to the west, possibly scattered, but just could be uniting in one area. We can find no information as to where Union General Reynolds and Scott may be, but we can be sure they are not anywhere near here. General Grant, as you may or may not know, was *removed* to a job out of the action and was to be found in an office in Washington, until Bull Run was lost. After that, he disappeared."

Here he stopped and reached into a box for a small cigar, which he lit and drew on with obvious pleasure.

"So we realise," he continued, while his audience began to feel somewhat dazed by the long speech, "that, with winter coming on, it may be difficult to launch an immediate attack on Meade's force here. There is inevitable concern about the unknown forces to the west, but, again, winter may possibly keep them where they are, although the thought that they could be rebuilding some strength in the meantime is very much on our commander's mind."

"Do forgive me if I have misunderstood," George spoke quickly, suspecting the Colonel might still not have finished his lecture, "but should we take it that General Longstreet has come to the conclusion that any real or serious action is unlikely for several months?"

Colonel Grey raised his eyebrows and then looked around the room.

"I think you should realise that, although the forces of the Confederacy now have a powerful upper hand in this sad conflict, events have moved more swiftly than even we could have expected."

The man appeared to be unstoppable. "Winter is coming. We have a Union force that is now severely wounded and shocked, dug in many miles away from here. We also very likely have some further splinters of the original Union armies scattered to the west of us and they will be, I am sure, equally disillusioned as well as drastically reduced in number; our information suffers from uncertainty and a lack of solid facts in that direction. Our whole land is bleeding and longs for respite. We assure you, and your government, that we will continue to build up our presence between here and the farmland closer to Gettysburg, and our battle readiness, as well as trying to improve the hazy nature of what little information is reaching us from the west."

"I am sure we can appreciate that," Ernest now put in, "but we are wondering what we can do now and in the winter to come, to assure our government in England that the invaluable action our navy has just taken on your behalf is likely to be followed by the Confederate Army's swift reciprocal measures here on land in order to bring this savage conflict, that is creating such cost to both your country and our own, to a final solution."

The colonel prevented Ernest from adding anything else.

"I am not a Confederate general, thank God, but on behalf of those who are, I am authorised to say that we will do all we can to let you see the excellent state of our army here and, when appropriate, what actions we shall be taking in the future. You are already in a position to talk to anyone you wish in this camp and to report your findings to your government. We shall try to take you forward to see our preparations for future action and the General will also talk to you about the wider context and what he sees for the future." He paused and then added, as an after-thought, "As you would expect, since this has to be the most confidential and privileged information, your report to your Prime Minister will have to be agreed by General Longstreet before it is despatched."

Neither Arthur nor Ernest said anything, although George knowingly muttered, "Ah."

# Chapter Twenty-Nine

## December 1861

More than two months had passed in what was now a massive military camp confined in the depths of winter. No one was amused when George informed them that in (38) the furious winter of 1777/78 George Washington's army had been similarly stuck in Valley Forge for months. Eighty-four years later, the heavy snowfalls and freezing temperatures of the winter of 1861/62 had prevented any action, beyond that of the all too frequent and hated training of the Confederate troops, both in and beyond the confines of the camp. The Envoys were bored beyond belief. The only small piece of good cheer was that it had briefly stopped snowing.

Arthur was never quite sure whether it was less cold when it did snow or whether that was just an illusion. Winter back at home did not often produce very much snow at all, just cold, wind and rain intermingled from time to time with sleet, but Waterhead Hall had always been kept warm with blazing fires of coal from local mines, logs gathered from their estate and the new wonders of 'centrally fired heating'.

Arthur's mind turned, as it had so often recently, to wonder: *what is Mother doing today at home; has she been able, at last, to accept Betty's dreadful loss of the baby;..... is Maggie coping with life in the town, since the mills must have been shut for months and hunger surely would be stalking the streets and homes of those now without jobs or money;...... Is Father now in an inevitable state of anger and despair seeing his beloved mill silent and the reserves of profit draining away week on week;....... is the family managing to retain their comfortable lives through all this?*

Here in Pennsylvania winter was a totally different beast from Oldham. It began when the spectacular leaves of autumn had fallen and it would end: who knew when? As Arthur sat just inside their tent pulling the blankets around the layers of more or less every piece of clothing they possessed, began to fantasise that snow would probably still be here next August.

Just inside the multitude of partly open door flaps, small fires were competing to stay alight against a freezing wind. Soldiers not on duty huddled in tents and huts, seeking any relief from the freezing air, while those on duty resembled clotheshorses draped with coats and blankets, as well as sacking tied over their boots in an attempt to keep the snow out and helping to keep them standing upright on the eternal whiteness covering the land. Ernest and George had trudged up the slope to the headquarters half an hour ago, crossing the lanes between tents that were now covered in deep, trampled, frozen snow and ice.

Arthur had agreed to take on the journal again and up to date that was more than simply anything to relieve the boredom. It was now the record of what they had seen since sending the last telegraph to London and arriving here more than two months ago. It was difficult to write with freezing, numb fingers, even inside two pairs of gloves. There was, however, hardly anything he could constructively write about. He now gave up the attempt and put the pencil down; pen and ink had been abandoned two months ago when conditions started to freeze the ink. He flicked back through the pages of what was his fourth journal.

The three of them had found the first month or so truly informative and the weather not unpleasant. They explored the vast camp and talked to a great variety of officers, infantry soldiers and cavalrymen, as well as the amazing variety of women and children from so many different places and backgrounds. They met and talked to more butchers, bakers, cooks, washerwomen, carpenters, smiths, genuine doctors and quacks, surgeons and women with some basic skills at caring for more sick and wounded than they would have encountered in a lifetime at home. They had met those supplying alcohol to the troops and those pedalling moonshine. They had been present, and horrified, at the public punishment of soldiers who were charged with various crimes or even trying to escape the camp to get back to their homes; men who had been tied to cannon wheels to receive ten, twenty or more lashes, others thrown into the camp's equivalent of jail, with no comforts of any kind, little food and, as winter increased its grip, the threat of dying of the cold.

They had spoken to General Longstreet once and seen General Robert E Lee from afar when his visited the rear-guard camp. Arthur and Ernest now shared the task of keeping the journal at that time as fully as possible, although Arthur made sure he only contributed information or recollections that had caused his brother to speak out against something, avoiding his own take on slavery.

The sole interview with General Longstreet had been of shorter duration than they had hoped, having waited two months to meet with the illustrious commander of the rear and reserve guard. While the General had been generous in his compliments about what England had done for the Confederacy so far and what information the three English envoys were gathering to send by telegraph to London once they felt they had something positive to report and before the journey to the railhead cable office became impossible, as indeed it did in the middle of October. The general's views on what might or might not be expected to happen when the army could escape the vice-like grip of winter were rather vague, but the Envoys felt they had to agree with his conclusions.

"It is our intention during this rather cool weather to ensure that our soldiers keep alert, healthy and in good spirits," General Longstreet had felt able to confide in them two months ago. "Any of the insane attempts by Meade and his Yankees to attack defences have been shown to be pointless and costly for them in terms of their dead and wounded. Those we have taken prisoner are in a parlous state, being half-starved, in ragged clothing and with no will to fight. Once we of the Confederate command deem the time to be right, we shall advance on all fronts and fall down on them like a wolf on the fold."

Only Arthur was aware of the reference to Lord Byron's poem 'The Destruction of Sennacherib', while the military history to which the reference gave enlightenment, would probably have been pointless to pass to the Secretary of State for war in his London office.

What was of much more interest to them two months ago, before the winter prevented their movement from camp, was an expedition that Colonel Grey had managed to arrange for them in early October. This enabled them to travel forward to see for themselves what Confederate strength lay between their rearward encampment and the rest of the army stretching towards Gettysburg, where they were also allowed to observe the considerable outward defences before the town: entrenchments, walls, mounds and artillery emplacements collapse into the harbour; they looked as if they had been there for years.

They had also spent another week out of camp at the beginning of September, this time travelling in the relative comfort of a coach, accompanied by Colonel Grey and two lieutenants. They had first crossed the sixteen or seventeen miles from the rear-guard encampment to the most forward position of the Confederate army, several miles to the south and east of Gettysburg. However, they soon discovered that the whole of the area of farmland, woods and gentle hills was occupied by troops in grey uniforms. Some parts had relatively small groups on duty in outposts, while other encampments were of several thousand men.

Much of the farmland had been transformed with defensive works: trenches, earthworks, foxholes, farmhouses turned into fortresses, high and solid wooden barricades, featuring forward facing, savage looking spikes and crisscross barriers with *cheveaux de frise* of sharpened logs. These covered hundreds of yards at a time.

They saw many wooden lookout and signal towers and hundreds of field guns, cannons and mortars, again behind redoubts of earth and rock. In the journal, Ernest described it as '*a hundred square miles that had become one mighty fortress that seemed it could easily withstand an advance of an army twice the size of the Union's and equally could destroy the enemy in the process*'.

They were able to talk to private soldiers as well as officers and noted the high level of confidence and belief in the Confederate cause amongst all concerned. Ernest had added a note to the journal that: "*The cause of this, I suspect, has not a little to do with their being well fed, accommodated in tents and huts, at least partially out of the threatening winter weather and having been rested for many weeks.*"

George had cautioned that this was all very well, but that, as he said, "*It is important to look for evidence that their troops are assiduously being drilled and trained on a daily basis to be prepared for battles that are surely yet to come.*" In fact, they were able, just a few days later to have been permitted, '*To observe at last this important training and serious troop preparation on all the fronts we have now visited*'.

Two other pieces of vital information were also revealed to them, which they were asked to convey to London. They learned of these instances when they had the chance to meet the extraordinarily self-confident and extrovert Brigadier General James (Jeb) Stuart. They had arrived at his cavalry headquarters one evening in September 1861 and were surprised to be invited to dine with one of the heroes of Bull Run. During the evening, where wine and whisky flowed, they learned that the Union General Sherman, also present at Bull Run, had just resigned from his army post and had then actually shot himself. It was said by Jeb Stuart that General Sherman could no longer bear to see '*his boys so reduced to cripples or even corpses by battle*'. It was Sherman who had then said '*War is cruelty*' and his departure from this world seemed to confirm it.

More significant even that all this, however, was the news that Abraham Lincoln, who had retreated from Washington DC after Bull Run, had set up his headquarters in Pennsylvania and had now been visiting his forces there, well away from any potential battle. There was a rumour that he had claimed he '*would lead my brave lads into the final battle that would turn the war and crush the Confederacy for ever*'. Ernest had not failed to note in the journal that this had further incensed the Confederates, who now bragged how they would '*string old Abe up from a sour apple tree*' when they caught him, which they promised whoever was listening would not be too far away.

Once back in their own camp as autumn gave way to winter in October, which was by then witness to the first flurries of snow. he Envoys had prepared a much-shortened version of events since they had left Washington DC and this was now ready to send over the wires to Lord Palmerston in London. At the telegraph station at Hanover Junction, they watched the clerk laboriously spell it out and dispatch it. They felt, as always, the relief that it appeared to at least have started its journey satisfactorily. They were unaware that it was the last cable they would be able to send for many months.

Meanwhile, they would wait until spring to hear the news that Prince Albert had died of typhoid on December 14. Their Queen would no longer express any concern for the American Civil War as she plunged herself into the intense and heartfelt mourning for her beloved Albert that would last for many years; some said for the rest of her life.

# Part Two
## 1862/63

# Chapter Thirty

**February 1862**

By late February the camp, now named by its occupants as *Davis Town* after the president, was almost as established as a genuine town might be. Those selling supplies may not have been in shops, but rather tents, huts or even carts; its eating places were hardly restaurants; its barber shops were found outside tents in every lane; its medical facilities were at best in requisitioned farm houses and at worst under canvas. Even so, its population was greater than in many towns back home in Lancashire.

Discipline was probably better imposed than in most towns, since military rules and regulations were often harshly imposed. There were two jails, one for the punishment of soldiers and one for civilians, although that stockade would eventually serve as a secure holding place for Union soldiers taken prisoner in battle.

Mid-February had seen a break in the heavy snows of the previous months and was a chance to put details of troops onto the lanes to clear the passage of snow and ice for people, as well as for carts and waggons. As for the level of comfort on exposed farmland in a hard winter, it could only be said to be just better than having to live with no shelter out of doors. The best accommodation, naturally reserved for higher-ranking officers, was in farm houses and barns, where it was possible to be warmed a little by fires and protected from snow storms by reasonably sound walls.

Lower ranking officers, the lieutenants and captains, were generally garrisoned in temporary buildings of rough-hewn planks and canvas. For the remainder of regular soldiers, either volunteers, three-month enlisted men, or those who joined the army for indefinite periods, shelter for these was the thickness of canvas, with floors of snow-covered earth or, if you were more fortunate, a groundsheet. The lanes between tents and huts were too numerous to all be named and the snow that gathered in drifts there made movement hazardous for weeks at a time.

Attempts were made by cavalry officers and their men to provide some shelter for the lines of horses by searching out the areas that were wooded. Those who owned their own mounts, usually with private soldiers to act as grooms, had the benefit of tarpaulins that were sometimes obtained by methods that were often not revealed, but could provide some cover to the horses of cavalrymen of higher rank like Jeb Stuart. The fitness of cavalry horses could mean the difference between life and death for both horses and their riders in battle.

The three Englishmen, by now accepted by neighbouring Confederate soldiers as inevitable members of their part of the camp, had begged or borrowed, or even bought, a few small improvements to their comfort, which included thick military overcoats and a hearth and metal chimney stack so that they could light a fire inside the tent, although firewood was in short supply at times. They had paid an exorbitant price to a local farmer at Harper's Junction for three larger and thicker blankets than those supplied by Major Meredith. They soon learned to spend as much time as they could in the canteens, cookhouses and even the few saloons that existed on the outskirts of Davis Town.

It was a week before the end of the month and, with the snow having stopped its assault for a few days, the lane past their tent, although icy, was at least passable on foot.

Ernest, who had grown more and more morose as the days passed, claimed he had never been so cold in his life and was not afraid to ask George and Arthur: "What the hell are we supposed to be doing here, we have very little to write up, except frost bite and foul living conditions, but we can't actually *report* anything to London anyway!"

Neither of the other two Envoys replied and they retreated as usual to the canteen just as soon as it was open in the morning. At least it was fairly warm in there, with its steaming cauldrons and hundreds of bodies each giving off a little heat. The rest of the day was filled with cold and boredom. George tried everyone he thought he could persuade to let him join a regiment in preparation for battle, but he was always refused, on the grounds that he was '*too important*' to risk injury or illness with the common soldiery. George himself had to accept that for a British officer to volunteer to serve in a Confederate regiment would hardly be acceptable, politically, in London.

One evening, as February slipped its frozen feet into March, they left the comparative warmth of a saloon and Arthur was able to excavate his pocket watch to declare that it was after ten o'clock. The moon was full, the sky clear and the temperature starting to freeze the moustaches and beards both brothers had by now grown, although George maintained his shaven face was '*as a soldier should appear*'.

They had reached their tent and had managed to start a small fire that gave off some heat, when they heard what sounded like a not uncommon commotion in the distance towards the northern edge of the camp or it might be, also not unusually, a fight between men who were feeling the cabin fever of the confinement of winter quarters.

However, when it was followed by the sound of rifle fire from the same quarter, the occupants of tents and huts as far as the eye could see by the light of the moon, began to appear outside on the streets. As the noise of panicking voices percolated the cold air, shouts and even screams became louder and the crack of rifle fire increased. This became more rapid and there was a surge of bodies towards the source of the turmoil, about a mile away. As the Envoys reached the bottom of their lane and the more sturdy buildings of canteens, saloons and officer's quarters there, bugles began to sound the call to arms.

George managed to grab the arm of a lieutenant running past and shouted the obvious question of what was happening? The reply was also shouted above the melee. "We are under attack! Bloody Yankees!" and then to the confused crowd of soldiers, "Get your guns, you bastards! You know what to do. Get your platoon together and rally to your officer. NOW! Or I'll have your hides flayed!"

In the chaos of several thousands of men realising what was happening and following orders for such an eventuality or other hundreds becoming desperately confused and terrified as they attempted to gather their wits, and probably their courage. The majority by now tried to follow orders, which were really supposed to apply in a planned battle, when officers would be in command and could order them what to do and where to go. Whatever emotions were uppermost, everyone realised that the shouts of such a multitude of soldiers and the increasing frequency of gunfire meant that somehow and somewhere what was once a distant prospect of death and injury had now moved insanely close.

George and Arthur having rushed outside along with the inhabitants of every tent and hut around them, now stood outside the empty saloon, having no idea what they ought to do. George shouted to make himself heard, "We'd better stay here until we can find some officer who has an idea what is happening and where we ought to be."

Immediately after this, they both realised that Ernest was not beside them to hear his advice; he was nowhere in sight. They both ran haphazardly and, as it happened, pointlessly, dodging between the crowds of armed soldiers heading in different directions, but while it was obvious that Ernest could probably be just yards away and they would not be able to see him, it was equally true that he could have been carried away on the tide of soldiers, as well as the panicking women and children, who were caught in the maelstrom that was sweeping more and more residents out of the camp towards its northern edge.

It seemed to be an eternity, but was in truth just twenty minutes, when shouted orders from officers were at last heeded and the battalions, regiments and cohorts of Confederate soldiers began to coalesce into a recognisable semblance of order. In the distance at the upper end of the camp came the sound of cavalry on the move, although neither George nor Arthur could see much beyond the next few rows of tents. What they could see some distance away at the lower edge of the camp, were the now constant flashes of rifles in the distant woodland, illuminating the clear night sky.

Within the next few minutes, the somewhat more orderly mass of men who had, until recently, filled the lanes, had moved away to the north and west, where there now seemed to be a raucous conflict in progress. As the two young envoys stood, unsure of what to do, three mounted officers came at a gallop down the lane. Two passed them, intent on wherever they were going; the third pulled his horse to a halt, skidding perilously on the icy roadway.

"What the fuck you doing standin' there? Why are you not in uniform?"

As the officer shouted down to them, he had pulled a pistol from the holster on his saddle and pointed in menacingly in their direction, his eyes almost as wide and close to panic as those of his horse. George managed to string a few words together that the officer apparently accepted, as he pulled his horse around and galloped away, going out of sight into the darkness.

By that time Ernest had, in fact, also been carried forward by the mass of soldiers that tumbled down the lane leading away from the saloon, now empty. He could not see where he was being carried to in the darkness, shouts and screams of orders impossible to understand, while the sound and sight of gunfire, which was getting nearer by the minute, was both terrifying and disorientating. Once this crowd was out of the confines of lanes of tents, it began to scatter, running in the direction of officers shouting orders and the cry of bugles.

Ernest came to a halt at the edge of a wood, bent over and coughing violently as he tried to breathe. Once he could stand upright, he realised how cold he was since his overcoat had disappeared and also that only about four or five hundred yards away were lines of soldiers running through the trees, some in grey, but some in blue, blazing the night into day and creating clouds of smoke over what appeared to be tangled groups of soldiers, it being impossible in some places to distinguish between grey and blue uniforms.

Ernest was jerked into action as mini balls and bullets began to thrash through the branches above and beside him, most hammering harmlessly into the tree trunks. He dropped to the ground and crawled further into the cover of trees, but there was no protection there either as the deadly wasps of lead whistled ever closer. As he crouched as far away as he could from the heart of the action and, while trying to keep under the cover of trees, he could hear the crashing of bodies coming smashing through undergrowth and low branches behind him. He turned in terror, praying that they were advancing Confederate soldiers, but who could, of course, assume he was another Yankee invader, as he was not wearing the grey of the south.

He could hear nothing above the screaming noise of a raging fight, nor see anything other than the outline of trees in the light of discharging rifles that now lit up the darkness continuously. What was behind him and what was in front became one nightmare surrounding him, as he cowered against a tree trunk. When something hard struck the side of his head, he had a fraction of a second to be aware of it and then blackness and silence descended.

The Union soldier who had used his rifle butt to fell him, then moved swiftly on, caring only for the surprise the advance the skirmishers were inflicting on the damned Rebs.

It took almost another half hour for General Longstreet and the other senior officers in command of the rear-guard camp to make sense of what was happening and to restore a semblance of order to what had at first been a chaotic reaction, followed for a while by a ragged defence of Davis Town. However, once orders were able to get to officers at the scene of the attack it became slowly possible to organise those Confederate soldiers, regardless of their platoons or divisions, into defensive positions between the Union skirmish force and the main camp. By that time, the attackers were already a scattered force penetrating the north western edge of the camp, setting fire to lines of tents and with the flames already threatening to invade much more of the camp.

The commanding officers struggled to understand how a Union force had been able to move around the western edge of the whole Confederate rear guard force with no alarm being raised and then get within striking distance of Davis Town before anyone knew of their existence; these officers vowed that heads would roll for this negligence. Much later, it was realised that it was probably a relatively small Union force that had come across their western flank and that had inflicted carnage before any organised defence was in place.

Three hours passed before Longstreet's front line officers and men were able to drive the Yankees back from the main camp itself, by which time the Confederates had an overwhelming force involved in the action. The invaders, as suddenly as they had arrived, melted into the darkness and, although several platoons pursued them for about a mile, it was clearly impossible in the dark to go any further.

When dawn broke at a little before nine o'clock, it was possible to make a count of their own dead and wounded, as well as the Union casualties left behind and the prisoners taken. The ledger that was eventually drawn up in the Confederate farmhouse headquarters could only be an approximate record, at least for the time being. A colonel was in charge of the count, as bodies were gathered and the wounded taken to hospital tents. The tally at eleven o'clock that morning was reckoned to be: Confederate dead 252, wounded or missing over 300, prisoners taken by the Union possibly 3; Union dead left behind 74, wounded 27 (it was thought that many wounded had been carried away by the more able bodied), Union prisoners 15.

General Longstreet addressed his senior officers at midday.

"I want every one of you to draw up an account of how this could have happened. We have over ten thousand soldiers here, fresh, well-armed and anxious to whip the Yankees once and for all and we suffered a surprise attack by a few hundred bloody Union lovers out-flanking our entire army of more than eighty thousand and creeping up on us without any alarm being sounded!"

Major General Pickett managed to utter three words, "If I may—"

Before Longstreet rounded on him and, raising his voice even closer to a shout, spat out, "No, sir, you may not! I want answers, not excuses...*and* I want outlying posts established, *at once,* manned day and night, as well sentry patrols, both close to camp and covering a belt a mile wide around the camp, which should have been in place long ago, as I ordered."

The General was now pacing ever more quickly up and down the room and heaven help any officer who got in his way.

"This day will live for ever in the annals of shame for the army of the Confederacy. I shudder to think what President Davis will have to say if, when, he hears of this. I don't want any more words from any of you, just get out there and I expect to see every damned soldier here working from dawn to dusk until they are able to be called soldiers of the Confederacy once again."

From that afternoon onwards, all soldiers and officers in the camp, apart from General Longstreet and the most senior commanders, were left in no doubt that there was always a man of higher rank than themselves, an officer who was now intent on driving them to the edge of exhaustion, often without sleep or food, in order that General Longstreet might eventually be satisfied that Davis Town Camp was ready for any attack, skirmish or battle, be it by day or night, whether in freezing or sweltering weather.

Failure was met with punishments that varied from forced marches to being ordered to stand sentry duty all night in temperatures below freezing and where a man found sleeping on duty could expect to feel the lash on his back. It took a month for the General to be satisfied enough to report his eventual satisfaction to General Robert E Lee, commanding the Confederate army and based in his own headquarters somewhat closer in the direction of the town of Gettysburg. Here he was able to enjoy the comparative luxury of a requisitioned mansion, once the property of an unfortunate wealthy Pennsylvanian, whom he described as 'another stinking Union lover'.

Once it was light, it was possible to see the devastation that had been wrought over-night throughout a significant part of the camp that had suffered the most from the Union attack and whose burnt out ruins were now all too obvious. George and Arthur scoured the whole area at their wits ends, trying to discover what had happened to Ernest during the night's chaos. Their search for any information was made all the more difficult by what seemed to be every Confederate soldier in the camp being marched, drilled, shouted at for incompetence and then marched, drilled and shouted at again.

No one had time for the anxious enquiries from two Englishmen about one missing non-military, and hence unimportant, man. After several hours of waylaying soldiers, officers and the many still remarkably unperturbed women, designated by unattached soldiers as 'camp followers', all claimed either being unable to help or with no time for such a trivial enquiry when comrades were either dead or in the dubious care of surgeons in hospital tents.

Eventually, the two Envoys made their way to General Longstreet's headquarters and there endured what seemed like hours of waiting in the cold morning for the commander's adjutant to make a brief appearance. During those few minutes, he could spare them he made it obvious that he could not be expected to be able to account at this early stage for every man in camp last night. In the end, he did consult some papers on a table amongst many others lying scattered there. These appeared to be inscribed with hundreds of names presumably of the dead and wounded and he felt he had done his duty by assuring them that an *'Ernest Tissiman'* definitely was not amongst them.

"I'm sure you will find that he got separated from you in the confusion of the attack and will appear alive and well soon enough," he said, as he folded the papers and disappeared into another room in the farmhouse.

Arthur and George trudged back to their tent, which thankfully was nowhere near the devastation of so many others further away and discovering it was just as cold inside as it was outside and so made their way to the canteen, which, like several others, was even busier than usual; two similar buildings had been severely damaged. With mugs of hot coffee and some hard biscuits, they retreated to a table, already half full. After a mouthful of unsweetened coffee, Arthur was clearly struggling to put his dismal thoughts into words.

"I just cannot believe that my brother is probably dead and lying in some ditch or woodland right now." He let out a long sigh. "What do you think? Run through with a bayonet? Shot and so badly wounded, it took him hours to die in agony or…" Here he turned away from George in a vain attempt to disguise the effect this was having on his countenance.

George found that he couldn't find any words of comfort or optimism after such an horrendous night that even he, at least for a while, had believed it must be the forerunner of a massive, surprise Union offensive that would reverse all the Confederates had gained so far. Eventually, as he tried to remind himself of all the battles he had survived, but also all the friends he had lost in India and the Crimea, he leant across the table and put his hand on Arthur's arm.

"Arthur, it is hard for me with so much of my life spent soldiering and with so many years of bitter experience of battles far away from our own country, really to understand how you feel. After a time you see friends killed, maimed and captured, battlefields strewn with bodies, but where some still struggle to hold on to life against all the odds. It hardens you I suppose to feel anything. All I can say is that *if* your brother, whom I am sure you love, was killed last night by Union soldiers, I am sure he would have fought for his life and hopefully taken some of them with him. But I am surprised that his body has not been found today. After all, the skirmish was all either within this camp or very close to it. Hold on to the thought that he may well be alive, but just maybe was taken prisoner. In that case, there must still be a chance that you will see him again."

Arthur heard what George said, but made no attempt to give any indication that he had listened to it. He continued to gaze into his mug of what was now cold coffee. George knew that Arthur's thoughts were obviously in a dark place far from the real world.

# Chapter Thirty-One

**Six weeks later**

Sergeant Tommy Flynn and Corporal Frank Witherspoon of the Mississippi Vipers were paying an early morning visit to the prisoner stockade that had been built inside an ancient barn, with large parts of its roof missing, on the northern edge of Confederate Camp Davis. The dawn was only just breaking in the eastern sky. The two Confederates were in high spirits, partly because they had started the day, not unusually, with long swigs of moonshine and partly because, after a long winter, the like of which did not exist in their bayou country home way out beyond the town of Jackson, it looked as though the Arctic weather was loosening its grip. Here in Pennsylvania, there were the first signs that spring just might be in the air.

As they got closer to their assigned post, Flynn turned to Frank, who had been his subservient companion ever since their childhood, and put his finger to his lips, which made Frank snigger with delight, as he knew what was coming and it wasn't standing guard duty on the prison stockade, which was what they were supposed to be doing this morning.

They crept quietly up to the solid door, reinforced with extra planks nailed to it and an iron bar across it, its end slotted into a solid hasp that boasted a large padlock. Frank was now barely concealing the laughter that was trying to escape his mouth and Tommy slapped at him to try to keep him quiet.

Having produced from his pocket a key ring with two keys on it, Sergeant Flynn inserted the larger key and slowly eased the padlock open, attempting to keep it as silent as possible. They then both gently and quietly eased the old door just an inch out of its frame. They paused long enough to control their drunken delight and then Tommy gave the signal by miming the opening of the door.

Frank waited again until he raised three fingers and then slowly lowered one, then the next and, as the third dramatically went down. They wrenched the door open and began to scream the rebel yell at the top of their voices. Both had unsheathed bayonets in their hands and as they crashed inside, they stabbed them in between the wooden bars that were lashed into a grid from the floor to meet the rough planks of a ceiling, ten feet above, forming a large cage. They continued to yell and shout and also to rattle the bars with their bayonets.

In the dim light, the bodies incarcerated there could be heard falling over each other, swearing and shouting back insults. Men's faces began to appear out of the gloom, keeping away from the bars, looks of fear on some, hatred on others. They had months of matted beard growth and close up, it was obvious that they were all in various pieces of uniform, often torn, that gave way to faces and exposed arms and legs caked in dirt. Where any colour could be seen, and there was not much, it was blue, but it was mixed with dried mud and, in many cases, showing holes and slashes. Filthy pieces of blood-stained cloth had been used to bind what were clearly wounds or to act as slings to broken or torn arms. All in all, the stockade had the appearance of cage containing dirty, injured and potentially dangerous animals.

"Get back, you filthy fuckers!" screamed Flynn, as he thrust the bayonet as far through the bars as he could reach.

"Yeah! Do it!" Witherspoon added in a weaker imitation of his sergeant.

The prisoners were forced to move back out of reach. Flynn then produced a Colt revolver from the holster on his belt and waved it slowly backwards and forwards across the cage front. To emphasise his power over them he cocked the gun. "Now then… Shut the fuck up or I'll plug every one of you!"

The crowd of dozens of prisoners grew quieter, as they assessed if he would actually shoot and the considered opinion seemed to be that he would; what had he got to lose? Flynn then pointed the pistol at a middle-aged man, who could well have been wearing the remains of an officer's uniform jacket.

"You! Yes, you there in that fancy jacket! Now you come here…*sir*!"

The man who was leaning against the back of the cage, lifted his head and looked at the gun and then at Tom Flynn. "You talking to me?"

"Damn right I am. Now you move your arse over here when I tells you."

The Union officer smiled, adjusted his torn jacket across his shoulders and then stood to attention. He looked around the cage, seeming to be reviewing the quality of his companions and briskly marched towards the front of the cage and only stopped when he was pressed against the bars, forcing Flynn to take a hasty step backwards.

"At your service, sergeant!" Then in a much quieter voice, "You piece of rebel shit."

His stare bored into the surprised eyes of Tommy Flynn, who recovered quickly.

"You'll regret that. Corporal, cover that doorway with your pistol. If one of them even thinks about moving towards it, shoot them in the belly. Now *officer*, you go and stand by that door." Here he indicated a wooden door about three feet high on the left side of the cage. "The rest of you get back!"

There was some shuffling of feet, but no serious signs of movement. Flynn raised the Colt and fired about six inches above their heads. The echo bounced around the barn's walls. However, it had the desired effect and, reluctantly, the men moved away from the bars.

Flynn crossed to the low door, found the smaller key on the ring and, with his left hand, inserted it into the second padlock, keeping his pistol trained on the officer as he undid the lock and pulled the door open wide enough for a body to slide through.

"You, smart arse, get yourself through this here door…slowly. Corporal, you keep the rest of 'em covered."

The officer smiled again and dipped, almost elegantly, to step through the doorway, which was instantly slammed and locked behind him. Flynn, the Colt held inches from the man's chest, grabbed his arm and spun him around against the wall. He then jabbed the barrel against his head.

"Corporal, take them shackles and fix his hands behind him. Mind you're not too gentle with this piece of Yankee scum."

Witherspoon rammed the irons onto both wrists and then tightened them until the man gave a gasp, but slowly resumed his smile. The corporal pushed him hard towards the barn door. Flynn, looking suitably satisfied and with his Colt back against the man's neck, said, "You won't be smiling for long, not if I have my way."

The war, now close to its third year, was creating tens of thousands of prisoners in both the blue and the grey and a far greater battle than Bull Run was already in many thoughts. The subsequent battles and skirmishes that were looming elsewhere would undoubtedly generate tens of thousands more to fill the jails, compounds and stockades of both Union and Confederate armies.

What the Union soldiers in Davis Town Camp stockade were enduring was repeated in different forms, some even worse, some marginally better, across thousands of square miles of what was once called the *United* States of America. The question in the New Year of 1862 for more or less every Confederate soldier within twenty miles of Davis Town was: "How much longer have we got to wait here, doin' nothin' and givin' them damn Yankees, time to lick their wounds clean?"

Another of these prisoner of war camps was the Union's in Pennsylvania, but not more than thirty miles to the north of Confederate Davis Town. The Pennsylvanian *Arendtsville Prisoner of War Camp* was, in fact, not a camp at all, but a two very large farm barns, whose original use was to store fruit and vegetables in one and cereal grain in the other. When farmer Johnathan Hegerty's farm was commandeered by the Union army in the village of Arendtsville, about seven miles north-west of Gettysburg, he and his family were forced to find somewhere else to live. A regiment of the Massachusetts Rifles was billeted in the village and its surrounding orchards and fields. The barns were then originally planned to be used as officers' accommodation, but as prisoner numbers grew north of Gettysburg, with more and with more being moved into the area that originally stretched from Washington through New England, prisoners were shuttled from camp to camp, as the army under the control of the Union shrank. Arendtsville eventually expanded to become the only Union prison camp north of the Potomac and east of the Shenandoah Valley.

The first task forced on newly captured Confederate prisoners from Bull Run and dozens of other conflicts fought north of Virginia in the first years of the war, was building, and gradually extending, the high stockade made from tree trunks that enclosed a large open area around the two barns, but eventually several others. This was originally frozen grassland, but it turned to frozen mud beyond the gateway into the prison. The barns had the advantage that they were of solid boards and at least partially of waterproof construction, bur with the large double doors of each torn off they were as cold inside as out. Needless to say, any fruit, vegetables and grain had been removed from all barns very early on by the quartermasters to help feed their own troops.

This left the barns barren and empty; ideal for the despised Confederate prisoners. Sleeping quarters, so called, were simply earth floors and the only comforts were those blankets and coats that a few of the men had managed to carry with them on the long marches into captivity. A few cattle drinking troughs had been dragged in from the surrounding fields and became the only washing facilities available. These were once filled with fresh water, but after a few months had been changed only once. No lavatory facilities were provided; buckets, the floor or the area outside were used as needed. The result, as time went on, was an appalling stink that could be smelled from hundreds of yards around, especially downwind and, inevitably, the rapid spread of diseases such as typhoid and cholera.

There were a few surgeons and their assistants, as well as many women, who were mostly ex-slaves who had reached Washington DC on the *underground railroad,* the route for escapees from plantations to safe houses leading them gradually north. Their role was now to help nurse the sick, injured and dying Union soldiers.

The surgeons generally refused point blank to step through the stockade gates and so risk being hugely out-numbered by hundreds, and gradually thousands, of gaunt Confederates in clothes so torn and ragged that they no longer could be identified as uniform. However, the Union medics were far more afraid of the diseases the prisoners carried than they were of any attack that these men would probably find physically impossible to inflict on them.

Once a day at times that could vary greatly, a platoon of Union soldiers, chosen for their sadistic natures, forced the prisoners into long lines to get their hands on possibly a small piece of corn bread, a lump of raw sweet potato or a stale hard cracker; no meat or vegetables were wasted on the '*Rebel scum*', who had so disloyally defied President Lincoln.

In the barns, there were also old barrels containing water that was less and less wholesome as time passed. These were frequently empty and only occasionally changed with what was supposed to be drinking water. The result of this misery, starvation and the frequent savage cruelty of guards was a great mass of emaciated men, living, often fighting and dying like wild animals.

Into Arendtsville prison camp in the early hours of a bitterly cold March morning came a man, barely alive, with his head wrapped in a filthy piece of torn shirt, stained with his own blood, which had also dried across the side of his face. The man must have been dressed at one time in good quality civilian clothes, but these, or what was left of them, were now hardly recognisable as such, being torn and tattered and bearing a crust of mud and ice; he wore no items that could be identified as military clothing. Two Union privates encouraged him, and all the other Confederate prisoners, to keep moving on the journey to the prison camp by frequent blows of their rifle butts and shouted threats and insults. Especially in the case of the man with no uniform, this caused widespread laughter among the group of skirmishers returning from what they clearly regarded as their successful reconnoitre and their justified bringing of death and destruction into Davis Town Camp.

Unlike the unfortunate prisoner the Union wounded, of which there were about twenty from the skirmish into the Confederate camp, were taken at once into the hospital set up in a farmhouse and manned by surgeons, ready to do the best they could to treat the wounds received from rifles and swords in the woods miles to the north. Their originally white aprons were rapidly stained with Union blood, but the identical rebel liquid was disregarded and probably infected.

So it was that Ernest Tissiman was violently hurled into the horror of the Union at Arendtsville by the young Union infantry soldiers, boys really, who on the long march in the dark from Davis Town, had shown a savage and vicious malevolence to the English *spy*, who, now sprawled on the trampled snow inside the prison's stockade gates.

He curled himself into an exhausted ball in the sadly unfounded hope of receiving no more blows and kicks as the price for not being dressed in the blue of the Union. His wish was now to be left to die on the cold ground and to escape the nightmare he had lived through from the moment he had been left stranded in the woods, dropped by a blow to his head and surrounded by the advance of the Union skirmishers.

He guessed that he was probably no more than twenty miles from his brother and his tent home at that moment, which he had unfairly complained about so loudly. When he was at least able to think again, he was in the nightmare of dragging his body for what seemed more like a hundred miles from Davis Town and a world away from his real home in Oldham; the mill where he had, until recently, been responsible for so many hundreds of cotton workers, and he was now unbelievably not even on the same continent.

However, even Ernest had to accept that he was now in a Union prison camp as he drifted into the relief of unconsciousness. This was not to last for long as he became aware of hands pulling at what was left of his clothes and trying, he realised, to steal even these. As he came fully out of the blackness, he saw the legs and bare feet of men around him and their hands trying to take his ripped jacket and his badly damaged boots off his body. As one boot was successfully torn off the thief then became the target of others, whom he could see more clearly now. Three of them tried to wrench the precious prize from the new owner's grasp, while others fought over the remaining boot still on Ernest's other foot. The men scrabbling at his body were skeletally thin, with gaunt faces and dirty beards. They were dressed in rags that must at one time have been grey uniforms and had eyes that were sunk into their heads. They did not speak, but uttered savage grunts and screams as they fought for the prizes of clothes that Ernest would never have even considered giving to the poorest and most destitute of Oldham.

Semi starvation was soon feasted upon by diseases that spread rapidly through the prison: typhoid, diphtheria and cholera were the worst and created the most mortality. This was the reason the Union guards were moved out of the entire stockade and so away from any direct contact with prisoners, for fear of infection. What little food was occasionally thrown through the bars was stale and often mouldy or inhabited by maggots. What had once been a daily distribution by armed soldiers of a little basic food ceased two days after Ernest arrived. Any attempt at medical care he was told by others had never been given. Prisoners who could still walk were forced to carry the dead out of the stockade and drop them into pits, where lime was scattered over the bodies before earth covered the unmarked mass graves.

Ernest eventually simply gave up. He had no strength left and tried to cover as much of his head as he could with his hands and let the scavengers take whatever they wanted; he drifted again into welcome unconsciousness. When he came around, he thought he must be dreaming, since the blows had ceased and he was lying on ground that he slowly realised was not covered in snow and ice, but simply earth. He was aware of what he realised was stark reality and not a dream, but through just one eye. His left eye seemed to be glued shut and when he slowly managed to lift his hand to explore his face, he could feel some sort of crust over it; he rubbed it and, in spite of a sharp pain, managed to prise the eye-lid open. He could now see that far above his head in a dim light were old beams supporting what must be a roof, although fretted by holes where tiles were missing. He was lying with his back against a rough, hard wall. He could feel the cold from the earth floor seeping up into his body. It took him several minutes to realise that another body was propped against the same wall a few feet away from him.

His mind, still working very slowly, revealed a man sitting there staring at him, yet another skeleton with rags of a grey jacket hanging from his shoulders. What was left of his trousers stopped in ripped strips well above his ankles, while his feet were bound with pieces of cloth that could have been grey at one time, but now looked a mixture of smeared black and a deep red.

Ernest focussed at last on the face and met sad eyes, set deeply in a skull-like face and lips that seemed to be sucked into his mouth. The surprise came when those lips broke open into a smile, which admittedly disappeared within a few seconds. He could not shift his gaze from this vision of inhumanity, whose eyes stared unblinking into his own.

"I reckon you might be back with us," the mouth mumbled. "You're one lucky son of a bitch, you are. I thought they'd done for you, but either you're stronger than you look or the good Lord hasn't completely deserted you yet."

The soft, hesitant voice belied the man's appearance by sounding not unlike that of Daniel Hayward. However, Ernest realised he must be just another southern gentleman, although his emaciated appearance made that hard to believe.

Slowly, Ernest formed the words, "Who are you? Where am I?"

The shadow of a man slowly, clearly painfully, replied, "I am, sir, Major Jerimiah Whitworth of the Second Tennessee Volunteers, late of the Battle of Bull Run, Washington DC, Oak Ridge and Davis Town. You and I, sir, are prisoners of the bloody Union in Arendtsville, Pennsylvania. May I ask to whom I have the honour to be speaking?"

Ernest was now beginning to feel once more the intense pain in his head, which must have been dulled, as he came back to consciousness, but was now sending agonising shards through his skull like knives being pushed into his brain. He gasped and held his head in both hands, as he rocked backwards and forwards. The man, whose name he had heard whispered through his waves of pain, looked searchingly at him and grimaced as if he too were feeling similar agonies.

"Hey! Come on, soldier, don't give in to it, you've got a long fight ahead if you're going to survive this place. There are thousands here worse off than you and me, because they've been here longer."

Ernest felt the waves recede somewhat. "I am not a soldier! I don't fight for either of your damned armies! I am an Englishman, God dammit!"

As his voice rose to a shout, so the hammering pain intensified and he dropped his head and arms between his knees, somehow fighting back the tears that sprang into his eyes. His words had apparently so shocked the major that he shuffled himself away from the wall and swung around to look directly at Ernest.

"You're English? What in God's name are you doing here?" A pause and then, "Why you must be one of those bloody newspaper reporters I reckon! Who do you write for? Not the *London Times* is it, like that other fellow who was at Camp Davis, what's his name?"

"You mean William Russell, I…ah! My head is bursting! Do something!"

"I can do nothing for you, my friend. Do I look to you like the smartly dressed gentleman and soldier I once was, fighting valiantly for Dixie in my fine uniform?"

Ernest wasn't listening, being only aware of some devil destroying his brain from the inside. Major Whitworth, seeming to appreciate that there was nothing he could do for the semi-corpse beside him and tried to continue the conversation, which was, of necessity, now one sided. He remained silent for a minute or two before continuing.

"Yes, you see here a victim of sheer bad fortune. You must also have been at Davis Town, I reckon, so you know how chaotic that was. I stumbled into half a dozen Union skirmishers in the pitch dark. Can't remember when that was. Anyhow, before I knew it, they had me on the ground, took away my pistol and cutlass and then dragged me away through the trees. I didn't have time put up a fight and I didn't even see any action. How's that for a day in the life of a victorious Rebel from Bull Run?"

He looked at Ernest, but could see no reaction and so leant back against the wall and closed his eyes; sleep was the only escape from this place where he was now resigned to breathe his last.

Major Jerimiah Whitworth, whose father Ebenezer was the fourth generation of Whitworths to own the cotton plantation at Bowling Green, near Memphis, close to the Mississippi river. He had recently helped manage the estate, but when the winds of war grew stronger, he had joined the Confederate regiment gathering twenty miles from his home, while his social station took him directly to the rank of major in the Second Mississippi Volunteers. He was a God-fearing young man and well educated by the standards of the day; as loyal a Confederate soldier as Jeff Davis could have hoped for.

However, by February 1862, with one bloody battle behind him and several skirmishes following that, he had lost much of his natural charity and the thrill to be fighting for the southern cause. He now despaired at what he had seen of his fellow human beings in both battle and victory. He felt that today he was both hardened and realistic. He knew that neither he, nor this Englishman, nor most of the men in this prison who had lost most of their humanity by now, would survive for much longer. At first, he had felt a violent anger at his situation, but that had shrunk to nothing and he was resigned to await the day, probably quite soon, when he would simply fade away. He had quietly accepted that he was going to die in this hell on earth.

# Chapter Thirty-Two

## February/March 1862: Virginia

It seemed to the millions of men under arms in both the Confederate and Union armies that God, whom both sides believed was on their side, had decided at this historic time in their history to inflict an Arctic winter on the eastern United States above the 35th parallel. As a result, Pennsylvania and the states to their north, as well as even Virginia and Kentucky to the south were frozen solid with no sign of amelioration any time soon.

General Longstreet's Reserve Confederate army of some twenty-five thousand soldiers, now battle hardened, had pursued General Meade and the Army of the Potomac northwards in the autumn of 1861. It had then driven the Union government and its President to flight as far as the remaining Union parts of northern Pennsylvania. The cat and mouse pursuit had been halted when the severe winter of 1862/63 had frozen all the states from Virginia northwards and both armies had no choice but to dig in and wait for the weather to change; it did not oblige for many months.

General Longstreet was ordered by General Robert E Lee, the commander of the Confederate army, to:

*"Consolidate the position of your army in southeast Pennsylvania".* (The next lines missed due to the telegraph endlessly repeating the word 'line')

*Be prepared to repel any attempt by General Meade to break out of the area around Gettysburg. Be alert to any attempted advance south by General McClellan into our lands well south and west of Washington."*

Longstreet, although severely frustrated by his forced confinement by the winter weather, was also confident that General Meade was equally confined to the Confederacy's northeast. Both Generals were forced to wait, they assumed for only a month or two, until each could finally attempt to tear the other limb from limb.

At the same time and in weather, less wintry, although lashed by rain storms around the Confederate capital at Richmond Virginia, was Robert E Lee, who had decided to rename the Army of the Confederacy, a large part of which was now marooned in Pennsylvania; it would now be known as the *Army of Northern Virginia.*

President Jefferson Davis had agreed with Lee's confident prediction that the outcome of the war would undoubtedly be settled once and for all in his own home state. General Lee had also assured his president that, above all else, Richmond, the heart and soul of the Confederacy, would never at any cost be allowed to fall into Union hands. Jeff Davis gave the honour to the Army of Northern Virginia, under the command of Lee, of ensuring that no Yankee army would ever again be allowed to hold sway in Confederate Virginia. Command General Lee said that any Union intrusion would be swiftly chased out of any state that it might have temporarily occupied.

By the early winter months of 1862, in spite of the Union's defeat at Bull Run and the rout of a major part of its army, driven from Manassas through Washington DC and into Pennsylvania, other parts of the Federal Army of the Union had gained ground in other United States in the southwest. Since this Yankee army had never before been brought together in one place, it was difficult for the Confederacy to estimate its numbers, but Lee and his commanding generals believed that there were perhaps still many thousands of Union soldiers in western Virginia, largely in the Shenandoah Valley, only fifty miles south-west of Washington. The Confederacy was also aware that Union divisions were in parts of Tennessee, Kentucky, Florida and those states bordering the Mississippi River: Louisiana, Arkansas, Missouri and Mississippi itself. While it was, indeed, winter in all these states, none experienced anything as severe in the winter months as did Virginia and New England. Those far away to the south and west only knew winter as a time when an extra coat might occasionally be needed.

Arthur and George were marooned with Longstreet's army in Pennsylvania and throughout those long months, from October 1862 to late April 1863, they were unable to send any telegraph cables to London, since it was either impossible to travel to Hanover Junction or overhead cables had been brought down by the weight of ice clinging to them.

Towards the start of that winter, however, George and Arthur did meet a Confederate Lieutenant, Gerald Cornwell from Kentucky, who had been transferred from western Virginia along with some regiments of mixed cavalry and infantry. The Kentucky Mountain Brigade of three thousand soldiers would be the last to undertake the journey of one hundred and fifty miles to reinforce Camp Davis before winter set in and travel became more or less impossible.

The remaining two Envoys met Lieutenant Cornwell in one of the officers' canteens, where they happened to sit next to him one evening. He seemed very young to be a lieutenant, but did not appear to want to sit with the other junior officers of his regiment. George was keen to try to find out what was happening far away in the south of Virginia and the young, sandy haired officer, regarded by him as a *boy*, was happy to oblige. He explained that their Kentucky Brigade had arrived south of Richmond and had been stationed for several months on the banks of the James River opposite Hampton, on its opposite shore.

(39) "It would have been March last year," said Cornwell, as he started to light up the cold evening with his story and then continued unhindered, "just after we arrived, when a whole bunch of us got to see a real incredible spectacle of the conflict at sea, where the James runs into Chesapeake Bay. There were a lot of Union and Confederate war ships out in the bay, which was fairly calm. This meant that they all moved with difficulty under sail, so it wasn't a real roaring sea battle, I must admit. Those of us Rebs not on duty and crowding the shore were able to laugh at the clumsy ships trying to sink each other. If you was from Kentucky like me, you wouldn't get to see these great sail boats back at home. Anyhow, they were firing these cannons out of portholes in the sides of them and, although most of them missed, a few was hitting each other. Not really doing a lot of damage, I can tell you."

Lieutenant Cornwell was really getting into his stride by then and neither George nor Arthur made any attempt to interrupt his excited story.

"Well, that went on for an hour, I guess, and then out of nowhere like, there comes I suppose a boat, but like nothing we'd ever seen before. The only thing like those other slow old ships was the stars and stripes flag flying from its top. It was grey all over and we reckoned it was metal, iron I guess."

Arthur was eager to question something or other, but young Cornwell talked right over him, his voice rising and now gesticulating with both arms.

"It was weird! It don't have no masts nor nothing like that. It was like a flat piece of metal, just a foot or two above the water, with a great round turret towering up in the middle. There was a big gun barrel sticking out of that and sort of a chimney with smoke coming out. There was no sailors to be seen and yet it was moving through the water faster than them other boats. It fired a shot at one of our Confederate ships and damn me if it didn't hit it!"

George managed to get a few words in as the enthusiast drew breath.

"We came over from England on a ship with an iron hull and a steam engine to power it and—"

"Yeah, well this weren't no man-o-war. No sir! It was like something that someone made up, like. Like a picture of something that wasn't real…and then! Then we saw, and I can tell you we were on the very edge of the river by then. We saw, coming from the other side of the water another one! But, no! You was going to ask if it was the same. No, it was not! It was another metal monster, but different. This one had our stars and bars battle flag flying on top and, instead of a gun tower it had, like a metal tent, you know, like this one we're in now, and the tent thing went right along it, from front to back…and another funnel with smoke! But, no, just wait a minute…along the sides were, like window shutters that was open and each one had a cannon sticking out! They were belching fire and smoke as cannon balls shot out! Our folks won't never believe we saw them, but they was real; I swear on my life they was!"

George and Arthur were actually finding it hard to decide how much of this was true and how much might be fiction, maybe something like Mr Jules Verne would write. Arthur was the first to try to understand if all this was really true.

"Did these iron monster ships hit anything with their cannon balls, or maybe you couldn't see from so far away."

"Oh no," the lieutenant assured him, "we was maybe a mile away, but the sea was almost flat and the sky was clear, although it was damned cold I must say. I reckon you find it hard to believe, eh? But it was real all right and one of them shots, from our Dixie tent-thing, did hit a Union sail boat and knocked its mast right over!"

There was no time to ask any more questions as the other officers from the Kentucky Brigade were all starting to leave, commanded by one older, more senior officer shouting for Lieutenant Cornwell:

"Get your arse over here, boy. We've got better things to do."

It was almost two years later that Arthur read a rather more accurate account of the Naval Battle of March 1862 off Hampton Roads, in which the only two wholly iron ships of the Civil War exchanged a few shots before returning to their home ports, never again to be seen a battle; the Union iron warship was the *USS Monitor,* while the Confederate forerunner of modern warfare at sea was the *Merrimack.*

In late 1862 and through much of 1863, many members of the Democrat Party, the majority of whom could be found in the Confederate states, although a sizeable and equally outspoken number lived in Union states and were all campaigning against the Civil War with the growing catalogue of death and injury it was causing. This gave rise to several south and mid-west Union States threatening also to secede from the Union, which in turn disturbed the Union President and Commanding generals. Demands were voiced by these Democrats in both north and south to restore: *"The Union as it was, the Constitution as it is."*

Abraham Lincoln, President since November 1860, as a result of this widespread disquiet decided to bring forward his long intended 'Emancipation Declaration'. This, put baldly, declared that every slave in the US, including the southern Confederate states, was now 'Free'. He had expected some serious uprisings among southern slaves, but this did not come about as he had hoped. There was disquiet, but it was smothered, at least for the time being.

The Union Commanders, notably Generals McClellan and Grant persuaded Lincoln at the start of that appalling winter of '62/63 that they could, indeed, now counter the Confederate forces; although they had to admit the terrible losses of both men and spirit from the time of Bull Run, which they called Manassas, the rout that followed, the loss of Washington and the flight of a large part of the Army of the Potomac to Pennsylvania; these were serious setbacks. General Ulysses S Grant simply, if rather optimistically, summed up the situation: *"We must now put fire in their rear!"*

What he intended to begin just as winter gave its first warnings, was to use the larger part of the Union army, now split from Meade in the north, to storm through Virginia, take Richmond and, at the same time further outflank the Confederacy by coming at them from the west and the Mississippi at the same time, rolling up the southern states as they went; this, in theory, would be while the main Confederate force was confined by winter in Pennsylvania It was an audacious plan in reality, but should be proved a success, or not, over the next nine months.

# Chapter Thirty-Three

## March to December 1862

During the spring of 1862, General Ulysses Grant was confirmed as the overall Commander-in-Chief of the Union armies, although General Meade would remain as Commander of the much reduced in size Union Army of the Potomac, which was presently marooned in Pennsylvania.

Meade, however, still had sufficient influence, as well as communication ability, in May 1862 to appoint Major General William Sheridan with his Army of the Shenandoah and who was then to move southwest of Washington with some 25-30,000 troops, as Commander of all the forces in the West; albeit his force was definitely not *one* army, but disjointed divisions, battalions and regiments of armies from all over the western United States.

Facing off against Sheridan was Confederate General Robert E Lee with his Army of Northern Virginia. He was supported by General Joseph Johnston with his Army of Tennessee also in northern Virginia, a combined force of some 25,000 if ever joined with General Jackson's army. Along with Lee and Jackson, Generals Beauregard, Ewell and Wade Hampton were also destined to make their marks on this campaign.

So it was that these various armies of the Confederacy and Union were involved for over nine months in the numerous battles and confusion, known as the *Campaign of the Shenandoah Valley,* which culminated eventually in a messy withdrawal of both sides from the valley; they would not meet again until the next year at the small town of Gettysburg.

The Shenandoah Valley campaign was in reality not just one campaign involving various battles, but was actually several separate campaigns, set in the same large area and that lasted for nine bloody and generally pointless months. The Campaign brought death and destruction to this once beautiful and vast valley and to the Virginian inhabitants in its numerous towns and villages, farms and woods.

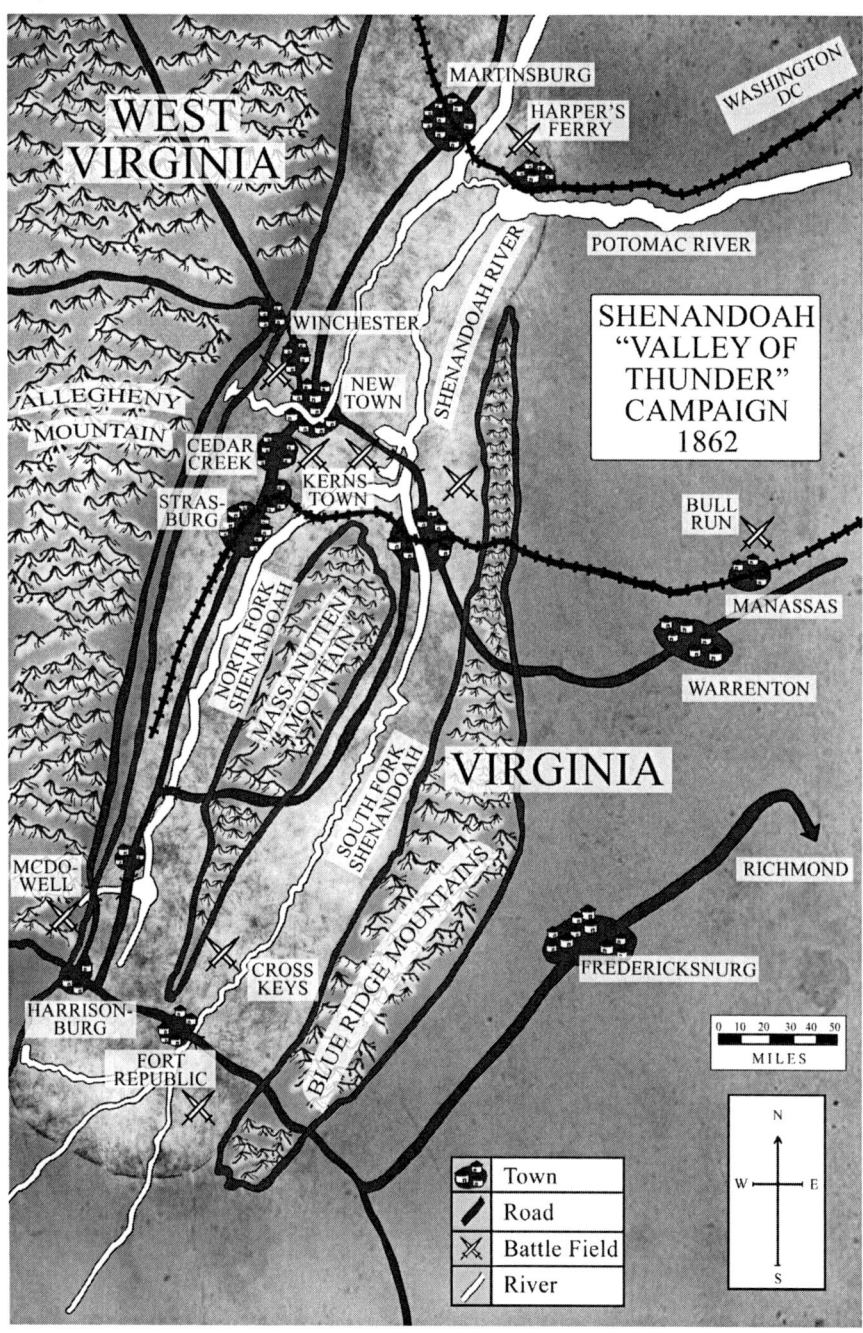

MARTINSBURG

HARPER'S FERRY

WASHINGTON DC

WEST VIRGINIA

POTOMAC RIVER

SHENANDOAH RIVER

WINCHESTER

NEW TOWN

SHENANDOAH "VALLEY OF THUNDER" CAMPAIGN 1862

ALLEGHENY MOUNTAIN

CEDAR CREEK

KERNS TOWN

STRAS-BURG

BULL RUN

NORTH FORK SHENANDOAH

MASSANUTTEN MOUNTAIN

MANASSAS

WARRENTON

SOUTH FORK SHENANDOAH

VIRGINIA

MCDO-WELL

RICHMOND

CROSS KEYS

BLUE RIDGE MOUNTAINS

FREDERICKSNURG

HARRISON-BURG

FORT REPUBLIC

0  10  20  30  40  50
MILES

| | Town |
| --- | --- |
| | Road |
| | Battle Field |
| | River |

N
W — E
S

Both warring sides had a very similar aim: to score a victory in the valley of such overwhelming proportion that the enemy would be driven out, fleeing

311

for their lives, either to the northeast if a Union victory or south-west if it were Confederate. The conflicts, which grew bloodier as time and optimism passed, began around the town of **New Market** (not the town of the same name in the Bull Run valley) in March 1862 and ended at Cedar Creek in December, by which time, winter had fastened its grip. General Thomas Jackson reckoned later that he had marched his 17,000 soldiers for over six hundred and fifty miles by the time they reached Cedar Creek at the end of the campaign.

The Shenandoah Valley is a ten thousand square mile elongated bowl, its high mountainous sides prevented the conflict spilling out into the surrounding Virginia countryside. There was violent bloodletting somewhere in the valley more or less every day for many months.

Both had problems setting up supply lines and maintaining them. The result was that it was not unusual for of starvation from time to time, or worse still, to run short of supplies of ammunition. Both sides fought tooth and nail over bridges, railheads, towns and hamlets, not to mention seizing food and drink at gun point from terrified farmers and families.

In March of 1862, General Jackson was led to believe that Union General Shields, who was occupying **Kernstown** had '*only a handful of men holding the town*'. In truth, he had over ten thousand. Jackson, believing a small force to be a fact, assumed that taking the town would be a simple matter and threw his own force of three and a half thousand against the superior enemy with no further confirmation. Once over the initial shock, the Confederates were making strong headway in this bloody battle, when one General Garnett, without any order from Jackson, withdrew the whole force and left the field. Jackson court-martialled him as soon as he was able to gather his scattered army into safety. The court-martial was then suspended due to General Robert Lee's next action starting immediately; Garnett proved himself in several later conflicts right up to Gettysburg and his trial was 'forgotten'.

Not long afterwards, Union General Banks, with a force of around four thousand, attacked Jackson, who commanded at that time sixteen thousand near Winchester. With outstanding skill and well-disciplined soldiers, Banks managed to force Jackson to retreat and, yet again in this civil war, there was failure to pursue the enemy and Jackson was able to regroup.

Perhaps a conflict late in the campaign in November 1862 summed up the poorly managed troops on both sides. Union General McDowell's army of the Potomac was forty thousand strong and was heading for Richmond via

Fredericksburg under the command of a Union General Fremont. General Jackson was quick to move his own force in an attempt to cut Fremont off before he could attack the poorly defended Confederate capital. However, starvation among Fremont's soldiers, poor communication, blocked mountain passes by snow and bad roads stopped Fremont in his tracks. Jackson had leap-frogged the stranded Union and then rapidly organised a 'ring of fire' around Richmond. A severely disappointed Lincoln wrote in a mood of brooding defeat: "*It was all a matter of legs.*"

The final conflict at Cedar Creek was typical of many others: a Confederate force under General Earley surprised a Union brigade, also there at the end of November 1862, defending an area around their large military camp resulting in the Union force retreating rapidly. Earley's men were exhausted and starving and their officers failed to prevent their falling on the Union camp and its supplies like wolves on carrion. Before order could be restored, the Union managed to regroup and returned to surprise the Confederates stripping the camp of its food and drink, as well as its supplies of bedding, arms and ammunition. The Confederates were, in turn, chased out of the camp, many suffering death or severe wounds, but the Union was too tired, or possibly had no will, to take on the pursuit for more than a few hundred yards; shades of Bull Run perhaps in many minds? Union and Confederate belligerents were more concerned with licking their wounds at that point, filling their bellies and finding somewhere they could stop to rest.

The Campaign in the Shenandoah Valley, was fought so bitterly and for so long, but resulted in neither side achieving any really major advantage. The Confederates named it the 'Valley of Humiliation' for the Union, while the Union claimed victory in the "Valley of Thunder" anyway, although they left the confines of the valley speedily, rather than advancing. General Grant ordered the Union forces then to continue to move southwest, to avoid the Confederate forces around Washington, and to aim for the back door to Richmond, which would be their principal target when the long winter thawed and allowed large movements of armies again. Many officers, from majors to commanding generals, would, however, have learned a great deal to their advantage when the greatest battle of the war eventually erupted.

*

General Robert E Lee moved his forces directly and rapidly towards Richmond, which the Confederates would defend while both sides dug in to try to survive the harsh winter that soon arrived and which would be the challenge to both Union and Confederate armies far greater than any actual battle.

By January 1863, Lee's army was well dug in to the south of Richmond and had drawn some of his Confederate force from in and around Washington to regroup nearer Richmond as a defensive force to the southeast of Washington, so filling in the space between it and the Confederate capital. Lee was confident that this flank of the army, as well as the larger force now spread below Richmond, in conjunction with the winter weather now looking set in for months to come, would force the Union to leave the Army of the Potomac in Pennsylvania until the spring thaw. He also banked on the declining Union strength to the west to realise it no longer had the power needed to overwhelm the Confederate ranks now holding most of Virginia, with the exception of Chesapeake Bay and its river valley. By the winter of 1862/63, the Confederacy held most southern states from North Carolina and Tennessee and then to the south and west through Alabama to the borders of the state of Mississippi.

General Lee and President Davis, whom he was able to visit frequently that winter, had no idea as the January winds, rainstorms and snow turned Virginia into a veritable unassailable fortress, of a highly secret Union plan to outflank Richmond from its south east where the Rappahannock, James and York Rivers flowed and which the Confederacy had failed to garrison in nearly sufficient strength to withstand a concerted attack.

It was Union General George B McClellan who had devised this audacious plan. He had been furiously disappointed and angered when Union General Ambrose Burnside had been defeated at Fredericksburg, attempting to set up a similar surprise attack on Richmond. McClellan now ordered Burnside to get his not particularly large, nor indeed particularly powerful, force to come at Robert Lee in a shock attack at what was believed to be their weakest point. They would cross the Rappahannock unobserved and then pour north up what McClellan believed was the lightly guarded peninsular below Richmond.

He had told Burnside when he briefed him for the mission during an especially heavy rain and sleet storm:

*"I am giving you this vital mission, Ambrose, partly because I believe you can achieve its end and partly to give you the opportunity to make amends for*

*the unfortunate outcome at Fredericksburg."* It is unrecorded how Burnside regarded the mission: poison chalice or golden egg?

January 1863 in the part of Virginia that included the eastern seaboard, Chesapeake Bay and the numerous rivers that flow into it, including the James, York and Rappahannock, had arrived with torrential rain and sleet, rather than the snow and ice that prevailed a little further north in the Virginia-Pennsylvania border lands.

Burnside had charge of just fifteen hundred men, including some cavalry and several artillery pieces and gun carriages. The plan was that they would firstly advance unchallenged down the Pennsylvania bank of the Rappahannock, while the cavalry would move immediately west to distract any Confederate defensive troops that might be in that area and hopefully draw in others to die on their sabres.

Burnside and the remaining force would by then have reached a small Union base towards the river's mouth, where pontoons would already be in place across the Rappahannock. By the time they arrived there, the rain and sleet had reached storm proportions. Burnside, still determined to proceed, was sheltering in a Union telegraph hut when he received a cable from President Lincoln in Pennsylvania. This read:

*'No major movements are to be made without informing the President'.*

The unfortunate general could not understand how Lincoln knew about his mission. In fact, he had been betrayed by another general who regarded Burnside as *'too inefficient to command'*. The Union plan was to bring up a large force after pontoon bridges had been built and then to cross at Fredericksburg, destroy Richmond and the Confederate army there commanded by Jackson.

Nevertheless, Burnside disregarded the cable that no one should pre-empt the main attack and began to cross the river in a rapidly growing and violent storm, while General Lee's sharpshooters on the far bank were able to pick off many of his men on the pontoons.

Having crossed the Rappahannock with serious losses, he gathered what was left of his force on the far bank. He then began to *'march'* through darkness, storm and over ground that was now as much as three feet deep in soft, wet and very cold mud. Gun carriages were down to their axels even as soldiers tried to drag them through the mire. Conditions were like a '*scene from Hell*' one surviving Union sergeant later wrote to his brother. As man after man collapsed and drowned in the mud, artillery was abandoned. Visibility was down to a yard or two. Progress was by then less than half a mile an hour.

General Burnside eventually gave the order for the survivors to retreat, which took many more hours. The mission was christened '*The Mud March*' by his many critics. It had been a military disaster and the ruination of General Ambrose Everett Burnside's military reputation.

Three months later in April 1863, Union Commander-in-Chief Grant sends orders to General Meade north of Gettysburg. This was telegraphed in code as top secret. Grant had devised another plan intended to catch the Confederacy napping and that would very likely cause them immediately to move their army south from Gettysburg to defend Richmond. This, in turn, would release Meade and the Army of the Potomac to burst into Virginia and, with Grant's forces cause '*The utter and final destruction of the Confederate army*'; '*if at first you don't succeed...*' was perhaps his hope for this follow-up plan.

Meade was ordered by Grant to send General Winfield Scott with a brigade of at least seven thousand cavalry, infantry and artillery to depart the Union's huge, slightly thawed winter encampments and march fifty miles due east, thus avoiding the Confederate army to his south. He was then to turn south for another thirty miles to reach Chesapeake Bay at all times ensuring the Confederates got neither sight nor sound of his Union brigades. In preparation for his arrival, Grant had arranged for more than a hundred flat bottomed boats suitable for carrying both men, horses and artillery to be ready to take the Union force for seventy or eighty miles to the confluence with the James River. They would be accompanied by Union war ships, drawn from the blockade of the Confederacy out in the Atlantic.

If anyone had dared to question General Grant, which naturally no one did, he would have demonstrated his certainty that the movement of this large number of troops would be absolutely unknown to the Confederacy who, he was assured, had no presence in that part of Pennsylvania.

Once at the mouth of the James River, the whole force would be landed at the old Fort Monroe on the south-eastern tip of the peninsular where, fifty miles away to the north-west stood Richmond. Fort Monroe had once been a stronghold of the Union, but they lost it to the Confederacy in late 1861, at the same time as Washington was occupied after Bull Run. Grant had *reliable* information that since then it had not been occupied by the Confederacy, which apparently considered any attack from the sea by 1863 to be impossible.

General Joseph Johnston was in command of the Confederate defence force on the peninsular south-east of Richmond and in fact had a similarly large force to the Union on the huge spit of land, well dug in at Williamsburg, Yorktown (the historic site of the surrender of Great Britain in 1781 at the end of the War of Independence) and along the rivers James and York, on both sides of the peninsular. With General Scott's landing at Fort Monroe, the short Peninsular Campaign, which was to last until late June 1863, was launched.

In reality, Grant's optimism was not as well-founded as he had assumed. Robert E Lee was an exceptionally fine commanding officer and in Joseph Johnston, he had an equally experienced and hard fighting general. However, neither Grant nor Lee was to take any active part in the campaign, but placed their trust in their senior generals at the sharp end of the campaign. The result was that, by the time Scott had trans-shipped his brigade of Union soldiers all the way to Fort Monroe, which took far longer than he had anticipated, he was relieved to see that his information from General Grant was correct and there were no Confederate troops in the immediate area. The brigade set foot on land at last on May 10 1863.

Unfortunately for Winfield Scott, Johnston was made aware of their arrival within twenty-four hours and dispatched regiments from both Yorktown on the east side of the peninsular and from Lee's Mill on the west to, '*Meet Scott with fire and brimstone*', as General Johnston put in his cables to local garrisons.

The conflict that Generals Grant and Scott were so sure would create a swift victory on the peninsular and then destroy Richmond, sending the Union marching victoriously through Virginia, never really unfolded into any formal battles, but moved sluggishly up the peninsular giving no overwhelming results. Scott was initially as successful as he had been sure he would be: he pushed the first Confederate force back to Lee's Mill. He then swung west in an attempt to take Yorktown, a much larger conurbation. A savage fight took place there between fairly well-matched numbers, but again with no obvious outcome, except that the Union was able to leave the exhausted Dixie lads still holding the town and march north again unopposed. They eventually reached Drewry's Bluff, some distance to the north, but by then Confederate Johnston had gathered a much larger force to cut off their advance. This was the closest to a major battle in the Campaign and lasted, off and on, for several days.

The result was that General Johnston turned the invaders decisively and was then able to pursue them, not as they had hoped towards Richmond, but north-west which was their only possible line of retreat, away from Richmond and into Pennsylvania. The Union stood fast again east beyond Hanover Court House, but only briefly. It is probably likely that Johnston would have tried to continue the chase, maybe all the way to Gettysburg, but General Lee called a halt as the Union army began to scatter across a region where many rivers crossed its route, they hoped and prayed making their way was no threat towards what they dreamed was still a Union Pennsylvania.

Robert E Lee was, by then, aware that the Union was determined to try to concentrate all its available armed force in the area north of Baltimore in eastern Pennsylvania, where they already had a large army camped in and around the area north of Gettysburg, commanded by General Meade.

General Joe Johnston had been wounded near Hanover Court House and Robert E Lee was inevitably aware of this and did not want Johnston's army chasing the Yankees north, leaving the Confederates very possibly without their Commanding Officer.

Hence, the so-called Peninsular Campaign petered out and Union Commander-in-Chief Ulysses S. Grant was driven to '*bouts of pessimism and depression about the future*'. His close friends were aware that he blamed himself for this failure and in the great battle now inevitably to come, he would probably play very little or no part.

It was now early June 1863 and Abraham Lincoln, attempting to control the Union army from his headquarters well north of any action, could only agree with senior generals like Grant, McClellan and Meade, who were able to contact him at a distance by telegraph cable, an outline plan for the summer of 1863. The President was under the illusion that this had already been agreed between the generals. Lincoln had no choice but to accept that it should go ahead.

The Union plan for the forthcoming summer could well have seemed an act of desperation, but it alone might well have had a slim outside chance of final success: bring all Union armed forces, or at least those within eight or nine hundred miles of Pennsylvania, together as one overwhelming army to face the Confederacy, where, in Lincoln's words in July 1963: "*The future of our Union States will be decided by blood and courage for the rest of the history of America.*"

# Chapter Thirty-Four

## May 1863: Davis Town Confederate Camp

Major Thomas Wilberforce Parish had remarkably survived the winter of 1862/63, the worst that New Englanders could remember. However, the numbers of his compatriots in the Davis Town prison camp had greatly declined, as so many had life torn from their bodies by cold, disease and starvation.

Tom Parish had eventually given up his name to Captain Jessie Jones during his numerous sessions of interrogation and had been deposited once again into the cage inside the stockade on a day when the sleet was causing even Tom Flynn and Frank Witherspoon to doubt that spring and the long-anticipated battle would ever arrive.

The major had used whatever physical and mental strength he had left to resist not just hours of questioning, but also the offices of Flynn and Witherspoon, who had assumed, unknown to their senior officers, the responsibility for adding a rougher form of persuasion.

In the weeks since his capture, he had at first been treated reasonably well, at least by the standards of the crude prison camp. He had refused to give any hint of what the Union command knew of the strength or battle plans of the Confederates, nor of any plans that the Union had in mind. His only answer had consistently been the give his name and rank. This meant that very quickly, Captain Jones had washed his hands of the prisoner and he was handed over to Sergeant Flynn to *try to persuade him to change his bloody stubborn attitude'*.

After what seemed like months, but was actually only about a week, Flynn and his loyal corporal had locked shackles to his ankles, with two iron cannon balls attached, thus making any movement either impossible or very painful. They had then starved him for days at a time and, as a result, had been satisfied with his growing resemblance to a skeleton. When this failed to achieve the desired result they had expected, namely that he quickly supply details of the Union Army's defensive positions, numbers and firepower, as well as if or when they intended to attack the waiting Confederate force; then something even more physical was obviously required.

It was a month into their scheme of reducing the prisoner to a compliant shadow of the man he once was, when Witherspoon came up with a suggestion, joyously received by his sergeant.

"You know them cows we had back on your dad's farm. Well, what did we do to 'em before we drove 'em to Jackson?"

Flynn needed only a moment's thought before a grin lit up his face. "Yeah! Damn right! Get that fire real hot, Frank."

Two days ago, they believed they had been given *carte blanche* to get the major to give up all he obviously knew. They had taken over a small hut well beyond the southern edge of the camp, where screams would not bother anyone's sleep. With the fire roaring and a metal rod lodged in its now red-hot heat, they tied the major to the centre post, took the iron from the fire and, waving under his nose, asked their questions once more; the man remained as silent as the grave he now longed to inhabit. Flynn insisted on having the first branding and applied the iron to the prisoner's cheek. As he cried out to his God, Witherspoon, within inches of his contorted face, said quietly, "That's a present from us to a damned Reb, so you'll remember us for as long as you live!"

Perhaps it was fortunate for Thomas Parish, who had once seemed so young, but as the branding continued through the afternoon, he eventually lost the power to utter any sounds and, so weakened was he that by the time the light faded completely his two interrogators realised with disappointment that he was dead. Their meagre wits eventually had them realising exactly the trouble they were now in.

Tom would no doubt have been delighted with the result, which was that the two Mississippi farm boys were court marshalled for acting without orders, but quite possibly in reality for failing to obtain the vital information that their superiors had expected them to extract. A furiously frustrated general ensured that finding them guilty was swift and inevitable and known to their fellows. Their punishment was, with a certain divine justice, that they were stretched upright between two posts, their shirts and coats removed, and received fifty lashes with the cat 'o nine tails, followed by having his forehead branded with a *C* for Criminal and then being hanged in front of their regiment.

Neither George nor Arthur, half a mile away in a camp canteen, were unaware of events in the distant hut, which was just as well, since it would be unlikely that Arthur would have failed to make a very vocal protest to General Longstreet if he had known. George, however, was inured to reports of the events there by years of service in the Crimea and India to see such brutal actions, which he had become used to regarding as 'necessary'. It would have been natural that he would have seen it as anything out of the ordinary in a military camp in a state of war.

The snow eventually began to retreat from the camp itself, but far later than anyone in Longstreet's army, some out of their minds with the months when the temperature never rose even close to freezing, could have expected. It was the first week of May when the solidly frozen ground began to thaw. The white world gradually moved away from the open ground, but still hid under the trees in the forests and woods and finally, by late in the month, disappeared, to be replaced by two weeks of almost continuous rain. It became clear to the two Englishmen that preparations were then urgently under way at last for some sort of genuine action, in spite of the downpours now replacing the snowstorms.

As May ended and the greenery of the late spring became obvious, so a new energy and drive seemed to have occupied the senior officers of the rear guard/reserve force in Camp Davis and, from what they began to hear rumoured from further towards Gettysburg, the same seemed to be spreading like wild fire through the larger part of the Confederate army to their north east.

Spirits rose from the lowliest private infantryman to the most senior general and this went on to infect even the civilians in the camp as well. Waggons of supplies began to pour in to the camp carrying everything from huge supplies of both fresh and tinned food, as well as more and more artillery pieces, new rifles, ammunition and, most recently, columns of non-military labour in the form of what they took to be poor, white labourers, whom they were told were only too pleased to help the Confederate cause, but had been promised some welcome dollars at the same time; the chances of their getting such material reward were not good. These men were quickly put to work in the camp on the preparation of artillery pieces, repairing waggons and limbers, while others went forward with working parties to dig more defensive ditches, faced with lengthy mounds of soil into which were buried the now traditional long, sharpened logs.

Arthur and George were allowed to travel forward, for a few miles, albeit protected by a small group of soldiers, with some of these work parties to see the considerable gun emplacements and defences being constructed over a wide area, spreading for several miles between the camp and the bulk of the army closer to Gettysburg. To their surprise, they saw no evidence of the Union army on these expeditions.

If they had been able to take to the air in one of the observation balloons still being prepared for use on the ground, and if then had been able to hang several hundred feet south-east of Gettysburg, they would have seen seventy-five thousand Confederate soldiers moving like ants over a vast area of fields, woods and hills, covering at least twenty-five square miles relatively close to the town of Gettysburg, all working feverishly in preparation for what would surely be a mighty battle.

Returning to the camp after their third foray into countryside that now began to resemble the preparation for a giant city to be constructed rather than a bloody conflict, Arthur and George discussed how best to communicate this rapid development to London. Events in Pennsylvania, in their opinion, would be the precursors to a conflict far greater than any battle or skirmish so far in the Civil War and must surely determine the future of the United States of America as a whole or in two parts. In the end, the text of the coded telegraphic message that was dispatched from Hanover Junction for the attention of Prime Minister Lord Palmerston in London to read urgently:

Cable sent to London from the Envoys in an agreed code, of which this is the translation.
*June 1 1863: Pennsylvania:*

*Preparations for battle by Confederacy for many weeks. 50-70,000 well prepared to face Union force less in size. More expected to join the Confederacy from south and west after Union defeats across whole area. Could be a force of up to 75,000. Site of probable battle well prepared by Confederacy. Rumoured Lincoln may lead his troops in battle. Union force here is all the organised army remaining in one place. Outposts of Union forces, may soon experience desertion by many Union soldiers. The*

*Confederacy confidently expects battle to be the final conflict. Blockade of southern ports by HM Royal Navy has had widespread success. Cotton should be reaching England by now. An equally possible surprise outcome to any battle could still be possible. We suggest English troops in S. Canada are readied to assist if needed. Suggest the fleet should remain in position until conflict over. We report that Elder Brother is missing after raid. Have no news of him. Will contact again.*

*Respectfully: A & G.*

Another three weeks passed with no sign of any military action from either side. The days were now longer and the sunshine was unseasonably very warm indeed, so that those still working on the defences and artillery positions were stripped to the waist and bathed in sweat. It was towards the fourth week of June that George and Arthur were told they could have one '*final*' visit to the forward lines since a '*great battle for the soul of America*' was anticipated by the Confederacy in the near future. They joined a small cavalry unit and rode northeast for the best part of a day, coming to Blackhorse Tavern in mid-afternoon. As they left Camp Davis several battalions were breaking camp and beginning to march in the same direction, but, having left them behind, they then came upon far greater numbers of grey uniformed soldiers, some moving forward towards the north east, while others were occupying the defensive ditches, mounds, walls and gun emplacements that stretched as far as the eye could see.

Their group of half a dozen cavalry riders had passed through open farmland, divided by wooden rail fencing and occasional trees and copses. By the time they reached Blackhorse Tavern, they had joined the dusty Fairfield Road that disappeared ahead in a straight line towards Westfield Ridge and then, they were told, Gettysburg itself. They stopped for the night in a barn close to the tavern, which they shared with about a dozen horses, but were able to take advantage of the packed tavern itself to satisfy their hunger and a mug or two of beer after a long day's ride.

By dawn of the next day, having enjoyed a hot mug of coffee and some fresh bread, courtesy of the now Confederate controlled tavern, they were back on Fairfield Road, trotting up the gentle slope to the top of a ridge. They stopped there and were able, with the help of a telescope, to survey the woods and hills to the north and east. Cemetery Ridge was pointed out, about five or six miles distant and, a little further over flat farmland, the tiny buildings that were the outskirts of Gettysburg, with its earth roads dividing it into a regular grid pattern of buildings. The captain in charge of their small troop handed George the telescope.

"If you look to the left of the town, that calls itself a city, in the north east you can pick out the dust rising from a straight road heading out from Gettysburg. You might be able to spot a rail line just beyond it."

"Yes, I've got it," said George, "I'm not sure about what might be human figures, but there are tiny signs of life of some sort on the road and, just maybe, they could that be horses and waggons as well?"

"Yes, sir. You're dead right. What you can see, about six miles away is the very edge of the Union army under General Meade. If you move the 'scope slowly and steadily to the left, that is the west, you might spot some earth works, lines of defence, but the artillery now positioned there is probably far too small to make out."

George was straining to make sense of what he could actually see and that which was by now partly obscured by a rising shimmer of heat haze. The strangest thing was to observe some of what lay out there miles to the west, as well as how much he could only imagine, all of it shrouded in silence from this distance.

Dust rose slowly from the roads. Battalions, regiments and divisions in the very far distance, they were assured all dressed in blue, must be on the move, but were doing so like insects on a far-off pavement. The captain handed his telescope to Arthur, who found it much harder to both control his horse with one hand and to focus the telescope with the other.

"It's like seeing a huge painting, but one that has the smallest of occasional twitches of life, that I believe I must have imagined."

"What you are seeing," said the captain, "is an army probably only about two thirds the size of our own and which is struggling to stop even more of its soldiers vanishing into the dark each night as they decide to stay alive and get home, rather than become corpses on those pleasant fields. Do you realise that it is reckoned that already over four hundred and fifty thousand Americans have died in places like this since the Union started this war?"

As he turned his horse to move on, George noticed Arthur staring unmoving across the miles separating them from the Union front lines. He turned his own horse back and stopped beside Arthur, who seemed unaware of his presence.

"What's caught your attention out there, Arthur? I don't see any real movement."

"I was just wondering if Ernest is maybe only a few miles distant, perhaps in some prison camp, or maybe he's in a shallow grave somewhere. I suppose we shall never know now."

"Don't despair yet," George said, slapping his back, "we are closer than we were months ago and if this battle goes as the Confederates predict, then you just might find him not too far, way over there, healthy and unharmed."

Arthur turned his horse and, as he started to trot away, shouted over his shoulder, "Your confidence is so ridiculous, it doesn't deserve any comment from me."

In fact, George was not entirely mistaken. Ernest was still alive, just, and at that moment was probably at least sixteen miles away well behind the Union lines. However, he was very weak and seriously scared when a guard entered the compound, grabbed him by the arm and forced him to stand up. He was then thrust with his face against the wall and, his arms dragged behind his back as his wrists were shackled together.

The guard yelled in his ear, "You come with me! Your expectation of living out this war has just lost any hope! Now move!"

He was roughly propelled forward by the point of a bayonet drawing blood on his back, now only partly covered by a ripped and filthy shirt. He stumbled out of the compound's gate and then across an expanse of ragged grass and earth towards a wooden farmhouse, that also looked as if it had seen happier days. The door had another soldier standing guard beside it, who laughed as he pushed the door open and Ernest fell up the steps and sprawled across the threshold of a stone-floored room. He was pulled to his feet and found himself facing a Union officer, seated behind a kitchen table, on which were scattered maps, some papers and a bottle of whiskey. The guard then punched the prisoner hard in his right ear.

"Salute the Major General, you rebel scum!"

"Stop that, this instant, private!" The general commanded as he jumped to his feet and the guard took several steps back, as if expecting to be hit himself.

"Get that chair by the wall and put it here." As he hesitated, the officer raised his voice again, "At once! Help the gentleman to sit down, remove those shackles and then get out of here before I lose my patience and confine *you* to the lock up."

As wonderful as it was to be freed from the iron cuffs and to be sitting on an actual chair, Ernest remained certain that this was all some sort of trick, probably prior to his execution. He kept his gaze on the floor and his mouth closed, but he had by then noticed another officer, originally standing well behind the general, but now stepping forward to sit beside his superior officer, who spoke with a quiet and confident voice.

"I am Major General Humphreys and this officer is Colonel Wood. We have the honour be officers in the Union army of the Potomac, under the command of General Meade. I hope you will be prepared to reveal your name in return."

Ernest had learned by now that no one imprisoned in this appalling place should offer any piece of information willingly and so kept silent and his eyes lowered.

The Major General did not, as he had anticipated, scream at him and order a guard to beat him around the head. Instead, Arthur heard only a quiet voice that even hinted at a smile behind it.

"Let me save you the trouble, sir."

Ernest's head shot up as if by a reflex and he stared at the man, unable to conceal what was genuine shock.

"Young man, I am aware that you are not a Confederate rebel, which is extremely fortunate for you. You are English and certainly not a military man. Am I correct?"

Ernest stared at him in silence. *How could he possibly know this?* That was followed to by another quite foolish thought: *Did this mean that he had been seized by mistake and would be released and returned to Camp Davis without delay, maybe even with an apology?*

"I understand your reluctance to speak, sir, but that could mean that we, the Union, may be now forced to assume you are a spy for the Confederacy, albeit that you are not from their disgusting, enslaved states... Are you a spy, Mr Englishman?"

Ernest's mind was by now racing. To agree he was a spy would clearly be a very dangerous thing to do. In fact, it would probably lead to his immediate

326

execution. Equally, he could not betray his own country and reveal why he was here.

"I understand your hesitation. I am a reasonable man and do not wish you ill." He then leant forward and pulled a piece of paper towards him from the top of a pile nearest to Ernest and which he had already guessed was the translation into clear words of a coded telegraphic cable; he had seen something like before it at the Hanover telegraph office. It had several lines with well-spaced letters and words impossible to make out.

Major General Humphreys appeared to be rereading it and slowly at that.

"This cable was intercepted by a telegraph station north of here in Pennsylvania, a state, of course, within the Union. The cable itself, in a code fairly easily transcribed into English by Colonel Wood here, was sent from somewhere further south on May 15, but can you perhaps guess where it was addressed to? No?"

The Major General stared at Ernest, an encouraging smile on his face, reflected the genuine shock in Ernest's own expression, which he was unable to conceal.

"Well, as you may already know, it was addressed to a telegraphic cable office in London, England... In spite of your shocked countenance, I assume this is something you are already aware of, is it not?"

Ernest felt what he had heard so-called 'therapists' in England propose a feeling in the brain that was 'other-worldly'. If that meant what he felt now, as if he were outside his body looking down at himself, he then understood that it must be real. He saw himself agonised by fear and self-doubt: *how did I ever get into this? How did that man crack the code? Am I actually going mad?*

"Now, sir, we need you to be sensible and give your confirmation of what we have surmised. In return for that simple assurance that we are correct in what we believe to be the truth, the Union and its President, Mr Lincoln, will be happy to convey you, unharmed, to a ship in New York that will carry you home to London. I am sure you will agree that could hardly be a fairer, nay a more generous outcome to the unfortunate situation in which you find yourself."

Ernest had managed to convince his voice to resurrect itself, although he had no sane idea of what was really happening to him or what he could do about it. He started to speak at last, albeit hesitantly.

"I am, as I would have hoped you could tell, an English gentleman. I have no knowledge about cables or telegraphs. My employment as a manager in the English cotton industry has no need of such new-fangled inventions. I have become caught up in your tragic war, but play no part in that. As you correctly surmise, I am not a soldier and never have been… I demand to be released immediately."

There was then a long pause, when no one spoke. The Major General exchanged looks with Colonel Wood and then got up and, leading the colonel to the far corner of the room, they both looked again at the copy of the telegraph message; they spoke in hushed tones that Ernest could not make out. They eventually returned to stand behind the table opposite Ernest.

"We are most disappointed in your foolish, ill-mannered attitude. As a result, and at this most significant moment in our country's history, we have no choice but to pass you to others who may be a little less generous in the manner in which they require you to divulge the information the Union reasonably requires. Guard! Take the *gentleman* into the care of Lieutenant Richmond."

The last Ernest saw of Major General Humphreys and Colonel Wood was as he was dragged out of the door and down the steps of the farmhouse to what he assumed would undoubtedly be his torture and death.

# Part Three
# Gettysburg 1863

# Chapter Thirty-Five

## Gettysburg: Summer 1863

After the long and arctic winter of 1862/63, the summer of 1863 in Pennsylvania was to become one of the hottest and driest anyone in the small town of Gettysburg could remember. By June, the grass had changed from spring green to a withered brown and fast flowing streams were now mere trickles or dried up traces in the dust. Nevertheless, the harvest of fruit, especially the famed local cherries and peaches, promised to be finer than ever as the fruits sucked up the heat day after day. Remarkably, it also remained unnaturally peaceful even after April saw the end of the harsh winter and still with no battle in prospect through May, June and into July.

The inhabitants of southern Pennsylvania, who had not already fled their homes and farms at the advance over their land of tens of thousands of armed soldiers, now began to believe, as months passed with no advance of the secessionists, that the war had come to a state of stalemate. They even hoped it might actually end here and perhaps now with some sort of armistice or surrender, since you could always trust Honest Abe to sort something out when things got out of hand. It seemed to those boasting of a knowledge of the history of wars in other parts of the world that their enemy now, like so many in the pages of the past, was simply too frightened in the face of a powerful army like that of the Union, to do anything other than sink to their knees and beg for forgiveness.

Most Pennsylvanians, caught up in the first armed conflict in their homeland for more than almost a century, began to think that just possibly the rumoured '*final great conflict*' might not be about to crash about their ears. A war that pitched brother against brother or son against father had at first seemed fanciful, to many something only the news sheets believed, although as real news reached them over recent years of a face-off at Charleston and then the slaughter at Bull Run and the Union retreat through Washington DC, it had become real, but still far distant; even when the Union army arrived near Washington in the Shenandoah Valley They now started to pay some attention to news of numerous far-off battles that sounded as though neither side was scoring great victories and stolidly assured each other that it could never spread this far north or could it?

The early summer of 1863 seemed to the citizens of Pennsylvania that it might have been a blood bath in states like Virginia, as they were made aware of battles that far off between the '*damned rebels*' and the brave patriotic boys of the Union. They tried to discount stories in newspapers of bloodshed from the hills and mountains of Kentucky and Virginia to as far west as the Ohio River. They read these reports of real battles, descriptions of thousands of men and boys being killed and wounded, even occasionally met people who claimed to have seen some fighting, but of course, they knew that Pennsylvania and the rest of New England would always have the upper hand in the unlikely event that war came their way.

They might remember hearing about the 'minor skirmish', with no loss of life, at Fort Sumpter in far off Charleston two years ago, but that had been laughed off as a brilliant trick by Abe Lincoln's generals to fool the Rebels into believing that the Union army was too weak to fight.

Then there was Manassas, although the Confederates had the nerve to call it *Bull Run*, which was of course just the southern newspapers trying to scare the good citizens of the Union states. Remarkably, there were still many in the northern New England states that expected it to be reported soon that this *far off war* would soon end and they would never have to experience the rumours of death and destruction on the soil of the Union ever again.

There came a rude awakening to the truth when, in the autumn of '62 and the spring of '63 they started to come across whole families moving along the dusty farm roads in southern Pennsylvania heading north to escape the Confederate army that had, temporarily of course, occupied the capital. Those who bothered to speak to these folk bore back horrific tales of the disaster at Manassas and then accounts of hordes of savage Rebels that they were assured would soon be on their heels all over New England. This was followed pretty closely by flowery and rather vague newspaper reports, where you had to read between the lines to discover that battles in the Shenandoah Valley had been fought, but surely that had resulted in the retreat of the rebels? Then in West

Virginia, Harper's Ferry and further south at Lynchburg on the James River similar stories had spread: *had thousands of their boys really been killed?*

As the month of June1863 grew hotter, so citizens in and around Gettysburg, all fiercely loyal to the Union and President Lincoln, began to realise that the impossible just might be happening and might well even be on their doorsteps. Panic began to creep into many thousands of hearts. During the last three weeks of the month, a large part of Pennsylvania south of Baltimore saw a mass of civilians following those from Washington and fleeing north. A few chose to remain closer to their homes, sheltering in woods and even under farmhouses and barns, away from Gettysburg itself, but where they believed, or perhaps simply hoped and prayed, that no battle could ever reach them and where they could keep an eye on their houses and farms and somehow protect them from marauding Rebs.

While small villages, hamlets and farms began to empty en-mass as the inhabitants fled towards to New York and even Ohio in the hope of finding the Union government safely installed behind a heavily protected border in the hands of Union forces.

Unfortunately, at the same time a contrary rumour was swiftly spreading through the air like a poisonous disease, threatening honest and patriotic citizens, saying that the Confederacy had '...*over a million men preparing to destroy Abe's army and then they could wipe out the entire civilisation that had been the United States of America'*.

Not surprisingly, Ernest had no such information, nor had he, in fact, any information about the current state of the war in waiting, nor of Arthur and George, nor even whether Longstreet's regiments were still at Camp Davis. His world had shrunk to just one room in a small farmhouse that, as far as he could tell, was miles away from the Union headquarters. All he could see through the gloom of the late afternoon were four stone walls, a ceiling that looked ancient and cracked, and a window that was boarded up from the outside, so that only a vestige of light penetrated his cell. He could make out one wooden door, which he was quite certain was locked. The only furniture was a small round table with a chair pushed under it and another chair, to which he was tied facing the table. He had begun to wonder if he had gone deaf, since the world around the farmhouse was absent of any sounds that, at least, could penetrate the walls. Had he misjudged the distance he had been marched from the Union Headquarters?

The silence was broken by the sound of a key in the door lock. The door was thrust open, crashing against the wall, and immediately let in the light of an oil lamp, carried by what he took to be a Union officer; two other soldiers, carrying rifles came in behind the tall, almost gaunt man in blue uniform. He had a ginger moustache and beard, but with virtually no hair on the rest of his head. He wore the jacket of an officer and Ernest had no doubt that this must be the threatened Lieutenant Richmond.

All three soldiers ignored Ernest, not even glancing in his direction. The two privates were posted at the door by the officer while he placed some papers, a pen and a small bottle of ink on the table, all taken from a leather satchel that hung from his shoulder. He then arranged them symmetrically. He carefully hung the satchel over by second chair by the table, took off his jacket, which he arranged over its back. He looked at the seat with some annoyance and, taking a kerchief from his pocket, blew away a cloud of dust that had settled upon it. Ernest felt the need to scream in frustration, but managed to both keep silent and to force his expression to be that of boredom, keeping his eyes away from the table and slowly looking around the room. Lieutenant Richmond, if indeed it was he, having ensured all his belongings were neatly placed, picked up the papers and started slowly, maddeningly slowly, to read them. There being three pages, this took a considerable time. Only once he had placed them back in front of him did he lift his eyes to direct a steady, confident look at Ernest, but remained unspeaking. Ernest returned the compliment and stared directly into the lieutenant's eyes, managing not to blink. In so doing, he noticed for the first time the man's large nose, somewhat out of proportion to his face and exaggerated by the moustache below it and the almost bald brow and crown above; he could feel a laugh rising in his throat, but pushed it away.

The officer gave a small cough and muttered something like, "Mmm…"

He was silent again for several minutes and then picked up the top sheet of paper from the table, which he appeared to read again, although Ernest was sure he must now know it by heart.

"You claim to be English. Where do you live in England?"

Ernest hesitated, unsure whether it would be better to remain silent or try to persuade this odd-looking man that he was an innocent Englishman, caught up in a war by accident. He chose the latter.

"My name is Ernest Tissiman and I live in Oldham, a cotton milling town in Lancashire. If you know where the great city of Manchester is, Oldham is nearby."

"What is your profession or trade in Old Ham?"

"My family owns one of the largest cotton mills in Lancashire, which, as I assume you know, is the heart of the cotton industry in England, as well as being the largest cotton manufacturing industry in the world."

"I am informed that these mills use slave labour to produce its cotton cloth. How do you condone…"

Ernest, forgetting his inability to stand, fell forward, but was able to control the movement and now almost shouted his reply.

"The cotton mills of England do *not* employ slaves. You should know full well that slavery was made illegal in England in 1833 with the powerful help of many Englishmen, including Mr William Wilberforce, a Member of the English Parliament. I strongly object to your suggestion that Lieutenant Richmond cut him off and looked at him with a half-smile on his face. "So I may take it, may I not, that you have no connection with these damned rebels, the Confederates of the southern *cotton* states and strongly resent my suggestion that you favour the practice of slavery?"

Ernest hesitated long enough for the lieutenant to prompt his reply, "Well? Have I not stated your English principles correctly?"

"If you meant that slavery is no longer to be found in the great country of England and all of Great Britain, then you are correct. Just as you are a soldier and thus give your life to the success of your military campaigns and the commands of your senior officers, so I am a cotton merchant and manufacturer and have given my poor efforts to trying to ensure that the trade of manufacturing cotton is carried out efficiently and profitably for *all* concerned."

The lieutenant got up from his chair with some enthusiasm, walked around the table and stood beside his prisoner.

"Can you then explain, to a simple soldier like myself, what you are doing here in the United States of America, deeply involved in a war between the righteous Union and the foul, rebelling, slave owning Confederates?"

At that moment, his anger at Ernest, seemed to burst from his mouth as the words became louder and louder. He grabbed the face of the pale Englishman and put his own face within inches as he spat out his accusations.

"You were captured in a Confederate camp on the eve of a battle whose aim it is for your friends, those same Confederates, those supporters of slavery, to kill and maim the men folk of tens of thousands of Christian mothers, who will weep tears of rage and their desperate sorrow that they will never see those sons, husbands and fathers, who your friends will slaughter, soaked in blood on the fields they have so loyally fought to defend from this evil!"

Two days later, Ernest, to his continued sense of shock, found himself still alive and guessed he had remained well back from the front-line northwest of Gettysburg.

Lieutenant Richmond, having failed to get any further response from him, other than the repetition time after time of his original statement, had washed his hands of the prisoner and condemned him to solitary confinement and a diet further reduced from his previous meagre prison rations.

Ernest had been suffering increasing pain from his wound, which he suspected was, unsurprisingly, infected, and that was added to his near starvation in the months since he had been taken prisoner. After his initial interrogation by Lieutenant Richmond, he was moved again to sit on a brick floor and lean against a stone wall in another part of the farmhouse; he was at his lowest ebb.

The strength he had somehow mustered to get him through his interrogation to date had now entirely deserted him. He was so physically weak that he could not even attempt to rise to his feet, while mentally he could no longer pretend that he had any future; his life was destined to be cut short at the end of a rope, he was certain, probably in the next few hours.

The following morning, he was lifted to his feet by two young soldiers and, unable to walk, was carried to a waggon. The waggon, with him as its only cargo, made a slow, jolting journey of over an hour before stopping in what he could make out was a small, almost deserted town; deserted, he soon saw, of ordinary citizens, but busy with Union soldiers in its dusty streets. The waggon had stopped outside a church and his wandering consciousness assumed he was about to be buried in its graveyard. At that point, the world went black and he descended into complete and grateful unconsciousness.

He became aware again as he slowly saw, through the dim light, an arched ceiling some distance above him and then a figure, that at first his muddled brain told him was an angel, but although this angel was young and dressed in white, she had a black face, which his bible pictures of childhood had never included. He knew he was either dead or dreaming, since his narrow view was surrounded by silence; even as the mouth of the angel moved, as if speaking, but no sound emerged.

Very gradually, he began to hear a dim whisper of voices and, as he was able to hear more and more, a clattering of what could have been several metal buckets carelessly being dropped on a stone floor. His vision eventually cleared and so did his hearing. What he vaguely remembered as a silent angel now put her hand on his brow and he could hear her speaking.

"…and you look a might better young 'un."

She smiled at him and her whole face lit up, as she turned to another older woman, this one, with a white face and fair hair, did not smile, but also gently laid the palm of her hand on his forehead.

"Well, I'm not so sure that I would say he was a lot better, Eliza, but at least he's not dead yet."

Ernest wanted to know what was going on, but although opening his mouth and his brain instructing him to speak, all that came out was a rasping sound that terrified him, since he was apparently now dumb.

"Don't you try to speak, now, sir. You'm alive, so thank the Lord for that."

The angel with the black face he saw now also had black skin on her hands and arms. *She was what Paul Hayward had called his workers: a 'negro' for God's sake. Was he somehow back at Cotton Hall? But he'd seen no church there.*

"You move over now, Eliza. Let me look at him properly. And you go get the doctor, Major Cook over there, up the end of the aisle."

As the first angel almost ran off, the other one now stopped him from trying to speak again.

"I was told you were English, young man. So I'm not expecting to hear some Dixie drawl from you. You just tell me, as best you can, what your name is."

Ernest, still struggling to grasp where exactly he was, tried to decide why he was lying down looking at a church ceiling above him and why there seemed to be nothing holding his wrists behind his back. His vision had by now cleared considerably, as well as his hearing. He began to cough and that caused a burning pain in his chest. He managed to splutter out his name and was relieved to realise that he had not entirely lost his voice. The woman, whom he could now see was probably as old as his mother, put her arm under his back and lifted him forward, as if he weighed nothing more than a pound of sugar. With her other hand, she pulled a somewhat soiled pillow up behind his head and let him rest back on it.

He could see that he was covered by a fairly clean sheet and was lying on a straw mattress supported by boards. He began to look around the church and saw the inside of a fairly small, very simple building: just one large, high room made of stone and painted white. Above him was a high beamed roof. Dozens of chairs had been piled haphazardly closer to the walls, while he could see dozens of these mattresses lying on the stone floor, all of them with men in various stages of injury lying or sitting on them.

A rather short, stout man was now hurrying towards him, with the girl-angel trying to keep up with him. He was dressed in boots and blue uniform trousers and jacket, but with a white shirt, open at the neck; there were stains of some sort on the lower part of the shirt that he suspected were blood. The older lady moved aside and the man came to squat beside Ernest, moving his head slowly from side to side as he seemed to be examining his face.

"Well, well. This is sure a first for a Union surgeon: an Englishman, no less. How are you feeling, son?"

Ernest felt both relief and surprise when he found he was actually able to speak, albeit somewhat quietly and hesitantly.

"I suppose I feel…not sure…strange. I'm not certain where I am or how I got here. Did you say *surgeon*? Does that mean I'm dying?"

"No, no. At the start you were more or less, but, by God, I guess you've come through the worst."

Ernest realised how dry his whole mouth and throat felt and maybe that was what made his speech sound so odd to him. "Could I have a drink…if you please?"

The officer, or maybe what he would call a doctor, looked at the young black woman hovering a few steps away and nodded at her. She hurried off.

"Let me explain a few things to you. They told us your name is Ernest *Tissiman*? Is that correct?"

"Yes. I'm afraid it's an odd name, but I am English." Ernest felt it very difficult to get words out and realised they still sounded odd.

"Yeah. That's what I was told." He was handed a tin mug of water by the girl Ernest still called an *angel* in his mind. He drank greedily.

"I reckon you need to go a bit slower with that, Mr Tissiman."

The mug was taken from his hand, with just a hint of unspoken reprimand.

"I think I need to give you a little information before I look at how we might be able to make you feel more comfortable. What is the last thing you can remember about where you were or what happened to get you here?"

Ernest was silent, as he tried to force his memory to come alive and, a little vaguely, it obliged.

"I think the last thing I can remember properly was being in a room, a small room, with some officer, who was trying to make me tell him who I was and why I was here… no…no, that's not all. I can remember, but it's more like a dream and with bits missing… I was in a fight, with rifles going off…and then I was in a frightful prison camp… I was hurt somehow… There was blood and an ugly wound… yes…there was pain, awful pain. There was not much food. I was dying. I wanted to die; it was all so…terrible. Maybe that was before the room with the officer, or was it later? I can't remember exactly." His mind relapsed into confusion and he realised he was crying, silently at first and then sobbing desperately.

# Chapter Thirty-Six

Major General Joseph Hooker, known to the army of the Potomac as 'Fighting Joe', was not at that time held in the highest esteem by General George Meade, the then commander of the Union army. Hooker had until very recently been himself the commander of the principal army of the Union, but had been soundly defeated by General Robert E Lee of the Confederacy in a particularly bloody battle in West Virginia the previous winter. Hooker was still an officer in the army of the Potomac, which by the summer of 1863 was the only Union force that could be called an army, but he had been obliged to give up his overall command to general George Meade, after he and the remains of his force had limped into Pennsylvania earlier that spring, struggling through snow and ice to get there at all.

He was a beaten man, a *'useless general'* as so many even of his own men said, albeit under their breath, or when promised they would be quoted incognito by the press when they 'let slip' his fall. Joseph Hooker needed to show that he was not the fool that he was only too well aware was the opinion that other generals now had of him, relegated to the lower echelons of general command by Meade.

Fighting Joe had been instructed only yesterday by General Joshua Chamberlain, Meade's second in command, to make his way without delay to the small town of Brownsville, about seven miles northwest of Gettysburg. His mission was to ensure an Englishman, one Ernest Tissiman, captured during the previous winter's daring a raid on the Confederate Camp Davis, was alive and had been safely moved to the military hospital at Brownsville. Hooker should see that he was well cared for and, the hardest pill to swallow, he must explain to him what his situation now was.

He had been briefed on what had happened to this 'gentleman', once considered a spy, and what General Chamberlain wanted him to understand his situation was today. To those who much later were required to investigate why

Hooker received no written orders and why he claimed that those he did receive verbally were so brief and hurried that he could not be blamed for any misunderstanding of them; so could not possibly comprehend what he was accused of being responsible for. It was possibly fortunate that he was killed, believed by many to have been murdered, shortly after the battle at Gettysburg, his body never found even in the state of Maine, where he was last seen just outside his home town of Cincinnati a month after the last day of the battle, alive and well, but not in uniform.

By the time General Hooker arrived in Brownsville, which he described as soon as he saw it as 'more of a township than a town', Ernest had been in the hospital there for six days and was now in an actual bed, and a clean one at that, appropriately he felt, next to the altar. He was responding to being warmer and having the tattered clothes that had hung on him when he arrived there, changed for reasonably old, but also reasonably clean, shirt and jacket and cotton trousers. His wound was being properly dressed, while his other symptoms, which had until very recently seemed life threatening, were less apparent now that hot food and local milk were reviving his constitution. Nurse Eliza was in charge of keeping him warm and well fed, as well as changing his dressings. He had learned from her that she was not, in fact, a nurse, although that did not stop Ernest from calling her by that title.

She had explained in a quieter moment late one night that she had been freed from a tobacco plantation where she was a nursemaid to several of the '*master's*' children. A large force of the Union army had arrived in the region of the plantation where she had been all her life until the summer of 1862. The officer in command was apparently in charge of a regiment that arrived out of the blue soon after a battle at a place called Manassas. They had killed most of the white families on surrounding plantations, including her master and his missis, burned down their big houses and declared all the slaves now to be '*Free*'. They were on a rampage of revenge for the battle at Manassas, from where they had sensibly retreated south, rather than north like most of the doomed Union army.

She admitted that their acts of terror terrified her because she had no other home and no place to go to; she had been born into slavery on the island of Jamaica and then sold as a very young woman to a plantation owner there. She had managed to persuade the Union officer, who was charged with '*ridding the states of the white trash*', that she was experienced in nursing and for that

341

reason was eventually taken north as the regiment joined the slow retreat towards New England. She eventually finished up in the Brownsville hospital.

General Hooker arrived outside the Brownsville church accompanied by a major, two captains of cavalry and ten privates. Such a contingent of clearly important Union soldiers caused something of a stir around the church, heightened by the disturbance caused when all of them, bar two soldiers left with the horses outside, followed the general in marching through the church door, their boots clattering on the stone floor and their sheathed swords inevitably swinging against the piles of chairs and pews. The volume of their voices filled the church and echoed, as they bounced from the roof. All other conversation stopped and the soldiers were aware of dozens of pairs of eyes fixed on them, many looking scared of so many armed soldiers in their midst. Joseph Hooker deliberately tried to make himself rather more important than he now was and raised his voice, quite unnecessarily since the place was already silent.

"I am Major General Hooker. Who is in charge here?"

He then looked around accusingly, as if preparing to run his sword through anyone who dared to provide the wrong answer. The younger nurses gasped with shock, while Eliza, her hand to her mouth to stifle the scream that was trying to escape, hid behind two large nurses, also dressed in white gowns.

"I said *who is in…*"

"I think we all heard you quite clearly the first time."

Major Cook stepped briskly forward, wiping his hands on a cloth and held out his hand to Hooker. This was obviously a mistake.

"How dare you, sir! How dare fail to salute a senior officer, a line general to boot, and offer your hand, as if you were some village yokel. Who the hell are you, sir?"

Major Cook stood to attention, clicked his heels together and, having handed the bloody cloth to a nurse beside him, presented a smart salute.

"My apologies, general, I was foolishly paying too much attention to these desperately sick and wounded men to appreciate your importance."

The general seemed lost for words for several moments and the officers and men behind him, with difficulty, rapidly assumed suitably serious expressions.

"That is insubordination, sir. You are a soldier and under my command. I could have you court martialled before you knew what had hit you."

Here he hesitated, looked questioningly at one of the other officers, but receiving no response, turned back to bark at Major Cook.

"I will deal with you later."

Major Cook remained at attention. General Hooker looked somewhat disconcerted, glanced at his own major, received no response and eventually was forced to address the doctor once again.

"Yes, well, exactly. You need to take care, sir…yes, take care. For now, I need to speak with a Mr Tissiman and that has to be in private. Organise that at once… Well, don't just stand there. Do as I command."

All the other staff, who had by then gathered around to view the spectacle, were told to get back to their duties, while Major Cook and Eliza moved Ernest, who by now could walk with assistance, to what would have been the minister's vestry, through a door to the side of the altar. Since the room contained simply an upright chair and a store cupboard, they helped Ernest to sit on the chair, but at least with a pillow placed at his back. The patient was left there, while Major Cook went back into the body of the church and pointed the general in the direction of the door to the vestry, before hurrying off as fast as possible.

General Hooker was taken aback when he saw that the only chair was a small and straight-backed wooden one and was already occupied by Ernest. The Union major, who had followed him into the room, tactfully stood in the far corner. The general took several minutes to study the small, almost empty vestry in the hope, perhaps, that another chair, more suitable to his rank, would be instantly provided. Ernest observed the scene through half-closed eyes.

General Hooker muttered, "Very well, then," and made the decision that the best course of action was to stand, which he consoled himself meant that he had a commanding position looking down at Ernest.

He cleared his throat noisily and Ernest took that as his cue to open his eyes and looked unblinking and silent at the general, who, as he started to address him, began almost to *march* up and down the narrow room.

"Very well. I have been…er…been instructed to inform you, by no less than General Meade, the commander of the Army of the Potomac, that your description of yourself as an Englishman from Lank Asher appears to be true."

Ernest showed no sign that he had even heard the man, who paused and then continued.

"What is more, General Meade is prepared to accept that you were sent to the United States by your father, Lord Tissiman, who we believe owns he town of Lank Asher. We understand that his lordship is very concerned by the Union's blockade of the southern ports that has stopped the supply of raw cotton to the cotton mills in England. His concern is shared apparently by your Queen Victoria."

He paused again and Ernest felt that he might have forgotten his lines, but he continued his speech.

"The government of the United States has no argument with England, I understand. As soon as this, em, disagreement with some states of the Union, is settled…and settled it will be in the very near future…we, that is the United States of America, would, of course, wish to continue our trade with England and, to that end, have already, as a gesture of good will, removed our great naval fleet so that the cotton trade in England may resume immediately. We would be obliged if you would inform your father, and through him your queen, that this has been done."

With Ernest's obvious lack of interest and frequently closed eyes, the general stopped pacing and moved three steps closer to him and peered down at him, placing what he apparently hoped would be seen as a friendly hand on his shoulder. Ernest came instantly to life with a cry of, "What the hell…!"

Hooker jumped back as if he had been stung, opened his mouth, presumably to give his prisoner a severe reprimand, but thought better of it before any words could escape and quickly turned his expression of anger to one of compassion.

"Forgive me. I did not intend to frighten you…son." To this, he received no response, although Ernest did now look at him.

"Yes, well, as I was saying. As soon as you are considered well enough by the doctor… Major… I forget his name, but you will then be escorted to a suitable ship to transport you back to Lank Asher."

He clearly expected a display of gratitude, but received none. Ernest simply said, "I see."

He hoped that his face did not betray his surprise and his nervous feeling that this could be a trap of some sort. However, the officer seemed too nervous for that to be true.

"I suspect," Ernest eventually continued quietly, "that you might prefer me not to mention to Queen Victoria and the Prime Minister, the degree of suffering I have undergone at the hands of the Union army. However, you will oblige me now by doing everything possible to get my body and mind back to a state of health whereby I can at least walk without aid and feel I have a chance of not dying at your hands."

The general started to say something that might have been intended to reassure Ernest, but he was stopped before he could utter a word.

"No, please don't interrupt me." Ernest had now begun to feel strongly that a sea change was taking place in his situation. He immediately pulled himself upright and spoke with a firm voice, looking the general in the eye.

"I *expect* to be assisted with all speed to be moved to more suitable accommodation with a nurse to care for me; I would prefer Nurse Eliza for that. I believe Major Cook, given discretion over necessary treatment, can have me well enough to travel within the next week or so. At that point, I need to be taken to the nearest sea port where a ship is available that can take me directly to either Liverpool or London."

Ernest's smile was not reciprocated by General Hooker.

He nevertheless continued in a firm voice, "I believe that all this can be swiftly accomplished so that I am able to send a telegraph message, *prior* to my departure, via the *London Times,* assuring the English Prime Minister that the Union government has treated an Englishman here in a supportive and friendly fashion. After all, we would not want his *Lordship* to mistake this for another Augusta affair, would we?"

It was clear from the reaction of the general that he was well versed in the fiasco of the *RMS Augusta* and how the boarding of that English vessel, and the forced removal of the two Confederate diplomats on board, was what had caused England to send their fleet to disband the blockade by force. Ernest was amused that the general's consternation somewhat belied his statement a few minutes ago that it was the Union which had voluntarily removed its ships from the sea-lanes outside ports like Charleston.

There followed several moments of silence as Ernest stared meaningfully at the general, while he in turn looked anywhere except at Ernest, apparently suddenly becoming fascinated by the interior construction of the vestry and then needing to adjust his uniform jacket cuffs, as well as moving his sword an inch along his belt. Eventually he gathered himself and Ernest could feel him resisting the reflex to shake his head to clear his thoughts. A decision had obviously been made and he advanced hurriedly towards Ernest with his right hand outstretched.

"I think we agree, sir, that a…misunderstanding may have occurred, which I have been able to…em…correct."

Ernest deliberately made him wait a few moments before allowing the handshake to proceed. He then spoke in a tone he considered to demonstrate false generosity.

"Since we now understand that the situation was an *error,* shall we say, I am satisfied that everything will be put to rights, as I have agreed."

He felt he was not mistaken in believing that the general only just resisted wiping his hand on his jacket as he turned towards the door. Ernest stopped him in his tracks as he placed his hand on the latch and raised his voice, so that the general had no difficulty in hearing him.

"Do not make the mistake, general, of being in any way tardy with putting in place appropriate orders concerning the actions you have agreed to undertake. We do not want any further *misunderstandings,* do we?"

His sometime enemy turned and sharply replied, "Naturally, it will be done. You have my word as an officer and a gentleman. Good day to you, sir," and with that he opened the door and Ernest heard the sharp sound of his boots as he moved down the church aisle and then his crisp command that demanded Major Cook's presence to receive his commanding officer's instructions regarding their English guest's welfare.

Within an hour of the general's departure, Ernest was relieved to have been removed permanently into the vestry and an actual bed had now also been carried there. Nevertheless, he was not as comfortable as he had hoped to be. Major Cook found it impossible to conceal his anger at being overruled by General Hooker and being forced to shift just one of his patients, and an Englishman at that, into what was to his mind a *private ward*, where he had his own dedicated nurse for this Englishman's personal care.

Once installed, Ernest took the opportunity, now that he was feeling stronger, to go out into the church itself with the intention of apologising to the major, but as soon as he stepped into the aisle, he could not fail to notice the murmurings of anger, maybe even jealousy, from other patients. He realised, of course, that it was preferable to the alternative of his execution, which he had expected a few hours ago, and decided that it would be safer if he kept himself to himself, hoping it would not be long before he was travelling north and then on the way back home to England.

When he came back into the vestry, he found Eliza already there. She was kneeling on the floor and putting what he took to be medical supplies into the cupboard. She had made up his bed, now with a pillow and clean sheets. There was a metal jug of water and a mug standing on the chair beside the bed. She jumped up as soon as she realised he was behind her and stood with her hands held in front of her. Ernest had noticed the indoor slaves at Cotton Hall all did the same thing when any of the Hayward family passed them. He felt suddenly awkward that she was treating him in the same way that she would have shown her respect, or more likely fear, for her previous masters.

"Nurse Eliza, please, I am not your master or anything like that. You are a nurse and you are helping me to recover my health, which was damaged by Union soldiers, nothing to do with you."

Finding words was really difficult, Ernest had no idea how to address a person he had learned over a year ago was called a *negro slave*; not just a servant, not even a young woman. He was in a state of genuine confusion. In the twenty-nine years he had lived in Oldham, as well as visiting Manchester, Liverpool and even London, he had never even seen a slave. He knew of slavery, understood it's outlawing in England before he was born, but seeing its reality in Carolina and Virginia, he had somehow not connected the slavery there with what had many years ago existed in his own country. With a young woman who had been a slave for her whole life, now standing unspeaking with eyes downcast in front of him, he was made to feel confused and very uneasy.

"Nurse Eliza… I'm sorry; I don't know your family name."

He looked at her, smiled and hoped that she would speak to him, tell him her other name, so that he could use it respectfully, as he would with any young lady at home who was a stranger to him. She raised her eyes and must have noticed his smile and perhaps that was what persuaded her to speak.

"I'm sorry, sir. I don't have no more names. My family calls me Eliza, just like my ma is my ma, my sisters is Ruth and Honesty and Jane, my brothers is Jerimiah and Joseph. That's all I got. No, pa. My pa was sold somewhere else. I am no nurse. I was just mindin' the mistress's babies. That's all."

After a few heartbeats, she shrugged her shoulders, as if to dismiss her family.

Ernest took the jug of water and the mug off the chair and then sat on the bed. He looked at her, standing like a statue.

"Miss Eliza, will you please come and sit on this chair. It would help me to explain to you how I feel now, although I'm better than I was before...please."

Eliza looked uncomfortable, as if he had just made an improper advance to her or perhaps threatened her; she did not move. There seemed to be an impasse. Ernest suddenly gasped and clutched at his wound, now in truth healing well. It proved impossible for her to ignore this and she quickly came to his side and reached down to examine the gash that a sword or bayonet had caused, although it was now sewn together and covered with a bandage. She carefully opened the bandage and looked closely at the jagged, but closed, wound that was no longer inflamed.

"There don' look like no bleedin' nor nothin." She then felt his forehead, which was, not surprisingly, quite cool. "An' you don' feel hot. I'd best go get the doctor...the major." She started towards the door, but Ernest pulled himself upright again and his smile returned.

"No, Eliza. No need for that. I feel much better now. Although it would help a lot if you could just spare just a few more minutes just to talk with me."

As the days passed, very slowly it seemed to Ernest, he felt more and more as if life were returning to him, both in body and mind. He was certain that this was, more than anything else, due to the ministrations of Eliza his wound was also kept clean. Major Cook, initially visited him every day, but that gradually became unnecessary, as he was clearly gaining strength. He could now walk with only a slight limp and his body was filling out, thanks to a diet of meat, bread and fruit, as well as warm milk, which tasted as if it had come straight from the cow.

Miss Eliza, which was how he insisted in addressing her, not only spent time caring for his medical needs, but also began to spend time talking to him and seemed to be more and more relaxed in his company as each day passed. By the end of the first week of his sojourn in the vestry, she often sat beside his bed and talked about her life and about the little she could remember of her first childhood years in Jamaica. Then the tobacco plantation years, where at first she helped clean the master's grand house and the worst possible tasks of cleaning ovens, laying fires and persuading spiders, snakes and other bugs to quit the kitchens. By the time she was thirteen or fourteen, she was moved upstairs to help the nursery maids in looking after the three children under the age of five, who had been born regularly by her mistress. This woman she regarded as 'the meanest, cruellest bitch in the whole world'. She also described the living conditions of house slaves to Ernest, as well as those of her two brothers, who worked in the cotton fields and lived in the slave huts there, along with her mother and two older sisters whose lives also revolved around the valuable crop.

Until he had arrived in Charleston, Ernest had known virtually nothing about slavery in the southern states of the Union, nor that it was unpaid and badly treated humans in those states, forced into slavery, often from birth, who provided all the labour to produce the raw cotton that arrived in huge bales at Crompton Mill, there to be made into thread and cloth that he and his father sold for a considerable profit. He had somehow managed to separate in his mind these slave labourers from those hundreds working at Crompton Mill. Until meeting Eliza, it never occurred to him that the slavery of the southern states, which enabled him to have such a comfortable life, was not so far removed from the cotton workers in Lancashire, who sweated long hours just to avoid starvation.

It was just before dawn the next day that Ernest, who had lain awake on and off through the night, now troubled for the first time by thoughts that deeply worried him: *the poor of Oldham, whom he had never questioned were lucky enough to be employed by Tissiman and Sons, but who, if they showed any sign of slacking, any breath of dissatisfaction with their lot, could lose their jobs and its meagre wage to be sent back into awful poverty. There were thousands in Oldham alone who were on the edge of starvation, who lived in places they called home that he would never even want to see. What right had he, or Betty, to whom he realised he had hardly given a thought for months, to complain if the fire were not lit at the right time, or if dinner were a moment late. God help him, the baby that he had worried might take away some of the love and respect Betty had for him, her husband, had then been born too soon and he was disgusted to admit it to himself how that was a secret relief or had he really managed to keep it hidden?* The self-satisfaction he had felt for his comfortable world was beginning to evaporate, like the night outside.

Indeed, now the dawn had decided, as it did every day, that its light would rise above the horizon and, he felt inappropriately, a perfect summer day began to spread sunlight through the window. He felt genuinely guilty and that he certainly did not deserve the life he had lived.

Half an hour later, Miss Eliza tapped on the door and came in with a bowl of water and a towel.

"Time for a wash and then some breakfast, sir."

It was said with the brightness that seemed so natural to all the women who worked as nurses in this place, an optimistic sound that was intended to cheer up even the truly sick and dying. She put the bowl on the table and then came over to where he still lay with his head on the pillow, although with his eyes wide open.

"And how are you today, sir?"

She stood with that ever-present smile and a questioning expression, an expression that always to Ernest seemed so genuine and honest. He hoisted himself to sit up and smiled back at her.

The thought suddenly materialised in his head that she was a sort of black Florence Nightingale, the famous nurse whom he had read about at school and remembered how she had apparently greatly improved the care of the sick and wounded in the Crimean War. He was then able to dig back through his memory to remember that it was another Crimea nurse, sometimes called a *doctress*; Mary Seacole, who was black like Liza and who had been really responsible for changing how the wounded and sick were treated so much better. He had even read about her in the *London Times* just five or six years ago, how she had set up a whole new, far improved way of treating soldiers on the battlefield. He could not imagine that surely any soldier, fighting for his life in such a place, would have had any concern for something as unimportant as the colour of her skin as she worked tirelessly to keep him alive? That, he realised, was what the world should be like, but he was sure, especially in the last few months, that it was not so in the Confederate world.

He realised that Eliza was staring at him and he guessed that he had been lost inside the strange memories she had caused to surface in his mind.

"You'm a thousand mile away, sir. Some great thoughts I's sure."

"Yes, Miss Eliza, I think they were."

He forgot that she had asked him a question and had looked at this remarkable, young woman for far longer than he realised. He shook his ongoing thoughts away and hurriedly returned to reality.

"Now, I need to get out of this bed and get some clothes on. It's time I rejoined the world and stopped lying here feeling sorry for myself and wishing, I suppose, it was not as it is."

# Chapter Thirty-Seven

## Davis Town & Gettysburg: July & August 1863

It was the last day of July and twenty or so miles still lay between Davis Town and Gettysburg town itself. If the fictional balloon had then been hoisted close to Gettysburg on that morning its pilot would have seen the huge area of flat fields and rocky hill slopes, as far as the eye could see, on the very edge of readiness for battle.

There were about 65,000 Confederate soldiers and officers now in what had once been Union territory, as well as civilian workers, wives and camp followers, newspaper reporters and even a small number of daring Union citizens, who were in the general area to witness the 'greatest battle in American history', some in hiding, some as spectators; all believed that they would see an end at last to this civil war. From the earliest days before the battle, this was known as Confederate *Robert E Lee's battle: his brainchild and he owned it, win or lose.*

On that same day the Union Army of the Potomac, numbering probably about 45-50,000, was spreading out for another fifteen or so square miles to the north and north-west of Gettysburg, although the Confederate armies covered an even greater area. The rapid movement of these huge forces, said by observers to be the greatest ever assembled in one place on American soil, stirred the dust on miles of country roads into brown swirling clouds which could be seen for many miles, in some areas blotting out the sun. The noise of more than a hundred thousand marching feet, the sound of numerous military bands and of men, excited or scared or both, heading directly into the dragon's mouth of death or glory. This sent aloft a rolling, often confusing and continuous level of sound across the countryside and into the very streets of the now virtually deserted, and so far unimportant, town of Gettysburg.

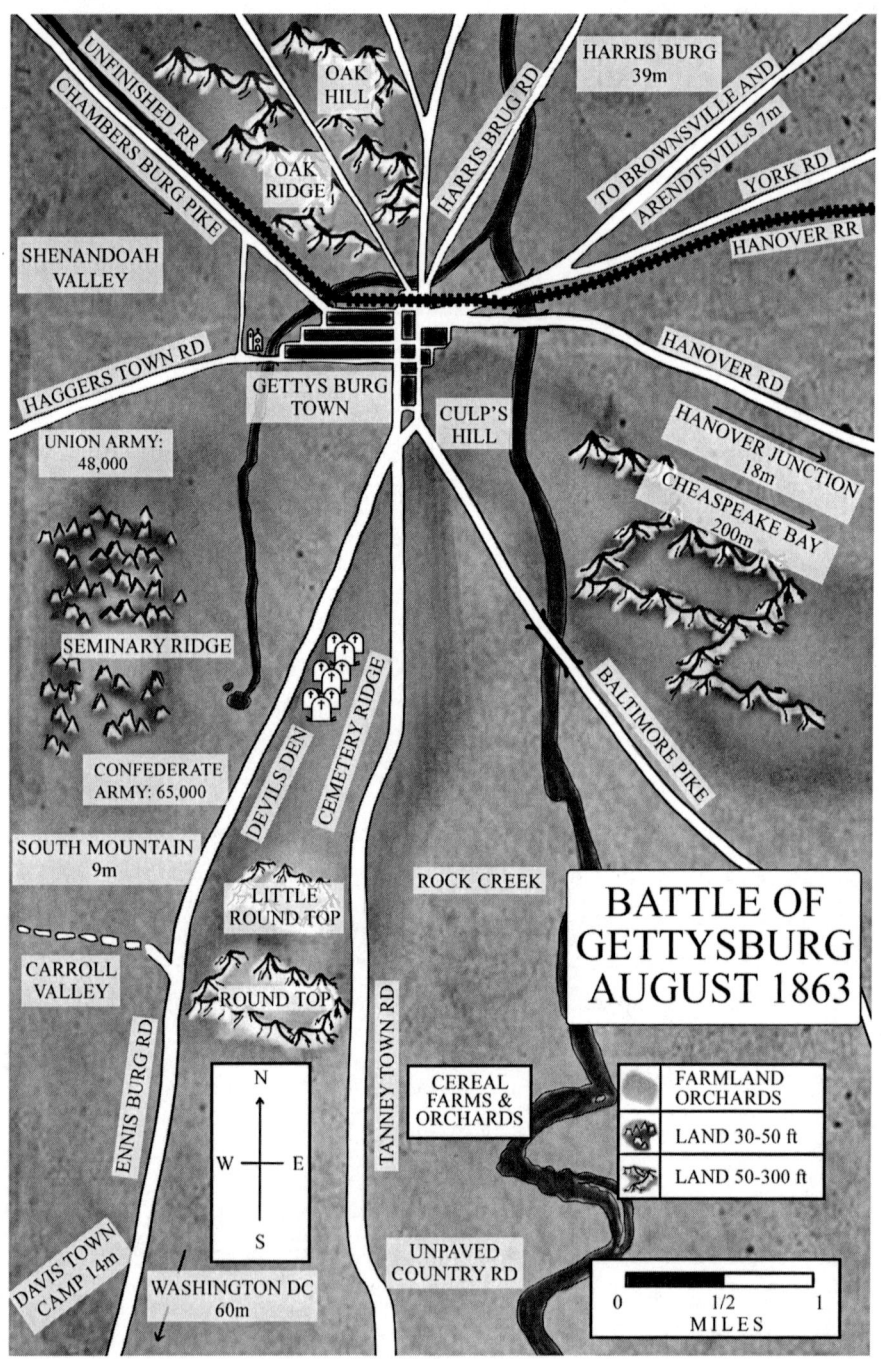

UNFINISHED RR

CHAMBERS BURG PIKE

OAK
HILL

HARRIS BRUG RD

HARRIS BURG
39m

TO BROWNSVILLE AND

ARENDTSVILLS 7m

YORK RD

OAK
RIDGE

HANOVER RR

SHENANDOAH
VALLEY

HAGGERS TOWN RD

GETTYS BURG
TOWN

HANOVER RD

UNION ARMY:
48,000

CULP'S
HILL

HANOVER JUNCTION
18m

CHEASPEAKE BAY
200m

SEMINARY RIDGE

BALTIMORE PIKE

CONFEDERATE
ARMY: 65,000

DEVILS DEN

CEMETERY RIDGE

SOUTH MOUNTAIN
9m

LITTLE
ROUND TOP

ROCK CREEK

CARROLL
VALLEY

ENNIS BURG RD

ROUND TOP

**BATTLE OF
GETTYSBURG
AUGUST 1863**

TANNEY TOWN RD

N

W   E

S

CEREAL
FARMS &
ORCHARDS

FARMLAND
ORCHARDS

LAND 30-50 ft

LAND 50-300 ft

DAVIS TOWN
CAMP 14m

WASHINGTON DC
60m

UNPAVED
COUNTRY RD

0     1/2     1
MILES

Most of the Confederate rear guard regiments commanded by General
Longstreet had left Davis Town camp the previous day, although leaving

behind a skeleton force who were happy in their belief that they would not be called upon to take part in the battle that all now knew was probably just a day or two away. As soon as he reached what would be the battlefield, General Longstreet's command was changed, by the direct order of Robert E Lee, from the Rear Guard to the Reserve Army of more than 10,000 or so cavalry, and some infantry, being readied for battle.

The Confederate defences that Arthur, Ernest and George had witnessed being constructed over the past few months, were now filled with the men of General Robert E Lee's Confederate army, all buoyed with confidence and excitement that they would be part of the Dixie Army of Northern Virginia that would make sure, once and for all, that their southern states could live peacefully as a separate and independent country. They would surely whip their northern neighbours into submission and send them back to their own lands with their tails between their legs.

If it had been possible to ask all the men in this huge armed mass of humanity which of them expected to die in the next few days, it probably it would have been a minority who considered the possibility that death would actually touch *them*.

George had done all in his power for the last week, once everyone knew that the battle was about to become a reality, to persuade every senior Confederate officer at Camp Davis, from General Longstreet himself down to Colonel Grey and Major Meredith, the officers with whom the Envoys had had the most contact, to allow the two remaining Englishmen to move forward with the army towards Gettysburg and the area that was likely to see the start of the battle. The answer had so far been a curt 'absolutely not' from General Longstreet, who spoke to them briefly in passing; while Major Meredith was able to explain that an officer of his rank 'could not possibly grant such a request'.

However, when George and Arthur had found Colonel Grey preparing to leave the camp the day before with his regiment, he had given them what seemed to be a more hopeful hearing. In the end, he had reluctantly agreed, providing they signed a letter to confirm that they held the army of the Confederacy in '*no way responsible for our injury, death or capture in the forthcoming battle near Gettysburg, Pennsylvania, August 1863*'.

They had the authority, at least of Colonel Grey, to accompany him and a few of his senior officers as far as the rear lines of defence that were about fifteen miles distant in the direction of Gettysburg, but probably several more miles away from the expected site of the start of the battle.

With Grey's regiment ready to march at any moment, the Envoys had to rush to get what clothes and possessions they thought they would need, especially including George's telescope and the diary record that Arthur had been attempting to keep since Ernest had involuntarily given it up. As so often in the last months, their thoughts turned to Arthur's brother whom they were sadly sure must be dead. Arthur mourned him in his heart and, too late, greatly regretted the times they had disagreed.

The day was hot and, although they were both mounted on cavalry horses, they had left coats behind in the camp. They trailed behind the Colonel himself and just ahead of a band playing the tunes of Dixie that had accompanied the army for two years, but the Confederate General William Smith now changed the predominant tune from *Dixie* to the fairly new march of *Rally 'Round the Flag*. This tune and its simple words had become popular with the Army of Northern Virginia, although it was rumoured that the Yankees had it as well and were claiming it had been played by their marching bands for over three years. Perhaps this demonstrated, to those who were willing to think about it, how closely Confederate and Union were intertwined in reality. The same General Smith was also responsible for telling the few local citizens that: "*The Confederate Army found Virginia too warm, so we have moved north into these Union lands for cooler air.*"

George and Arthur rode out of Davis Town and into a part of their lives that certainly filled Captain George with excitement, but for both also held a considerable trepidation, although for Arthur the frequently unanswered question of why he had agreed to leave home in the first place was more than ever on his mind.

The anthem was shouted from a thousand throats surrounding the two Englishmen, as they rode towards the fateful battle of Gettysburg:

*Yes, we'll rally 'round the flag boys,*
*We'll rally round again,*
*Shouting the battle cry of freedom.*

*We'll rally from the hillside,*
*We'll rally from the plain,*
*Shouting the battle cry of freedom*

\*

On August 1, Ernest was actually outside the hospital in Brownsville about to board a coach to Harrisburg, a town half way to New York and at that time still under the control of the Union stars and stripes. He had politely thanked Major Cook for the contribution he had made to his greatly improved state of health, made sure he had the clothes and dollars he had been obliged to sign for, as well as a letter to the telegraph clerk giving permission for Ernest to use the cable facility at Harrisburg to contact England.

He was taking one last look at the church-cum-hospital, much relieved that he would not be seeing it again. As his hand was reaching for the coach door, Eliza came running out of the hospital door and then, in her rush, slipped on the step down to the road, but was saved by Ernest from falling to the dusty street. She pulled back from him in embarrassment and concentrated assiduously on brushing herself down.

"Thank you, sir. I's real sorry for... I's..."

"Please, Miss Eliza. There's nothing to thank me for. I just stopped you maybe finishing up on the road, that's all."

Eliza seemed struck dumb and uncertain what to do next. She was wringing her hands, looking first at the safety of the doorway behind her and then at Ernest, who had come to her rescue. He now felt he needed to fill the gap of silence that had grown between them.

"Miss Eliza, I'm pleased you came out since I just wanted to thank you for all your kindness towards me here. You should make sure you continue nursing once this awful war is over... I wish you every good fortune."

He then held out his hand to her, which she looked at as if it were the strangest of objects and then half turned, taking a step to go back inside. She hesitated for a moment longer, looked back again, then took two quick steps and flung her arms around Ernest's neck. She immediately gasped, put her hand to her mouth and ran back into the church as if she were being pursued by demons.

Ernest was rooted to the spot by the emotion he felt. Once inside the coach and watching the houses of Brownsville pass the window, now mostly deserted of all but military personnel, he tried to understand what he was feeling: was it simply surprise or was it something more? He had no idea why he felt as if he were leaving someone of real importance here in America, someone who had somehow got deep into his heart. Memories of his wife back in England, he ignored entirely.

As the coach picked up speed once out of the town he first heard and then saw a Union regimental band coming the other way. To his surprise, they were playing '*Dixie*', which he assumed was with some sort of sarcasm, since the troops marching behind the band were yelling and whooping with delight and amusement.

*

Many miles from Ernest's coach on the road to Harrisburg and well into the south-western farmland beyond Gettysburg, Arthur and George had dismounted on a slight rise and were looking at what Colonel Grey informed them was Cemetery Ridge in the far distance. With the aid of George's telescope, they could see it was a hook-shaped escarpment stretching from what was known locally as Devil's Den, with its outcrops of huge rocks with slits and voids between them, and then curled around just short of Gettysburg town.

The colonel told them that the dusty track they had reached from Camp Davis was the Ennesburg Road that eventually led into the town. The ridge, as well as others that they could see further distant, was covered in large patches of woodland, while where they now were to the south-west was gentle farmland with wooden farmhouses and barns, most with rail fences marking out the fields and orchards. It would have been a peaceful pastoral scene had it not been for the vast number of soldiers in grey and buff uniforms now gathered along fences and ditches, as well as large groups of field artillery behind the defences that had been built over the past months. The larger, well-ordered groups George pointed out as whole divisions, as well as some more battalions and corps, were often drawn up on more open ground, most with Confederate battle flags or other standards, whose designs represented their individual units.

"It's probably not a very suitable comparison given that these thousands upon thousands of soldiers are down there getting ready to kill and maim each other," remarked Arthur as he peered through George's telescope and scanned the miles of farm and woodland, "but it reminds me of looking down on the battles that Ernest and I used to play as children on the nursery carpet with his lead soldiers on rainy afternoons. They looked so small down there, covering the carpet, soldiers in different colour uniforms with cannons and some cavalry, all so inoffensive at a distance just like those down there; just like toy soldiers with toy cannons and toy horses, all set out here on a giant carpet in this glorious sunlight."

Colonel Grey was close enough, along with his entourage of senior officers, to hear Arthur's remarks.

"I almost agree with you, sir. I was proud of my collection of lead soldiers as a boy and pretending I was the general able to knock them over, to kill some here, some there, just as I pleased. Today might look like those battles on the floor, but I regret that only God Almighty knows what will be the outcome here, how many will be slaughtered or wounded or lost. I can only pray that He knows *our* cause is just. I hear that General Lee is already christening this a *Harvest of death* and I assume that is exactly what it will be."

The colonel seemed to be somehow relishing this moment of stillness, of a battle still far away, of men and horses and cannons moving silently on a dry carpet, some of it grass, but much being field after field of grain crops already pale yellow in colour, with trees poking through in places. There were tiny doll's houses scattered across the carpet, that would soon erupt with fire and fury, with death and mutilation, smoke, the hail of bullets and the explosions of thousands of shells plunging into the ranks of men, some in grey, some in blue.

The colonel lifted his own telescope to his eye and moved it a little higher. "There, captain, can you spot that haze almost on the horizon?"

George had now taken his own telescope back from Arthur and was looking in the same direction as the colonel.

"Yes, I can, but is it just haze from the heat of the day or am I imagining that I can see what might just be minute figures moving or swaying as it were?"

"No, you are not imagining, captain. What you can see, I'd say almost six miles distant, is most likely the end of the Union front line. I can't distinguish bodies, but there must be thousands of them."

Both men were now fixed on a spot to the northwest, before the town of Gettysburg. George could make out farmland, then small woodlands, possibly a river and a straight line that looked man made.

"Is that a railway line I can see just in front of those tiny lines that are swaying slowly in the haze like short grass, but now I appreciate must be men?"

"Yes, that's the rail line that will soon reach into Gettysburg from the west, but at the moment is only partly built. You've got sharp eyes, sir."

Colonel Grey then snapped his telescope shut and put it in his jacket pocket. He wheeled his horse around. "We had better get back to the regiment gentlemen. I estimate that we have about four hours of good light left, but not enough time for any action to take place today, I'd be prepared to wager."

The cavalcade of six officers spurred their horses and galloped back down the Ennesburg road towards where their regiment was stationed about three miles away and hidden for the moment by thick woodland. George and Arthur dutifully followed, their minds trying to conjure up a picture of what the next twelve hours might bring to this quiet landscape.

Two or three hours later, they were happy to be trotting into Camp Davis when a shout stopped them.

"Captain Fitzwilliam, sir… Stop, sir!"

George and Arthur both came to a halt at once as they had been making their way towards the lanes of what were now the largely empty tents and huts that had made up Davis Town Camp. They swung around as a breathless Major Meredith almost ran into them. He bent forward to catch his breath.

"It seems you are in somewhat of a hurry, Major," George pointed out through a broad smile.

"Yes, of course I am, captain. I have just been instructed by Colonel Grey to inform you that all the regiment, apart from a skeleton force left here, will be moving up in the next few hours. The Colonel informs me that he is now able to grant permission for the two of you to advance a short distance with the regiment, but that I am to accompany you closely at all times. We shall be taking a small group of cavalry with us as well."

"I'm sure you know that we have been hoping to hear that, major," Arthur said, "but can you tell us how far from the battlefield we shall be? We shall certainly be required to inform the gentlemen in England exactly what happens here in the next few days."

"Yes, sir. My orders are clear. Firstly, you are not to be placed close enough to any action that could put you in danger, but a place has been reconnoitred from which you should be able to observe the course of events, albeit from a distance. If that position is in any way threatened, which is, of course, possible, I shall extract you immediately."

Arthur now felt a sudden, and unexpected, wave of both fear, but also a thrill at the prospect of danger, probably that would test his courage once again, just as it had at Bull Run. These emotions were mixed with a sense that he could soon be one of the many thousands who would be part of an event that could change the very course of history.

He doubted that George felt anything similar, since it would be yet another of many similar events in his life where he had seen, heard and become part of the lives of men being torn apart amidst blood and shredded flesh, the roar of cannon and rifle fire, the flash of steel blades and bayonets, but from which he had so far emerged with his life; just another day in a life of so many similar days in his past career.

They agreed to meet Major Meade at seven o'clock the next morning at what remained of the horse lines and from there they were told they would ride through the morning to the edge of what would undoubtedly soon be called the Battle of Gettysburg.

# Chapter Thirty-Eight

**The Battle of Gettysburg the First Day: Friday 3 August 1863**

Confederate Major Meade was commanding what he described as 'an elite cavalry group', made up of a captain, a lieutenant and six privates, as well as George and Arthur, riding out of Davis Town the next morning, having watched as General Longstreet's regiments march away earlier, Confederate flags proudly fluttering in the breeze and several bands striking up *Dixie* among other stirring marching favourites. By eight o'clock, the sun was above the hills to their right and the small party set off in the same direction as General Longstreet, but after an hour turned due west into the gradually dimming light as clouds floated in to obscure the sun. They were now following a country road towards a line of hills about six miles away at the end of what the major informed them was known as the Carroll Valley.

"What might look to you a ridge of hills is actually known as *South Mountain*," the captain riding next to Meade pointed out. "My Aunt Lizzie grew up around here and always found it amusing to tell us of what she called a *mountain* near her uncle's farm. Those of us who grew up in the great Blue Ridge Mountains of Virginia would have called it a gentle rise, not a mountain at all." Polite laughter followed.

They entered the valley and the sides gradually closed in as the road began to rise. After a mile or two, the gradient became steeper and the road, now more of a track, began to zigzag to cope with the slope. Arthur could not imagine why anyone called this a road, since it surely could not have accommodated anything much wider than two horses abreast. There was no sign of any hint of civilisation as the forest closed in, which made the dying light gradually disappear between the trees.

The climb had taken well over an hour when they were suddenly almost blinded, as they navigated the next hairpin, by the dazzling spotlight of the sun suddenly appearing on the clear horizon as they burst out of the trees onto a grassy plateau. The clouds were painted in red, as the sun seemed to settle on the far off line of much higher hills. The party came to an unsteady halt, partly due to the sudden light and partly because their mounts were sweating from the climb and were obviously relieved not to be pushed any further. Major Meade swung his horse around so that he faced east, away from the sun's last rays. The rest of the party followed him and then stared out across what must have been almost ten miles of countryside, farmland and woods and there, in the far centre of that distant view, every building that made up Gettysburg picked out in the clear evening light, but looking like a child's toy town.

"My God! What a view," exclaimed George, who already had his telescope slowly moving across the landscape, revealing the whole of what would, within a few hours, be a battlefield, a scene of carnage, death and destruction, but which was now in the fading light a silent scene of pastoral beauty. Arthur had pulled his horse up next to George's grey and was staring at the same view, which had robbed them all of words for several minutes. "It's as if God had decided to show two sides of a coin," he said, but seemed unaware that he was speaking, allowing his mind to wander from the present to the near future in silence.

"What do you mean?" George asked, as he lowered his telescope.

"It just struck me. There below us is one side of this farmland, as it is now and, if you just wait for the sun to rise again, you will see the other side of the coin: farmland bathed in blood."

The land below them in the distance had already slipped into shadow as the sun disappeared behind South Mountain and its range of hills. These stretched from behind them, all the way to the waiting Confederate Army of Northern Virginia, past Gettysburg to its northeast and then curled west into the night; here the Union Army of the Potomac also lay in wait that night.

For well over one hundred thousand men, now in the darkness of the warm evening, it was unlikely that this night would bring any sleep, much less rest, to either side.

Believing that the darkest hour was just before dawn, both armies were by that time in the positions that the battle plans of their commanding generals decreed they should occupy in readiness to resist the most powerful advances.

All waiting during those overwhelming first hours believed their comrades on the fields and hills that night would be part of a decisive and conclusive confrontation as soon as it was light. In fact, it was destined to be the greatest battle fought in America's recorded history.

While General George Meade, a very distant second cousin to Confederate Major Meade, was the man chosen by Abe Lincoln to command the Union army, he had caused some consternation and even confusion among his colleague generals by having signalled that he himself was still many miles away in the early hours of the third of August (. What made this worse was the fact that he was bringing the much-needed reinforcements in excess of ten thousand men with him.

General Joe Hooker, who accompanied Meade, quickly took the opportunity to enhance his career prospects after what he believed was his success with the 'Englishman' at Browneville, by persuading Meade on the day before that he should take a small group of cavalry and 'ride like the devil', in his own words, to be ready to take command if by any chance the Rebels started the battle early and without giving any consideration to General Meade, who felt he ought to arrive with his reinforcements to a hero's welcome just before the battle started.

Union General Hooker, as well as Generals McClellan, Burnside, Meade and Pope, were considered by Confederate General Robert E Lee as 'inferior commanders', while their own leaders, Generals Stuart, Longstreet, Hill and Jackson were 'the finest fighting force on earth'.

General Joseph Hooker was, in fact, just in time to take command of the Union force on Wednesday the third before Meade could get there. Both Hooker and Meade were only too well aware of another factor that was now working against them: the citizens of both the north and south had recently become far more strongly anti-war than they had been previously; they were known as Copperheads. This meant that the Army of the Potomac had reduced support from the civilian population, even less now than they had had after Bull Run.

In addition to Union Generals Meade and Hooker, there were no fewer than a dozen other senior ranking Union generals ready and waiting to lead their regiments, divisions and battalions into battle. However, the celebrity Union general Ulysses S Grant was notably absent from this number. He had been relegated to commanding a desk by Lincoln after being mistakenly outspoken in expressing, in Lincoln's presence, his belief that *'this war is now a hopeless waste of American lives'*.

The Confederate force, much larger in terms of the numbers of fighting bodies that the Union, was commanded by another celebrity, General Robert E Lee. An additional fourteen other senior Confederate generals were destined to play their part in the leadership of the men of Dixie on the field of Gettysburg. One of these was General James Longstreet, the commander of the Rear-Guard, now the Reserve Force. Surveying the presently peaceful fields of Gettysburg on the evening of August 3, he foretold the future outcome of the battle with firm belief and considerable brevity: *"I'm going to whip them or they will whip me."* Looking forcefully at the thirteen other generals, he added, "You can't lead from behind."

Robert E. Lee was, at much the same time, impatiently waiting for General Jeb Stuart to arrive. He was already half a day late in bringing his cavalry and support waggons to join the waiting army. When he did eventually arrive, only hours before the next dawn, Lee managed to quell his anger and forgave the extrovert cavalry general in view of his expected importance in the next days.

Of the twenty-seven senior generals on both sides, more than a third would be dead or seriously wounded in three days' time.

Although two and a half years had passed since the Confederacy attacked Fort Sumpter, their army still remained less well-equipped with modern weaponry than did the Union. In August 1863, a few Confederate infantrymen were still carrying muzzle-loading muskets of some age; many of these fired mini balls of lead, rather than bullets. Confederate Lieutenant General Wade Hampton from Carolina would have been aware of this, but no doubt discounted it. It was remarkable that he had been a witness to the first shots of the war at Fort Sumpter and now here he was on what he sincerely prayed was the last battlefield at Gettysburg. He had his own company of men now, known as 'Hamptons Legion'. This consisted of 12 companies, made up of infantry, cavalry and artillery soldiers.

The Union had, from the beginning of the war, the vast majority of factories producing iron and steel, which meant that rifles, mostly repeating in operation, such as the Springfield, Enfield and Spencer weapons, were faster to load and more accurate. The boys from Dixie would undoubtedly have been vehement in their response to this fact by declaring that their roaring attacks held more terror for their enemy than any rifle could and that they were certainly raring for a fight, while in their opinion the Union army was mostly ready to slink off back home.

Officers carried swords, sabres and Colt or Remington six shot revolvers. The artillery corps, probably used to better effect that day by the Confederacy, had smooth bore canons, also bronze field guns of various calibres, many by now with rifled, more accurate barrels, firing solid balls, explosive shells, shrapnel and spherical case shot. Both sides were also equipped with very short, wide barrelled Howitzers, while the 'machine' gun's early forms were present in the shape of the Gatling and Agar guns, that could fire the contents of a box full of shells or bullets rapidly and without pause.

As the Confederate armies had grown since Bull Run, they had also come under stricter and more professional command by the time of Gettysburg. That, and the boost to morale of numerous victories, created a new pride in their uniforms and hence the hotchpotch of unmatched and many very *individual* items of kit had largely disappeared, but the majority of the men in grey began to appear as smartly turned out as those in blue.

In fact, by August 1863, with so many desertions and even whole companies simply turning their backs and walking away, the Union army at Gettysburg would certainly not have looked as crisply turned out as it once had been; their morale had taken a terrible beating. Incredibly, a minor general, James Harrison, honestly looked forward to the battle soon to come as '*a picnic, a chicken fry, a parade*' for the Union. To exacerbate its own confusion the Union army also included a regiment dressed in French African Uniform: white *kepi* caps, white or red trousers and red jackets. Soldiers on both sides were often unsure whether these were friend or foe. Many Confederate soldiers and officers would also be shocked in the next few days to see black faces among the throng of the Union army, these most likely being either escaped or freed slaves from the south.

Nevertheless, a Confederate officer introduced his battalion of soldiers to some Maryland women of Union persuasion, whom they met on their way to Gettysburg, in these words: "*Here we are ladies, as rough and ragged as ever, but back again to bother you.*"

# Chapter Thirty-Nine

## The Second Day: Saturday August 4 1863

The first real action of the definitive opening day of the battle occurred just before dawn on Saturday August 4 1863, within the huge area that would eventually be trampled by hundreds of thousands of feet and hooves. Just as well since it would soon be drenched in both Union and Confederate blood, while men in both blue and grey were awaiting in terror, as well as some gallant optimism, for the first light of dawn that would act as a starting pistol for the struggle to come. Very few in the next days would have time to notice that the blood shed by men on both sides was exactly the same colour. Joseph Cotton, a volunteer in the Confederate ranks, who survived the first day of action, described it in a letter to his mother as: *'a skirmish, compared with the days to follow'.*

Confederate Brigadier General Johnston Pettigrew, previously Governor of South Carolina, was the commander of his own South Carolina brigade. He was a proud, finely dressed officer in his thirties and had positioned his brigade within a few miles of Gettysburg the previous evening. He observed in the light of lanterns and torches that many of his men had what to him seemed an inappropriate variety and quality of foot ware, much of it in a state of serious disrepair. He had been informed by a colonel in his brigade that Gettysburg boasted many shoe maker's shops with brand new boots and shoes in their windows and stores. This unfortunately turned out to be very far from the truth, particularly in a town from which more or less all of the inhabitants had fled.

That night, General Pettigrew selected a corps of about fifty cavalrymen, including himself and several other officers, to take part in a pre-dawn raid on the town that he was assured was empty, to obtain a supply of new footwear to make his brigade truly fit to fight.

They approached the quiet outskirts of the town under the cover of darkness and along roads, even inside the town, that were often unpaved, being simply made of earth and stones. Hence, they moved as quietly as possible through the apparently deserted streets with their shuttered and locked houses and shops. To Pettigrew's growing frustration, he was unable to locate any appropriate shops displaying anything he was searching for in boarded or empty windows. It was just beginning to grow light when his small party reached the middle of the town without being challenged.

Suddenly, as they turned a sharp corner, in the dim light almost colliding with Pettigrew's men, there appeared dozens of other uniformed cavalry, but these were dressed in blue, not grey. Although Pettigrew had no way of knowing it, they were commanded by General John Buford, whose intention it was to get a foothold in the town before daybreak.

The shock of the unexpected confrontation on both sides took only moments to turn into a furious street battle. Fighting on horseback in such narrow thoroughfares proved chaotic. Hand to hand fighting on foot became inevitable as dozens of cavalry horses soon created a massif logjam. Rifles and pistols were repeatedly used at very close range, as were the swords of officers. Men were frequently attempting to kill each other with their bare hands, knives and the swinging of rifles like clubs. The noise of a bloody fight in such a restricted area was exaggerated a hundredfold by the whinnying screams of terrified horses, many terribly wounded or killed in the melee.

If there were any residents of the town still inside their homes as fighting erupted, they would have kept as quiet as they could for fear of being slaughtered by 'them evil Rebs'. The screams of wounded and dying men and horses filled half a dozen of the small streets with enough uproar to wake the dead. After an hour of the confused attempts of dozens of men to kill each other, those of each side who were still able to walk gradually started to make a fighting retreat towards their own lines, only some of them able to find horses to take with them.

Undoubtedly, both Union and Confederate soldiers would have told stories of how their opposite numbers, who had not been killed, had fled for their lives. No new shoes were available for General Pettigrew's brigade to wear in the battle that would start in earnest within the next few hours. The residents of Gettysburg, who had not already fled the town with all the possessions and food they could carry, now hurriedly quit the town as if the devil himself were at their backs.

Before the dawn broke, General Hooker issued an early order to all generals: "*All commanders are authorised to shoot any man who does not hold his ground.*" This chillingly foretold, even before the fighting began, that the ordinary soldier's killers would not only be in front of him.

The horror of the day began in earnest with a massive bombardment by the Confederate artillery, that had been positioned on Cemetery Ridge and particularly on Little Round Top hill. This had a clear, uninterrupted view across the farmland towards Gettysburg and the line upon line of Union infantry below, drawn up across the fields like '*giant hedgehogs*'. This description caught exactly what the infantry looked like to those manning the artillery batteries with their bayonets fixed or in lines extending two, three or even four deep for hundreds of yards through the golden barley..

The roar and smoke of the cannons, field guns and howitzers seemed to wake the men on either side to the realisation that a far more deadly and serious a battle than they had experienced elsewhere was suddenly upon them in shocking earnest.

The Confederate guns were positioned for nearly a mile along the open grassy ridge while those around the cemetery gatehouse on the highest point were scattered among the gravestones of Gettysburg's Evergreen graveyard. General Robert E Lee, viewing the huge number of cannons stretching along the ridge, was able to assure the officers in charge of the line that '*our artillery could hold this position against any Union assault*'. He had then dispatched the order to open fire, along with the words: "*Give them hell, boys!*"

In spite of the rain of iron cannon balls and exploding shells falling closer and closer to the Union's front line, their Generals, including Winfield Scott, were able to urge the men forward from the right wing of the Union army so that they could then fight to gain most of the town of Gettysburg, albeit with heavy losses. General Chamberlain, commanding his Maine regiments from the saddle, bellowed his encouragement: (39a) "*Stand firm you boys of Maine, for only once in a century will men be required to do so much as you for freedom.*"

George and Arthur observed the start of these offences from the slopes of South Mountain, but in the now clear light of early morning, with the distance appearing to slow the movement of the armies and reduced the sounds of battle to a murmur. It seemed that the two huge forces were simply '*lobbing stones at each other from a distance'*, as Arthur described it. The Confederate artillery position high on the distant ridge was wreathed in smoke and hence the hundreds, if not thousands, of shot and shell falling on the Union infantry seemed to come out of nowhere.

The small Confederate party of which George and Arthur were part, high above the far-off battle, noticed two major movements in the next hour. Firstly, there appeared to be a sudden influx of blue clad infantry out of nowhere that now poured into the rear of the Union lines; they resembled water gradually filling a lake from its far side. These Union reinforcements were, in fact, those commanded by General Meade, who had moved more quickly than expected after finding a safe route from the west that avoided Washington. The observers on South Mountain had no way of knowing that what they were seeing was the arrival of the desperately awaited Meade's Reserve joining the fray. Nor could they know that these thousands of men had been force marched from Shenandoah for several days and were in truth utterly exhausted.

The second major movement that the Envoys could see was the sudden advance of the Union lines that had until then been stationary on the edge of the wide swathe of farmland south of Gettysburg. The presence of the reserve battalions provoked the front lines, which had been firing continuously from static positions, suddenly to begin an advance; whether this was caused by the pressure from behind of thousands more men in blue, or by a planned order, was unclear. In fact, General Hooker had taken the opportunity, before handing over command to General Meade actually to order a general advance across the farmland, towards the gentle rise of the lower slopes of Cemetery Ridge.

On the top of that ridge was the Confederate Commander-in-Chief, Robert E. Lee, along with his second in command Major General Richard Stoddert Ewell. Lee had commandeered a nearby stone-built farmhouse up there as his Headquarters, from where he was able to look down and across the battlefield, towards the Union lines. It was there that Lee spotted a notice attached to the wall of the nearby imposing Gettysburg Cemetery's gatehouse, which caused him to laugh heartily. It read: *'Any persons using firearms in these grounds will be prosecuted'*.

At the same time, General Pettigrew, now reunited with the main Confederate force after his escapade into Gettysburg town, joined the survivors in his two brigades of cavalry in an unauthorised attack on the Union left wing: the first charge of the battle. They came at full gallop down the hill on to the so far unchallenged infantry now slowly advancing across the farmland towards the lower slopes of the ridge, a mile or so away. These packed ranks of infantry were already providing unmissable targets for the ceaseless artillery barrage from the Confederate guns high above them. The unfortunate Union soldiers then received a second punishing shock to their flank as General Pettigrew raced with his cavalry, seemed to come out of nowhere, screaming with swords and sabres that cut bloody red gaps into their ranks.

George realised what a uniquely remarkable position they were in as he looked across the valley at the battlefield, rapidly expanding in action to both right and left, clouded with the smoke from artillery and rifle fire, where all the hundreds of thousands of figures moved like his lead soldiers of childhood on a green baize table, now set up for a war that was certainly no game.

Sounds reaching them from such a distance, even the explosive noise of bursting shells and the virtually constant crackle of rifle fire, were no more than a background noise to be heard from their eyrie, gazing at what seemed a surreal scene playing out before them. By late morning, the Envoy's party had dismounted and, leaving two soldiers in charge of the horses, had moved to the front edge of the small plateau. Not only George, but also the three Confederate officers, had telescopes focussed on individual parts of the developing battle.

It looked as if the Union infantry lines had held on to their newly advanced positions, almost half way across the farmland towards the lower slopes of the ridge. General Pettigrew's cavalry charge had appeared gloriously heroic from afar, but was now bogged down against the Union line. It was possible to spot numerous dead and maimed horses, whose riders, if still alive, were struggling in the hand-to-hand fighting going on in the melee of dead and wounded soldiers and horses. Pettigrew himself was incredibly fortunate to survive the charge in more or less one piece: he suffered a wound to his right hand, which cleanly removed three of his fingers, obliging him to retreat from the action. His cavalry corps was less fortunate: they took some sixty percent killed and another twenty percent wounded.

A Confederate infantry advance had now emerged from concealment behind the cover of woodland and rocks on the lower slopes of Cemetery Ridge. They hit the Union right flank, although even from afar it was obvious that the men in blue were putting up strong resistance, which was slowly pushing the Dixie boys back.

The Confederate barrage from the top of the ridge had by then virtually died out, presumably because both friend and foe were now becoming bound together in fierce fighting on the level farmland, crushing acres of yellow wheat and barley underfoot and staining it with blood. The ridge and Little Round Top hill were yet to be trampled by any Union advance now encountering its mass of obstacles in the form of rocks, scree and boulders, as well as multiple trees and scrub, covering the slopes they would have to fight their up if they were ever really to challenge the Confederates in this, so far, the most fiercely contested part of the battlefield.

As the afternoon wore on the Confederate commander, Robert E Lee, dispatched Generals Ambrose Hill and Richard Ewell to use their cavalry brigades, so far held in reserve on the Confederate right wing, just below Culp's Hill. They were ordered to charge the Union advance that had begun from outside Gettysburg and towards the rocky outcrops of Devil's Den, crossing the Baltimore Pike as they moved forward.

'Old Bald Head', as Richard Ewell was known to his men, had already proved a remarkably able commander and he and Ambrose Hill, with several brigades of hardened cavalry, now drove the Union advance backwards on the Confederate right, spectacularly quickly. The sight of the Confederate cavalry, swords and sabres viciously slicing through bewildered infantry was close to a massacre and resulted in a retreat of the right wing of the Union force, or rather those still standing and who had suffered chaotic panic.

Those Union infantry who made it back to the outskirts of Gettysburg were punished even there, as Confederate cavalry, now filling the narrow streets, soon left heaps of Union bodies against the buildings. General Hill's charge, which had got somewhat out of hand by this time, was eventually brought under control and the cavalry withdrew to just outside the town, to await infantry reinforcements. In fact, these never arrived and by nightfall Gettysburg had been abandoned by both sides, to become a no man's land once more.

While the Confederate group of observers on South Mountain prepared to camp there for the night, commanders and their generals on both sides of the battlefield shrank their forces back just sufficiently to be separated along what was now a ragged front line, in places more or less on the edge of the lower slopes of Cemetery Ridge at its south-west extremity. In the east this left Gettysburg unoccupied, but with opposing forces facing each other across the town. Both sides put in place thousands of pickets keeping watch on either side of the no-man's land, which was less than a mile wide, and for most of the night was in pitch darkness, forsaken by moon and stars. Few would sleep that night as every soldier in the valley and on the hillsides expected to be faced with a sudden attach out of that darkness. In fact, on that first battle-proper night, perhaps through exhaustion or perhaps through fear, no such surprise forays were launched by either side.

Waggon trains ferrying wounded to casualty stations and field hospitals moved throughout the short summer night through exhausted masses of the surviving combatants to find the equally horrendous conditions of surgeons cutting off the limbs of screaming men, who must have wished they were amongst the piles of dead. Doctors, some possibly qualified as such, and nurses, most of whom had never lived through such conditions. These women did their best to patch wounds not fatal and to accept the far more frequent fact of so many boys dying under the knives and saws of the surgeons.

A new reality to those barely hanging on to life in such places was that this now horribly real war had also become, in some ways, *a woman's war*. The number of both Confederate and Union women working in the casualty stations of this battlefield ran into many hundreds, their ministrations badly needed by vast numbers of frightfully wounded men. The Union had its Sanitary Commission, made up of women nurses, working in large tents behind the lines; the Confederates also had many women nurses, but not so well organised as their enemy. They were all to be the precursors of many more in the future.

The army commanders of both sides spent that sleepless night trying to assess the situation and making plans for the next dawn. Undoubtedly, many men no longer able to stand attempted to sleep where they happened to be and mostly failed to find any blessed relief; the lucky ones were relieved to find some food and, more importantly, water.

So called 'minor' wounds were left untreated for those lucky enough not to be on the surgeon's tables and being still on the battlefield might have seemed the better option. Soldiers so far relatively unscathed and still very much alive might have thanked God for their survival. Those who had been held in reserve regarded themselves as the fortunate, but others who had been in the pure hell of the fighting might well have called them cowards. Thousands were involved in sentry duty, while comrades tried to sleep or, more likely, to experience the relief that they had survived the day, although in the darkness of that night relief was soon to be swept away in the waking dread and the brief sleeping dreams of what tomorrow might bring.

# Chapter Forty

## The Second Day: Saturday August 4 1863

During various late night strategy meetings Union General Meade, in conference with senior generals Hooker, Chamberlain and Reynolds, had come to the conclusion that the first day's fighting had really achieved little, apart from the great numbers of dead and wounded. What must now follow needed to be a return to proven 'traditional' infantry tactics. As far as he was concerned, this meant putting the maximum numbers of men available to take the low ground between their Union positions and Cemetery Ridge. The belief was that, provided the Union could put more men and more firepower into an advance than the Confederates had to defend their positions, then the Union would inevitably succeed. An advance up Cemetery Ridge would follow as night follows day and, with God unquestionably on their side, a victory could be achieved before the sun set again.

General Hooker was a lone voice asking Meade how many men he was prepared to sacrifice for such a victory. Meade's angry reply, backed up by his fist hammering down on the table at every pause, was: *"All our loyal soldiers of the Union would be proud to die if only their deaths ensured that the bloody secessionists would be trodden for ever into the earth of Pennsylvania!"*

General George Meade, commander of the Army of the Potomac, was not a man that even another senior general would argue with and the strategy for August 4 was thus determined without question.

Before dawn on that still Saturday morning over twenty thousand Union infantry were moved into position; a great bristling hedgehog four deep and almost two miles long. Although there were many different divisions making up this huge force, armed with repeating rifles and bayonets, interspersed with artillery pieces, it had been necessary to appoint commanders of each division, since the whole, now widely spread infantry force, was too large for General

Meade himself to be able to guarantee its control in his own hands alone with any real confidence.

As the light grew enough for the Union commander-in-chief to see if anything had changed in the Confederate position, he could hardly believe his eyes when he saw that the Rebels had brought up a remarkably large number of their own infantry, presumably from their rear reserves about which he had been warned. These were now spread along the gentler lower slopes where the ridge met the farmland. There were very considerable numbers, but instead of being in one great bristling hedgehog of bayonets catching the first rays of the sun, the Confederates were in blocks with ranks four or five deep, but with avenues of open space between them.

Union General Joshua Chamberlain was on his black horse regarding the huge, so far peaceful, acres of farmland with their network of wooden rail fences between the fields. Next to him sat General James Wilson, one of the cavalry commanders.

"What do you think of that, Wilson?" Chamberlain asked, without moving the telescope from his right eye.

"I believe the gaps between the infantry are significant, sir. If I were commanding that Confederate force over there, which thank the Almighty I am not, I would hazard a guess that somewhere not too far away, but out of sight at present, that damned traitor Lee has cavalry concealed. That could be what those empty lanes are for."

Chamberlain chewed on the remains of the cigar in his mouth without speaking. He scanned Cemetery Ridge slowly with his telescope from the copses of trees and stonewalls on the far right to where the ridge bent in its 'fish hook' shape and then the steep knolls of Little and Big Round Top which blocked the view to the left.

"Dammit!" he barked around the cigar that had now gone out; he threw the remains to the ground in exasperation.

"I can see nothing but the Rebs in those haphazard formations. There's no cavalry there Wilson... No, absolutely no cavalry! Our boys are going to be on a rabbit hunt out there today, mark my words."

No sooner had he pronounced this judgement than the Union artillery right along the line began to open up. Initially shells fell short and the Confederates started to whoop with laughter. Their own batteries on the top of the ridge then began to reply and the notorious Rebel Yells could be heard.

As the artillery commanders on both sides began to find their range, Meade gave the initial order for his personally planned line of infantry to advance. Within minutes, the peaceful pre-dawn became a wailing scream of shells exploding among the advancing men on foot, which inspired officers to try to push them into running. Those who faltered or refused were often shot by those same officers. Inevitably, with individual commanding generals in charge of each section of the line, orders were never going to coincide, except by chance, and that proved to be the case.

In fact, as the infantry battle was now frantically engaged once more, a stray Union shell overshot the Confederate infantry force and hit General Lee's stone farm headquarters on the top of the ridge. Apart from inflicting extreme damage, it also killed three officers and General Ewell himself was lucky to escape unhurt, although covered in stone dust and wood splinters.

The Union line, as predicted by some Union generals, was proving far too long to control as a co-ordinated movement and hence it wavered like a ribbon in the breeze, some units far ahead of the more tardy. Confederate cavalry generals Johnson Pettigrew, still in the saddle with his right hand heavily bandaged, George Pickett and Jeb Stuart, watched from their positions, each about a thousand yards from the neighbouring cavalry commander. Concealed behind the crest of Cemetery ridge General Longstreet, in command of these concealed cavalry brigades, stared down through the smoke of battle at the lanes between the infantry squares and remarked to an aide at his side: *"My heart is heavy. I can see the desperate and hopeless nature of this charge and the slaughter it will cause."*

As the Union force continued a gradually more haphazard advance, it changed from a great spiked hedgehog, that had started as a genuinely threatening line supporting the accuracy of General Meade's plan, swiftly to become a mass of thousands of increasingly confused Union infantry moving at different speeds and even somewhat different directions. Meade, astride *Old Baldy,* could now observe the many already dead or wounded that were impeding the progress of those still standing, but pissing their pants as the reality of their situation began to come home to them: Rebels both in front and beside them, with Rebel shells and cannon balls punching great holes in their ranks.

George, Arthur and the Confederate troops watching from the plateau on South Mountain could see the smoke of exploding shells as they fell like rocks dropped into a pool of minnows and so preventing the confused and slow advancing Union force from seeing through the fog of battle. Hundreds of the Union infantry were by then leading a charge within a few hundred yards of the lower slope of Cemetery Ridge, while others were entangled in the melee of slaughter being wrought by the Confederate artillery batteries from their commanding positions a few hundred feet above them.

By this time, the three generals of the Confederate cavalry were desperate to be released and to order the charge of over a thousand mounted men, who had been waiting for their moment of glory. General Longstreet was the overall commander of the cavalry generals and a hurried request had reached him by messenger asking him to confirm the order to charge. Rumour would have it that he had immediately said that such a charge was now '*not needed*', but after a few moments of thought he changed his mind and simply nodded to the messenger.

At that moment George, distant from the raging battle, could clearly make out what looked like six waterfalls of horses and men in grey released to flood down the ridge. They came through the gaps deliberately left between the forward Confederate blocks of infantry and then spread out to thunder down the short distance towards the mass of Union soldiers just below them.

Very many Union officers were now scattered amongst their divisions, already greatly depleted by artillery fire; they then were shocked to see what was now trotting over the top of Cemetery Ridge and then immediately spurring into a full charge, which was further speeded by gravity as the horses felt the ground drop away beneath their hooves. The Union generals had no time to issue any order. Not that it would have been heard even if they had had the time and breath to deliver it. The bombardment from the Confederate guns had ceased a few minutes before the cavalry became all too terrifyingly obvious.

Many of the Union infantry did try to hold their ground, using their bayonets simply in defence to thrust upwards into the bellies of the horses now on top of them. The speed of the charge rendered defensive rifle fire virtually impossible, although officers found their revolvers were somewhat more effective.

The swords and sabres of Jeb Stuart's '*ghost*' cavalry, whose fearsome reputation had gone before them in the form then of wild talk in the Union ranks the night before. They appeared out of the concealing smoke and immediately began to hack the men in the blue uniforms to the ground. Many of those whose limbs had been severed must have wished they had been killed outright. Nevertheless, the fighting was not all one sided and once a rider had been unseated or his horse brought down, he often became the target for the bayonets or rifles of the Union men on foot.

It was only much later that this remarkably effective action gained the name of *Pickett's Charge.* General George Edward Pickett himself always maintained after the battle that he was only one of three commanders of the gallant cavalry and deserved no more to be honoured than any other Dixie general that day.

From South Mountain, all the miles of farmland between the initial Union advance and the slope of the ridge could be seen buried beneath churning bodies as thousands of men struggled for their lives in what became a vast hand to hand battle, with the Confederate cavalry now embroiled in the heart of it. They were trying to hang on to their advantage of both surprise and being on horseback above the infantry, at least while the charge continued to crash its way into the wall of Union bodies, both dead and alive.

There were undoubtedly numerous cavalry deaths, but there were still large numbers that now forced their way through the Union's ragged lines and then turned and came back from their rear, creating even more havoc. While General George Pickett was second in overall command of these massed cavalry regiments, giving his name to posterity for it, the entire force would eventually be praised for:

*"An action of outstanding courage, resulting in the blow that turned the Battle at Gettysburg firmly in favour of the Confederate Armies of Northern Virginia and Tennessee."* The commendation was awarded by General Robert E Lee, Commander of the Confederate Army at Gettysburg, August 1863.

*Pickett's Charge* had undoubtedly caused grievous damage to the Union army as a whole and to their single massive infantry force in particular. The force that General Meade had pinned so much faith in, expecting them to scale the slopes of Cemetery Ridge and destroy the Confederate guns on its crest, as well as the troops supporting that artillery. As expected by the Commander-in-Chief, he should by rights be gloriously victorious by the end of the day.

The body count at the end of August 4 could only ever be an estimate and both sides undoubtedly inflated the numbers of the dead and wounded of their enemy. However, it was likely that close to 15,000 Union soldiers were dead that day, wounded or missing as darkness fell on the summer's night. The Confederate losses were less, but even so, the cavalry regiments, as effective as they had been, were probably reduced by several thousand.

The early evening did not show any real sign of sufficient darkness to stop the fighting until after ten o'clock. In the six hours or so after Pickett's Charge, the Union officers still alive on the field managed to engender some remarkable resilience in what remained of their infantry regiments. With the Confederate cavalry retreating behind the crest of the ridge, those Union officers, who notably included Generals Joseph Hooker and Ambrose Burnside, saw a window of opportunity and gave orders to advance and take the hill at all costs. This pitted them directly against Robert E Lee, who had so far directed the Confederate force from his position close to the cemetery gatehouse at the top of the ridge. The remainder of his reserve regiments of infantry, who had, until then, sat the battle out behind the crest, were now brought rapidly forward under the command of Generals Gustave Beauregard and General James Longstreet, lately commander on the reserve force brought up from Camp Davis, and now resumed his role as Commander of Cavalry, with Beauregard as his second in command. He sat close to Robert E Lee through much of the battle on the top of Cemetery Ridge.

Although the light was more or less gone by that time, George and Arthur still had a clear view across the whole landscape around Gettysburg, now littered with the dead and dying, as well as the shell craters that pockmarked the area. George, perhaps thinking how he would have felt having survived such a brutal charge, remarked:

"To see those Union boys charging like very devils up that slope, I reckon they're filled with at least enough anger to take on anything the Confeds can now throw at them."

Indeed, it was obvious, even from that distance, that there were still large numbers of blue uniforms moving rapidly up the lower slopes in the semi darkness. In fact, many had moved a good distance up the ridge before the Confederates met them head on. The hand to hand fighting then grew frenzied. Even bayonets often proved too cumbersome to be effective and the Dixie boys reverted to Bowie knives, which many of them carried, to slice into the re-energised Federals with whom they seemed now to be literally face to face.

Within an hour or so, the battle had split into numerous smaller conflicts, some hardly removed from where they had started, but others pushing up the ridge, particularly onto the rocky slopes of Little Round Top. Here, not really visible to George, but for Robert E Lee dangerously moving ever closer to his own position south east of the Round Top hills.

By ten o'clock in the evening, the fighting was still desperate, but soon after had come to a standstill in most areas as it became very difficult to see more than a few feet as the darkness descended. Hundreds of bodies, in both blue and grey, littered the slopes, while the seriously wounded, unable to move, provided even more obstacles for the combatants than the rocks and trees, themselves marked with the blood of American sons, fathers, husbands and brothers.

As real darkness began to invade the slopes and fields, officers, or at least those who were still able to convey commands to exhausted men, tried to take positions that they could defend now that the sun had entirely disappeared behind the western hills. With the light gone and visibility reduced in what was by then the darkness of a summer's night, the crack of rifle and revolver fire was reduced considerably, but never ceased entirely all night long.

Where larger groups of soldiers had come to a standstill, it was possible for some to drop to the ground and gain some relief, defended as they were by others still standing around them, but very few would have any sleep, or even rest, before the dawn signalled the battle itself to struggle on.

Sharpshooters were the greatest danger, since they seemed able to move between outcrops of rocks or through trees in silence like ghosts and then pick off victims at will, before again disappearing into the night. There were also numerous skirmishes during the hours of darkness involving groups of soldiers suddenly attacking, or being attacked, out of the darkness; there was no moon that night. The fear that this engendered in more or less every man, whether private or general, was palpable. No one who survived the fourth of August 1863 at Gettysburg would ever forget the phantoms that stalked the darkness drawing the blood of soldiers, regardless of whether they were Union or Confederate.

In the early evening of August 4, Major Meredith had for several hours tried to insist that his small party accompanying George and Arthur must start to ride back to the Davis Town Camp before it became too dark to see, but George in particular had been so rooted to the spot overlooking the battlefield and the equally awful and incredible sights passing below them, that this had proved impossible to force on the two Envoys. The major at one point, as the sun was just dipping below the crest of South Mountain, had threatened that he and his men would now be forced to leave the two Englishmen alone on the mountain if they did not mount up immediately.

George, handing his telescope to Arthur and turning to face the officer who was torn between abandoning those whom he was commanded to protect and staying for a second night on the mountain, with very mean supplies of food and water, patiently addressed the major. We are perfectly safe up here, as you well know," he insisted. "You only have to look at the scenes we have witnessed today to know that the Union is not about to launch an attack in this direction, in fact probably not in any direction. *We* have a duty to our Prime Minister to be able to report on the outcome of this battle, which will most probably be the final outcome and end of this war."

"For God's sake, Captain Fitzwilliam…" was as far as Meredith got, before George stepped very close to him and, spoke in a lowered voice not audible to the soldiers standing in a group by their horses on the other side of the clearing.

"Mr Tissiman and I," he said clearly and slowly, "are citizens of Great Britain and her Empire. We are bound by duty to remain here. If you wish to *retreat* to Davis Town Camp, that is up to you and your conscience. Please feel free to do as you wish, but we shall stay here and see this thing through to its bitter end."

Arthur had not said a word during this increasingly confrontational war of words, believing that anything he could add would be pointless. Major Meredith turned on his heel and marched off towards his men, but after a few yards, turned and came back. He drew a deep breath.

"Very well, sir. I bow to your demand, but do not say that I did not warn you that to stay here another night would be…*inadvisable.*"

# Chapter Forty-One

## The Night of the Third Day, 4–5 August 5 1863

None of them would be privy to the extraordinary decision that would be forced on General Meade and the Union Army now at their headquarters at around midnight, as Saturday the 4th turned into Sunday August 5th.

General George Meade had been in an urgently called strategy meeting for over two hours by two o'clock on the Sunday morning. The sounds of distant rifle fire had continued to disturb the still air ever since darkness had forced the real battle to hold its breath until the first faint rays of light would undoubtedly witness its full-blown start all over again.

Meade and the generals around him were too experienced in the ways of war to admit to any sense of panic, but none of them could find words that would give genuine encouragement to facing the day ahead. Meade's most senior generals had so far failed to agree about how to proceed. No one had dared suggest that they might be forced to ask for a truce or cease fire, although the word *surrender* was certainly not going to poison the lips of any man present.

General Meade by this time was at his lowest ebb and had decided to call an end to any further discussion or suggestions about possible plans of action. He then issued the command, which he made clear would brook no argument:

"All officers commanding troops in the Army of the Potomac today are to throw every Union soldier still standing into a single attack stretching from Gettysburg to the far south-western end of Cemetery Ridge at dawn. Any man who takes even one step backwards is to be shot on the spot."

At that moment, the farmhouse door of the Union Headquarters crashed open and a young major, whose name none of them knew nor cared about, almost fell into the room. His uniform jacket was ripped and there was dried blood down the side of his face. He looked from one general to another, clearly unsure who was who. He simply addressed the crowded room as a whole.

"Sir! Sir I'm in charge of the guard half a mile up the road and we've just seen a carriage come in at speed with Union cavalry all around it, sir, and…"

Meade had by then turned from the table and found himself only a few feet from the sweating, dirt stained major.

"What the fuck are you talking about soldier? Do you have any idea who you're talking to? I'll have you…"

"No, sir. I mean, yes sir. We all saw it, sir. There's a man in the coach and it's stopped just around the corner here and seems to be waiting for something… I mean, the man in the coach is, probably is… I think it *is* the President, sir. Mr Lincoln, sir and he's…"

Generals Winfield Scott, Joseph Hooker and Joshua Chamberlain were now also crowding around the major, who looked to be in a state of horrified shock. The door to the farmhouse was still open and then gradually the whole room of officers grew silent, as they became aware of the man standing in the open doorway: a tall man with a pale, bearded face and a stovepipe hat still on his head, which had caused him to stoop in order to step over the threshold.

Like most Americans, whether Union or Confederate, Abraham Lincoln was easily and instantly recognisable, since there was hardly anyone at this time in the war who had not seen a drawing of him or even a photograph. General Meade and many others in the now silent room had also met him and some, like Meade, more than once.

It was that general who was the first to overcome the shock. He quickly gave a formal salute and warmly shook the hand the president extended to him. He then cleared the room of all but the three most senior generals. He also quietly ordered that the sergeant who had so dramatically broken the news of Lincoln's arrival should be temporarily confined to another room upstairs in the farmhouse, until the reasons for the president's decision to travel from Harrisburg to a battlefield, which was still the site of an ongoing, bloody conflict, could be ascertained. None of the four officers remaining had any doubt that Lincoln had embarked on a life-threatening risk by abandoning his original journey that would have taken him far to the north into New England.

It was over an hour later that General Meade had persuaded the President and Commander-in-Chief of the Union to move to an adjoining room, where he could rest after what had apparently been a long and arduous journey. He then called the remaining generals back to the meeting room, having increased the guards both on the building and the surrounding area by several hundred, as well as ensuring that no one other than the generals was anywhere close enough to be aware of what was going on in the headquarters farmhouse. Once this had been achieved, the room reverted to an anxious silence.

"Gentlemen," General Meade addressed them quietly and solemnly, "as you are aware President Lincoln has honoured us with his presence here at this critical moment in the history of the United States of America and has done so with no regard for his own safety. I suspect that you may not be surprised to hear his reason for this selfless action."

Several officers either nodded or muttered their understanding to neighbours, but then silence again descended until Meade began to speak again.

"The President has told me that it is his firm intention, in spite of his never having served in a military role, to be clearly seen by his army, on this never-to-be-forgotten day, in a truly active role. In other words, it is his avowed intention to *lead his soldiers into battle*."

Immediately, the words left his mouth there was uproar among the seasoned generals of the Union Army. Meade made out shouted remarks, such as, '*This is lunacy!*', '*We must not allow the President, the figurehead of the Union, to lay down his life*' and '*You must stop this, sir, it is your duty to do so*'.

"Gentlemen!" Meade shouted at the assembly and pounded the table to reinforce his command. That had the desired effect and obedient quiet was restored.

"I naturally agree with your understandable and loyal sentiments. Mr Lincoln is a brave man and, as we know, has proved in the past that he will take any personal risk to ensure the safety of our Union and its citizens."

Another pause allowed more sentiments of agreement to be aired, but Meade continued.

"However, I intend to do all in my power, and I am sure with the support of all of you, to *persuade* the President that, while we applaud his presence on this battlefield, his most effective part, assuming he would refuse to travel back to Harrisburg, must be to be seen as our soldiers move once again into the fray at first light. Seeing their President here, standing proud and giving them his blessing before they begin on what must be a final victory, will, I am sure, be the most valuable thing he could do to ensure that victory."

When Arthur was shaken awake where he lay on the grass of South Mountain, he could barely see the trees ten yards away, since the night's slow retreat towards dawn was only just visible. He could, however, clearly see George standing over him and offering his hand to help him stand. As he hazily came awake and was aware of where he was, he could just make out a faint orange glow in the eastern sky in the distance over Cemetery Ridge and, once he was on his feet, he could also hear the movement of men and horses close behind him. George passed him his canteen and Arthur realised how thirsty he was.

"You must have slept better than I did," said George. "There are many thousands of men very much awake not more than five or six miles away, although I suppose by this morning there are rather less than there were yesterday, actually alive, I mean, and able to realise they are facing another dawn."

All the members of the small group were by then making their way to the front edge of the plateau and staring out into the semi darkness. The irregular sound of rifle fire had been heard off and on all night, but was now fast becoming much more frequent and any pauses were rare, hardly ever present anywhere within their hearing for more than a few seconds. The only sights to be clearly seen were the flashes as rifles, muskets and revolvers discharged raggedly along the miles of farmland and ridge slope that could now be dimly seen against the very slightly lighter sky. George had been scanning the battlefield with his telescope, which he now passed it to Arthur.

"If you hold it really steady, I think you'll be able to see some vague movement all over the land down there; not so much individual figures as something more resembling living shadows."

Arthur could, indeed, see the shadows George described moving against the darker land and the more or less continuous muzzle flashes. He then almost dropped the telescope as several horses, tethered twenty yards behind them, suddenly whinnied and hooves could be heard stamping on the dry ground. Every man jerked around, probably imagining a sudden attack from behind by a Union skirmish group, but then realised that a dozen large birds, which must have been in the trees overnight, suddenly took flight. Some nervous, relieved laughter quickly followed. By the time they focussed their eyes back towards the east, pale light was dawning and they could see, although still not clearly, what must have been tens of thousands of miniature figures now moving across the farmland towards the ridge.

General Lee had been awake all night and now sat astride his horse, surrounded by other senior Confederate officers in front of the cemetery gatehouse. His telescope revealed the movement of soldiers across the miles of battlefield to both his right and left. He was aware, and had been for several hours, that the Union was planning a final, desperately powerful, full frontal advance on his position on Cemetery Ridge. He was also aware that the ridge was no longer clearly either Union or Confederate. Reports reaching him overnight reinforced his view of the previous evening that there were many strongholds of Union forces right across the ridge, even touching Gettysburg itself.

Four miles to Lee's west, and certainly not visible to him, George Mead was trying to see that his order for a mass advance at four o'clock was fully in place and now, at a quarter past that hour, the Union Army was moving forward at a steady and orderly pace. Staring, as he was, directly into the first rays of the rising sun, Meade's vision was not as perfect as he would have wished. The plan he had forced into place was that the mass advance towards the east across the last fields would trigger the Union strongholds already on the ridge, especially on Little Round Top, to break out of their overnight positions, destroy any opposing Confederates and then be an advance party up the final slope to the crest. Once there they would overwhelm the artillery and drive the undoubtedly large mass of Lee's force, by then hopefully confused, to retreat at full speed through the hills and woods into the risen sun.

However, what Meade saw was not exactly his perfectly executed plan. He was fortunately not aware of the words of a young Confederate sergeant on the same battlefield, who had just stepped across a wooden fence and had disturbed a rabbit, which skittered away from him, generating his quiet words in return: "*Run old hare. If I was a hare, I'd sure run away too.*"

General Meade had started the day when it was still dark with what he considered a success. His meeting with Mr Lincoln had proved that the powers he wielded as a previously successful Union general were strong enough to persuade the President that he, General George Meade, a Brigadier General of many brilliant battles fought in the distant past, had long ago proved that he understood military matters far better even than his president. Abraham Lincoln had reluctantly, after a long-drawn-out discussion, eventually agreed to show himself to his troops behind the lines, rather than risk his invaluable life in the roar of battle. This was a task he would carry out just before dawn and he was clearly delighted to be able to be face to face with his brave lads.

President Abraham Lincoln, accompanied by General Meade and an impressive number of other senior officers, had left the headquarters farmhouse a little later than intended and the early shine of dawn was in the eastern sky. He had insisted on being mounted for the ceremony, as were all the senior officers. They moved slowly towards the waiting mass of Union men, who were being organised into the positions they were to occupy for battle on what they were being assured would be the *'last day: the day we whip those filthy Rebs!'*. Many appeared unconvinced of this. They had no idea that President Lincoln himself was less than a mile away.

As the entourage of officers escorting their president approached the rear of the lines, orders were shouted to, *'Make way! Officers coming through!'*

*'Step aside!'*

*'Clear a way for officers.'*

Lincoln, as ever, was a head taller than his honour guard and gradually as the entourage slowly advanced through the ranks, he and his stovepipe hat began to be recognised. At first, it was with disbelief, then astonishment and within minutes cheers started to echo into the semi-darkness. It was soon impossible to stop hundreds, then thousands, breaking ranks, trying to touch their president, or even his horse, waving their caps in the air. For the first time in three days, smiles sprung onto the faces of the exhausted and dispirited soldiers of the Union. Many more thousands would wish that they had been near enough to see this spectacle.

Lincoln soon found his horse had been pushed up against a cannon still attached to its gun carriage. Before he could be stopped, he took his feet from the stirrups and, almost gracefully for such a tall man, stepped across onto the top of the carriage.

By now, it seemed that there were many thousands of men pushing to get closer to this living symbol of the Union. He held up his hands to try achieving some quiet so that he could be heard; to no avail. A young bugler, who was standing next to the artillery line saw what was happening and raised his bugle.

He blew '*Reveille*' and in moments, the great crowd became quiet. Abraham Lincoln looked across the waves of soldiers around him.

"My friends!" his distinctive voice, raised but not shouting, magically created near silence. "My friends, you brave soldiers of the Army of the Potomac, I am honoured to be with you on this auspicious day, the day when at last the blood that has stained our land for three years stops flowing. The victory that *you* will achieve before the sun sets this evening will live in the memories of future generations." A great cheer burst forth again and Lincoln waited for it to die down before continuing.

"Remember, you cannot fail unless you quit and I know you are not quitters." More cheers punctuated his words. "You have a job to do and I know you will do it well. You hold the responsibility for tomorrow in your hands and that means you cannot evade today… God fights with you today! He does so because he respects the righteousness of our cause. I am His servant and I know you will honour Him now." His audience was quieter as the Almighty was invoked. "I tell you now that I *know* what is right in this great battle, so stay with me throughout whatever is to follow… but, if I am wrong, then leave me." He lifted his hat from his head and waved it in the air as he turned full circle from his rather precarious position.

Cheers and cries of '*Good old Abe*', '*God bless you Abe*' and '*We'll finish 'em now*' as many more surrounded him while his escort pushed forward to protect him. Someone leant down to help him back into the saddle. General Meade made the decision that this was the time to leave.

"Leave them to avenge all the death and spilled blood," he said to General Hooker, whose horse was pressed close to his. "They're ready for anything now. Thanks to the President we can't lose today."

It took some time to prise Lincoln away from his much-refreshed army and for officers to get some order back into the lines, and by then dawn was well above Cemetery Ridge. By the time that happened, the President and a corps of cavalry were on the road to the nearest Union controlled railhead, from where the President and his small escort would hope to go on to Harrisburg by train in safety.

Abe Lincoln was too far away by then to hear the noise of the desperate battle under way again over the fields, woods, hills and farms he had left behind.

General Meade had taken Generals Hooker and Chamberlain, as well as a small group of colonels and majors, to just under a mile back from the field of conflict. They had placed their new battle command post on a gentle rise in the ground there, giving them a reasonable view of the farmland in front and the slope of Cemetery Ridge beyond.

"There they go!" Meade cried at the top of his voice, his telescope swinging along the line of advancing Union infantry. "I knew they wouldn't let him down... I told you all would be well. The Almighty is with us today...and, of course, with Abe Lincoln."

From where the General stood, it was sadly not possible, even with the help of a telescope, to judge whether Lincoln's appearance to the troops was making any significant difference to the quality of their fighting resolve. The bulk of the infantry, who had not spent the night on the slopes of the Ridge and Little Round Top, had advanced, although somewhat haphazardly, about half a mile across the fields, although the rail fences still standing were causing delays in some areas.

As far as Meade could tell, the fighting on scattered parts of the slope and Little Round Top had certainly taken on a deadly appearance, but it was hard to distinguish blues from greys. Nevertheless, the union commander seemed still to be in positive mood. Training his telescope on the top of the ridge he thought his eyes must have been deceiving him, when he thought he saw numerous puffs of grey smoke appearing in the sky just in front of the ridge edge, but that was followed by the roar of explosions. Within seconds the ridge, all the way from the western edge to just before Little Round Top, was obscured by hundreds more plumes of smoke and the crash of artillery fire. To his horror, his hand frozen with the telescope to his eye, Meade saw iron cannon balls and explosive shells smash into his infantry not yet within reach of the crest. It was clear to him that death and injury were being caused, not only by the explosions of the shells, but also by flying iron and stone as well.

"By God, Mr Hooker, the devils have pulled in even more cannon. Look at the havoc they're spreading through our men! Both of you! Instruct your officers down there to go forward at full speed. Get to the shelter of the hill!"

Hooker and Chamberlain, who had also been watching the scorching fire raining down on the infantry, pulled their horses closer together and Meade could see urgent gesticulation, but could not hear what was being said. By now, the field of Confederate artillery fire was well over a thousand yards wide.

"Get on with it!" he shouted at them. "We have no time, no time at all!"

He turned his own mount to get closer to his two generals, but as he did so they moved away and he saw them, urgently shouting orders to messengers, who galloped off towards the action, now almost a mile away. The party of officers around him moved with him, as he went forward a short distance and then came to a stop again. He could see a figure of an officer he vaguely recognised galloping through the infantry bogged down at the rear by falling shells. He lifted the 'scope to see more of what looked like encouraging valour in a senior officer. He then realised it was the full hair and beard of General Joshua Reynolds, but at the same moment the ground opened under Reynold's horse as a shell exploded directly beneath it. Meade was unable to look away; the explosion shredded the front of the horse and Joshua Reynolds simply disappeared. Another officer in blue hesitated and avoided the blast, but then spurred onwards; Meade recognised General George Custer.

# Chapter Forty-Two

**The Fourth Day, Monday August 6 1863**

Steady as the statues on the graves just beside him, General-in-Chief of the Confederate Army, Robert E Lee, sat unmoving on *Traveller,* his grey war-horse, which had been his mount for many battles in the Civil War to date and before. General Lee and Traveller stood in front of the cemetery gatehouse unmoved by the roar of shot and shell, half a dozen senior officers and two generals close beside him.

The bellow of the artillery, some as close as ten yards from his position, made any speech impossible. Lee sat expressionless, his grey beard just touching the front of his uniform coat: decorated with gold epaulets, buttons and the swags on his belt. He knew that two hundred and sixty artillery pieces of various types were drawn up just behind the edge of the ridge and each was delivering a shell every two minutes into the mass of Union soldiers who had now virtually stopped again below, just where the slope began to rise in front of them.

The slaughter he observed was horrendous and, he had to admit to himself, gratifying. He was later to comment to a young officer about what he had seen at that hour: "*It seems obvious that a corps commander's life does not count when lives are taken so randomly.*"

Every moment, it seemed dozens of men in every direction were mown down and even more could be seen with limbs blown off; in one case, in Lee's central field of vision, a head was thrown into the air.

Robert Lee had been part of too many scenes like this in his long career to allow any emotion to show on his face and some said there was no feeling in his heart either. He took out his pocket watch, carefully checked the time and put it away again. He turned Traveller until he was close against General Alexander, commander of the artillery, and shouted something in his ear. He received a nod and a raised hand to confirm Alexander had heard him. Lee then moved the short distance until he was next to General George Pickett. He similarly gave some sort of instruction or order and Pickett moved away and then picked up speed as he galloped, along with two other less senior officers, towards the northeast part of the ridge, at what was known as Devil's Den. This was nearer to the brutal, close combat fighting going on a couple of hundred yards down the rocky slopes and on nearby Little Round Top. The officers disappeared from Lee's view at that point, but he knew the order would be carried out when Pickett calculated the time was right.

Meanwhile, General Pettigrew, still smarting from the debacle of Friday in Gettysburg, was leading what was left of his regiment from the front, embattled as they were nearly half way down Little Round Top, fighting for every rock and tree. As they started to move towards two nests of Union troops and some sharpshooters on their left, the private carrying the Confederate infantry colour, was shot through the head from close range and crumpled to the ground, still clutching the flag. Pettigrew, being very close, immediately dismounted and vaulted over a rock to retrieve the colours.

A major in grey just behind him shouted a warning, *"No one can take up those colours and live, sir!"*

As Pettigrew bent to pull the staff of the flag from the dead man's hand a bullet passed so close to his cheek that he felt the rush of air and a high-pitched whistle, before the bullet hit another rock. General Pettigrew carried the regiment colours for the next three hours and came out of the battle unscathed and with his honour restored, except to those whose very recent memory was still alive.

General Lee checked his watch as the hour hand moved up to twelve noon and within a few minutes, he was satisfied to observe Generals George Pickett, Jeb Stuart and Isaac Trimble move forward from behind the ridge, each in command of a troop of cavalry numbering, by Lee's orders, over 600 men. Each troop advanced over the ridge and then moved as swiftly as it was possible down the slopes, in Pickett's case, down Little Round Top; Jeb Stuart dropped down into Devil's Den and Trimble into what later became known as the Valley of Death.

Lee had taken a calculated risk in ordering large numbers of cavalry to attack on the downward facing, rocky and screed slopes, rather than their habitual killing fields of flatter ground. He believed that the Union soldiers fighting their own separate battles on the hillside would never expect cavalry to come at them from above again and, equally shocking, would find their sudden appearance, looming high above their men on foot, would put the fear of God into the '*dammed Yankees*'.

It was only a matter minutes after the three troops of cavalry crested the ridge that Lee could see Pickett's and Stuart's men come within the sight of the Union. He was proved right in that the attack certainly took the enemy by surprise and that on its own was significant, since the surprise caused them to divert their attention by trying to combat the mounted Confederates, which in turn meant that they could not concentrate any longer on close combat with the Confederate infantry.

However, Lee was soon disturbed to see that, perhaps as no real surprise, the horses were making heavy weather of the slope and the obstacles of slippery scree, rocks, outcrops and trees. He could see dozens, just in the two areas visible to him that were sliding uncontrolled on the dry soil, unhorsing their riders and then crashing into infantry of both Union and Confederate colours.

It was General Stuart who had insisted that the so called 'charge' should be accompanied by rebel yells as loud as possible and undoubtedly the vision of horsemen swinging sabres and screaming at the top of their lungs sent many Union soldiers running down the slope for fear of their lives.

The fighting on both Little Round Top and Devil's Den began to assume a picture of chaos. The dust rising from the horse's hooves filled the air, accompanied by smoke from the rifles of the infantry. The result for General Lee, even when he moved to the very front edge of the escarpment, was that after half an hour he could make little sense of whether his cavalry were actually pushing the Union troops back down the slope and on to the farmland below, or not. He had sent messengers with each troop and so far had had no news from General Trimble in the valley towards the north east, the 'Valley of Death' the name it would be appropriately known by to history.

As if there were not enough death being dealt out on the slopes of Cemetery Ridge, the Confederate artillery continued to keep up their bombardment of the farmland below, which effectively put a wall of flame and explosion between the fields and the slopes of the ridge and that in turn virtually stopped any Union infantry advancing to join the fight from the farmland, while closing the door on the retreat from the ridge itself.

Two more or less separate actions were now taking place within a short distance of each other and the slaughter in both was beyond anything even the most seasoned of soldiers had ever seen before. Any so-called *advance* was limited to a few yards. Union soldiers were shoulder to shoulder, rank touching rank as they made useless efforts to push forward, carrying a forest of flashing steel bayonets, for which there was no room to kill the enemy with a vengeance.

On the confederate side, scattered along the slope, one young survivor later wrote to his wife, '*An ocean of armed men were sweeping upon us from below*'. He did not mention that they were 'sweeping' at a snail's pace and often were pushed back just as slowly.

By two o'clock on the Monday afternoon, General Lee had received messages from each area of battle along the ridge and had sent back orders that when the artillery fire ceased that would be the signal for both Confederate cavalry and infantry to advance as fast and strongly as possible down the slope; in Lee's words: "*Show no mercy. Clear the Yankees off this field once and for all.*"

Before Lee's orders to close down the artillery came into effect the barrage actually increased in rate of fire, so that there was virtually no time gap evident between shells leaving the muzzles of the artillery and others smashing into the Union army, as well as the ground itself, which appeared to heaving like a living creature breathing and exhaling. As this happened, a great moan seemed to spread through the union line as each explosion seemed to take out whole groups of men at a time. It was no exaggeration for those fortunate enough to be away from this bloody scene to be able to report that, "*Entire regiments disappeared in a few minutes. Legs, arms, knapsacks and rifles were thrust high into the clear air.*"

In the heart of the struggle on and around the Ridge, infantry soldiers were so close to their enemies that they fired directly into their faces at a range of a few feet. Headless bodies lay underfoot, those still standing were tangled amidst the dead and dying. It was, as one report would tell: "*A struggling mass, red with blood.*"

One Confederate captain screamed to those of his corps still close to him, "*Go home, boys! Home is down there, beyond the Union line!*"

When, just after two o'clock, the barrage of artillery fire suddenly stopped right along the ridge, it felt to those still able to hear anything as if the blanket, which had been keeping the sounds of hell close to the ground and that had smothered them all day, had been lifted and suddenly the cries of men could be heard, the sound of rifle and musket fire, even the beat of horses' hooves as they reached the flatter ground. The smoke that had wreathed the battlefield gradually cleared as a brisk wind got up from the west. General Lee on the eastern side of the battle, and General George Meade still miles away from him to the west, could see what lifted the heart of the army in grey and drove the one in blue to despair.

The combined Confederate force of infantry and a much-depleted number of cavalry were forcing the Union army back away from the ridge and across the open fields towards where they had so confidently started that morning. Raymond Laferty, a Confederate Corporal, told his wife when he reached home a month later that, *"Cheer after cheer rose from the boys in grey, making the heavens throb."*

The Confederate infantry were now reinforced by the reserve corps, now under the command of General Beauregard, being brought up from behind the ridge. These were men who had been kept out of the fight for so long that they were desperately eager to kill as many Yankees as they possibly could before dark.

It was equally true that many of the Union men were putting up a brave rear guard fight, but larger Union numbers had already turned tail and were running away from the fight, not towards it. Others could be seen throwing down their weapons and, hands in the air, surrendering in the hope of receiving mercy from Confederates, who were now intoxicated by the thrill of killing so easily and by the excitement of what seemed to be victory at last.

# Chapter Forty-Three

## The Afternoon and Evening of the Fourth Day, Monday August 6 1863

High above and to the west of the dying battle, the soldiers of the Envoy's observation party on South Mountain were loath to admit the relief of seeing a potential Confederate victory as they watched from far off the toy soldiers of the Confederacy begin to sweep the Union in front of them like fallen autumn leaves. Neither Arthur nor George could find any thrill or delight by what they saw; the sight, and almost the smell, of death was all too real.

To George, it was another dreadful moment of watching an enemy crumble and die in blood and gore, while to Arthur, it was an appalling and unnatural shock, even after seeing action at Bull Run, now to see so many bodies lying across the previously peaceful fields and gentle hillsides; he felt as if he were seeing the end of the world in miniature. He turned away from the shocking sights in the distance, walked back and sat on the ground close to the horse line. His head drooped into his lap as the full horror of what human beings could do to each other in extremis caught up with him.

George was far too involved with what he was watching on the battlefield to notice Arthur's departure. By four in the afternoon, he had not moved from the same spot for several hours. Taking the telescope from his eye for a moment, he looked across at Major Meredith, who was standing next to him, equally enthralled by what they could see.

"It seems to me," George remarked, "that we are probably watching the last hours, not just of this battle, but of the war itself. What's your opinion, Major?"

"I am relieved to say sir, that I am convinced from what I can see below at this moment, that you are right."

Meredith paused, staring across the hundreds of acres between them and Gettysburg, littered with the tiny spots, tangles and heaps of bodies and with the Confederate army in full cry behind what might be generously called the retreat of the Army of Potomac, but looked far more like a rout.

"The thought of getting home again is sweet," he said, "as I am sure it is for every man here today who will survive, but the question in my mind is whether the prize is truly worth the heavy price paid?"

The Commanding Generals of the Confederacy and Union were now watching a spectacle from their positions, Lee on the top of Cemetery Ridge and Meade, who had moved with his entourage, back almost as far as their Headquarters farmhouse. What they saw was identical. What that sight meant to each was diametrically opposed; success and relief for one, defeat and disaster for the other. Cloud had now come up with the wind to blot out the sun, which meant that the light had changed considerably and the temperature had dropped.

General Lee looked at the sky above and behind him and at what was yet to come from the east. He leant across to General Edward Alexander, now re-horsed, who was watching the bloodletting in front of him with similar emotions no doubt.

"Look behind you, Alexander. Do you think that is rain coming up?" Alexander turned his horse the better to study the darkening skies.

"Well, sir, if I were at home on the plantation, I'd reckon we were in for some pretty serious rain, but you never can tell in alien places like Pennsylvania."

"That is not entirely helpful, sir, but since it coincides with my own view, I think we should act on it."

He then called up a messenger and sent him to bring General Ewell over to him immediately. When the three were together, a historic conversation followed; the result of which sent messengers racing down the ridge, now cleared of Union troops, and who then proceeded towards the mass of Confederate forces advancing at walking speed for some and, for cavalry, with brief charges; all this to drive the Union towards an uncertain destination.

The three Confederate generals and their accompanying troop of some thirty or forty cavalry officers and men then began a measured descent to the fields below. They were soon moving amongst growing numbers of their own army and were cheered by many as they passed by. General Lee was pleased to see, a few minutes later, a cavalry corps, led by George Pickett and Jeb Stuart, break away from the pursuit and head north-east as fast as the advancing numbers of infantry in their path would allow them. The destination, that Lee had ordered, was to clear any remaining Union force out of Gettysburg town itself.

Half an hour after messengers had been dispatched from the remains of the Gatehouse on the ridge, bugle calls echoed across the whole width of the Confederate army and multiple officers were shouting the order to 'Cease fire'!

The front lines of the advance were halted and those behind at first jostled those in front and then were also forced to stop. No officer was in a position to explain these commands, but they were required to establish order among the tens of thousands of soldiers involved. There was, not surprisingly, a degree of confusion, not to mention frustration, among men who now smelt blood and revenge within touching distance.

A corps of cavalry was ordered to move to the front of the infantry, partly to stop any hot-headed rush forward by the infantry, now behind them, and partly to show the fleeing Union that they could expect no mercy if foolish, pointless aggression came from them.

Generals Meade, Hooker and Chamberlain, who were at that time sitting on their horses a few hundred yards from their Headquarters, at first assumed this was some Confederate trick to keep the remains of the Army of the Potomac from a ragged and disorderly rush towards the hills in the west and thus kill them while they were closer at hand, but when the Confederacy seemed to be holding on to a cease fire, they relapsed into bewildered uncertainty.

The Union Headquarters was over a mile west of Gettysburg, which Meade had ordered to be abandoned by the relatively small force stationed there until two hours ago. Nevertheless, the Union Generals were far from alone in the area close to their original Headquarters farmhouse. A sizeable number of officers, both senior and junior, were trying to establish order among thousands of soldiers who had retreated that far and then been stopped from going any further by both threats and calls upon their loyalty.

The Union generals were well aware of the state of confusion, fear and the instinct to run and try to save one's own life. Equally, they were reasonably sure that most senior officers would never flee a battlefield, but the younger officers seemed to be fidgeting on the edge of desertion. No experienced senior officer ever doubted that the ordinary soldier would desert as soon as he safely could.

The eerie cessation of the ear-splitting noise of battle was also adding to the atmosphere that was close to terror amongst the thousands of Union soldiers, who were either uninjured or at least able to walk or somehow drag their bodies forward. It was impossible for their generals to take in what they now saw. Their officers were used to their commands being obeyed without question, then to see their men moving precisely as planned, but now they were robbed of their belief that discipline would hold and also in the inevitable victory of the Union.

They were also aware that thousands had stopped in their retreat, albeit now scattered over a wide belt of land stretching back from the actual battlefield for at least two miles, but many more thousands were already fleeing through the countryside beyond that, often having thrown their guns to the ground in the hope that unarmed they would be taken prisoner rather than shot in the back. The only real consolation to General Meade was the message that had been awaiting him on his arrival at the farmhouse and which reassured him that President Lincoln had been escorted by small group of cavalry, commanded by General James Wilson, to the nearest operating railway line to the north and was now, he hoped, safely on his way to Harrisburg and beyond.

General Joseph Hooker happened to be one of the few present close to the farmhouse HQ. He was facing Gettysburg and hence then witnessed a column of several dozen Confederate cavalry moving swiftly in their direction from the town, at the head of which were three cavalry officers holding white flags aloft.

By six o'clock that evening, the senior generals and officers of the Confederate Armies of Northern Virginia and Tennessee successfully brought some order to the mass of their troops, who were now being mustered along the miles of farmland below Cemetery Ridge. There were as many as fifty thousand or so now in a variety of positions on the flat farmland: those responsible for finishing the rounding up of Union prisoners and corralling them inside the temporary barriers provided by several hundreds of Confederate soldiers, as well as those responsible for a huge sentry force around the area. A more select number heavily guarded the acre or so around the Union Headquarters, now confining all their senior officers, either captured or who had, after the cease fire, given up their swords in a gentlemanly fashion.

Then there were those in charge of the organisation that evening of the huge numbers of Confederates who had to survive for a temporary period camped on the battlefield itself. Another large squad, under command of

Confederate quartermasters, w now charged with finding all the food available from the Union camps, as well as those of the Confederacy, to distribute from food centres along the massed ranks of exhausted, but equally elated, victorious troops. Finally, two corps were moved to patrol the farm buildings on the road into Gettysburg that were the temporary Headquarters of the Confederate command.

The next problem that needed to be dealt with, if time permitted before dark, was that of the numerous casualty stations set up to serve Confederate wounded during the four days of battle. Hundreds, if not thousands, were moved into Gettysburg town itself, where all buildings were commandeered by the Confederacy.

General Braxton Bragg, whose home was in Carolina, was given charge of the organisation of care for the wounded and the disposal of the bodies of the Confederate dead. This was what most other generals felt was a poison chalice, since it would carry no opportunity of giving any officer so selected the chance to shine at this glorious hour of victory.

Bragg had, in fact, commanded some of the artillery battalions during the battle, but was not trusted as a commander by either Lee or, for that matter, a number of other officers. There were in the region of fifty-five thousand bodies which by that Monday evening and the following days still filled trenches and ditches, hung over farm fences and lay around the numerous stone walls on the battlefield, as well as those more difficult to locate scattered across the slopes of Cemetery Ridge, lodged in gullies, stacked in copses or drawing their last breath behind stone boulders and outcrops.

It was no wonder that Bragg had to be replaced a few days later, as he appeared to have suffered a mental breakdown. When the Confederate and Union officials attempted, months after the battle, to make an estimate of the numbers who had suffered one way or another during the years between Fort Sumter and Gettysburg, they eventually provided information for posterity that 3,000,000 men had fought in the war, of which 750,000 had died, 475,000 were wounded and 400,000 were captured or missing on battlefields scattered across many states; Gettysburg accounted for over fifty thousand of the dead.

The darkness of the night of Monday August 6 1863 eventually settled over both the living and those holding on to life with difficulty, grey and blue alike, as well as those who had had the life ripped from them and were still lying across the farmland and slopes of the battlefield that was Gettysburg.

As the seriously wounded were treated to rough surgery in casualty stations, many having limbs sawn off without anaesthetic, their moans and screams echoing through the night, replacing the previous terrifying sounds of gun fire and exploding artillery shells. Union prisoners, guarded by mostly uncaring Confederate survivors of the battle, were huddled in congested crowds on the ground, fighting over buckets of water.

Meanwhile, General Lee and his most senior generals gathered in the relative comfort of an unscathed farmhouse to try to understand what they had achieved and what the future now held.

A summer downpour of warm, but torrential rain had been falling for several hours on the mass of men out in the darkness with no shelter. The rain eventually stopped and by the early hours of Tuesday, the moon broke through the clouds, while the stars glittered above, as ever unaware of what disaster or joy occurred on the small planet far below.

Robert E Lee had been lauded, cheered and applauded wherever he had ridden or walked during that Monday evening and night after the battle of Gettysburg came to a staggered and, for many, an uncertain halt. His first task was to discuss the agreement that had been reached earlier between both sides that a cease fire should come into immediate force and be followed at nine o'clock on Tuesday morning by a meeting at the Confederate Headquarters between General George Meade, accompanied by four of his most senior generals, General Robert E Lee himself and all the generals he cared to invite.

General George Meade, erstwhile Commander of the proud Army of the Potomac, was widely reported to have said, apparently frequently during the closing hours of August 5: (40) *"It is my entire fault. I have asked more of my men than I had a right to ask."*

Lee, like all those in the largest room of the now relatively calm headquarters, was exhausted and found it impossible to gather up any joy in victory or enthusiasm for what this might mean for the future of the Confederate States. There were a dozen other generals in the room, some collapsed into chairs, others leaning against the walls, some with wounds that had been temporarily patched up, while the obvious gaps, caused by generals who had died in combat or who were more seriously wounded, were adding to the downcast atmosphere. General Lee eventually accepted that it was incumbent upon him to say a few words at this hour of so-called victory.

"We have all lived through many battles in the past and probably at least one war in our time of service to our country. What we have seen and done in the last four days and the previous months and years, should not have been any surprise." The Commander-in-Chief paused and glanced around the room. "At moments like this, there is no victory. We have all lost something on these battlefields and that may well be a little more of our humanity. So I have to remind each and every one of you that this war, fought as a last resort and not of our seeking, might well be over, but we now have to deal with the peace." He paused again and took a drink from a glass of brandy.

"President Davis," he continued, "has been cabled frequently over the last week and is aware of the actions today. He is pleased that a cease fire was called earlier and that we shall meet with General Meade and some of his officers tomorrow morning. The intention is that an indefinite cease fire will be agreed. I shall also require General Meade, on behalf of the Union Army, then to surrender formally." His tiredness now seemed temporarily to overcome him, and he leant on the table to gather his thoughts.

He was soon able to go on. "Other more important details will also have to be agreed, such as the future of Union prisoners, the immediate handing over of Confederate prisoners not already freed and how casualties will be dealt with over the next week or more. It is imperative that you ensure that the army of the Confederacy is alert to the possibility that renewed conflict may break out as a result of Union treachery or stupidity." Here he took another drink and wiped his hand over his face.

"I should inform you, gentlemen, while on the subject of the Union, that we understand that Abraham Lincoln fled north through Harrisburg earlier today, but did not stop. If he does not flee the country entirely, no doubt he may be involved in an eventual treaty with President Davis and the Confederate States." Groans and muttered mentions of 'the coward' and 'bring him to justice' were heard in the ranks of the officers present.

"Now, there is just one imperative matter to be dealt with tonight. General Gordon, I need to pass this to you." Lee gratefully sat down and rested his arms on the table.

General John B Gordon was a long time trusted senior aide to Lee and now pushed himself away from the wall, where he was on the point of nodding off. "Yes General. What can I do to be of assistance?"

"John, I need you to find a suitable group to clear out the hay barn across the way and turn it into somewhere we can hold these talks tomorrow morning. I'm sure your legal mind is well aware what we shall need: tables, chairs, someone to record everything said and agreed, and a draft document of indefinite cease fire and surrender, that I will need to see to read no later than, let us say, five o'clock in the morning. I will leave it all to you."

"Very well, sir. I will get started as soon as we finish here."

"I've ordered some sort of food and drink to be prepared before anyone leaves to attend to what I am aware must be pressing duties for all of us."

These were Lee's final words that awesome night and he did not add anything else or ask for comments. Some bread and cheese was brought in, as well as beer and more brandy. The meeting broke up before midnight.

# POSTSCRIPT

## Historically, One Hundred and Fifty Years Later...

In the American Civil War, which lasted in reality two more years until 1865, the sombre account of lives lost or ruined was: approximately *3,000,000 fought or took part in the war. Of these 800,000 died, which was more than 25% of the population of the whole country at the time.* It is possible that if it had ended in the summer of 1863, as this novel conjectures, the horrifying number of dead would probably have been partly reduced.

The outcome of the war for Senator Crittenden of Kentucky is a fitting epitaph to represent the millions of Americans who suffered death, loss and injury in the American Civil War:

*(41) Senator Crittenden had two sons, both army generals in the Civil War, although one chose to fight in the Confederate and one in the Union cause; both were killed before the war ended.*

\*

You, the reader, are now invited to think of what the outcome of the American Civil War, as it is posed in this novel, could possibly have been after the final battle of the war at Gettysburg and how it would have affected the future of the country, or countries, which called America home:

# Reading Group questions for discussion
# What Were the Likely Outcomes?

There are a variety of possible endings to this fictional account of the American Civil War. The author suggests the theory that events could easily have been different to those that in reality occurred in history. In essence just one fact needed to have happened differently: events immediately after the Battle of Bull Run in 1861. The story of *Rally 'Round the Flag* could then possibly have been true.

At the conclusion of the Battle of Bull Run (or Manassas), as recorded in history, the Union army knew they had been defeated and were indeed in a state of panic as they trudged, scampered and hobbled back towards Washington in the mud and pouring rain of July 1861.

In historical reality, the Confederate army command decided NOT try to pursue them and the Union was then able to consolidate their position and strength for the next four years of conflict and, as a result, won the war.

*But what could have happened if this decision had been reversed? If Robert E Lee's advice that 'once you've got 'em on the run, keep chasing 'em' had been acted upon in reality? (42) Could the American Civil War have then ended differently as a result? Would world history also have been changed?*

\*

The author has left the story hanging after the 'final' battle of the war at Gettysburg (where in 1865 the historical war also ended). What do you, having read this account, feel would have been the military and political outcome if it had ended in 1863 as this novel suggests?

The story poses the probability that the cease fire and then the surrender of the Union should have happened within a day or two after the Battle of Gettysburg ended (Tuesday August 7 1863), but what would have happened then? Make up your own mind and choose the option below that you think most likely then to then have taken place on that day or soon afterwards:

1. Two days after Gettysburg, Abraham Lincoln comes back from somewhere beyond the border with Ohio. He meets with President Jeff Davis of the Confederate States at Richmond, Virginia. There a treaty is agreed and signed to the effect that the Union is formally to surrender and give the seven or more secessionist states of the south a permanent separation from the Union States of America and entitle them to hold all those secessionist states as an independent country, called the Confederate States of America, to live and trade as a free country from that day onwards...or...

2. Great Britain is called upon by the Confederacy to chair a peace conference at Montreal in Canada to settle a 'fair peace' for both sides in the war. This conference, chaired by the British Secretary of State for Foreign Affairs, takes four months of bitter argument to come to a settlement similar to No.1 above, but it is the British Government that insists, as an integral part of the treaty, the Confederate States of America must agree to make slavery illegal and to emancipate all slaves within its borders, thus bringing it in line with Great Britain and the Union States of America...or...

3. The Montreal Peace Conference takes place, but fails to reach any settlement between the Union and Confederacy and breaks up in chaos as the Union gathers all its surviving military forces not killed or imprisoned after Gettysburg and attempts to invade the Confederacy, in particular Richmond. The outcome, that lasts two more years, is that the Union is finally victorious and forces the Confederacy to surrender. The USA assumes the completeness of all its states and emancipates slaves in both Union and Confederacy...or...

4. The Montreal Peace conference fails to agree any settlement, but Great Britain immediately deploys a large army, which had been mobilising in Canada. This army advances into New England, as well as using the full power of the Royal Navy's ships that then blockade Union ports on the Atlantic and Gulf of Mexico coasts. This, with a minimal amount of further fighting, forces the Union to cease any further aggression and thus has to accept No.2 above.

**What happened to the fictional characters after 1863?** In late 1863, **Captain George Fitzwilliam** resigns his commission in the British army and volunteers to serve in the Confederate army. He lives in Carolina when not on military service further afield, until he dies in 1900.

**Ernest Tissiman** reaches Oldham soon after the Battle of Gettysburg is fought. There he discovers that his father died a month earlier and has left Crompton Mill and Waterhead Hall to him in his will. Not unusually at that time, John's wife would be entitled to live at Waterhead for her lifetime. Ernest makes some half-hearted attempts to improve the lives of his mill workers.

**Elizabeth Tissiman**, Ernest's wife, has been in *mental distress* caused by his absence, as well as by her miscarriage. In 1866, two years after Ernest's return to Oldham she gives birth to a healthy baby girl. Ernest insists she is called Eliza and her birth helps the marriage to continue until Ernest dies in 1891.

**Arthur Tissiman** also returns to Oldham, arriving in December 1864. He receives the thanks of Lord Palmerston for his part in providing the Prime Minister with invaluable information about the progress of the Civil War, but that thanks had to remain officially unrecognised, since his role, and that of both Ernest and George, could never be revealed outside the cabinet. Arthur tells Ernest, in no uncertain terms, that he wants nothing to do with the cotton industry, now booming again in England. His father has left him an inheritance £1,000 and with this large sum (at the time), as well as his determination to improve the lot of factory workers, he establishes a cotton milling 'village' south of Manchester, similar in its philosophy, both then and later, to those in Paisley, Bourneville and Port Sunlight. He pays particular attention to two schools he founds in the new village of 'Crompton'. Arthur marries Maggie in 1869 and they had five children by 1876.

# Postscript

In 1903, Prime Minister Lord Salisbury died. He was the last peer to hold that position. Earlier in that year, reviewing his premiership, he had expressed regret over what he believed was 'British folly' not officially to espouse the Confederate cause in the American Civil War of forty-two years earlier.

'*If we had interfered*', he wrote, '*it might have been possible to reduce the power of the United States to manageable proportions, but two such chances are not given to a nation in the course of its career*'.

(*By the first of the 'two chances',* he presumably meant the American War of Independence of 1776-81.)

# INDEX

Sources & References

## A timely reminder of how the past colours the future

| No. Ref. | Page No. | |
|---|---|---|
| (1) | 10 | Abraham Lincoln's speech on June 16 1863: '*A house divided against itself will not stand*'. His opposition to slavery would lead to emancipation of all slaves in 1863. SOURCE : Google |
| (2) | 11 | Words of 'Rally 'Round the Flag'; 1862 by George Frederick Root for the Union, but adapted by WH Barnes for the Confederacy SOURCE: Google. |
| (3) | 13 | Abraham Lincoln's speech in 1860 departing to become President in Washington DC from his Home in Springfield. SOURCE: 'The Coming Fury' by Bruce Catton |
| (4) | 13 | Jefferson Davis (Confederate President) accepting his election with some reservations. SOURCE: Google |
| (7) | 14 | Reference to 'Uncle Tom's Cabin' by Harriet Beecher Stowe 1862 – popular with opponents of slavery. Illustrations by Hammat Billings. SOURCE: Wikipedia |
| (8) | 19 | 'Cottonopolis' became the nickname for Manchester: manufactured in the UK, sold to the Empire and much of the world. The centre for the manufacture of cotton thread and cloth. SOURCE: Google |
| (9) | 19 | 'Tissiman' name: real name of a Bishop's Stortford family, Originally, Huguenots from France/Belgium, who fled from religious persecution. The original 16th century shop still bears their name. They were related to the author. SOURCE: Google and in the printed family history. |
| (10) | 21 | Refers to the 'Pickwick Papers' by Charles Dickens; Published 1837 in monthly magazines, then in book form. SOURCE: Google |

| | | |
|---|---|---|
| **(11)** | 27 | Coal-fired boiler supplying hot water through radiators re-invented from the Roman original by William Strutt in 1793 and refined in the 19th century by Thomas Tredgold.<br>SOURCE: Wikipedia |
| **(12)** | 44 | Description of Werneth (Oldham) by a young Surveyor in 1861-65. He noted that Oldham had no municipal funds and that unemployment and Typhus were rife.<br>SOURCE: Google |
| **(13)** | 68 | Manchester Exchange first built in 1727 in a warehouse for cotton business transactions and then with several new constructions between 1806 and 1809 and enlarged with a splendid dome in 1851 by Alex Mills after a visit by Queen Victoria.<br>SOURCE: Google |
| **(14)** | **See p14** | See Reference (7) |
| **(15)** | 96 | Lord Sidney Herbert of Lea was the Secretary of State for War from 1861 and a Liberal MP; Lord Palmerston wittily was called 'Lord Pumice' behind his back. Prime Minister at the same time and known for his 'abrasive' style; and also known as 'Lord Cupid' for obvious reasons.<br>SOURCE: Google |
| **(16)** | 97 | The Queen's Own Royal Hussars were known by this title until 1993, when they merged with Queen's Own Irish Hussars and soon became just The Queen's Royal Hussars.<br>SOURCE: Google |
| **(17)** | 116 | 'Confederate States': The first seven to secede were: South Carolina. Mississippi, Florida, Alabama, Georgia, Louisiana and Texas – the original 7 were in place by 1859/60 and were joined by Virginia, Kentucky, Tennessee, North Carolina, Arkansas, Missouri, Maryland and Delaware soon after the Civil War began in 1861.<br>SOURCE: Wikipedia |
| **(18)** | 132 | 'Champion' Roger Prior was a Confederate Congressman from Charleston. His appearance on the hotel balcony in that town was true history, before the siege of Fort Sumpter. He shouted, *"You have at last annihilated the cursed Union,"* and thus became 'Champion Prior'. SOURCE: 'The Coming Fury' by Bruce Catton, published by Phoenix Press. |
| **(18a)** | 142 | Taking "tokens of war" from a battlefield was, and even is today, common and from early times onwards. |

| (19) | 172 | *The London Times is the most influential newspaper'* SOURCE: 'The Coming Fury' by Bruce Catton, published by the Phoenix Press. |
|------|-----|---------------------------------------------------------------------------------------------------------------------------------------|
| (20) | 172 | *'The most respected reporter'* is William Russell of the London Times. SOURCE: 'The Coming Fury' by Bruce Catton published by Phoenix Press. |
| (21) | 178 | Richmond, Virginia became the Confederate capital and seat of government in 1861. SOURCE: Google |
| (21a) | 178 | The real Senator for the Confederacy at this time was Ian Cameron. The author has changed his name to 'Ivan Cameron' for a brief appearance in Richmond. SOURCE: Google |
| (22) | 182 | In 1720 a company (South Sea Co,) borrowed £30 million (£3,000,000,000 in 2021) from the government. In return they underwrote the loan. National Debt Shares rose x10 And then Crashed. Many suicides followed. SOURCE: Google |
| (23) | 183 | Great Britain agreed that a *"state of belligerency"* now existed between England and the Union, not a state of war SOURCE: 'The Coming Fury' by Bruce Catton, published by Phoenix Press. |
| (24) | 191 | The new President Lincoln was observed at this moment to have an expression, not of pride and optimism, but of *"sober reflection"*, tinged with sadness. SOURCE: 'The Coming Fury' by Bruce Catton, published by Phoenix Press. |
| (24a) | 192 | These names of "military units" were often given by the soldiers themselves, were rarely formally listed, but persisted throughout the Civil War in many corps and regiments throughout the War. |
| (25) | 200 | Just before Bull Run General Beauregard announced to his more junior generals: "I do say that our men will not do well when battle is joined: they have not had a long march, as has the Union, but we are badly trained." SOURCE: 'The Coming Fury' by Brian Catton, published by Phoenix Press |
| | | |

| (26) | 200 | Reference to Colonel/later General Jeb Stuart reporting General Jackson's seizure of rail cars and locomotives at Harper's Ferry from the Union and managing to move many of them into Confederate hands.<br>SOURCE: 'The Coming Fury' by Bruce Catton, published by Phoenix Press |
|---|---|---|
| (27) | 209 | Reference to the not uncommon audience of civilians who would travel to the scenes of battle to watch the 'show' as if it were a play or concert and a performance where one could enjoy a picnic at the same time. Tolstoy describes the phenomenon in 'War and Peace'<br>SOURCE: 'The Coming Fury' by Bruce Catton, published by Phoenix Press. |
| (28) | 214 | 'An impressionable soldier' marching towards Bull Run, described to his wife by letter *'the Union column, a great column of soldiers seemed to fill the roadway without break like a bristling monster lifting himself by a slow, wavy motion'*<br>SOURCE: 'The Coming Fury' by Bruce Catton, published by Phoenix Press |
| (29) | 214 | Mary Chestnut, wife of the soldier above, wrote to him: *"This is our first battle Summer. Please God, it is our first and last."* |
| (30) | 216 | Captain Alexander shelled in the same area. Colonel Bartow shows outstanding bravery, even bravado, when his horse is killed under him and, on foot at the height of battle, he seizes the flag dropped by another and then carries it, uninjured himself, for the rest of the day, calling his men to follow him. |
| (31) | 224 | General Jackson is described with some of his Legendary charisma and leadership: *'There's Jackson, standing like a stonewall'* gives him that epithet as 'Stonewall Jackson' for the rest of his life, as well as *'Old blue eyes'*, since he could apparently use them to look through the smoke of battle with clarity.<br>SOURCE: 'The Coming Fury' by Bruce Catton, published by Phoenix Press |
| (32) | 225 | Of even more note perhaps was his advice to his battle commanders: *"Once you get 'em running, keep at 'em."* Advice that could have helped the Confederates to victory and would very likely have the same result for the Union in reality. SOURCE: 'The Coming Fury' by Bruce Catton, published by Phoenix Press |
| (33) | 230 | Union General Scott sees the terrible retreat of the Union: *"Just look at these foul men, covered in mud...retreating after Bull Run soaked through with rain."*<br>SOURCE: 'The Coming Fury' by Bruce Catton, published by Phoenix Press |
|  |  |  |

| (34) | 231 | William Russell of the London Times reports on the Battle of Bull Run and then takes advantage of the new trans-Atlantic cable to send his words in a few hours to London.<br>SOURCE: 'The Coming Fury' by Bruce Catton, published by Phoenix Press. |
|------|-----|---|
| (35) | 244 | The *Augusta Incident:* basically factual in that the two Confederates aiming to reach London, persuade the UK government to assist the south, here credited with their real names and only the captain of the UK, MS *Augusta*, is in fact the name of the Union captain. |
| (36) | 254 | Benjamin Disraeli was the Tory Leader of the Opposition to the Liberal Government. Disraeli proved forthcoming in such debates as described fictitiously on this occasion.<br>SOURCE: Google |
| (37) | 263 | The Prime Minister (Palmerston) declared during the debate that the UK *'is not about to commit an act of war'* but will move *'our troops in Canada to the border with the USA as an act of self-defence'*<br>SOURCE: Google |
| (38) | 277 | This was an historical reference to the American War of Independence: in the extreme winter of 1777/78 George Washington, commanding American forces, imprisoned by snow and ice at Valley Forge, where he and his men had camped to await some abatement of weather: thousands perished.<br>SOURCE: Google; Wikipedia |
| (39) | 306 | This young officer gives a true account of the first all-iron-clad American (Union and Confederate) warships that briefly shocked the military world by their design.<br>SOURCE: Google/ Wikipedia |
| (39a) | 369 | Union General Chamberlain made his mark on the battle of Gettysburg when, as commander of battalions, he rallied his section of the Union army with appeal to *'stand firm you boys of Maine'* to which they responded with valour.<br>SOURCE: 'The Coming Fury' by Bruce Catton, published by Phoenix Press |
| (40) | 402 | The author puts words into General Meade's mouth when he has to accept defeat; they were actually spoken *during the battle when things were going badly for t*he Union. He said with desperate self-blame, *"It is not entirely my fault."*<br>SOURCE: 'The Coming Fury' by Bruce Catton, published by Phoenix Press |
|  |  |  |

| (41) | 405 | This is a fitting monument in reality, as well as used in this fictional account: Senator Crittenden's two sons, both generals, one Union and one Confederate: both were killed in the Civil War. SOURCE: 'The Coming Fury' by Bruce Catton, published by Phoenix Press. |
|------|-----|-----------------------------------------------------------------------------------------------------------------------------------------------------------------------------------------------------------------------------------------------------------|
| (42) | 406 | In this fictional account: If Jackson's advice in actual history, to "keep 'em running" had been followed by the Confederacy in this novel, after Bull Run, then it is likely that would have changed History and allowed the Confederacy to win the Civil War. |